ANYBODY'S DAUGHTER

Books by Pamela Samuels Young

Vernetta Henderson Mysteries

Every Reasonable Doubt (1st in series)

In Firm Pursuit (2nd in series)

Murder on the Down Low (3rd in series)

Attorney-Client Privilege (4th in series)

Angela Evans Mysteries

Buying Time (1st in series)

Anybody's Daughter (2nd in series)

Short Stories

The Setup

Easy Money

Non-Fiction

Kinky Coily: A Natural Hair Resource Guide

PAMELA SAMUELS YOUNG

ANYBODY'S DAUGHTER

GoldmanHOUSE
PUBLISHING

Anybody's Daughter

Goldman House Publishing

ISBN 978-0-9892935-0-1

Copyright © 2013 by Pamela Samuels Young

For information about special discounts for bulk purchases, please contact the author or Goldman House Publishing.

Pamela Samuels Young
www.pamelasamuelsyoung.com

Goldman House Publishing
goldmanhousepublishing@gmail.com

Cover design by Marion Designs

Printed in U.S.A.

For three amazing women on the front lines
in the battle to save our daughters.
Thanks for all you do.

Commissioner Catherine Pratt, Los Angeles STAR Court
Los Angeles Juvenile Defense Attorney Sherri Cunningham
Los Angeles Juvenile Defense Attorney Shirley Henderson

"There is no trust more sacred than the one the world holds with children. There is no duty more important than ensuring that their rights are respected, that their welfare is protected, that their lives are free from fear and want and that they can grow up in peace."

—Kofi Annan
Former Secretary-General
United Nations

PROLOGUE

Brianna sat cross-legged in the middle of her bed, her thumbs rhythmically tapping the screen of her iPhone. She paused, then hit the *Send* button, firing off a text message.

ready?

Her soft hazel eyes lasered into the screen, anticipating—no craving—an instantaneous response. Jaden had told her to text him when she was about to leave the house. *So why didn't he respond?*

She hopped off the bed and cracked open the door. A gentle tinkle—probably a spoon clanking against the side of a stainless steel pot—signaled that her mother was busy in the kitchen preparing breakfast.

Easing the door shut, Brianna leaned against it and closed her eyes. To pull this off, Brianna couldn't just act calm, she had to *be* calm. Otherwise, her mother would surely notice. But at only thirteen, she'd become pretty good at finding ways around her mother's unreasonable rules.

She gently shook the phone as if that might make Jaden's response instantly appear. Brianna was both thrilled and nervous about finally meeting Jaden, her first real boyfriend—a boyfriend she wasn't supposed to have. Texts and emails had been racing back and forth between them ever since Jaden friended her on Facebook five weeks earlier.

It still bothered Brianna—but only a little—that Jaden had refused to hook up with her on Skype or FaceTime or even talk to her on the phone. Jaden had explained that he wanted to hear her voice and see her face for the first time in person. When she thought about it, that *was* kind of romantic.

If it hadn't been for her Uncle Dre, Brianna would never have been able to have a secret boyfriend. When her uncle presented her with an iPhone for her birthday two months ago, her mother immediately launched into a tirade about perverts and predators on the Internet. But Uncle Dre had teased her mother for being so uptight and successfully pleaded her case.

Thank God her mother was such a techno-square. Although she'd insisted that they share the same Gmail account and barred her from Facebook, Brianna simply used her iPhone to open a Facebook account using a Yahoo email address that her mother knew nothing about. As for her texts, she immediately erased them.

A quiet chime signaled the message Brianna had been waiting for. A ripple of excitement shot through her.

Jaden: hey B almst there cant wait 2 c u
Brianna: me 2
Jaden: cant wait 2 kss dem lips
Brianna: lol!
Jaden: luv u grl!
Brianna: luv u 2

Brianna tossed the phone onto the bed and covered her mouth with both hands.

OMG!

She was finally going to meet the love of her life. Jaden's older brother Clint was taking them to the Starbucks off Wilmington. Her mother kept such tight reins on her, this was the only time she could get away. Jaden had promised her that Clint would make sure she got to school on time.

Turning around to face the mirror on the back of the door, Brianna untied her bushy ponytail and let her hair fall across her shoulders. The yellow-and-purple Lakers tank top her Uncle Dre had given her fit snugly across her chest, but wasn't slutty-looking. Jaden was a Kobe

Bryant fanatic just like she was. He would be impressed when she showed up sporting No. 24.

Slinging her backpack over her shoulder, Brianna trudged down the hallway toward the kitchen.

"Hey, Mama. I have to be at school early for a Math Club meeting."

Donna Walker turned away from the stove. "I'm making pancakes. You don't have time for breakfast?"

Brianna felt a stab of guilt. Her mother was trying harder than ever to be a model parent. Brianna had spent much of the last year living with her grandmother after her mother's last breakdown.

"Sorry." She grabbed a cinnamon-raisin bagel from the breadbox on the counter. "Gotta go."

Donna wiped her hand on a dishtowel. "It's too early for you to be walking by yourself. I can drop you off."

Brianna kept her face neutral. "No need. I'm picking up Sydney. We're walking together."

Brianna saw the hesitation in her mother's overprotective eyes.

Taller and darker than her daughter, Donna wore her hair in short, natural curls. Her lips came together like two plump pillows and her eyes were a permanently sad shade of brown.

Donna had spent several years as a social worker, but now worked as an administrative assistant at St. Francis Hospital. Work, church and Brianna. That was her mother's entire life. No man, no girlfriends, no fun.

Brianna wasn't having any of that. She was *gonna* have a life, no matter how hard her mother tried to keep her on a short leash like a prized pet.

Donna finally walked over and gave her daughter a peck on the cheek, then repeated the same words she said every single morning.

"You be careful."

Brianna bolted through the front door and hurried down the street. As expected, no one was out yet. Her legs grew shaky as she scurried past Sydney's house. Brianna had wanted to tell her BFF about hooking up with Jaden today, but he made her promise not to. Anyway, Sydney had the biggest mouth in the whole seventh grade. Brianna

couldn't afford to have her business in the street. She'd made Sydney
swear on the Bible before even telling her she'd been talking to Jaden
on Facebook.

As she neared the end of the block, she saw it. The burgundy
Escalade with the tinted windows was parked behind Mario's Fish
Market just like Jaden said it would be. Brianna was so excited her
hands began to tremble. She was only a few feet away from the SUV
when the driver's door opened and a man climbed out.

"Hey, Brianna. I'm Clint, Jaden's brother. He's in the backseat."

Brianna unconsciously took a step back. Jaden's brother didn't
look anything like him. On his Facebook picture, Jaden had dark eyes,
a narrow nose and could've passed for T.I.'s twin brother. This man
was dark-skinned with a flat nose and crooked teeth. And there was
no way he was nineteen. He had to be even older than her Uncle Dre,
who was thirty-something.

Brianna bit her lip. An uneasy feeling tinkered in her gut, causing
her senses to see-saw between fear and excitement. But it was love, her
love for Jaden, that won out. It didn't matter what his brother looked
like. They probably had different daddies.

As Clint opened the back door, Brianna handed him her backpack
and stooped to peer inside the SUV.

At the same horrifying moment that Brianna realized that the man
inside was not Jaden, Clint snatched her legs out from under her and
shoved her into the Escalade.

The man in the backseat grabbed a handful of her hair and jerked
her toward him. Brianna tumbled face-first into his lap, inhaling sweat
and weed and piss.

"Owwwww! Get your hands offa me!" Brianna shrieked, her arms
and legs thrashing about like a drowning swimmer. "Where's Jaden?
Let me go!"

"Relax, baby." The stinky man's voice sounded old and husky.
"Just calm down."

"Get offa me. Let me go!"

She tried to pull away, but Stinky Man palmed the back of her head
like a basketball, easily holding her in place. Clint, who was now in the

front seat, reached down and snatched her arms behind her back and bound them with rope.

When Brianna heard the quiet revving of the engine and the door locks click into place, panic exploded from her ears. She violently kicked her feet, hoping to break the window. But each kick landed with a sharp thud that launched needles of pain back up her legs.

"Let me goooooo!"

The stinky man thrust a calloused hand down the back of Brianna's pants as she fought to squirm free.

"Dang, girl," he cackled. "The brothers are gonna love you."

"Cut it out, Leon," Clint shouted, turning away to grab something from the front seat. "I've told you before. Don't mess with the merchandise."

"Don't touch me!" Brianna cried. "Get away from me!"

She managed to twist around so that her face was no longer buried in Stinky Man's lap. That was when she saw Clint coming toward her. He covered her mouth with a cloth that smelled like one of the chemicals from her science class.

Brianna coughed violently as a warm sensation filled her body. In seconds, her eyelids felt like two heavy windows being forced shut. She tried to scream, but the ringing in her ears drowned out all sound. When she blinked up at Stinky Man, he had two—no three—heads.

Brianna could feel the motion of the SUV pulling away from Mario's Fish Market. She needed to do something. But her body was growing heavy and her head ached. The thick haze that cluttered her mind allowed only one desperate thought to seep through.

Mommy! Uncle Dre! Please help me!

DAY ONE MISSING

"Sex traffickers often recruit children because not only are children more unsuspecting and vulnerable than adults, but there is also a high market demand for young victims. Traffickers target victims on the telephone, on the Internet, through friends, at the mall, and in after-school programs."

—*Teen Girls' Stories of Sex Trafficking in the U.S.*
ABC News/Primetime

CHAPTER 1

Day One: 8:00 a.m.

Angela Evans zigzagged her Saab in and around the slow-moving cars inching up Hill Street, ignoring the blaring horns directed at her.

"Shoot!" She pounded the steering wheel.

The lot where she normally parked for court appearances had a *Full* sign out front. It could take another twenty minutes to find a place to park. Twenty minutes she didn't have.

She spotted a two-hour parking meter a few feet ahead and swerved into it. Grabbing her purse from the front seat, she tumbled from the car, not bothering to put change in the meter. She'd just have to deal with the fifty-dollar ticket.

When she rounded the corner, the line of people waiting to enter the Clara Shortridge Foltz Criminal Justice Center was at least fifty deep. The line for attorneys and staff was half as long. She strolled up to a middle-aged white guy in an expensive suit near the front of the attorneys' line and flashed him a hopeful smile.

"Cuts? Pretty please?" she said, trying to catch her breath. "I'm way late."

The man grinned and allowed Angela to step in front of him. A few people behind them had started to grumble, but by that time she was already dropping her purse onto the conveyor belt and walking through the metal detectors.

She jogged down the hallway and squeezed into an elevator seconds before the doors closed. The car shot straight to the fourth floor. When she finally reached the courtroom, Angela frowned. Shenae was supposed to be waiting outside.

Inside the courtroom, Angela was glad to find that the judge hadn't taken the bench yet. She grew incensed, however, as she scanned the gallery. Her client was sitting off to the right, next to a man in a sports jacket and tie. Angela presumed he was the detective who had picked her up from the group home. On the opposite side of the courtroom, Angela counted four women and five men. The whole rowdy, tattooed group looked as if they'd just broken out of county jail. One of the men craned his neck in Shenae's direction and scowled, confirming exactly what Angela had assumed.

She marched into the well of the courtroom and straight up to the deputy district attorney.

"Why haven't you cleared the courtroom?" she demanded. "If you don't get them out of here, I'm advising my client to take the Fifth."

"Good morning to you, too, Counselor," Monty Wyman replied with a forced smile. "I was going to do it. We haven't started yet."

Wyman was in his late twenties, with sandy hair and black-rimmed glasses. His doughy midsection publicized that exercise wasn't high on his agenda.

"If you want my client to testify, do it now." Angela cocked her head and smiled. "Pretty please."

Wyman had spent the last six months of his young legal career in the sex crimes unit. He knew how traumatic it was for a twelve-year-old child to face her pimp in court. It irked Angela that the defendant's homies were even allowed to be in the same building as Shenae.

Angela walked over to Shenae, greeted her with a hug, then escorted her to a bench in the hallway.

"You okay? You still want to do this, right?"

Shenae's timid eyes fell to the floor. "Uh, yeah." The thin, gangly girl never made eye contact for more than a few seconds.

Six months earlier, Shenae had been arrested for solicitation to commit prostitution. She was one of a dozen under-aged girls forced into prostitution by a pimp named Melvin Clark. Yet the justice system treated *her* like the criminal.

Angela represented Shenae in juvenile court on the solicitation charge and had arranged for her to be sent to a group home. As part of a special program, if she did well in school and stayed out of trouble for at least a year, the charge would be dismissed.

Angela was in court today to lend moral support.

"If I tell 'em everything I did, are you sure they're not gonna arrest me?" Shenae asked.

"Yes, I'm sure." Angela placed a hand on her shoulder. "I've already negotiated that with the prosecutor. You have full immunity. That means nothing you say can be used against you. Ever."

Just then, the defendant's cohorts were ushered out of the courtroom by the bailiff. Angela pulled Shenae close, blocking her face from the glares of her would-be intimidators.

Wyman stuck his head into the hallway. "We're ready."

Shenae wrung her hands. Her khaki pants and black sweater seemed a size too big. Her hair was gathered into a small puff that sat atop of her head, drawing attention away from her sad, round face.

"I know it's scary," Angela said softly. "But you can do it. You did really good when we practiced last week. Candace will be here any minute."

Angela glanced down the hallway, praying that Candace Holmes would indeed appear. "Just keep your eyes on Candace or me. And whatever you do, don't look at Melvin."

As if conjured up by magic, Candace Holmes raced up to them. "Sorry," she panted. "I had another client on the fifth floor."

Candace, who was not much taller than Shenae, worked for Saving Innocence, a non-profit group that provided an array of support services to sexually trafficked children. She was here today to serve as Shenae's witness advocate.

Candace swept her reddish-brown bangs off her face and bent to look Shenae in the eyes. "I'm proud of you. I know you're going to do great."

Angela opened the door of the courtroom. "Let's go."

Shenae didn't move. She looked up at Angela. "I…I would feel better if I could take your purse up there with me."

Angela glanced down at her camel-colored Dolce Gabbana bag. "My purse? Why?"

"It's a nice purse," Shenae said, her lower lip quivering a bit. "If I had it with me on the witness stand, I would look important. Like you."

A pained look passed between Angela and Candace. Angela handed the bag to Shenae and led the way inside.

The judge, jury and defendant were all in place now. Melvin, dressed in a suit and tie, sat next to his lawyer, a veteran public defender who'd obviously pulled the short straw. A portly man with a hard face, Melvin looked much older than twenty-eight. He glanced back at Shenae, but turned around when his lawyer tapped him on the arm.

Judge Willis Romer, known for both his shoe-polish-black hair and for nodding off on the bench, peered through his thick lenses. "Call your first witness, Mr. Wyman."

"I call Shenae M to the witness stand."

Shenae slowly rose to her feet and marched down the aisle, followed by Candace. After taking the oath, Shenae propped Angela's purse on her lap and curved her small fingers around the pearl handle. She sat arrow straight, chin forward, her face blank of any emotion.

Candace was sitting in a folding chair just to the right of the jury box, facing Shenae.

"Ladies and gentlemen of the jury," the judge began, "Ms. Candace Holmes is a witness advocate. She is here for emotional support for the witness, who is a juvenile. You should give no weight, pro or con, to her presence."

Wyman rose from the prosecutor's table and smiled warmly at Shenae. "Can you tell us your name for the record?"

"Shenae Mar—"

Wyman held up both hands. "That's okay. Since you're a juvenile we don't need your last name. Is it okay if I call you Shenae?"

The girl smiled. "Yes."

"And how old are you?"

"Twelve."

"Do you know the defendant, Melvin Clark?"

Shenae nodded.

The judge leaned toward Shenae and spoke in a fatherly voice. "Shenae, we'll need you to speak out loud. The court reporter can't take down a nod of your head."

"Oh, I'm sorry. Yeah, I know him."

As instructed, Shenae did not take her eyes off of Candace, not even to face the judge.

"And how do you know Mr. Clark?" the prosecutor asked.

Shenae swallowed. "He was my pimp."

Melvin shifted in his seat, then angled his head and stroked his stubbly chin.

"Where did you first meet Mr. Clark?"

"At the Kentucky Fried Chicken on Crenshaw and Imperial. He bought me some chicken and fries cuz I was hungry."

"How did Mr. Clark know you were hungry?"

Shenae's slender shoulders rose, then fell. "I guess cuz he saw me eat somebody's leftover food after they walked out."

For the next few minutes, Shenae stoically recapped her tragic young life. At ten, she'd been placed in a foster home after her mother's boyfriend molested her. In the foster home, she was physically and verbally abused and ultimately ran away. She was eleven when Melvin offered to let her stay at his apartment.

"At first, he was nice," Shenae explained. "He didn't even try to have sex with me or nothing. He took me shopping and let me buy whatever I wanted."

"Did that ever change?" the prosecutor asked.

Shenae lowered her eyes. "After about a month we started having sex. But by then, he was my boyfriend, so that was okay."

One of the jurors, an older black woman who'd been carrying a Bible, puckered her lips.

"And then what happened?"

"One day, he told me that cuz he spent a lot of money on me, I had to make some money for him."

For the first time, Shenae stole a quick glance at Melvin. She clasped the handles of the purse even tighter.

"How did he want you to make money for him?"

The courtroom grew quiet as Shenae's eyes watered. "He put me on the track."

Angela took in the jury. A few faces appeared shocked, others displayed confusion.

"Tell the jury what the track is?"

Shenae began to gently rock back and forth, still holding onto the purse. "Where johns go to pick up ho's for sex."

"What did you do on the track?"

Shenae did not answer for a few seconds. Wyman waited.

"At first I…I just sucked…I mean…I gave blow jobs. I got fifty dollars every time. I gave all the money to Melvin. But later on, he put me in a motel room so johns could come there to have sex with me."

"I see a tattoo on your neck," the prosecutor said. "M-M-M. What does that mean?"

Shenae's hand absently caressed her slender neck. "Uh, it means Melvin's moneymaker."

Two female jurors gasped.

"How many men did you have sex with on a single day?"

"A lot," Shenae sniveled and wiped away a tear. "Sometimes up to twenty."

Several jurors winced. The black woman cupped a hand to her mouth.

"Did you want to have sex with those men?"

"No."

"What would happen if you refused?"

Shenae was weeping softly now. "Melvin would beat me."

Judge Romer spoke with genuine sympathy in his voice. "Shenae, are you okay? Are you able to continue?"

Shenae finally let go of the purse. She pressed both hands to her face and sobbed.

"Your Honor," Wyman said quietly, "we'd like to take a short break."

CHAPTER 2

Day One: 8:05 a.m.

When Brianna's voicemail clicked on again, Dre cursed under his breath and hung up.

That was the second time this morning that he'd tried to call his niece. He didn't even know why he even bothered calling her. Anybody under twenty only used a smartphone for texting. Talking took time away from their texting.

He chuckled to himself, then pecked out a text.

call me

Dre and his buddy Gus were installing tile in the bathroom of the two-bedroom house he'd recently picked up at an auction. The two men had done time together at Corcoran State Prison. Gus was good with his hands and Dre was happy to have the help.

Dre reached for a towel and wiped sweat from his shaved head. He was surprised when he didn't receive an instantaneous response from his niece. The girl was usually glued to her phone.

Brianna had gotten a real kick out of the fact that *he* had called *her* to help him pick out a nice restaurant for his date tonight. His niece wasn't your average thirteen-year-old. She was smart as a whip and knew almost as much about sports as he did. The fact that she looked more like him than his own son was another reason he loved her to death.

Dre had asked Brianna to go on the Internet and find him a nice restaurant in Marina Del Rey. He wanted just the right place for his reunion with Angela. Not super casual, but not too highbrow either. Brianna had given him three great choices.

Dre wanted to let Brianna know which restaurant he had selected. But he hadn't told anybody that he was hooking up with Angela tonight.

"Hey, man, what's going on?" Gus asked. He was in his late forties, with a lean, muscular body, perfected during his time behind bars. "Why you smiling so much today?"

"Didn't know I was smiling." Dre stroked his goatee. He was close to six feet with the kind of body built for hard work.

"Yeah, you were. Smiling *and* whistling. So what's up?"

Dre grabbed another tile and carefully set it into place. He wasn't sure he wanted to spill the beans about his plans tonight. It was as if doing so might jinx something. But he was excited as hell, so he had to tell somebody something.

"I'm taking Angela out tonight," Dre said.

Gus nodded, but left it at that.

"You don't have nothin' to say?" Dre asked.

"Hey, bruh, who you go out with is your business."

"Sounds like you think it's a bad idea."

"Ain't for me to judge."

Dre was surprised at Gus' response. His buddy was never one to keep an opinion to himself.

"Well, I'm asking."

Gus set aside the tile he was holding and looked over at Dre.

"You put it all on the line for that female and she left you hangin'. So if you ask me, hookin' up with her again might not be the best decision you could make."

This was no doubt the same reaction Dre would receive when he told his sister and mother that he was seeing Angela again. Unfortunately, they'd never gotten a chance to meet her. If they had, they'd surely feel differently. The only thing they knew about her was what they'd seen in the news reports. And that was bunk.

When Dre first met Angela at the Spectrum Athletic Club, she was weeks away from marrying some control-freak judge. She eventually broke off the engagement and they'd hooked up. Angela's ex, however, had refused to accept the breakup and started stalking her.

In the midst of that drama and before Dre could tell her himself, Angela found out that he'd been in the business of dealing crack cocaine and had served time for possession with intent to sell. She then broke it off with him too.

Worried about her safety, Dre stayed close and had been there to intercede when Angela and her ex were wrestling over a gun. The judge took a bullet to the gut and Dre took the rap. The media immediately jumped on the story. A love triangle involving a federal prosecutor, a superior court judge and a drug dealer made salacious news. No charges were ever filed because the shooting had been ruled self-defense.

Dre had been both pissed off and hurt by Angela's decision to move on, but the girl *was* a lawyer. Part of him understood her reluctance about having a relationship with an ex-con. He still kicked himself for not having been up front with her about his situation from day one.

It still amazed him that a woman he'd only known for a few weeks could take hold of his heart the way Angela Evans had. As hard as he tried, he couldn't shake his feelings for her. It had been three months since he'd last seen her. Last week he'd gathered the nerve to ask her out to dinner and to his relief, she accepted.

Now that he was getting a second chance at being with her, Dre didn't care what anybody thought. He was taking it.

He checked his smartphone again. Brianna still hadn't texted him back. She was probably already in class by now. He called her again anyway. No answer.

Dre couldn't wait to tell her about his date. At least Brianna would be happy for him.

CHAPTER 3

Day One: 8:10 a.m.

Clint glanced in the rearview mirror. Brianna was stretched out across the backseat, still knocked out cold, her head resting in Leon's lap. Leon was alternately snoring and smacking his lips.

The grab had worked precisely according to plan. Clint just hoped it wouldn't take too long to break in Little Miss Brianna. The girl looked like she had a lot of fight in her.

He punched a button on his cell.

"We should have her on lockdown in a few," Clint said into the phone. "This one's real fresh, man. Got them light eyes. She's gonna bring in some long dough."

He barked several instructions, then hung up.

Clint was relieved that everything had gone so well. You never knew what could happen when you were snatching a girl in broad daylight. So far, the Facebook scam was working like a charm. His boss was a genius.

Clint smiled to himself. "Mo' money, mo' money, mo' money."

Leon yawned from the backseat. "How far away are we?"

"A long way," Clint said. "Just shut up."

Leon ran a hand over Brianna's rear end. "This girl is bangin'."

"Don't mess with the merchandise," Clint snapped, eyeing him in the rearview mirror.

"I'm just sayin'." He stroked Brianna's face.

A phone began to ring. Leon looked around, then realized the sound was coming from Brianna's backpack.

"Don't answer it!" Clint shouted. "Give it here."

Leon pulled the iPhone from an outside pocket on the backpack and tossed it to Clint. The caller ID read *Uncle Dre*. He turned it off, then placed it on the console between the seats.

"I'm hungry," Leon complained. "We need to hit a drive-thru."

"We ain't stoppin'. I ain't about to risk nobody seeing that girl tied up in the backseat."

Clint shook his head. His cousin was such a screw-up. But what did he expect from a crack head? His boss would have a big problem with Clint having brought someone into the operation without his personal approval. Hopefully, he would never find out. This was the second and last time he planned to use Leon. His regular cohort, Darnell, had to make a run to Oakland to pick up some new girls. Clint didn't want to reschedule "Jaden's" hookup with Brianna. Leon had worked out okay on a last-minute grab a couple of weeks ago in Inglewood. So Clint had called on him again.

It took close to an hour in rush-hour traffic before the SUV exited the Harbor Freeway at Gage. Clint drove a few more miles and slowed when he reached a yellow house that was little more than a shack. Except for a group of boys strolling along the sidewalk, the street was empty. Clint hit a button opening the electronic gates, then steered the Escalade down a short driveway and parked on the grass behind the house.

Leon hopped out first, followed by Clint. Leon bounced on his tip toes as Clint pulled a money clip from his front pocket and peeled off fifty bucks.

"You can go now." Clint shoved the money into Leon's hands.

"Thanks, cuz!" Leon gazed excitedly at the bills. "When you gonna need me again?"

Never. "I'll let you know. Just make sure you keep your big mouth shut."

Leon was already trotting back down the driveway. Clint knew exactly where he was headed. To get high at one of three neighborhood crack houses.

After first opening the back door to the house, Clint easily collected Brianna's limp body from the backseat and hurled her over his shoulder.

The house was stuffy and night-time dark, even though it was still morning. Every windowpane in the place had been painted black. He flicked on a light switch in the kitchen and marched down a narrow hallway. He stopped outside the second bedroom on the west side of the house. Using a single key, he unlocked the three deadbolts on the door.

Inside, a low-watt bulb hanging from the ceiling provided minimal light. A naked girl with wild blonde hair sat huddled in a corner hugging her knees to her chest. Her face was clear and smooth, but her chest, arms and legs bore red, black and blue markings that stood out against her white skin. The filthy mattress where she sat was the only piece of furniture in the room.

"I brought you some company," Clint announced. He dumped Brianna on the mattress next to the frail girl.

"If you're ready to act like you got some sense, I'll bring you something to eat."

The girl, who looked to be close to Brianna's age, didn't respond.

"Well?" Clint said.

"Yes," she mumbled. "I want something to eat."

"Okay then. You better get with the program. Next time, just do what I tell you or I'ma beat your ass again."

He pointed toward Brianna.

"When the new girl wakes up, you tell her the deal. Let her know that if she plays along, everything'll be fine. But if she plans on being hard headed like you, life is gonna be rough."

CHAPTER 4

Day One: 11:30 a.m.

Angela and Candace sat facing each other in a booth at the California Pizza Kitchen in the downtown Wells Fargo complex. Angela mindlessly stabbed her Cobb salad with a fork. Candace ignored her Thai chicken pizza. They hadn't exchanged a word in over ten minutes.

Diane Sims slid into the booth as Candace moved over to make room for her.

"I tried like hell," Diane said in a breathless rush, "but I couldn't get to court in time."

Diane was Shenae's social worker. She wore her hair in long braids and had a fondness for African clothes and jewelry. The three women had bonded over their efforts to help Shenae and several other young trafficking victims.

Diane turned from Angela to Candace.

"Uh-oh. Based on your dreary faces, I guess things didn't go well in court this morning. How'd she do?"

Angela forced a smile. "After a short meltdown, Shenae actually did great. Even when Melvin's attorney tried to attack her on cross, she didn't back down."

"Okay, then," Diane said, treading lightly, "Why do you two look so sad? The jury didn't believe her?"

"They believed her," Candace said. "They came back with a guilty verdict in just over an hour."

"Then why the doom and gloom? We should be celebrating. There's one more pimp off the street."

"Let's see," Angela said, laying down her fork, "let me give you three reasons *not* to celebrate. One, Melvin will probably be out of jail in about nine months or less exploiting a whole new stable of girls. Two, one of Melvin's homeboys told Shenae outside the courtroom that he was going to kick her ass for *lying on the witness stand.* And three, Shenae's social worker just called to give us the news that she's got syphilis."

Diane propped an elbow on the table and cupped her forehead. The table fell silent again.

"And just for good measure," Angela said, "I'll throw in a fourth reason: I have another dozen clients just like Shenae."

Candace swung her head from side to side.

"Even when we win, it feels like we've lost," Angela muttered.

Diane was always one to look for the bright side. "The tide is changing," she said. "The criminal justice system is finally waking up. Every other week I read something in the newspaper or see something on TV about human trafficking. What we do is important."

"I know it's important," Angela said. "I just wish it wasn't so heart wrenching."

"I say we change the subject," Candace proposed.

Diane smiled. "I second that."

"I have a date with Dre tonight," Angela blurted out. She stuffed a forkful of salad into her mouth and started chewing so she wouldn't have to speak.

Her two friends didn't utter a word.

"Go ahead," Angela prodded. "Say what you have to say."

Diane was never one to hold her tongue. "So you guys are getting back together?"

"I never said that." Angela paused. "But what if we were?"

Diane picked up the menu and started studying it. "I guess that's your business."

"You guys went through a lot," Candace said gently. "Just make sure his past is really in the past before you get involved with him again."

"Thanks for the advice. I'll be sure to do that."

"Girl, don't give us attitude," Diane said, lowering the menu. "We're just looking out for you."

Angela finally smiled. "I know."

Andre "Dre" Thomas had been there at a time when Angela had needed him most. If he hadn't stepped in to protect her, she might not be alive today. The media attention surrounding the stalking situation with her ex, as well as a case that had spiraled out of her control, prompted Angela to resign from her job as a federal prosecutor. For the time being, she was handling the defense practice of a friend who had to leave town to tend to her dying mother. Angela would figure out her next career move later.

Learning of Dre's drug-dealing past had been a blow that still left Angela reeling with uncertainty. For months, she had hoped her feelings for him would fade. They had not. There was far more than a physical attraction between them. Dre made her feel safe, strong and worthy.

Truth be told, Angela didn't just want Dre Thomas back in her life. She needed him in her world.

CHAPTER 5

Day One: 1:00 p.m.

Brianna's eyes fluttered open and she took in the unfamiliar surroundings. The room was close in size to her own bedroom, but that was the only similarity. She was lying on a bare, damp mattress. A strong, putrid smell made her want to puke. The dirty gray walls and faint lighting reminded her of a horror movie.

She tried to lift her head, but she was so woozy, her first attempt failed. Gripping the edge of the mattress, she finally managed to sit up.

"Are you, okay?"

Brianna jumped at the sound of the soft voice behind her. She looked over her shoulder at the naked white girl sharing the mattress with her. Her sad eyes were bleary and her hair looked as if she'd just run through a wind tunnel.

"Where are we?"

"I don't know." The girl started to whimper.

"What do you mean you don't know? Where are your clothes?"

"They took 'em. They're gonna take yours too."

"Who?"

The girl hugged her knees and sniveled. "I don't know."

"What's your name?"

"Kaylee."

"How long have you been here?"

The girl began to rock. "I don't know. It seems like a long time though."

This didn't make any sense. "Where do you live?"

"In Oakland."

"Oakland? That's a long way from here," Brianna said, although she didn't know where *here* was. "This is L.A. How did you get here?"

"I met this guy named Jaden on Facebook. I told him how my foster mother beat me for talking back. So Jaden said I could come live with him and his brother. He was supposed to pick me up in downtown Oakland. But when I walked up to the car, a man grabbed me and put a nasty-smelling rag over my mouth. When I woke up, I was in a room with a bunch of other girls."

Brianna gasped.

"They brought you all the way here from Oakland?"

"Not at first. They kept me there for a while."

"You need to call somebody to come get you."

"Like who? Don't nobody care about me. And anyway, if I did have somebody to call, they wouldn't let me. They not gonna let you either. This is like a prison."

"I'm getting out of here!"

Brianna crawled across the mattress toward the wall and struggled to get to her feet. To keep her balance, she palmed the wall until she made it to the door. But there was no doorknob. Just a hole where a doorknob should have been. She pounded on the door with both fists.

Kaylee ran over and tugged on her arm. "Stop it! You can't do that! They're gonna beat you just like they beat me."

Brianna eyed the bruises all over the girl's body. She pointed in distress at a red splotch of skin just below Kaylee's collarbone. It looked as if she'd been burned.

"What happened to you?"

Kaylee's eyes followed Brianna's. "It's a tattoo. They put it on all the girls. They're gonna do the same thing to you too."

"No they're not!" Brianna cried. "Where's Jaden? Does he know these men?"

"You so stupid! There ain't no Jaden. They tricked you just like they tricked me."

"What? What are you talking about? Why would they do that?"

The girl buried her face in her hands and fell back onto the mattress.

Brianna kneeled next to her. "What's going on?" Brianna shouted. "Tell me!"

"They gonna make us have sex with men," the girl blurted out. "For money. That's what they made me do in Oakland and now they gonna make me do it down here!"

"What are you talking about? They can't do that."

"Yes, they can." The girl rocked back and forth as she cried. "They already have. A real nasty-looking man tried to have sex with me yesterday and I scratched him. That's why they beat me and threw me in here. We have to do what they say!"

"I'm not doing that!" Brianna cried, her anger squashing her fear. "I can't. I won't."

"You don't have a choice. They'll kill you if you don't."

"Yes, I do have a choice!"

Parallel tears rolled down Brianna's cheeks as she tried to comprehend what was happening to her. She was still a virgin and proud of it. She wasn't having sex with anybody. This had to be some kind of sick joke.

"I'm not staying here," Brianna declared through her tears. "My Uncle Dre's coming to get me. You just wait and see."

CHAPTER 6

Day One: 7:30 p.m.

Dre stared across the table at Angela, an eager smile stretched across his lips. From the second he'd knocked on her door at exactly seven that evening, he'd been trying to tamp down his excitement. Unfortunately, he couldn't help himself.

He could tell by her furtive glances around the restaurant that Angela was impressed with his selection. Café Del Rey had a chic, relaxed vibe with the added plus of being able to gaze out at the boats docked along the marina.

"It's good seeing you again," he said, taking a sip of his Pepsi.

She was still as fine as ever. Dre liked her pert nose and natural spiral curls. Her low-cut coral sweater matched the color of the blush that highlighted her cheekbones.

"Same here."

Angela's words came out flat, nonchalant. But then she cocked her head and smiled with those lips. Those full, soft lips that he hadn't been able to kiss for three months.

Dre had started to believe that Angela didn't intend to see him again. Ever. But his heart knew better. Despite all the drama that had gone down, there was still something special between them.

"So how's the law business?"

Angela tinkered with her napkin. "I'm handling a lot of juvenile cases now," she said. "It's kind of depressing at times. What about you? How's *your* business?"

Dre stiffened and palmed his glass with both hands. That was a dig. The kind of dig black women knew how to fire off with the skill of a sharpshooter.

"You know I'm not about that anymore." He smiled so the hurt wouldn't show on his face. But the edge in his voice gave him away. "I quit dealing before we broke up."

"Well, that's good to hear."

Dre turned away and gazed around the restaurant. It hadn't been like this before. Bland conversation, long gaps of silence, the air so thick with tension you could hardly stand to breathe it. He should just ask for the bill and take her prissy ass home. Only Dre didn't want to take her home.

"So what kind of juvenile cases are you handling?"

"Most of my clients are minors charged with soliciting prostitution."

"Any dude who'd mess with a child is sick."

"Absolutely. These girls are victims, but they're treated like criminals. The johns only get a slap on the wrist and the pimps rarely get prosecuted because the girls are too afraid to testify against them. But one of my girls did really well in court today. I'm proud of her."

Dre's smartphone vibrated. He ignored it.

A waitress with bright-pink lips and matching nail polish walked up to the table. "How are you guys doing tonight? Have you had a chance to peruse the menu?"

They both listened as the woman recited the specials. Dre ordered chicken piccata. Angela chose the grilled tilapia.

"How's your son?" Angela asked.

Dre beamed. "Growing up way too fast." He pulled his smartphone from his pocket and showed her a picture. "This is Little Dre and my niece, Brianna."

"Wow," Angela said. "Both of them look just like you. She has your hazel eyes."

"Yep. She's more like my daughter than my niece. Smart as a whip too. She wants to be a lawyer. Maybe I can bring her down to your office and you can talk to her sometime."

"Sure."

He swiped through a few more pictures.

"Who's that?" Angela pointed to a woman pictured with Dre and Brianna.

Dre smiled. "That's my sister, Donna. I'm taking them all to a Lakers' game next week. Why don't you—"

The smartphone vibrated again. This time, he read the screen, then placed it face down on the table.

"My sister, Donna," he explained with a shrug. "She can wait."

Angela arched a brow and gave him a *yeah-sure-it's-your-sister* smile.

Dre frowned. "You don't believe me?"

Angela responded with a hunch of her shoulders.

"I've never lied to you."

Angela chuckled. "Depends on whether we're talking about a straight-out lie or a lie by omission. Like your never telling me you were a drug dealer."

"An ex-drug dealer," Dre corrected her. "And I did plan to tell you." He scratched his jaw. He didn't like being judged.

"If you're still trippin' about everything that went down, then why'd you come tonight?"

Angela waited a long beat. "Because I missed you."

Dre smiled at the first green light of the evening and exhaled the anxiety right out of his body. He leaned in over the table. "Angela, I—"

The loud vibration of his smartphone cut him off a second time.

He grimaced. "My sister's a drama queen. Whatever she wants can wait."

"Sure it's your sister." Angela clasped her hands and set them on the table. "Guess I'm not the only woman who misses you."

"I'm not seeing anybody. I haven't been with anybody since you."

"If you say so."

"It's the truth."

Angela propped her right elbow on the table and extended her palm. "If that's really your sister, then let *me* return her call."

Dre briefly looked away.

He had babes jockin' him every day of the week. He didn't have to take this crap. Still, he turned back to her, picked up his smartphone and placed it in her outstretched hand.

"Go 'head. Knock yourself out."

Angela redialed the last incoming number.

As she raised the smartphone to her ear. Dre locked his arms across his chest and leaned back in his chair.

"I'm a friend of Dre's," she said, her eyes on him. "He asked me to return your call."

Dre's lips angled into a smug smile as he waited for her doubt to fade. But in seconds, Angela's expression went from skeptical to distressed. Her eyebrows fused into a single line and when she pressed the palm of her free hand flat against her chest, Dre sprang forward.

Knowing Donna, she might think it was funny to pretend that she was his woman, not his sister. If she did that, he'd never get Angela to trust him again.

"Hold up. What's she saying?"

Angela raised her hand, quieting him.

Dre waited a few more seconds, but couldn't take it. As he reached across the table, ready to take the phone, Angela thrust it into his hand.

"You better talk to your sister." Angela's voice echoed the same level of panic that now filled her eyes. "Brianna didn't show up at school today and nobody can find her."

CHAPTER 7

Day One: 8:45 p.m.

Angela spotted the patrol car halfway down the block the second Dre turned onto Magnolia Street. She glanced over at him, anxiety rumbling in her chest. Dre had an innate distrust of cops. But if something tragic had really happened to Brianna, they would need the help of law enforcement. Dre would need to keep his animosity in check.

The Volkswagen Jetta screeched to a stop and the driver's door swung open even before Dre had turned off the engine. Angela tumbled out of the car and had to jog to catch up with him.

As she trailed behind, Angela wished she were meeting Dre's family for the first time under better circumstances.

A woman's hysterical shriek pierced the air as they reached the front door.

"What do you mean we need to wait? Somebody took my baby! You need to do one of those Amber Alert things."

Dre opened the screen door and stepped inside. His sister was standing toe-to-toe with a red-faced officer who was shaped like a fireplug.

"I'm sorry, ma'am, but there's no evidence that your daughter's been taken. We don't have enough evidence to proceed with an Amber Alert."

"She hasn't come home! Of course she's been taken!"

"Ma'am, I really need you to calm down. You don't know for sure that your daughter didn't run off. Does she have a boyfriend?"

"No she does not! And my daughter wouldn't run—" Donna spotted Dre and rocketed into his arms.

A frenzy of words shot from her mouth as if they'd been fired from a machine gun.

"Brianna was supposed to walk to school with Sydney, but she never came over and they didn't really have a Math Club meeting and she doesn't know where Brianna is and—"

Dre's fingers curved around Donna's shoulders. "C'mon, sis, you gotta calm down. We're gonna find her, okay? Bree's gonna be fine."

"You don't know that!" Donna wailed, her nose runny. "Somebody took my baby!"

Dre led her over to the couch and forced her to sit, then gave an older woman sitting next to her a hug. "Hey, Mama."

Angela remained near the door, out of the way. Dre's mother gave Angela a curious look, but didn't speak.

"I'm Andre Thomas." Dre's tone was suddenly formal. "Brianna's my niece. There's no way she'd run off. What's being done to find her?"

"We don't really know that she's missing yet."

Angela stepped forward. "She didn't show up at school and it's after eight o'clock and no one knows where she is. That means she's missing. Don't you have some kind of protocol to follow for missing children?"

The officer grunted. "Yeah, but not for runaways. We—"

"My child is not a runaway!" Donna yelled. "She has no reason to run away. She's a good kid." She turned to Angela. "And who are you?"

Angela swallowed. "I'm—"

"This is Angela," Dre said. "A friend of mine. She's also a lawyer."

Donna's eyes registered recognition and Angela could practically see the news reports playing in her eyes.

Dre turned back to the cop. "And even if she did leave on her own, it doesn't mean she isn't in danger. She's only thirteen."

"But you don't know for sure that she's in danger," the officer insisted.

"And you don't know for sure that she isn't," Angela fired back. She'd been worried about Dre going off on the police and here she was ready to go ballistic herself.

"Call the TV stations," Donna ordered. "We need to get Brianna's picture on TV."

The cop's blue-green eyes rolled skyward. "I'll see what I can do."

"If my baby was some blonde-headed white girl, I bet there'd be cameras and news reporters all up and down the street by now," Donna cried. "But because my baby is black, nobody's going to lift one finger to find her. This is racism!"

The cop sighed and turned to Dre. "Do you have a recent picture of your niece?"

Donna started to rise from the couch, but Dre waved her back down. He glanced around the room, then snatched a framed picture from a sofa table.

"This is her most recent school picture. It's only a few months old."

The officer wrote down Brianna's height and weight and a description of the clothes she was wearing.

"We need to make some posters," Donna mumbled, seemingly to herself. "And call the TV stations."

"What about Brianna's father?" the officer asked. "Could he be involved?"

Donna shot up from the couch. "No, he couldn't! My husband died in Iraq defending this country!"

She crumpled back to the couch and into her mother's embrace. Both of them were sobbing now. Though eight years had passed since her husband's death, Donna had never fully recovered from the loss. At times, her severe bouts of depression had left her unable to work or properly care for Brianna. His sister would not survive another tragedy.

"We'll need to check her email and Facebook accounts," the officer said, continuing to scribble on his notepad.

"I don't allow her on Facebook," Donna sniffed. "We have the same Gmail account and I check her emails every week."

"Does she have a smartphone?" the officer asked.

"Yeah," Dre said.

"Then she probably has a Facebook account you know nothing about. Most teenagers do these days."

Donna was on her feet again. "I know my child! How dare you say—"

"Donna! Stop it!" Dre shouted. "This isn't helping."

He looked at the officer. "She has an iPhone which she never lets out of her sight. I'm sure she took it with her, but I'll check her room anyway."

Dre disappeared down a hallway.

The front door opened and a man and woman stepped into the living room. The man resembled Dre, but was both taller and younger. He sat down next to Donna and gave her a hug.

"Anthony, my baby's gone!"

"Don't worry, sis. We're gonna find her."

Anthony looked up at Angela. "Who are you?"

After a beat of silence, Dre's mother answered his question. "That's that girl who was mixed up with that judge and got Dre all over the news."

All eyes were pinned on Angela now. His family obviously didn't view her reappearance in his life as a good thing.

"I think I remember that case," the cop said, wagging his pen at her.

Before Angela could say anything, Dre stepped back into the room, his expression noticeably grim.

"I couldn't find her phone," Dre said, walking over to Donna. "But I found this underneath her mattress." He held up a pink spiral notebook. "Maybe she does have a boyfriend because some dude's name is scribbled on almost every page. So who the hell is Jaden?"

CHAPTER 8

Day One: 9:45 p.m.

The possibility that Brianna might have a boyfriend her mother knew nothing about sent Donna deeper into hysterics. It took some doing, but Dre had finally convinced her to take a sleeping pill. Now, as he glanced around his sister's living room, he wondered where all the people had come from.

While his brother and sister-in-law were in the kitchen unpacking food they'd picked up from a nearby barbecue joint, Dre's mother stood in a circle of her friends from Hope in Christ Community Church, holding hands and softly praying to Jesus. A host of cousins, neighbors and church folks he'd never seen before stood around the living room acting like they were at a Monday-night wake.

Dre didn't want any of them there. He needed to think, to plan. He'd already made up his mind that *he* was going to find Brianna. Screw the police.

He'd hated the I-told-you-so look on the officer's face when Dre produced Brianna's notebook with all the *I-love-Jaden* doodles. Just because Brianna *might* have a boyfriend they knew nothing about didn't mean she was a runaway. She was a smart kid. A happy kid. She had no reason to run off.

Dre walked into Donna's bedroom and Angela followed. Dre expected to find his sister sleeping, but she was sitting on the edge of the bed, rocking back and forth like a heroin addict coming down from a high.

"I wanna talk to Sydney," Dre said, more to himself.

"We already did." Donna was dried-eyed now. "She would've told me if Brianna had a boyfriend."

Dre shook his head in disagreement. "Sydney's her best friend. If Brianna has a boyfriend, Sydney knows about him."

Angela touched Dre's forearm. "Let's go talk to her now."

They walked the short distance to Sydney's house and repeatedly pressed the doorbell. Dre didn't care that it was approaching ten o'clock at night. This was important.

Sydney's father finally opened the door. His hooded eyes squinted at Dre.

"Hey, Winston," Dre said with forced collegiality.

Winston looked past Dre to Angela.

"This is my girl—uh, my friend, Angela. I know it's late, but we need to talk to Sydney."

An exasperated look crossed Winston Burns' face. "I'm really sorry about Brianna. But Sydney already told the police everything she knows."

"I need to talk to her for myself." Dre wanted to push past him and bolt into Sydney's bedroom. "It's important, man. Please."

"It's kinda late and Sydney's already asleep. Why don't you come back in the morning?"

Dre didn't want to come back in the morning. He needed to talk to Sydney tonight. After a few seconds, a soft voice broke the stalemate.

"Daddy, I'm not sleep."

Dre peered past Winston and saw Sydney dressed in a knee-length nightshirt.

Winston grudgingly stepped aside and let them in. Sydney's mother greeted them from a hallway.

Winston showed Dre and Angela into the kitchen, where they all converged around a small wooden table. Sydney sat at the north end of the table, with the adults lined up on all sides. The low-hanging light fixture gave the room the feel of a police interrogation.

"Sydney," Dre began, trying to conceal his distress, "you told the police that Brianna didn't have a boyfriend. Is that the truth?"

Sydney's eyes darted in the direction of her father.

"We know about Jaden," Dre said gently, not wanting to scare the girl. "We need you to tell us what you know. Brianna could be in danger."

Sydney hung her head. "Brianna didn't want nobody to know about Jaden. That's why I didn't tell nobody."

Winston glowered at his daughter. "You sat up here and lied to the police? Do you know that—"

Dre held up a hand, silencing Winston. "That's okay. Just tell us the truth now."

"Brianna met him on Facebook," Sydney said, staring down at the table. "That's all I know."

Dre's right knee bounced with angst. "Brianna had a Facebook page?"

"It was private, so her mother couldn't see it. She had a Yahoo account and a Gmail address too."

"Have you ever met Jaden?" Dre asked.

Sydney swung her head in a slow, wide sweep. "Nope. Neither has Brianna as far as I know."

Dre squinted as if a shock of light had suddenly blinded him. "How could he be her boyfriend if they'd never met?"

"People hook up on Facebook all the time." Sydney quickly added, "but I don't do that."

"Do you know where he lives?"

"Someplace in L.A. Not too far from USC."

"Did Brianna tell you they were planning to meet today?"

"Nope." Sydney raised her palm in the air. "I swear on the Bible. Jaden didn't like her to tell nobody their business. But she told me some stuff anyway."

"Like what?"

"Uh, well, he's an A student just like us. He's fourteen and he goes to Foshay Middle School and First A.M.E. Church."

Dre rubbed his chin. Finally they were getting some information they could use.

"Do you know his last name?"

Sydney smiled, glad to be of help. "Yep. Morris. Jaden Morris. He has one sister and his mother is a teacher at Crenshaw High."

"Did Brianna ever show you a picture of Jaden?"

"Yep," she said, blushing. "He's cute."

Her father grumbled and Sydney started twirling the ring on her baby finger.

"Uh…you wanna see his Facebook page?"

"Absolutely," Dre said.

Sydney ran to her bedroom and came back with her laptop, the screen already lit.

Her father grimaced. "Why is that on? I told you to turn that thing off an hour ago."

"Winston, stop fussing at the child," her mother said. "We need to concentrate on Brianna right now."

Sydney hit several keys on the computer, then turned it around for all of them to see.

Jaden Morris was a clean-cut kid whose Facebook profile described him as a Christian who was saving himself for marriage. He had 345 Facebook friends, was a Pisces, loved science fiction movies, and planned to be a lawyer. Dre scanned the postings on Jaden's page and found absolutely nothing that caused him any concern.

A knot of apprehension settled deep in Dre's stomach. "Do you know the passwords to Brianna's Facebook and Yahoo accounts?" Dre wanted to study Brianna's accounts for clues about Jaden.

Sydney hesitated, then gave up the information, which Dre noted in his smartphone.

"The boy sounds like a good kid," Sydney's father said. "At least she didn't run off with some thug."

Dre wanted to tell Winston to shut his trap. Brianna had not run off.

When his eyes finally met Angela's, he knew they were on the same page. It took a skilled criminal attorney or a street-smart hustler to recognize that this upstanding young man was not what he seemed.

CHAPTER 9

Day One: 10:15 p.m.

Brianna had lost all sense of time. She could not tell whether it was late night or early morning, the same day or the next. Her throat was so dry it hurt to swallow.

"Wake up," Brianna said, shaking Kaylee by the shoulder. "We have to figure out how to get out of here."

Brianna wished she was still drugged. That way, she wouldn't feel so cold and hungry and scared.

Kaylee sat up and hugged herself. "They ain't lettin' us out, so you might as well forget that. We have to do what they say."

"No, we don't," Brianna insisted. "We have to escape. Have you seen the rest of the house?"

"Yeah."

"Who else is here?"

"At least six other girls right now. But it changes every day. Some of 'em like it here. They're gonna try to get you to like it too. They rather be here than in a group home."

"I don't have to be in no group home!" Brianna started to cry. "Me and my mama have a house and I'm going home!"

They heard a rattling sound and the door opened. Two girls stepped inside the room. They were probably sixteen or seventeen, but their scant clothes and heavy makeup made them look much older. The shorter one had a pretty face and was wearing a short, red wig.

The taller one was toothpick-skinny and had tattoos up and down her arms.

"If y'all ready to act right, we'll let you out of here so you can eat." The tattooed girl threw Kaylee an oversized T-shirt. "Put that on."

Brianna decided to play it smart. She would pretend to go along with everything they said and when she got her chance, she was going to escape.

"I'm thirsty," Brianna mumbled. "Can I have some water?"

"Yeah, but then we gotta have a meeting. My name is Shantel," the tattooed one said.

"And this is Tameka. We in charge of the new girls. We gonna teach you what to do."

Shantel led them down a hallway into a messy kitchen that was half the size of the room where they'd been imprisoned. Half-eaten plates, balled-up paper bags, and other debris competed for space on the countertops. A roach hovered on the edge of the sink, surrounded by a cloud of gnats. The sour smell in the kitchen was as bad as the stench in the bedroom.

Brianna and Kaylee sat down at a scratched up glass table. Brianna began surveying the room for windows and doors that might serve as her escape. There was a kitchen window, a back door and a window in what looked like a family room adjacent to the kitchen. Every window was covered with iron bars.

"I see you lookin' around," Shantel said, fingering her long electric blue braids. "You try to escape and all you gonna get is an ass whippin'."

Shantel went to the sink, filled a paper cup with water and gave it to Brianna. She saw something floating on top and wanted to ask for a clean cup. Instead, she picked it out, then hungrily guzzled down the water.

"Okay, this house is all about the money," Shantel began. "The more money you make, the better treatment you get. Your first time with a john is gonna be a little scary. But after that, it ain't that bad. You probably been molested by somebody in your family anyway. So at least this way, you get paid for givin' it up."

"I haven't been molested!" Brianna shouted. "Nobody in my family would ever do that."

"Yeah, sure," Shantel said, rolling her eyes. "Then you must've been giving it up for free, which is stupid. Now you 'bout to make some money."

"I'm a virgin and I'm staying a virgin until I get married!" Brianna declared.

Tameka looked as if she felt sorry for her. Kaylee pressed her hands to her face, and started to cry again.

"I can tell right now that this little heffa is gonna be a big problem." Shantel pointed a gold fingernail at Brianna. "That mouth of yours is gonna get you in big trouble. Clint and Freda don't put up with no back talkin'."

"I don't care what you do to me. I'm not going to be a prostitute and you can't make me!"

Shantel laughed, held up her hand and gave Tameka a high-five.

"That's what they all say."

CHAPTER 10

Day One: 10:30 p.m.

Angela race-walked alongside Dre as he strode back toward his sister's house. Instead of turning into Donna's driveway, Dre headed for his car.

"We aren't going back inside?" Angela asked, as she opened the passenger door.

"Too many people in there. I gotta think." Dre slid behind the wheel, but didn't start the car.

Angela let him do that. They sat there in silence, Dre's head pressed back against the headrest, his hands gripping the steering wheel.

"You know what went down, right?" he finally asked.

"Yep. Jaden's no fourteen-year-old Christian." Angela had already surmised that Brianna could very likely be the victim of sex traffickers.

"I can't tell my sister what we suspect. She'll completely lose it if she thinks Brianna is in the hands of some pervert. I just have to fix this."

"How?"

Dre didn't answer for a long time. "I have no idea."

"I have lots of law enforcement contacts I can reach out to," Angela volunteered. "One of my FBI agent friends is doing some work with the LAPD's Human Trafficking Task Force. I can call him and—"

"Human trafficking? What're you talking about?"

Angela swallowed. "Dre, it's possible that Brianna's been kidnapped as part of a sex trafficking ring."

"She ain't no illegal alien. I'm figuring she was scammed by some pedophile."

Angela decided not to push the issue with Dre right now, uncertain just how much of her world she should share with him. Organized gangs were now deep into the sex trafficking business, snatching girls off city streets, not from other countries. She had no facts that Brianna was indeed a victim, but it was a real possibility. She'd call her agent friend anyway.

"I'll call Foshay in the morning to find out if there's a Jaden Morris enrolled there. I'll also check to see if his mother works at Crenshaw High."

"That's fine," Dre said. "But playing it by the book ain't gonna get Bree back."

It had taken Angela a while to admit to herself that she still wanted Dre in her life despite his criminal past. She truly believed that they could both start fresh. But Dre's statement only confirmed that the street would always be a part of him.

"So what are you saying?"

Dre glanced over at her.

"I'm saying that I ain't relyin' on the cops, the courts, the school or nobody else to get Brianna back. You see how that cop acted. He didn't even wanna take a missing person's report. *I* have to get Bree back. This is all my fault. So I have to fix it."

"That's crazy. How can you possibly think that this is your fault?"

"My sister kept super-tight reins on Brianna. I was the one always urging Donna to back up off her." His voice trailed off. "I was also the one who gave her that iPhone. She never would've been able to have a Facebook page if I hadn't done that."

"You can't think like that, Dre. If she hadn't had the iPhone, she would've found another way to get on Facebook. This is not your fault."

Dre stared straight ahead, as if focused on something down the block.

"I always teased Donna for being paranoid about child predators. But I guess she was right to be worried."

Angela could feel Dre's desperation and it terrified her. She knew he'd do whatever it took to find his niece—legal or illegal. While that concerned her, Dre had been there for her at a time when she'd needed him most and now it was her turn to stand by him.

He started up the engine and pulled away from the curb.

"Aren't you going to let Donna know we're leaving?"

"I don't have time to sit around crying and praying. I gotta go find Bree. I'll call Donna later."

They drove in silence all the way back to Angela's place in Ladera Heights. Dre escorted her to the front door of her apartment.

Angela fumbled with the key, but finally got the door open. "You want to come in for a while?"

Dre smiled. "What? You feelin' sorry for me now."

Angela smiled back. "Yep."

He pulled her into his arms and held her in a long embrace.

"Right now I have to focus everything I've got on finding Brianna." He finally let her go. "Can I get a rain check?"

"Sure. Where're you going?"

"I don't exactly know."

"Be careful, okay?"

"No problem there," Dre said with a melancholy smile. "Cuz what I gotta do is gonna require a whole lotta careful."

CHAPTER 11

Day One: 10:50 p.m.

By the time Dre left Angela's place and headed east on Slauson, it was approaching eleven o'clock. He thought about calling ahead, but decided against it.

As his Volkswagen Jetta chugged up the winding streets of Baldwin Vista, he gave some serious thought to upgrading his ride. Fancy cars were a pretense Dre didn't care about. But maybe it was time to up his game just a little. Especially since Angela, hopefully, was back in his life.

He reached the top of the hill on Cloverdale Avenue and rolled to a stop in front of a huge three-story home that had a view of downtown L.A. on one side and the Pacific Ocean on the other. He turned off the engine, dialed a number and waited.

"Hey, man, I need to talk."

"So talk."

"In person."

"Sounds serious. When?"

"Now. I'm outside."

As Dre had expected, Coop welcomed him into his home.

Cooper "Coop" Ford had been his unofficial mentor in the drug trade. Dre had modeled himself after this simple man who ran his operation like a business and had the smarts to get out when he'd collected enough cash to invest in legal operations. Coop now owned a chain of laundromats, several apartment buildings and two neighborhood bars, all in the hood. He treated his workers fairly and kept his businesses legit.

Greeting him at the door in a T-shirt, sweat pants and bare feet, Coop led Dre into his office, walking him down a marbled hallway lined with expensive African art. Coop had wooly salt-and-pepper hair. His penetrating eyes and the deep folds in his face conveyed a hard edge that seemed out of place in such posh surroundings.

After closing the double doors of his office, Coop perched himself on the edge of an antique desk. The impressive space had two walls of books that Coop had actually read. He was partially responsible for Dre's keen interest in biographies. Coop lived with a *wife* he'd never married and their two teenage girls.

Dre sat across from him on a cream-colored leather couch.

"What's up, youngster? You've got me a little concerned with this late-night visit."

"My niece is missing." Dre looked down at his hands. "She's only thirteen."

Dre quickly recounted everything they'd learned from Sydney. "I'm thinking this Jaden dude she went to meet was probably some sexual predator. Since he's operating in Compton, he's gotta be a brother."

"That's a crazy situation. I can't keep my girls off Facebook. I'll never understand why everybody needs to put all their business in the street."

"I gotta get her back," Dre said. "I'm trying to figure out where to start. I was hoping you might have a connection to some dudes who might know something."

"Man, I don't associate with perverts." He stood, grabbed a bottle of Brandy from a shelf and poured himself a drink. He raised the bottle in Dre's direction.

"You still a teetotaler?"

Dre nodded.

Coop took a long sip of his drink and returned to the same position on the edge of the desk. "Man, I'm truly feelin' your pain. I hate to do this, but I gotta put something on your mind."

Dre tensed. "I'm listening."

"The drug biz we knew is no more. These fools out here have no integrity. They ain't trafficking crack or meth. They're trafficking girls. Young girls."

Angela's comment about Brianna possibly being a victim of sex trafficking came back to him with the force of a solid punch in the stomach.

"I thought that craziness only happened to women from Mexico or the Philippines."

Coop shook his head. "Not anymore. Girls are the new crack, my brother. The Crips, the Bloods and even the Sureños, a Mexican gang, are in on it. They call themselves guerilla pimps. They're literally snatching girls off the street, breaking 'em down and forcing 'em into prostitution. Having 'em turn ten, twenty tricks a day. The younger the better. Pimping girls is easier, cheaper and less likely to get you shot or land you in jail for any serious time. And unlike a kilo, one girl can be sold over and over and over again. There's a ready supply and an endless demand."

Dre locked his arms across his chest. He didn't even notice that his leg was bouncing up and down. It had been hard enough for him to imagine Brianna in the hands of some pedophile. To think of her being turned out by a pimp was more than he could handle.

"There's only one dude I know of with the time or the brains to run a scam on Facebook like the one you just described," Coop continued. "You need to start with The Shepherd."

Dre squinted up at him. "Who the hell is that?"

"His real name is Rodney Merriweather. Smart young cat, barely thirty, if that. I heard he took a lot of flack from the roughnecks in his neighborhood growing up. So he hooked up with the Stoneside gang when he was at Dorsey High for protection. He went down south to college, then came home with some education and reunited with his boys. He started calling himself *The Shepherd* and talking himself up. The neighborhood dudes were impressed because he had a college degree and they started believing the hype. Eventually he was running things."

"Sounds like he just made up this persona and everybody fell in line."

"Basically. But the dudes out there today ain't like us, man. They're ruthless. They have no soul."

You had to be soulless to sell young girls. Dre was no saint, but he could never pimp women, much less children.

"Pimpin' is high tech now," Coop continued. "Cuz of the Internet. That's where they make the real money. Don't have to have girls walking the track. They arrange everything over the Internet. Set up a motel room and just run the dudes in and out. A hundred, two hundred dollars a pop."

Dre brushed a hand down the back of his head.

Coop reached over and squeezed his shoulder. "Sorry, my brother. But I had to be real with you."

"Where can I find this punk?"

"He owns a couple of liquor stores and runs City Stars on El Segundo."

"The strip club? I used to hang out there back in the day. I thought some older cat owned the place."

"He sold it several years ago. The Shepherd owns it now. The liquor stores and the club are just a front. His real operation is running ho's. I also hear he's also got loads of property, in South L.A. as well as the Valley. He drops in at City Stars from time to time. Easy to spot. Clean-cut-looking guy. Always flossin'. Drives a Bentley. But he runs three or four deep so you may have trouble getting to him. You should also talk to his old bottom bitch."

"His what?"

Coop smiled. "Sometimes it's hard to believe how square you are. Bottom bitch. A pimp's ride-or-die chick. Her name's Loretha Johnson. Used to be one of the baddest strippers to ever hit the pole. She's out of the game now. Runs a home that takes in ex-prostitutes. You might be able to find her walking the track in Compton trying to coax young girls off the streets. She'll probably have some helpful information about The Shepherd and I suspect she'll be glad to give it up."

"If he has Bree, I'm gonna get her back. Then I'm personally goin' after The Shepherd," Dre said, getting to his feet.

"You gotta approach this with your head on straight," Coop warned. "Getting your girl back should be the only thing on your mind right now."

"It is," Dre said as he moved toward the door.

He would find Brianna and bring her home. Then somebody was gonna pay.

CHAPTER 12

Day One: 11:15 p.m.

Loretha Johnson watched the young girl wobble along Long Beach Boulevard dressed in a halter top, cut-off jeans, black stilettos and sparkly red lipstick. She couldn't have weighed more than one hundred pounds. The awkward manner in which she forced her bony hips from side to side underscored her adolescence.

Standing in the doorway of an abandoned donut shop, Loretha waited for the right opportunity to approach. There was a steady trail of cars slowing down to check out the merchandise. She spotted two other girls on the opposite side of the street.

"You want a date, baby?" the girl in the halter top called out in a child's voice.

A beige Camry pulled over to the curb a few yards ahead. The girl scampered over, barely able to balance herself on her too-high heels. She bent low, allowing the potential john to get a glimpse of her non-existent cleavage.

Loretha clasped her hands, then absently twirled a finger around her shoulder-length locs. She sucked in a breath, praying that the girl didn't get in the car.

"Ten dollars!" the girl yelled, springing back to her full height. "You must be crazy! I charge fifty for a blow job."

She tottered away cursing as the man drove off.

Loretha glanced up and down the street, making sure the girl's pimp wasn't watching. With a kid this young—surely no older than thirteen or fourteen—her pimp had to be close by. If the girl was seen talking to Loretha, she'd get a beating. Hopefully, the pimp was busy keeping an eye on somebody else in his stable.

Confident that he wasn't nearby, Loretha followed the girl, remaining a few strides behind.

"You don't have to be out here on the street selling your body," Loretha called out. "You know that, right?"

Loretha pulled her sweater tighter across her chest and marveled at how the girl could look so comfortable dressed in next to nothing. It was barely fifty degrees.

"I'm from Harmony House," Loretha continued. "I can help you get away from your pimp."

Though the girl wasn't facing her, Loretha could see her body go rigid. She took a quick glance at Loretha over her shoulder.

"I ain't got no pimp," the girl snapped. "So just get outta here and leave me alone. My daddy warned us about you."

Good, Loretha thought. That meant the girl's pimp viewed her as a threat.

"Don't worry," Loretha assured her. "Your pimp's not around. I won't get you in trouble. I know you can't be seen talking to me. Just keep walking and I'll stay back."

"I told you, I don't have no pimp," the girl spat, continuing her stroll. "I have a boyfriend."

It would be a waste of time to explain to the girl that boyfriends don't sell their girlfriends to other men.

"If you ever need a place to go, you can come to Harmony House. All you have to do is call. Anytime, day or night, and I'll come get you."

The girl stopped, put a hand on her hip, but didn't turn to face her. "I already got a place to stay."

The bravado didn't fool Loretha either. She knew it was all an act.

"That's fine. But if you ever want to leave, I have a place for you to go. What's your name?"

The girl stepped off the curb and raised her hand high, trying to wave down a car that had reduced its speed. "You want a date tonight, honey?" she yelled out to the driver.

The man rolled down his window, gazed hungrily at the girl, then spied Loretha and sped off.

"You messin' with my business!" the girl yelled. She finally turned around to get a good look at Loretha, but kept moving. "Get the hell away from me!"

"What's your name?" Loretha asked again, matching the girl's steps stride for stride, but careful to stay a safe distance back.

"Lady, I gotta make my quota. Leave me alone!"

"I'm just here to let you know you have options. What's your name?"

The girl finally turned around. "Peaches. Why you messin' with me?"

"Nice to meet you, Peaches. I'm Loretha Johnson. How old are you, Peaches?"

"Nineteen."

The streetlight provided a solid glimpse of the cocoa-colored, plump-faced girl. There was no way she was nineteen. Up close, she looked even younger than Loretha had first thought.

"Why you out here tryin' to be somebody's fairy godmother?"

"Because I used to walk this track myself," Loretha replied. "I know what it's like."

That got the girl's attention. She glanced back at Loretha again. This time, her expression had softened, but only for an instant.

Loretha had indeed lived this life. Every horrible second of it. Older and wiser now, she was doing everything in her power to rescue others. One girl at a time.

She understood that Peaches and girls like her saw no way out. But to meet someone who had managed to escape, meant that it was possible for them to find their way to freedom too.

"I don't mean to hurt your feelings," Peaches continued, "but you don't look like you got what it takes. You must'a been out here a long time ago."

Loretha didn't take offense at the girl's intended slight. "Walking the track is hard work," she said. "Makes you age much faster than you have to."

It had been years since she'd strolled this very block, but the memory was like a deep wound. Though healed, the resulting scar would never go away.

These days, Loretha put extra effort into *not* looking pretty. Her skin was no longer porcelain smooth. Her hair still fell past her shoulders, but she didn't wear it bone straight anymore. Her locs were dyed auburn and were usually pulled back into a bun. She'd also picked up twenty pounds or so and found comfort in her bare face and loose-fitting clothes. Though her exterior appeared shabby, on the inside, she finally felt worthy. That was the kind of beauty she wanted these girls to experience.

Loretha's smartphone buzzed. She pulled it from her pocket, instantly recognizing the number. Another child who needed her help.

"I have to go, but I want you to call me. My number's easy to remember. It's 888-3737-888. Loretha pointed up the street. "I'm going to leave my card on the bus bench underneath that streetlight over there. I want you to pick it up and keep it with you. If you ever need help, call me and I'll come get you."

Loretha rushed past the girl, dropped her business card on the bench and turned down a side street toward her car. Minutes later, when her Prius reached the corner, the card was no longer on the bench.

She smiled and shook her fist in the air. "Thank you, Jesus!"

In Loretha's world, that simple act was a victory.

DAY TWO MISSING

"The average entry age of American minors into the sex trade is 12-14 years old."

—The National Report on Domestic Minor
Sex Trafficking: America's Prostituted Children
Shared Hope International

CHAPTER 13

Day Two: 12:05 a.m.

D re's next stop after leaving Coop's place was the 7-Eleven on Slauson and Angeles Vista. He withdrew four hundred dollars from the ATM and bought six bottles of 5-hour Energy. He had no intention of sleeping until he got Brianna back.

Though he wasn't certain that The Shepherd had anything to do with Brianna's disappearance, based solely on the information he'd obtained from Coop, he was now headed to City Stars to find out everything he could about the dude's operation.

Dre still couldn't get his mind around the fact that snatching little girls off the street and forcing them into prostitution was actually an organized crime. He tried, but couldn't fight the feeling that Brianna's disappearance was some kind of payback for the wrong he'd done. While he could honestly say that he'd never personally sold crack to a child, he'd surely impacted the lives of hundreds of children by supplying their parents' habit. Maybe this was God's way of punishing him.

Exiting the Harbor Freeway on El Segundo, Dre drove about three miles before pulling into the parking lot of City Stars. The neon sign out front boasted *The Best Topless Talent Around!*

After being patted down by the bouncer, Dre stepped into a dark entryway and handed ten bucks to the doorman and then walked through a turnstile and into the club. The bright lights from the stage and loud rap music attacked Dre's senses at the same time. The club looked almost the same as it had the last time he'd been there. Except back in the day, the place would've been clouded with cigarette smoke.

A topless girl was on stage slithering around a silver pole like a wannabe acrobat. Her enormous breasts bounced up and down in rhythm to the music. The small stage was surrounded by cocktail tables with red velvet club chairs. On the opposite wall, a bar ran the entire length of the room. It wasn't crowded at the moment since most of the married cats had probably gone home.

Dre felt like running up on stage and yelling that he wanted his niece back. Before he could plan his first move, a girl who was almost as tall as he was sauntered up to him. She was tightly stacked with a weave down to her butt.

"Hey, handsome. I hope we can spend some time together tonight."

She placed a hand on his forearm, then turned sideways so that her bare breasts pressed lightly against his shoulder.

"Not now," Dre said, brushing her aside as his eyes rotated around the club. He headed toward one of the high tables on the far side of the room. Before he could even get settled on a stool, a woman with flowers tattooed around the areolas of her plump breasts made a beeline in his direction.

"Hey, cutie, how about a private dance?"

A lap dance was the fastest way for a stripper to make some real cash. In his younger days, he'd had a crush on a stripper named Gypsy at the Barbary Coast. He didn't want to think about how much money he'd spent on lap dances with her.

Dre held up a hand waving the girl away. "Not now."

"Okay, baby," she said with a smile. "Maybe later."

Dre needed a few more minutes to evaluate his surroundings. He was surprised that there was only one bouncer inside. There was probably another one on the second level of the club.

His eyes were drawn across the room to a pretty girl who had an innocence about her. She appeared slightly uncomfortable, dressed in nothing but high heels and the bottom of a string bikini. She was probably new, Dre thought. He would start with her. They made eye contact. She smiled. When Dre smiled back, she pranced over.

"How you doing tonight, handsome?"

Up close, the girl was stunning. Her long hair was pulled back into a simple ponytail. Unlike the first two girls who had approached him, she wasn't wearing any makeup other than a bright red lipstick. He figured she was twenty-one, twenty-two, tops. He wanted to ask why she was doing this. *Couldn't a woman this hot find some dude to kick her down?*

"I'm doing pretty good now that you're here," Dre replied. "What's your name?"

"Katrina. What's yours?"

"Andre."

"Nice to meet you, Andre. Would you like a dance?"

"Absolutely."

Katrina took his hand and led him upstairs to the lap dance booths.

They walked past a small stage where a woman was jiggling short tassels from her nipples. Katrina directed Dre to a row of club chairs separated by high dividers. A sheer curtain provided a view of the stage and a modicum of privacy.

"Have a seat, sweetie."

Before Dre sat down, he made a show of taking out the stack of twenties he'd just withdrawn from the ATM at 7-Eleven.

"Looks like we're going to have a good time tonight," Katrina said, her eyes pinned on the roll of cash.

"How much?" Dre asked.

"Fifteen dollars a song," Katrina said.

He peeled off a twenty-dollar bill and handed it to her.

"You don't seem too excited," Katrina said coyly. "But don't worry. I'm sure I can get you going."

Dre wanted to tell the girl that she'd have to coat his Johnson in cement to get an erection out of him tonight.

She placed her fabulous rear end in his lap and started grinding against him in rhythm with the music. He placed a hand on her back, stopping her.

"Hold up," he said. "I wanna talk."

She glanced back at him with a baffled expression, then shrugged. "Whatever turns you on."

"I need information," Dre explained. "And I'm willing to pay for it."

CHAPTER 14

Day Two: 12:45 a.m.

Dre had definitely lucked up by selecting Katrina. She was new to the club and had no allegiance to The Shepherd or anybody else. Stripping was the fastest way for her to earn some tax-free cash to pay her nursing school tuition. She was more than willing to talk—as long as the money was flowing.

Six songs and a hundred and forty dollars later, Dre made his way back downstairs and found an empty seat at the bar. On both his right and left, half-naked girls were working hard to coax customers upstairs for a lap dance.

Dre shook his head as he listened to the women running their game. Based on what he was hearing, every dude in the place was *handsome*.

Katrina had confirmed that The Shepherd did indeed pimp girls. A couple of the strippers serviced athletes, celebrities and anybody else who could afford the higher price tag. According to Katrina, The Shepherd rarely visited the club, leaving his managers, Clint Winbush and Freda Kelly, to oversee his operation. Katrina had also heard from other girls that The Shepherd had taken his prostitution operation online. But she swore she'd never heard anything about The Shepherd kidnapping young girls.

"What you drinking?" said a female voice to Dre's rear.

He turned around. The bartender was a cute girl with at least eight hoop earrings in each ear. Unlike the strippers, she was fully dressed in a see-through mesh top and black leggings.

Dre's regular drink—a Pepsi—would send the wrong message.

"Brandy straight," he replied.

The two-drink minimum was how the club made the bulk of its profits.

"You got it, sweetie." The smiling bartender slapped a glass on the countertop and poured a shot.

Dre placed both forearms on the bar and leaned in closer.

"I'm lookin' for The Shepherd," he said in a low voice. "Is he here?"

The woman's demeanor turned from welcoming to frosty. "I don't know nothing about him."

"Doesn't he own this place?"

"I just work here, okay?"

"What's the deal? You scared of him or something?"

The woman took a step back, as if she feared Dre might hit her. "You asking questions like that, you need to talk to Clint."

"Who's Clint?" he asked, not wanting to give any hint that Katrina had already schooled him.

"The general manager."

"Okay, so go get him."

The woman turned her back to him and picked up a smartphone from a shelf along the mirrored wall. Dre tried to listen, but couldn't make out what she was saying over the music.

"He's coming," she told Dre, then retreated to the far end of the bar.

He turned back around to see Katrina take the hand of a greasy-looking white guy in a sweatshirt and lead him upstairs to the lap dance area. The sight repulsed him. It still puzzled him that such a gorgeous woman couldn't find a better way to make some cash.

It was a long wait before a man approached the bartender. Dre didn't look directly at them, but could see the woman pointing Dre out from the corner of his eye.

Clint had a short afro and was dressed in a nice-fitting navy suit. His expensive clothes and exaggerated swagger couldn't camouflage his ugly face.

"You the dude lookin' for Shep?" he asked, stopping a couple feet in front of Dre.

"Yeah. Who are you?"

Dre took in the man's thick gold chain, Rolex watch and huge diamond pinky ring.

"Clint Winbush. I run this place. What you want with Shep?"

"He took something from me."

Clint's lips see-sawed into a smile. "Is that right?"

"Yeah, that's right."

"And what's that?"

"My niece."

Clint took a smidgen too long to respond. It was as if he'd been knocked off balance and needed a few seconds to regain his footing.

"I don't know what you talkin' about. Neither does Shep."

Clint's smile stayed put as his eyes bore deeper into Dre's.

Dre saw evil in the man's hooded eyes. He knew something about Brianna. Dre could feel it.

"I heard y'all snatching girls off the street and turning 'em out. Young girls."

"I don't respond to lies."

Without taking his eyes off Clint, Dre picked up his drink from the bar. He raised it to his lips, but didn't take a sip. "I wanna talk to The Shepherd."

"He ain't here."

Their standoff was drawing attention. One of the bouncers headed over.

"So where is he?"

"I said he ain't here."

Dre visualized his hands around the man's neck. He did not know how he had expected Clint to respond to his allegation, but the denial was too weak. As weak as the man standing before him. This wide-nose punk was an underling, not a partner in this operation. He was a flunky who carried out orders, not someone who gave them.

Dre decided to use the opportunity to turn up the heat. He wanted a face-to-face meeting with The Shepherd and only The Shepherd. He raised his voice loud enough to be heard over the music.

"My name's Andre Thomas," he yelled to anybody in the vicinity of his voice. "The Shepherd snatched my niece and—"

Clint stepped back, making way for not one, but two burly bouncers. They moved into Dre's personal space, so close that he felt their foul breath on both sides of his face.

"You need to leave," said the goon on his right. He had a neck the size of a telephone pole.

Dre's hand reached toward the pocket of his jacket and the man's hand quickly gripped the butt of a gun stuck in his waistband.

"If you want it to get ugly in here, I can oblige you," the bouncer challenged.

Dre didn't flinch. "I was just reaching for my business card." He pulled it from his pocket and extended it to Clint. "Tell Shep that Andre Thomas is looking for him. He needs to call me. Right away."

When Clint didn't take the card, Dre placed it on the bar behind him.

"Get out," Clint said.

"I haven't finished my drink yet."

In what looked like a synchronized move, the two bouncers grabbed Dre by his biceps and started tugging him toward the door to the left of the bar.

Dre tried to pull away, but the men's hands felt like steel clamps around his biceps. He looked over his shoulder at Clint.

"The Shepherd has messed with the wrong family!" Dre yelled, just before they opened the door and threw him out of it. "You tell him I said his ass is mine!"

CHAPTER 15

Day Two: 1:00 a.m.

"Where's Cece?" Freda Kelly barged into the City Stars dressing room, hands resting on her meaty hips.

Half-dressed girls milled about the oblong room, fluffing their hair, oiling up their legs and piling on makeup. The air was thick with perfume and hairspray.

"She left already," Katrina volunteered.

Freda pouted. She resented the girls for their taut bodies and youthful faces. Freda had done okay in her day, but a twenty-nine-year-old, overweight stripper was more likely to pull a muscle than break the bank.

If a girl possessed the kind of beauty that stood out, Freda held even greater contempt for her. Katrina, with her high cheekbones, full lips and wide eyes, was the kind of pretty that didn't take work. God had done it all.

"You better not tell me she left," Freda said. "Not without paying her fee."

The strippers who danced at City Stars were independent contractors. They paid sixty-five dollars a day for the privilege of entertaining men at the most popular black strip club in the L.A. area. On most days, it took them only a couple of hours to break even and move into the black. On a night when the house was packed and the men were good and drunk, the girls could rack up several hundred dollars. Especially if they lined up several lap dances.

Katrina rolled her eyes and went back to applying her lipstick. None of the girls liked Freda and she knew it. Freda took pleasure in reminding them that she, along with Clint Winbush, were the powerhouses behind City Stars. But everybody knew they didn't own the place. They were just The Shepherd's lackeys.

"Look," Katrina said, "Cece's having a hard time. She's got two babies and a sick mother she's taking care of. Why can't you cut her some slack?"

"If I do that, then all of y'all will be skipping out on me without paying. Tell that girl don't show her face around here again until she has my money."

Freda stalked out of the dressing room and made her way to the back office. Clint was sitting behind his desk, deep in thought.

"You know that girl we took from Compton this morning?" he said in a low voice. "Her uncle came looking for her."

"What? How'd he know you took her?"

"I have no idea."

"You better call Shep."

"I ain't callin' nobody," Clint said. "He'll probably blame it on me. I told the dude I didn't know what he was talking about and had him thrown out. He ain't comin' back."

Clint opened one of six shoe boxes packed with money sitting on his desk. He started putting the bills into neat stacks by denomination. City Stars was a totally cash operation. No Visa, MasterCard or anything else. For customers who wanted a drink or a lap dance, but were short on cash, there was an ATM near the door.

"Looks like we're having a good night," Freda said, eyeing the cash.

"It ain't packed, but the brothers are drinking like fish. Mo' money, mo' money, mo' money!"

Freda peered at the screen of one of four laptops positioned on a long table against the back wall. "We just got online orders for six dates for Shantel and five of 'em are repeat customers."

"That's cuz Shantel knows how to treat her clients right," Clint said. "We need more girls willing to work hard like her."

The Internet Age made the pimping game a breeze. The smart pimps no longer had to send girls out on the track. Nowadays, the johns could use their smartphones, tablets or laptops to browse through pictures of hundreds of girls, then schedule a date online or via phone. Shep had a crew of six set up at one of his houses in the Valley who did nothing all day but schedule dates for his girls. There were far too many websites for the cops to keep up with, making the threat of detection miniscule.

"Wait until you see the girl we picked up in Compton," Clint said. "The clients are gonna go nuts over her."

"You're not worried about her uncle?" Freda asked.

"Hell naw. If he starts some trouble, we can trade her for a girl from Oakland or Atlanta and he'll never find her. I just hope it don't take long to break her in."

The girls usually came in the door scrapping like animals taken from the wild. But over time—once they realized there was no way out—they gave up and did whatever they were told.

"Why don't you go check on her?" Clint suggested. "I'm almost done. I'll be right behind you."

Taking her keys from her purse, Freda wondered how long it would take to break this one down. She hoped it happened fast because there was a whole lot of money waiting to be made.

CHAPTER 16

Day Two: 2:55 a.m.

"So where are you right now?"

Angela had called Dre three times since he'd dropped her off. It was close to three in the morning when he'd finally called her back.

"Hell if I know." Dre's voice had no life in it.

She sat up in bed and turned on the lamp on the nightstand. "You don't know where you are?"

Dre chuckled. "Hold on and let me check a street sign." Seconds later, he said, "I'm in Compton, headed north on Central. I've just been driving around. I think I've seen parts of L.A. and Compton tonight that I didn't know existed."

"Why don't you come over?"

"I wouldn't make very good company right now."

"Maybe I'd make good company for you."

"I can't. If I sat still, I'd feel like I wasn't doing everything I could to get Bree back. I gotta keep moving, keep looking. Even though I have no friggin' idea where to look."

"Anything I can do?"

"Yep. Ask the Man upstairs to send Bree home."

"Already done."

Angela held the phone tighter, as if that might bring Dre closer to her.

"So you've just been driving around ever since you dropped me off?"

"Naw. I hit quite a few spots over the last few hours. Been putting the word out on the street that I'm looking for my niece and that whoever took her is gonna have to deal with me. I actually think I know who may've taken her."

"You're kidding."

"Nope. You were right. It's highly likely that Brianna's been a victim of human trafficking. I'm pretty certain she's been grabbed by a pimp they call The Shepherd."

Dre told Angela about his conversation with Coop and his visit to City Stars.

Angela met his revelation with silence.

"I guess this doesn't shock you, huh?"

No, it didn't. It wouldn't do any good to share with Dre the atrocities some of her young clients had shared with her. She hadn't heard of The Shepherd, but she was well-aware that kidnapping and pimping girls—the younger the better—was now big business.

Neither of them spoke for a while, comforted by each other's presence even though they were miles apart.

Angela was now as scared for Dre as she was for Brianna. She knew the kind of man he was. Dre would do whatever it took to get his niece back. *Whatever* it took. He would not sit back and rely on the police for help. That was not in Dre's DNA.

A thought came to Angela. One that might help Dre find Brianna. "What's Brianna's phone number," she asked, reaching for a pen and paper from the nightstand.

"Her number? Why?"

"Just give it to me." She didn't want to tell Dre what she planned to do for fear of giving him hope that might not exist. She scribbled down the number.

"What do you plan to do next?" she asked.

"Hit a few more spots after daylight. I'm basically trying to call the dude out. I hear he's got a huge ego. He'll get in touch with me. Eventually."

"Dre, these sound like really bad people."

"I can be really bad too." He paused. "When I need to be."

They were face-to-face again with that gulf between them. The good girl-bad boy dichotomy. Opposites attract, they say. Dre would never be able to erase his criminal past and Angela would never be able to fully accept it. Especially, when it reared its menacing head, like now. So why was she trying to start things up with him again?

"I'm scared for you," Angela blurted out, her voice quivering.

"And I'm scared for Brianna," Dre replied. "I'm not worried about me or my life. I just want to save hers."

"Promise me you won't do anything crazy."

Dre didn't respond and Angela waited.

"Exactly how do you define crazy?"

Angela sighed.

"If these sick-ass cats do have Bree, my response won't be crazy," Dre said. "It will be a perfectly sane reaction. Not your kind of sanity, but the sanity of the streets."

CHAPTER 17

Day Two: 3:25 a.m.

After his call with Angela, Dre left Compton and drove back to L.A. He pulled into the drive-thru of a 24-hour Starbucks off Figueroa near USC and ordered a venti caramel macchiato with three extra shots.

"You have a very nice voice," the female barista purred at him from the speaker system.

Dre shook his head. He definitely wasn't in the mood to be hit on.

When he pulled around to the window, the clerk leaned out over the counter. "What's your name, handsome?"

Dre stared into the eyes of a cherub-faced teenager with a pierced tongue. Her heart-shaped lips were pale pink and she had on enough black eyeliner to patch a pothole. She looked almost as young as Brianna.

"How old are you?" Dre barked at her.

The girl jumped back, startled by his harshness. But it took her only a few seconds to regroup. "I'm seventeen," she said, puffing out her chest. "And how old are you, Mr. Cutie Pie?"

"Too old for you to be flirting with me." He flung a ten-dollar bill across the counter and through the window. "Give me my dang coffee!"

"Dang! Somebody sho' got up on the wrong side of the bed today."

When the girl handed him his drink, Dre snatched it from her, spilling it all over the side of the car door. He sped off without waiting for his change.

The clerk made him think of Brianna. He couldn't bear to think of his niece being held hostage in some grungy motel being raped by some sicko. He briefly closed his eyes, wishing he could erase the horrible images from his head.

As he drove, Dre debated whether it made sense to go this alone. Especially since he wasn't strapped. If he was going to confront The Shepherd, he would need backup. He'd also need some backup with balls. Too bad his brother Anthony was such a wuss. He could always count on his buddy Mossy. But for this job, he needed somebody who wouldn't be afraid to go down for the count if it came to that.

He made an illegal U-turn and headed toward Manchester. After turning onto Vermont, and then 85th Street, he parked on a street crowded with rundown apartment buildings and matchbox-sized homes. At least a dozen dudes were loitering outside the building where his cousin lived. Dre nodded a silent greeting as he moved past them.

He knocked hard on the apartment door. "Apache, it's me, Dre."

A bronze-toned man with straight black hair pulled back into a long ponytail opened the door.

"Hey, cuz. You know what time it is?" he said yawning. "I hope you got a good reason for disturbing my beauty sleep."

"Family business." Dre stepped inside the dingy apartment. "Serious family business."

"What up? Somebody died?"

That thought made Dre shiver inside. He refused to even consider that a possibility. "Naw."

Except for the 60-inch flat screen, Apache's apartment looked like a jam-packed thrift store. Furniture, clothes and boxes were everywhere. Dre had to push aside three large garbage bags on the couch to find a place to sit. He ignored his surroundings and told Apache the whole story.

"They can't mess with blood. We gotta get little shorty back. How you wanna handle this, cuz?"

"I need you to have my back."

"I'm down. Down all the way."

"You know anybody connected with Stoneside?" Dre asked.

"I got peeps everywhere and anywhere. You know that. A dude I know from Stoneside lives over on Budlong."

"Can we roll over there now?"

"Hell yeah. Let me get my piece."

Dre inhaled. He was a convicted felon and wasn't supposed to even be in the vicinity of a weapon. If they got pulled over, it would definitely mean jail time. To hell with that. He'd take whatever risks he had to take to get Brianna back.

Apache disappeared into the room and returned seconds later, Glock in hand. He slipped it into the small of his back and followed Dre out of the apartment.

"Man, why you still driving this piece of crap?" Apache asked as they approached Dre's Jetta.

Dre chuckled to himself. His cousin was driving a Benz, but living in a six-hundred-square-foot rattrap. "Cars are a luxury item I don't need."

As Dre opened the driver's side door, Apache stood back, as if even touching Dre's car offended him.

"I can't let nobody see me in this punk-ass ride. Let me go get my Benz."

"C'mon, man. We got business to take care of. Besides, the way you drive, we'll definitely get pulled over."

Apache grudgingly climbed in. "If we really wanna get the word to The Shepherd fast, we gotta go hard."

Dre didn't respond. He knew that. That was the only reason Apache was sitting in the seat next to him.

Twenty minutes later, Apache instructed him to park in front of a neatly kept house with a narrow driveway. Apache was already out of the car while Dre was still behind the wheel, surveying their surroundings. Even as a kid, his cousin had been fearless. That trait had only been bolstered after Apache survived being shot seven times in three separate incidents.

"Hold up," Dre called out. Apache had just stepped onto the porch. "I don't wanna start no trouble unless we have to."

"I know that," Apache said. "You carryin'?"

"Naw. That's why I got you."

Actually, even if it hadn't been a violation of his probation, Dre didn't trust himself with a gun. Not while he was on the edge of crazy.

Apache banged on a rusty iron door. "Hey, Deke, it's me, man. Apache. Open up."

They heard the fumbling of the doorknob, then the creaking of the door.

A gap-toothed man in pajama bottoms and no shirt appeared in the doorway. "Yo, man, do you know what time it is?" He opened the door just a crack.

Apache pushed his way inside and closed the door behind them. "You alone?" he asked.

"Yeah, man." Deke pointed at Dre. "Who's that?"

"My cuz. We need to find The Shepherd. You know where he lives?"

Deke raised both palms in the air. "Hey, man, don't nobody know where Shep lives. He keeps it like that."

"I hear y'all running women now," Apache said.

Deke's eyes darted from left to right. "Man, I don't know nothing about that."

Apache snatched the Glock from the small of his back and pressed it to Deke's head. "I need to know where I can find The Shepherd."

Deke froze, his hands at chest level. "C'mon, man. I thought we was cool."

"We are cool. But this is about my blood. My little cousin got snatched by The Shepherd. Since he rolls with Stoneside, I figured you might know something about it."

"Naw, man, I don't know a thing."

"You need to tell me something or I might have to pull this trigger."

"Okay, okay. But you gotta get that gun away from my head first. I can't think straight like this."

"Try." Apache pressed the gun deeper into Deke's temple.

Dre refused to breathe. He knew his cousin was more than capable of blowing the dude's brains out.

"Okay, okay." Deke started to stutter. "All I know is The Shepherd's been snatchin' girls and turnin' 'em out. A few days ago a crack head named Leon was bragging about getting paid fifty dollars for grabbing a girl in Inglewood."

"Where can I find him?"

"He usually gets high at a crack house near Hoover and Florence."

"Okay, we're going over there now."

Apache began to push Deke toward the front door.

"I can't go! Shep'll kill me if he finds out I helped y'all."

Apache cocked the gun and wrapped his free hand around Deke's neck.

To Dre's nervous ears, the cocking of the gun was almost as loud as a gunshot.

"Either The Shepherd can kill you later or I can kill you now," Apache said with a sinister smile. "So how you want it to go down?"

CHAPTER 18

Day Two: 3:30 a.m.

As hard as she tried, Brianna couldn't catch her breath. She was sitting on the mattress, her back against the wall, her palms pressed against her chest. She hadn't had an asthma attack in over a year, but she was certain she was having one now.

Kaylee crawled over to her. "Are you okay?"

"I...can't...breathe...Get help!"

At first, Kaylee just sat there, frightened and immobile. Then she hopped up and started screaming and banging on the door.

"Help, help! She can't breathe! She can't breathe! She's gonna die!"

Brianna's chest hurt so bad. She'd never had an asthma attack like this before.

The door opened and a woman wearing a nightgown stepped inside. She had a mean face and was probably her mother's age. A colorful scarf was tied around her head and knotted in front. She wore no makeup, but had long glittery eyelashes that looked like butterfly wings.

"What's going on in here?"

Kaylee pointed at Brianna. "She can't breathe!"

The woman walked over to Brianna and stared down into her face. Brianna's hands were gripping her neck and her chest involuntarily heaved up and down in short, jerky bursts.

"Oh my God!" The woman scurried out of the room. She returned seconds later with an inhaler and shoved it into Brianna's mouth.

Brianna sucked hard on the device and in a matter of seconds, was able to breathe normally again.

"Clint don' messed up again," the woman spat. "We don't have time for no sick ho's. You lucky I had that inhaler. One of my babies got asthma too."

Brianna reached up and grabbed the woman by her forearm. "They kidnapped us! Please, please, help us get outta here!"

The woman crouched down, stroked Brianna's face and pulled her close. "Listen, baby, my name is Freda and I'm gonna help you. But you gotta calm down first."

Kaylee lay curled in the fetal position sucking her thumb while Brianna cried and hiccupped into Freda's leg.

Freda took Brianna by the chin and smoothed her hair.

"You're not going to like it here at first," she said. "But I promise it's going to grow on you. If you behave and do what you're told, you're going to get a lot of nice things. How would you like some new clothes? I'll have one of the girls do your hair and nails. How about that?"

"No!" Brianna pushed Freda hard and she tumbled backward onto her butt. "Take me home. Now!"

"You're not going anywhere!" Freda shouted, struggling to get to her feet.

Brianna dashed for the open door, but Freda managed to grab her foot, causing her to fall to the floor, chin first.

"Ow!" Brianna yelled.

Freda dragged her back across the room and flung her onto the mattress.

"You need to understand something!" Freda snatched Brianna by the hair and slammed her head against the wall. "You're not going nowhere. We're your family now. So get used to it."

"No!" Brianna balled up her fists and pounded Freda's thighs, causing her to fall to her knees. Brianna then reached out and clawed Freda's face. "I'm getting out of here!"

"You stupid ho'! Clint, Clint!" Freda yelled, one hand trying to ward off Brianna, the other pressed against her injured jaw. "Get in here!"

Freda reared back to slap her again, but Brianna scratched Freda's face a second time and gripped a handful of her weave.

The man who had claimed to be Jaden's brother charged into the room. He untangled Brianna's hand from Freda's hair and hurled her across the room.

"I can't believe you let this little girl kick your butt," Clint said, laughing. "Wait until I tell Shep."

"You ain't tellin' Shep nothin'." Freda rubbed her cheek. "If she messed up my face, I'm coming back in here and kickin' her ass."

Brianna lay on the floor sobbing. "I wanna go home!"

Freda leered down at her. "I already told you, this *is* your home. So get used to it."

CHAPTER 19

Day Two: 3:45 a.m.

Loretha left the track in Compton and rushed over to juvenile hall. She filled out an endless number of forms, then spent the next few hours sitting on a hard wooden bench in a wide hallway with walls bright enough to startle a blind man.

She scolded herself for rushing down there. There was always a long wait. She should've spent a few more minutes with Peaches before abruptly running off. But the call of another young girl in need of her help always caused an excitement she could not quell.

Loretha pulled out her smartphone and sent yet another text asking how much longer it would be before they brought the girl out. A reply text advised that it would be about ten minutes. As it turned out, it was closer to thirty.

The sound of high heels click-clacking against the tiled floor made Loretha jump to attention. She glanced down the hallway and spotted her friend and social worker Sonya Moreno. Sonya's right arm was draped around the shoulders of a pouty young Latina. The girl's arms were defiantly folded across her chest.

Loretha briefly hung her head, prayed for strength and got to her feet. This girl was even younger than Peaches. When Loretha was part of this world, it was rare to see a girl as young as sixteen or seventeen. Now, girls that age were considered old. There were more babies walking the track than anything else.

"This is Carmen Lopez," Sonya said when they reached Loretha. The weariness in Sonya's voice matched the anguish in her eyes.

"I told you to call me C-Lo," the girl spat.

Carmen had large, dark eyes, curly black hair and a sullen attitude that said she'd rather be someplace else. Her spindly arms and legs gave her the appearance of a stick figure.

Sonya ignored the girl's rudeness. "And Carmen, this is Loretha. She has a place much nicer than the group home you went to last time. You're going to stay there until your hearing."

"I told you I don't wanna go to no group home!" Carmen shouted in a voice that sounded like Dora the Explorer. "Just keep me locked up. Big Daddy'll come get me."

Loretha placed a hand on the girl's shoulder. "Harmony House isn't anything like the group homes you've been to. I promise you'll like it. You'll make lots of friends there."

Carmen shrugged Loretha's hand off her shoulder. "I don't need no friends. I have six wives-in-law and that's all the friends I need. I don't see why y'all don't leave us alone. We ain't hurtin' nobody," she whined. "If you take me away, Big Daddy won't know where to find me."

The tears glistening in her eyes belied her bravado.

Loretha had once been as mouthy and rebellious as this child. She too had been glad to have a *Big Daddy* and other girls she called wives-in-laws, her first real family. Loretha could picture Carmen's wives-in-laws. A bunch of beaten-down little girls who were content to live in a crowded, rundown house, all vying for the respect and approval of a man whose only concern was the number of tricks they could turn in a twenty-four-hour period.

"Aren't you tired of being abused by strange men?" Loretha asked.

"I don't have sex with nobody but Big Daddy," she said, her face full of pride. "He don't make me turn tricks no more because I'm his favorite. I only do blow jobs and I make good money."

Loretha pressed a hand against the wall to steady herself. Her work drained her emotionally far more than it did physically.

"Do you get to keep any of the money?" she asked Carmen gently.

Carmen rolled her eyes and puffed out her chest. "That don't matter. Big Daddy gives me everything I need. He took me shopping to get this outfit last week."

Her *outfit* was a red Spandex skirt and a short top that exposed her not-so-flat stomach. Both were no bigger than a hand towel.

Loretha pointed to a dark spot to the right of her navel. "Is that a bruise? Did somebody hurt you?"

Glancing down at her waist, Carmen blocked it from view with one of her frail arms. "No. A trick did that. Big Daddy is nice to me. He's only slapped me a couple of times because I talked back to him. So I deserved it."

Loretha and Sonya exhaled at the same time.

"Have a seat while we talk," Sonya said, directing Carmen to the bench where Loretha had been sitting.

Carmen slumped down on the bench, her legs spread wide enough to reveal that she wasn't wearing any underwear. Sonya motioned Loretha several feet away, out of Carmen's hearing range.

"Vice officers caught her in a car giving a blow job to a guy behind a liquor store on Market Street," Sonya explained. "When the undercover cop moved in to arrest her, her pimp tried to take her away. They arrested him and the john too. She wouldn't ID the pimp and claimed she'd never seen the john before. Those two bailed out hours ago."

"How old is she?" Loretha asked.

Sonya folded her arms. "Fourteen. But she claims she's eighteen. This is her third arrest. Been in and out of six different foster homes over the last few years. Her mother kicked her out of the house after finding her in bed with her boyfriend. She was ten."

Loretha's cheeks expanded with air and she slowly let it out.

"She met her pimp walking home from school," Sonya continued. "He was obviously out scouting for girls he could groom. He took his time luring her in. The first time, he bought her some food and paid to get her nails done. Over the next three or four months, he started giving her money and taking her out on *dates*." She used her fingers to make imaginary quotation marks. "The movies, amusement parks, nice restaurants. Bought her a cell phone and clothes. Whatever she asked for, which wasn't much. Next thing you know, she's bragging to her middle school friends—on the rare occasion that she went to school—about her rich, older boyfriend.

Sonya paused and closed her eyes as if recounting the story was too much for her.

"You know the rest. They start having sex, then he convinces her to sleep with his friends. Weeks later, he wants her to prove how much she loves him by going out on the track to make money for him, supposedly to pay him back for everything he's done for her. Each time she's picked up for prostitution, we put her in a group home, but she runs right back to Big Daddy. At least he's one of the less-savage pimps. It's rare for him to beat his girls. By the way, Big Daddy is thirty-two."

Loretha grabbed both of Sonya's hands and squeezed. Without trading words, they both leaned in, their foreheads pressed together. They just stood there in silence, grieving for this child who had no idea she was even a victim.

"Hey!" Carmen yelled over to them. "Are y'all lesbos or what? Y'all need to get a room."

Sonya pulled away and threw her arm around Loretha's shoulders as they trudged back over to Carmen. "You're going to have your hands full tonight," Sonya said with a gentle smile.

Loretha laughed softly. "Unfortunately, it won't be different from any other night."

CHAPTER 20

Day Two: 3:50 a.m.

Following Deke's directions, Dre drove east on Florence. Minutes later they arrived at a boarded-up house with thigh-high grass, peeling paint and broken windows a block west of Hoover. In the backseat, Apache sat next to their captive, his Glock aimed squarely at Deke's stomach.

"Okay, I brought you here," Deke cried after Dre turned off the engine. "Now, y'all gotta let me go."

Apache raised the gun from Deke's stomach to his head. "Don't say another word. Just do what I tell you to do."

The three men exited the car. Dre popped his trunk and pulled out a flashlight.

"Let's go around to the back door." Apache had lowered his voice and lightened his steps.

With Deke leading the way, they traipsed along the side of the house. Dre was about to switch on the flashlight, but the spotlights dotting the roofline of a neighboring house provided them with more than sufficient lighting. They opened a gate and stepped into the back-yard, where the grass was taller than it was in the front of the house.

Pointing his flashlight toward the back of the house, Dre spotted a large window and a wooden door that had multiple holes in it. The door was opened just a crack.

Dre peered through the window, which was clouded grime. There was enough light from the house next door to see three figures sitting on the floor, their backs against the wall. They were either high or asleep or both. He could smell the strong scent of piss through the windowpane.

"There're three of 'em in there," Dre said.

Apache snatched Deke by the collar and pressed his face to the glass. "Is one of them dudes Leon?"

"Yeah, man. Please, can I go now?"

Apache didn't let go. "Which one?"

"The one in the middle. Now please let me go. If The Shepherd finds out I brought you here, he'll kill me!"

Apache jerked him away from the window. "Lay down on the ground and don't move. If I hear even a peep out of you, I'm going to shoot you in the head."

Dre aimed his flashlight at the door and Apache sprang into the house, gun drawn. "Hands in the air!"

The three men were suddenly wide-eyed, but apparently too high to follow directions.

"I said hands up!"

Three pairs of arms shot up, seemingly in slow motion.

"I heard you chumps been snatching little girls off the street."

The men were all tongue-tied.

Apache brandished the gun, slowly pointing it at each one of them.

"I wanna know where you been takin' 'em?"

"I ain't done nothin'," one of the men protested. "He's the one you want." He pointed at the man Deke identified as Leon.

"Shut up, fool!" Leon yelled. "You tryin' to get me killed?"

Apache pulled Leon to his feet, while the other men slithered to opposite corners of the room. He pressed the gun to Leon's temple.

"Did you snatch a girl named Brianna in Compton yesterday? And if you lie to me, I swear I'll blow your brains all over this room."

Leon's bottom lip quivered. "I just did what they told me to do."

"Who?"

"Just some dude. I don't know his last name."

Dre stepped forward. "That was my niece you took. Where is she?"

"She's at a place off Normandie. I don't know exactly where it is. I swear."

Apache lowered the gun from Leon's head and pointed it down at his bare feet. "You need to tell me who you're working with and where the house is, or I'm shooting off your toes one by one."

"I swear I don't know!"

Apache glanced at Dre. After several tense beats, Dre responded with an almost imperceptible nod.

Apache fired a single shot, blasting Leon's right foot. Blood spurted upward like a mini geyser. Leon screamed and dropped to the floor, grabbing his foot. The two other men cried out and hugged the walls.

"Start talking or I'm shooting you again. I got enough bullets to leave everybody in here with two stumps."

Apache pointed the gun at Leon's left foot.

"Okay, okay, don't shoot!" Leon begged and sobbed. "He's my cousin. I been working with my cousin Clint. He run City Stars strip joint."

Dre was so furious that he wanted to grab the gun and shoot Leon himself. He'd known when he'd looked into Clint's eyes that the punk had been involved in Brianna's disappearance and now his instincts had been confirmed. He wanted Apache to shoot the dude again.

"Where'd you take her?" Dre yelled.

"Sixty-second Street, off Normandie."

"That ain't good enough," Dre pushed. "We need the address."

"Man, I don't know no address. Clint drove, not me."

Apache fired the gun again. The bullet pierced the wall a few inches short of Leon's head.

"I don't know. I swear!" he cried, ducking, but still holding on to his bleeding foot. "It's bright yellow with lots of bushes and high gates all the way around. About halfway up the block on Sixty-second. I swear! It's the only house on the block with gates like that. Somebody's gotta get me to the hospital before I bleed to death!"

The pool of blood around Leon's foot was rapidly expanding.

"You working for The Shepherd?" Dre shouted.

"I don't know nothing about no Shepherd," Leon wailed, rocking and crying. "Clint hired me. I get fifty dollars every time I help him get a girl. I only did it two times. I swear!"

Dre stuck his smartphone in Leon's face. "Is this the girl you took?" he asked, showing him a picture of Brianna.

"Yes, yes," Leon cried, barely glancing at the photo. "Now get me an ambulance!"

"Is she still at the house?"

"I don't know! I swear. I just get my money and leave. I ain't never even been inside."

Dre gave Apache a nod that signaled that he was ready to leave.

Just for fun, Apache pointed his gun at the other two men and laughed. They screamed and rolled up as tight as water bugs.

"If anybody in here talks to the police about that sissy's foot," Apache announced, "I will hunt each one of you down and kill you. Count on it."

The other two men were trembling so hard the floor creaked.

When Dre and Apache stepped into the backyard, as expected Deke was long gone.

"Let's roll, cuz," Apache said, slapping him on the back. "We gotta go get little shorty."

For the first time since he'd walked into this nightmare, Dre finally felt real hope. He was close, real close, to bringing Brianna home.

CHAPTER 21

Day Two: 4:05 a.m.

Trying to sleep was a wasted effort, so Angela made some coffee and decided to get some work done. She'd hoped that her visions of a wild-eyed Dre roaming the streets, screaming threats and breaking down doors in search of Brianna would go away if she focused on one of her cases. That didn't happen.

Angela perused a few files, but was too wound up to concentrate. She would have to get it together soon because she had to be in court at nine. She spent the next few minutes alternately checking the clock and her smartphone hoping for a call or text from Dre. She was trying to wait until a proper hour to call her FBI friend, but finally decided this was too important to wait.

When her former colleague answered, he sounded as if he'd been awake for hours. As an FBI agent, Marty Shaw was used to early morning calls.

"Hey, Marty, this is Angela. Sorry to call so early, but this is important."

Marty had been a witness in one of the first cases Angela prosecuted as a young Assistant U.S. Attorney. After spending so many hours together preparing the case for trial, they'd developed a close friendship. Marty was now the federal liaison to the LAPD's Human Trafficking Task Force.

"Hey, Angela. What's going on?" His voice conveyed concern, but he also seemed glad to hear from her.

Angela had been nervous about how Marty might receive her call. She hadn't had much contact with any of her legal or law enforcement colleagues in recent months. Following the barrage of media reports about the shooting of her ex-fiancé and her relationship with a drug dealer, Angela chose to resign from the U.S. Attorney's office, where she'd been highly regarded.

She decided not to waste time with pleasantries or beating around the bush.

"I need a big favor. The child of a friend of mine's been kidnapped and possibly trafficked. I need help. Behind-the-scenes help."

An uneasiness suddenly seeped into his voice. "What kind of help?"

She quickly told him everything Dre had revealed to her. "The Shepherd's real name is Rodney Merriweather. Anything you can tell me about him or his operation would be helpful. I also need you to ping her iPhone. If we find her phone, we'll likely find her. She's only thirteen."

"Hasn't she been reported missing?"

"Yes."

"Then why aren't you working with the local police?"

"The family's done that. But they're not taking it seriously. They think she's a runaway. But she's not. She's a good kid. The officer who showed up barely wanted to take a missing persons report."

Marty heaved a sigh. They'd been close over the years. But disclosing information about an ongoing investigation could jeopardize his career.

Angela decided to play on his white guilt. "She's from Compton, Marty. A straight-A student. We both know that if this were a missing white kid from Pasadena or the Palisades, her disappearance would be leading the six o'clock news until the day they found her. I'm desperate. I really need your help."

Angela also knew that agents did stuff off the radar for family and friends all the time when traditional channels were taking too long.

"I can't tell you anything about our investigations," he said quietly. "You know that. Anyway, it's not like you can go track somebody down."

That wasn't true. If she turned over information about The Shepherd to Dre, that's exactly what he would do.

"Well, have you heard of The Shepherd?"

Marty remained silent long enough for Angela to know that he had.

"We've got our eyes on a few of these scumbag pimps. But I can't tell you any more than that. If you have evidence that somebody specific was involved in her disappearance, get me a name and I'll get somebody on it. But I'm not giving you any information so you can start running the streets like a vigilante. That will just come back on me."

"I'd never tell anyone you gave me the information."

Marty responded with an uneasy chuckle. "I can't risk it, Angela. If you get me some solid evidence, I'll follow up on it myself. Off the clock."

Angela rubbed her forehead. She was determined to do everything she could to help Dre find Brianna. Marty wasn't the only agent she knew. She'd just hang up the phone and keep dialing until she found someone willing to help.

"Okay, Marty. Sorry to put you on the spot. I shouldn't have asked you to—"

"I can't give you any information on our trafficking investigation," he said, cutting her off. "But I can probably locate her phone for you. What's the number?"

CHAPTER 22

Day Two: 4:20 a.m.

The location Leon had given them was less than fifteen minutes away, but for Dre getting there seemed to take forever. He drove cautiously, careful not to exceed the speed limit or even roll through a stop sign. He really wanted to floor the gas pedal, but with Apache carrying a Glock, they couldn't afford to get pulled over.

Dre was still a little antsy about having given Apache the go-ahead to shoot Leon. Despite the man's admitted role in kidnapping Brianna, Dre hoped he got to a hospital before he bled to death. If he'd been thinking straight, he would've realized that they needed the dude with them to locate the house. His Jetta headed west on Gage and made a left on Normandie. When he got to 62nd Street, he wasn't sure whether to go east or west.

Apache made the decision for him. "Hit a left," he said, pointing. "I just got a feeling it's this way."

Dre steered the car to the left and slowed to a crawl as he examined each house. His eyes bounced from one side of the street to the other, searching for a yellow, gated house.

"It's supposed to be in the middle of the block," Dre said when they reached the end of street. "It must be in the other direction."

"Maybe not," Apache said. "We got our directions from a crack head. Go up one more block."

Dre didn't need to be reminded that he had placed all of his hopes on an addict who'd been interrupted in the middle of getting high.

The car crept along the next block. There was one yellow house with lots of flowers in front, but no gates.

"There's no way we could've missed the kind of gates he described," Dre said. "I'm going the other way."

At the end of the block, he made a U-turn and drove in the other direction.

Dre's fingers tapped the steering wheel as he waited for the traffic to clear enough to allow him to cross the busy intersection at Normandie to make it to the other side of 62nd Street.

They eased along the first block. No yellow house. The next block either. Dre drove several more blocks, then zigzagged up and down the streets parallel to 62nd Street. With each turn, a bit of his hope faded.

"I think the dude punked us," Dre said.

"If he did, I'm going back and shootin' off the rest of his toes," Apache said. "Let's keep lookin'."

They drove up and down the neighboring streets for another ten minutes or so before Dre pulled back onto Normandie and parked in front of a liquor store.

"What you doin', man? Why we stoppin'. Let's keep lookin'. I gotta feelin' we're in the vicinity."

"I need to think," Dre said. Something that would be hard to do with Apache running his mouth.

"Man, when we find little shorty, we gon' beat them punks down!"

That wasn't the way it was going to go down. Once he got Brianna back, he was going to be slow and methodical about his revenge. He didn't need or want Apache's help for that aspect of the job.

He started up the car.

"Where we goin'?"

"I'm taking you back home," Dre said.

"You givin' up?"

"Hell naw. I gotta make a run to Compton. A buddy of mine used to deal in this area. He might know the house we're looking for. If he does, I'll call you."

CHAPTER 23

Day Two: 5:30 a.m.

The impressive mini-castles along Ocean Boulevard in Newport Beach were among Southern California's most prized waterfront property. One peach-colored monstrosity seemed glaringly out of place when compared to the neighboring homes. A low, gold-plated fence with goddess statues every few feet boasted an unwelcomed gaudiness. A black Bentley sat parked in the driveway next to a burgundy Jaguar. An intentional show of wealth that begged to be noticed.

Inside, The Shepherd plodded barefoot up and down the length of his great room, creating deep imprints in the plush gold-speckled beige carpet. The room was the size of two large garages, with high ceilings, fat leather chairs and a wall of glass that looked out over the aqua-blue waters. It had the feel of a model home that had yet to be lived in.

The Shepherd bore a baby face and the earnestness of a young TV anchorman. In sweats and a polo shirt, he resembled a college freshman. He'd created the look first, then altered his personality to fit it.

His two lieutenants remained silent as he paced. They were familiar with the unusual way in which their boss expressed his discontent. It was best not to speak while he simmered.

Pausing mid-step, Shep rigidly sat down in one of the leather chairs, his back facing the two men.

"This guy has no idea who he's messing with," he said, mostly to himself.

Shep was always careful to enunciate each syllable of every word. He never cursed and rarely raised his voice. He believed that a true leader always kept his emotions in check. He clenched and unclenched his fists as if he was practicing finger exercises.

"Nobody disrespects me."

After receiving Clint's call about Andre "Dre" Thomas' visit to City Stars, other calls followed. Jonesy, the manager of one of his liquor stores, reported that Dre had walked into the place and announced that The Shepherd had snatched his niece, so Dre was out for The Shepherd's blood in return. Several more calls reporting similar threats followed. Dre had gone all over town calling him out. And then Shep got word of the shooting of Clint's crack head cousin, Leon.

That had sent Shep off into an internal orbit. He slowly swung the chair around, his narrowed eyes locking with Clint's.

"What possessed you to bring someone into my operation without my approval, not to mention a crack head?"

"I...I was in a fix. He was the only person I could get at the last minute. He's my cousin. I didn't think it would be a problem."

"Well, it *is* a problem. Your cousin doesn't know how to keep his mouth closed. You should tell him it would be a good idea for him to disappear. If not, I will make him disappear."

As Shep continued to gaze at him, Clint seemed to shrink in size. He would've looked away, but Shep demanded eye contact. After a full minute of silence, Shep turned his focus on the second man.

"It's your job to thoroughly check out the girls, isn't it?"

There was no anger his voice. He might as well have been asking for a drink of water.

The second man had trouble meeting his gaze.

"Look at me when I talk to you," The Shepherd said evenly. "I spend a great deal of time planning my operation. You both know that. All of my girls are well-researched. Since I transferred everything online, we've never had a problem."

Clint fired off a sideways glare at the man everybody called *Large* because that's what he was. Clint's harsh look commanded Large to step up to the plate.

"That girl was a referral just like all the others," Large finally said, glancing at the floor, then quickly back at Shep. He had small ears and a head shaped like a bullet. "The information we got was that she didn't have a daddy and was back and forth between her mother and grandmother. I didn't check her out any further."

Only girls who fit their profile were targeted by "Jaden." It was preferable that they were from a group home, in foster care or, even better, runaways. But a troubled family life was a requisite. The likelihood of molestation for such girls was high, so sex wasn't foreign to them. They were also easily conditioned because they had no self-esteem to speak of.

"It's your job to research each girl's background, is it not?"

Large shrugged. "Okay. I messed up. But the referrals are usually good to go. We never check them out too hard anymore."

Shep laughed. It was never good when Shep laughed.

"So that's all you have to say? *I messed up.* Your lack of attention to detail is unacceptable. You can leave now."

Large trudged toward the front door and out of the house.

Clint finally spoke. "Man, this little trick ain't worth it. Got too much fight in her. She almost whipped Freda's ass. If she's related to this Dre dude, he ain't gonna quit until he gets her back. Let's turn her loose. We got six more girls coming down from Oakland in a couple of days and that dude in Birmingham wants to sell us some more girls."

Shep started pacing again. He was a thinker and Clint was used to letting him do that in silence.

As his No. 2 man, Clint was the only one besides Large and Freda, who knew the full extent of his operation and how everything worked. Shep and Clint had banged together all through high school. Back then, Clint supervised their drug runners, while Shep organized the distribution channels as well the finances. Shep had always been smart enough to stay out of sight, calling the shots. So he'd never seen the inside of a jail cell.

But slinging drugs posed more of a threat to his freedom than Shep wanted to bear for the long haul. They soon put crack and weed on the backburner and turned to the pimpin' game. Three years ago, they brought their operation into the Internet Age.

Shep stared up at Clint.

"I'm not very happy about this guy going all over the city disrespecting me. If he wanted his niece back, he should have come to me like a man. What do you know about him?"

"I made a few calls. His name on the street was Businessman because he ran a tight operation. He dealt crack, mostly to low-level dealers who didn't want to cut it themselves. Did a stint at Corcoran. He supposedly quit the game a few months ago and went legit. Brianna is his niece."

Shep slowly wrung his hands. Not in a show of nervousness, but as if he was slathering them with lotion. "I'm going to teach Businessman a lesson."

Clint threw up his hands. He was the only one in The Shepherd's operation who ever dared to disagree with him.

"C'mon, Shep! If this dude goes to the police—"

"Mr. Businessman is not going to the police. If he was going to do that, it would've already happened. He's a convict and convicts do not like the police. And if he does eventually decide to do so, when they run his record, they aren't going to do very much to help him. They might even think his drug dealing is the reason his niece is missing. And he knows that."

"Man, the girl has asthma and had a real bad attack early this morning. She could get sick and die or something. We don't need no girl dying on us."

Shep's eyebrows fused and his nostrils flared. But in seconds, he regained control of his emotions. "Why am I just hearing about this?"

Clint scratched his jaw. "She's fine now. But—"

"And she's going to continue to be fine because *you're* going to make sure she is."

Clint swallowed hard. "So exactly what you wanna do?"

"You said this guy *used* to deal. Sounds like he was smart enough to get out of the game at the right time. That means he's probably got some cash stacked away. A lot of cash, I suspect."

Shep smiled as he plotted. "We're going to expedite things with his niece. I want to send her on a date as soon as possible. But first, I want *you* to break her in. And I want it on video."

Clint felt his stomach churn. He didn't mind breaking in the older ones, seventeen or eighteen. But he had a problem doing the youngsters. That was for perverts. In his mind, pimpin' a child and screwin' one were two very different things.

"And after Ms. Brianna has had a little taste of being in the life, we'll hand her back. Then I want you to publicize *that* on the street."

"I really think you need to rethink this," Clint pleaded. "This is just one girl, Shep. Why risk all we got over her?"

"I don't plan to risk a thing. Right now, it's more important for me to restore my reputation on the street. Are you forgetting that I was the one who created this entire operation? How much money have I made you?"

Clint shrugged. Yeah, he was clockin' at least five grand a week, sometimes more. But that wasn't the point.

"It ain't about the money right now, man. It's about protecting the operation."

"Well, at least we agree on that. If I don't send a strong message in response to this affront, I'll have other fools out there thinking they can disrespect me too. "

Clint clenched his teeth. This was a bad move. A real bad move.

"And if Mr. Businessman wants what's left of his niece when we're done with her," Shep said with a smile, "he's going to have to pay to get her back."

CHAPTER 24

Day Two: 6:00 a.m.

Loretha had trouble keeping her eyes open. She was used to going 24/7, but at the moment, her body was screaming for sleep. She ended up having to wait another couple of hours before Carmen was officially released into her care.

She glanced over at the girl, who was asleep in the passenger seat, snoring softly. Whenever Loretha got her hands on a new girl, she was always hopeful that this one would be a child she could save. Not for a week or a few days, but for life.

Finally reaching Harmony House, she steered the car through electronic gates and down a long driveway. She pressed the garage door opener attached to the sun visor and waited as the garage door rattled open. Before driving inside, Loretha made sure the electronic gates had closed, then checked the rearview mirror and both side mirrors. She was always careful about making sure she hadn't been followed by some pimp.

This was Harmony House's second home in three years, and the best location so far. The two-story house in the Lafayette Square area of Los Angeles was a little known enclave of historic homes with a rich history of black wealth.

In the beginning, her neighbors had fought her efforts to disrupt their community with a "bunch of prostitutes," as one protester called them. But Loretha hit the pavement, and appealed to anyone willing to open their door to hear her pitch. The resistance soon faded and some neighbors had even volunteered to work as tutors and regularly donated food and clothes. A few others joined the board and helped them raise money to supplement the state grants Harmony House received.

The only downside to the location was that Loretha could only house fourteen girls at a time. The need was so much greater.

Loretha was surprised that the loud rumbling of the garage door hadn't wakened Carmen. She waited until they were safely inside the garage, then opened her driver's side door, which activated the car's overhead lights.

"We're here," Loretha said, gently touching the girl's shoulder.

Carmen shot upward, flailing her arms and yelling, "Get the hell away from me!"

Loretha had anticipated this reaction. In the early days, she hadn't been prepared for the girls' feral reaction when they were aroused from sleep. She gave Carmen the few seconds she needed to realize that she was not about to be raped. Again.

"You're safe," Loretha said softly.

Carmen shielded her eyes with her hand. "Turn off them damn lights."

The first thing Loretha would need to do was correct the girl's foul mouth. Harmony House had rules. But that could wait for now.

Carmen looked around. "That social worker said this was a nice place. Don't look all that nice to me."

Loretha climbed out of the car. "This is just the garage."

They maneuvered around boxes of supplies, clothing and canned goods. There was barely enough room for the small car. Loretha stuck the key in the door leading into the house. Before she could turn the knob, it opened.

Anamaria, one of two full-time house managers, greeted them.

"Can't believe you're still up," Loretha said with a thankful smile. She stepped into a wide hallway.

"Carmen, this is Anamaria. She helps me run this place."

Loretha could tell that Carmen was surprised to be greeted by another Latina.

"Welcome to Harmony House." Anamaria's Spanish accent had a melodic lilt to it.

"Yeah, whatever," Carmen muttered. "Ain't like I had a choice."

Loretha and Anamaria both smiled at the familiar insolence.

It would be their job to change that attitude and free the little girl inside this pretend-woman.

"I have the Hope room all ready for her," Anamaria said to Loretha.

It had been Anamaria's suggestion to name the rooms. Two years earlier, Anamaria had been a Harmony House resident. She was now one of Loretha's success stories.

Carmen gave a fake laugh. "The Hope room? Y'all are definitely buggin'."

As they stepped out of the hallway and into the foyer, Carmen stopped and took in the room. The walls and floors were nearly all solid mahogany with high ceilings and decorative window panes. The room exuded a regalness.

"Dang, this *is* nice!"

"Thank you very much," Loretha said. "Your room's upstairs."

As they ascended a spiral staircase, Carmen ran her hand along the polished wood banister.

They walked past closed doors, all labeled with words of inspiration. Trust, Peace, Safety, Love, Tranquility. Anamaria opened the door of the Hope room, then stepped aside so Carmen could enter first.

Carmen pressed both palms to her cheeks. "O-M-G!"

The room had twin beds with fluffy Hello Kitty comforters. The walls were bright pink with splashes of yellow and blue flowers. A pink teddy bear sat atop a pillow on the bed closest to the window and there were posters of Justin Bieber, Usher and Princess Tiana. A small rectangular desk rested against one wall.

"O-M-G!" Carmen said again. "How'd you know pink was my favorite color?"

She darted across the room and bounced up and down on the bed. She grabbed the teddy bear and hugged it to her chest. "Is this mine?"

"Absolutely." Anamaria opened the closet and handed Carmen a knapsack.

"This is yours too," she said, handing it to her. "It has toiletries, pajamas and other clothes. The shower is two doors down on the right."

Carmen grabbed the bag and looked inside. She pulled out a long-sleeved nightshirt with Brittany Spears' face on it. "I usually sleep naked, but I really like this. How'd you know my size?"

Anamaria grinned. "I just took a guess."

Actually, the majority of the girls wore a small because they were so undernourished.

"Okay, this is way too square for me," Carmen said examining a knee-length floral skirt. She stuffed it back into the bag, then gazed around the room.

"Oooooooh." She shot over to the desk, sat down and grabbed a paint set.

"I used to love to paint. That's the only thing I do good in. My third grade teacher, Ms. Harris, said I have imnate talent."

Loretha smiled at the mispronunciation, warmed by Carmen's youthful excitement.

"Can I have this too?"

"Of course," Anamaria said. "There's some paper in the drawer."

They watched as Carmen grabbed a sheet of paper and tore open the paint set. She dipped the paintbrush into a blue, then yellow pallet.

"What are you drawing?" Loretha asked, marveling at how fast Carmen had brought life to the blank page.

Carmen looked up at them with big, happy eyes. "I'm making a picture of me and Big Daddy. I'ma give it to him when he comes to pick me up."

CHAPTER 25

Day Two: 6:30 a.m.

Clint marched out of Shep's house pissed off at the task he'd been directed to carry out. They had a smooth-running operation that had been working without a hitch. But Shep's ego was about to mess everything up.

Inside his Escalade, Clint tapped a button on the navigation screen, which speed-dialed Freda.

"We gotta expedite everything," he said. "Shep wants to put Brianna out there A-S-A-P. So get her profile up online. Make sure you only use the body shots we took. Not her face."

"I know what to do," Freda fumed.

"Okay, then," Clint said. "Just do it."

Brianna's face would attract a lot more hits than her body because she looked so young, but photos of her barely budded breasts would do the job. There were enough perverts out there to have ten dates lined up within seconds of uploading her pictures. It would be stupid to post the face of an underaged girl on the Internet. That constituted child pornography, which carried much stiffer penalties than trafficking.

They'd taken extreme precautions to protect their online operation, running it through an international website with firewalls that made it next to impossible to trace any of the profiles The Shepherd posted back to him. Though Clint had tried to talk Shep out of branding his girls, he'd been overruled. As brilliant as he was, Shep's ego sometimes interfered with what Clint considered sound business judgment.

"That girl ain't ready for no dates yet," Freda complained. "It's going to take some time to break her down. And I wanna help with that process. I got a scar on my face because of her."

"I don't care about your face. It's your fault that you let a thirteen-year-old kid jack you up like that. And I didn't call you to get into a debate. Just do what I told you to do."

"I'm callin' Shep," Freda insisted. "We don't need to be—"

"You ain't doin' nothin'."

It pissed him off when Freda refused to take orders from him. Half the time, she acted as if *she* was running things.

"I just told you how it's going down. So do it."

He ended the call.

Clint thought it was a mistake to have a woman like Freda so heavily involved in their operation. On the other hand, it was good to have a female on hand, because it was easier for her to win the trust of the girls.

Though Freda could be just as callous as any dude, Clint knew she had ulterior motives. It wasn't just about the money for her. She'd been bucking to be Shep's bottom bitch ever since he pulled her off the pole. Nobody had really fulfilled that role for Shep since Loretha. And nobody *could* fill it like Loretha. That ho' had a business sense keener than Shep's. On top of that, you could trust her with your life. She always had Shep's back. No matter how many times he'd kicked her ass, put her down or threw her out, she always came back, begging to do better the next time.

Clint had been floored when Loretha finally turned her back on them and returned to the square world. After all the dirt she'd done, it amazed him that she was out there trying to save ho's from the life. He was equally surprised that Shep agreed to let her do her thing as long as she never tried to recruit any of his girls. Since they no longer had girls walking the track, it was unlikely that Loretha would ever run into one of their girls. Still, Clint had tried to get Shep to shut her down, but he refused.

Exiting the Harbor Freeway at Gage, minutes later Clint pulled up to the house where he'd deposited Brianna the day before.

Freda met him at the back door, hands on her hips. "I don't appreciate you hangin' up on me."

Clint continued past her. "Get outta my face."

"I don't care what you say. I'm still callin' Shep and tellin' him not to—"

He stopped and turned back to her. "Go ahead. Call him. Let's find out once and for all who has more pull. You or me. You keep trippin' and you're gonna find your ass on the street."

"You can't threaten me."

Clint shrugged. "I just did. Your problem is, you don't know when to shut your trap. That's why Shep don't have you staying at his crib. If you were really his woman, that's where you'd be."

Freda's lips tightened. He could see that he'd hit a nerve and that pleased him.

"And just in case you didn't know it, he's got Sareena living with him now."

That was a lie, but Clint wanted to mess with her head. Sareena was twenty-one, smart and sexy. Though Shep had claimed her as his own, he still shared her with his high-end clientele—businessmen, athletes and entertainers who were willing to fork over a few grand for an hour or two of what he got for free.

Freda's eyes glazed with anger. It had been almost a year since she'd shared Shep's bed.

"So go ahead," Clint said, continuing with his taunt. "Call over there with your attitude so I can remind Shep why he should keep Sareena as his main broad and not you. That girl knows how to keep her mouth shut and do what she's told." He paused. "In addition to having the baddest body on the planet."

Clint continued down the hallway, expecting a fiery retort that didn't come. Freda wouldn't question Shep about Sareena living with him. If she did, Shep might just put her ass back on the street. But nobody wanted a twenty-nine-year-old ho'. It was all about the young girls now.

He stopped halfway down the hallway, pulled the keys from his pocket and unlocked the three deadbolts. Brianna was huddled on the bare mattress in the fetal position, naked. The room smelled like piss. He wished he could open a window, but he couldn't risk the girl calling out to someone on the street.

"C'mon," he said, glaring down at her. "You're going home. Your uncle's been looking for you."

A smile ignited Brianna's drawn face. "I knew he would come get me!" she whimpered. "I knew it!"

"C'mon then. I got some clothes for you in the other room."

Brianna tried to stand, but her weak legs couldn't hold her up and she tumbled back to the mattress. She tried again and got halfway erect before Clint grabbed her upper arm and started moving toward the door. He dragged her across the hallway to the room he used when he spent the night at the house. It was one of only a couple of decent rooms in the place.

"What about Kaylee?" Brianna asked. "Can she come with me?"

"No," Clint snapped. "Kaylee was smart enough to get with the program. She's on a date right now."

Clint tossed Brianna onto the bed, then turned around to lock the door.

He hated what he was about to do. This girl barely had breasts. He doubted his dick would even get hard.

Pulling Brianna's iPhone from his pocket, Clint turned it on and fiddled with it until he found the camera. He was about to start the recording when something hit him.

Why did Shep want a video of him breaking Brianna in?

If the video got into the wrong hands, he would never see daylight. He and Shep went way back, but was his boy trying to set him up?

Brianna's weak voice interrupted his thoughts. "Where are the clothes?"

Perched on the edge of the bed, she glanced around the room. Her arms were crisscrossed in a futile effort to hide her nakedness.

Clint would give Shep a video of the girl all right. But his face wouldn't be in it.

Stepping up to the bed, he punched Brianna hard in the chest. The force of his blow sent her tumbling to the floor. He knew from experience that if he beat her before he had sex with her, she'd be much more compliant.

Clint reached down and grabbed Brianna's arm and tossed her back onto the bed. Instead of remaining there, she charged at him and sank her teeth deep into his forearm.

Clint yelped in pain and tried to pull her off of him. When he finally did, he saw blood seep through the sleeve of his shirt. "You crazy ho'!"

He backhanded her across the face. As he drew back to hit her again, Clint stopped mid-swing when he saw that Brianna's jaw was puffing up like a water balloon.

Damn!

Shep didn't allow hitting the girls in the face.

"My Uncle Dre's gonna get you." Brianna's words came out slow and garbled, as if she was drunk. Blood spewed from her lips.

With his right hand, Clint aimed the iPhone at Brianna and pushed *record*. Using his free hand, he yanked Brianna by the hair and slammed her head into the oak headboard over and over again.

Brianna used her fists to fight him off, but her punches felt like taps. The words coming from her bloody mouth no longer made sense.

Clint was careful to keep himself out of the video. He also didn't say a word so the recording wouldn't pick up his voice. He aimed the camera lower as he released Brianna's hair and started punching her in the ribcage.

She cried and gasped as her chest heaved up and down. Suddenly, she stopped fighting him and was struggling to catch her breath.

He hoped the girl wasn't having another asthma attack.

As Brianna fought for air, Clint backed away toward the door, his heart hammering, the camera phone still aimed in her direction.

No way this girl was going to die on his watch.

He stopped the recording, shoved the iPhone into his pocket and tore down the hallway. He found Freda sitting at the kitchen table, sulking.

"Get me that inhaler," Clint yelled. "Now!"

CHAPTER 26

Day Two: 7:45 a.m.

Angela pulled her SUV into the gated parking area behind the Kenyon Juvenile Justice Center in Watts and turned off the engine. She needed a moment of solace to brace herself for another heart-wrenching day.

Around seven that morning, Angela remembered a friend who was an administrator with L.A. Unified School District. Despite the early hour, she'd given her a call and asked her to find out if there was a teacher at Crenshaw High School who had a son named Jaden Morris. Her friend also agreed to find out whether there was a Jaden Morris enrolled at Foshay Middle School.

After saying yet another prayer for Brianna and Dre, Angela grabbed her satchel and climbed out of her car. She greeted the sheriff's deputy on duty at the rear door and passed through the metal detectors. As usual, the waiting area for juveniles who had matters before the court was as crowded as a hospital emergency room during flu season. She made a left at the end of the corridor and entered courtroom 264.

Juvenile court did not resemble traditional courtrooms. For one, there was no jury box, witness box or formal seating area for court watchers. Two long tables faced the judge's elevated bench. A couple rows of folding chairs served as the gallery. The court-assigned probation officer sat off to the right with the bailiff stationed near the door.

"Hey, Carol. What's on the calendar for today?"

The probation officer handed Angela a stack of papers. "The Public Defender's Office had conflicts on all six of those. So they're all yours."

Angela thumbed through the petitions. "This is crazy."

"You're telling me," Carol said with a shake of her head.

Angela quickly scanned the petitions. All six cases were juvenile girls picked up for soliciting prostitution. "Are any of them here yet?"

Carol looked down at a list on her desk, then reached up and flipped through the petitions that she had just given to Angela.

"That one, Jolita Allen, is in the back. Two others are in transit from juvenile hall."

Angela quickly read the scant paperwork for her newest client. This was the girl's second arrest for soliciting prostitution. After the first arrest over a year ago, she'd served six months at a juvenile camp. Angela entered a door to the left of the bench and walked down a hallway to the holding tanks.

"I need to see Jolita Allen," she told the deputy.

She followed him as he unlocked the cell.

Jolita stood up, arms folded. "When am I gettin' outta here?"

When Angela met a new client charged with soliciting prostitution, the girls typically displayed one of two demeanors: fear or defiance. Jolita fell into the latter category.

She was a tiny little girl, tiny even for fourteen. Her orange jailhouse jumpsuit swallowed her up. She was the color of vanilla ice cream and her dirt-brown hair was braided at the nape of her neck.

"Today's your lucky day," the deputy joked as he opened the door of the tank. "Your lawyer's here."

The guard escorted Angela and Jolita a few feet across the hall to an interview room which contained a table and three stackable chairs.

Jolita sat down lazily, plopped her right elbow on the table and rested her chin in her palm.

"I'm Angela Evans and I'm your attorney," Angela began. "I'm representing you on the solicitation charge. We need to go over some things before your arraignment today."

Jolita rolled her eyes.

"What I'm saying is very important. So I want to make sure you're listening to me."

"Yeah, I'm listening."

"Okay, then. What's my name?"

Jolita smiled for the first time. "Uh, tell me one more time."

"Angela Evans."

"Okay, okay. I'll remember."

Angela began, as she did with all of her juvenile clients, by reading the pertinent parts of the petition.

"You're being charged with Penal Code Section 647b, soliciting prostitution. You have a right to a trial or you can plead out. It's a misdemeanor punishable by six months in a juvenile facility."

"I can't go back to no group home," Jolita said. "You gotta get me outta here."

"Where do you live?"

Jolita hesitated, which told Angela everything she needed to know. She probably lived with her pimp, but wasn't about to admit that to her lawyer or anybody else.

"My friend, Nay-Nay."

"How old is Nay-Nay?"

"Same age as me. She live with her older brother. He's eighteen."

"What's his name?"

She hesitated again. "Ronny Green."

According to the police report Angela had read minutes earlier, Ronny Green was a known pimp.

"The judge isn't going to allow you to stay with them. Do you have any family members who can take you in?"

"Yeah, probably. My grandmother. But she on drugs."

"Then the court won't let you stay with her either." Angela exhaled. "Where's your mother?"

"I don't know."

She decided not to even ask Jolita about her father. "I'm going to see if I can find a suitable placement for you."

"Please don't let them send me to Dorothy Kirby. That's like being in prison. And the girls in there are crazy."

Her clients always begged not to be assigned to Dorothy Kirby Mental Health Center.

"Do you have a social worker?"

"Yep."

Over ninety percent of the juveniles picked up in L.A. County for soliciting prostitution had cases with the Department of Children and Family Services. The fact that Jolita had a social worker meant that she'd been neglected, molested or subject to some other form of abuse, making her ripe for the picking by a pimp.

"What's her name?"

"I forgot."

Angela folder her arms. "And what's my name?"

Jolita laughed, snapped her fingers and wiggled her neck. "Angela Evans. See, you thought I forgot. I'm very smart."

The tragedy of her work was that most of the girls Angela represented were indeed extremely bright. If they hadn't been raised in abusive, dysfunctional families, they never would have ended up in the hands of a pimp and likely never would have had any involvement with the criminal justice system.

Angela nodded her approval. "Very good. Let's go over the police report. According to the undercover officer who picked you up, you were standing on Long Beach Boulevard at four in the morning waving down cars. He claims you leaned into his car and offered to, quote, *suck him dry.*"

Jolita shot up in her chair. "He lyin' on me. I don't even talk like that."

"What about the rest of his account? Were you flagging down cars?"

Jolita slumped back in her chair. "Look, I was hungry. I was just trying to make some money to...to feed my baby."

Jolita's file didn't mention anything about a child. *Good God.*

"You have a child?"

"Yep. Deon is two," she said, glowing.

"Where is he?"

"He live with my Baby Daddy's Mama."

"I thought you said you were trying to get some money to feed your baby?"

"I was. Babies need a lot of stuff. You don't know how much Big Deon's Mama be sweatin' me. I try to give her some money every now and then."

"Where's Big Deon?"

"In jail. But he didn't rob no store. The police lied on him."

Angela didn't even want to guess how old Big Deon was.

"You're going to go before the judge to be arraigned in a couple of hours. We're going to plead not guilty and I'm going to see if I can get you in the STAR program."

"What's that?" Jolita asked.

The acronym STAR stood for Succeed Through Achievement and Resilience. The pilot program funded by a state research grant, treated juveniles arrested for prostitution-related charges as victims, rather than criminals, focusing on providing them with the resources to help them become independent, productive adults.

"It's a program that's going to help you get your life on track," Angela explained. "You're going to be closely supervised, and if you do everything the court requires you to do, the charges against you will be dismissed."

"I don't need nobody all up in my business."

"Would you rather go to Dorothy Kirby?"

Jolita made a sucking sound. "Nope. I don't belong in no crazy house."

"In the STAR program you'll have a treatment team that will—"

"I don't need no treatment? I ain't sick."

Angela ignored the interruption. "You'll be assigned a counselor and a mentor who used to be on the streets. You'll have to get counseling, go to school every day and meet with your probation officer and social worker when you're required to. Do you think you can manage that?"

Jolita feigned boredom, but Angela saw through it.

"That sound like it might be okay. So when can I get out of here?"

"When we go before the judge, I'll have to see where they can place you."

Angela would repeat this conversation with little variation at least five more times today. She had an active caseload of another dozen girls charged with solicitation whose cases were at various stages. Something was definitely wrong with the world.

Heading back into the courtroom, she asked the bailiff if any of her other clients had arrived yet. As the bailiff made a call, Angela checked her smartphone. No call or text from Dre.

She prayed that Dre found his niece soon. If he didn't, Angela didn't have to imagine the horrors Brianna would face. She knew them all too well.

CHAPTER 27

Day Two: 7:55 a.m.

D re's trip to Compton turned out to be a bust. The buddy he was looking for no longer lived at the same spot. He started up the car and was about to head over to his sister's house when another idea came to him.

Five minutes later he was parking his car across the street from Maverick Middle School.

Dre figured that Brianna may have talked about this Jaden dude to some of her friends besides Sydney. He also wanted a chance to speak to Sydney without her father breathing down the girl's neck. Maybe she knew more, but had been too afraid to say so in front of Winston.

As Dre crossed the street, he saw clusters of students heading for the entrance of the school. He pulled out his smartphone and walked up to three girls who were standing in a circle giggling.

"Excuse me," he said, "Do any of you know this girl?" He held up a photo of Brianna on his smartphone.

One of the girls immediately stepped forward. The other two, seemed wary of him and actually took a few steps back.

"That's Brianna Walker," the girl said. Her short hair was reddish-purple and the backpack she was lugging was almost as big as she was. "Why are you asking us about her?"

"Brianna's my niece. She didn't come home from school yesterday and I'm trying to find her."

One of the other girls put a hand to her mouth. Her eyes grew wide as she came closer. "Something must be really wrong then, because Brianna ain't like that. She's a good girl. She would never—"

"Excuse me, sir. What's going on here?"

A skinny white woman charged up to him. "Do you girls know this man?" The woman surveyed Dre from head to toe, her eyes simmering with suspicion.

"He's Brianna Walker's uncle," one of the girl's volunteered. "They don't know where she is."

The woman's eyes instantly softened. "You girls head on to class before you're late." She turned to Dre and extended her hand. "I'm Bonnie Flanagan. Brianna's one of my students. What's going on?"

Dre spent the next few minutes sharing what he learned from Sydney. A few minutes later, they were joined by a security guard and a lanky man dressed in a suit and tie. Bonnie introduced the man as Assistant Principal Richard Wainright. Dre repeated his story for their benefit.

The teacher pressed both palms to her cheeks. "I can't believe this. Not Brianna."

"She's one of our best students," Wainright said. "We'll do whatever we can to help you find her. Have you called the police?"

Dre nodded. "Yeah, but I don't think they're going to do much. Have they contacted the school yet?"

"Not that I'm aware of," Wainright said. "When they do, we'll cooperate fully."

"I came here hoping to talk to some of Brianna's friends. I want to find out if she spoke to any of them about the boy she met on Facebook. I'm pretty sure it's a scam and he doesn't exist, but maybe Brianna told them something that might be helpful."

"Unfortunately, we can't allow you to speak to our students," Wainright said. "Not without their parents' consent. But we can certainly talk to them for you and let you, as well as the police, know if we find out anything."

Dre's face flushed with gratitude. "I'd really appreciate that."

"I have Brianna for third period," Bonnie said. "She's a very popular girl. I'll talk to my students."

"I'll talk to the kids too," the security guard added.

Dre took out three business cards and a pen. "If you find out anything, please call me. I'll also give you my sister's number. But you should call me first. Brianna's mother isn't handling this too well."

"I can only imagine," Bonnie said.

Dre felt a tremendous emotional boost as he jogged back across the street to his car. The people he'd just talked to seemed to genuinely care about Brianna. He was certain they would do what they could to help him find her. And he could use all the help he could get.

He had just put the key into the ignition when he heard a quick buzz that signaled a new text message. He glanced down at his smartphone and saw that the text was from Angela. He quickly read it.

Although her message was no surprise to him, the reality of it took the wind out of him.

Angela had heard back from her friend at L.A. Unified. None of the teachers at Crenshaw High School had a son named Jaden Morris.

Foshay Middle School had never heard of him either.

CHAPTER 28

Day Two: 8:20 a.m.

The other Harmony House girls were already up and about, except for Carmen. Loretha marched up the stairs and gently knocked on the door of the Hope room for the second time that morning.

"Carmen, you have to get up now."

Even if the girls didn't have school, they had to be out of bed no later than eight-thirty. For Loretha, there was always the difficult balance of giving the girls their space, but ensuring that they respected the rules of the house.

She stepped into the room and found Carmen tangled up in the comforter. Loretha was about to wake her, when she noticed Carmen's painting. The child really did have talent. Loretha planned to do everything she could to nurture it.

Carmen had scrawled *Big Daddy and C-Lo* across the top of the page in red. The awkwardly drawn images, one big, one small, depicted a man and a woman. Carmen had painted herself with breasts much larger than her own. Big Daddy was smiling. The girl was not. That said it all. Loretha swallowed the lump forming in her throat and turned the paper face down on the desk.

Stepping over to the bed, she gently nudged Carmen's shoulder, then jumped back out the way.

Once again, Carmen shot awake, arms flailing. "Get offa me!" she screamed up at Loretha.

This time, it took her nearly a minute to collect herself.

"Oh," she said. "It's you. I thought…" Her words trailed off. She snatched the comforter to her chin and fell back to the bed.

"Time to get up," Loretha said. "We're having breakfast downstairs. It's after nine."

"You gotta be kidding." Carmen turned toward the wall, her back to Loretha. "It's too early to get up. I never get outta bed before twelve."

When you strolled the streets all night, nine o'clock probably felt like the crack of dawn.

Loretha ripped the covers off of Carmen.

"Hey!" The girl snatched them back. "I told you, I ain't ready to get up yet."

"The first thing you need to understand," Loretha said in a firm voice, "is that we have rules around here. And if you're going to live here, you'll have to follow them. You have fifteen minutes to get dressed and downstairs for breakfast."

"But we didn't even get here until—"

"You're wasting time. Now you only have fourteen minutes."

Loretha walked out of the room.

Thirty minutes later, Carmen sulked into the kitchen. That was a good sign. There were times when it took three or four trips to get a girl down to breakfast on her first day.

Loretha walked over and put an arm around Carmen's shoulders. "Everybody, this is Carmen."

"Welcome, to Harmony House, Carmen." The girls said in unison.

"Yeah, whatever. It's too damn early to be up."

"Our first rule is no foul language," Loretha said. "We'll go over the other rules later. You can grab a paper plate. The food is on the stove."

Loretha was glad that the six girls who had gathered for breakfast were not newbies. Two were on their second run, having gone back to their pimps, after a couple of months at Harmony House. But those few months were long enough for them to start questioning whether the street was the kind of life they wanted. They had returned badly beaten for some minor infraction that sent their pimp into a psychotic fit.

The other four girls had only been with Loretha for a few weeks. While they weren't physically with their pimp, they were still there psychologically. It would take time to reach them. To show them that they had options. Four other girls had already been picked up for school.

Carmen marched over to the stove and lifted the first pot.

"Uh, grits. I hate grits, but I cook 'em for Big Daddy all the time." She scooped a tablespoonful of scrambled eggs onto her plate and picked up a single piece of bacon. It always amazed Loretha how little these girls ate.

"Everybody," Loretha said, "please introduce yourself to Carmen."

The girls went around the table and said their names. One of the most outspoken girls, Little Kim, asked Carmen a question.

"So how long you been on the streets?"

Carmen bristled. "I ain't on the streets. My clients come to me."

Little Kim harrumphed. "Don't make no difference. You still spreading your legs for money. Don't try to act like you better than us."

"I didn't say I—"

"Hey!" Loretha interrupted. "Cut it out. Let's talk about something positive." She turned to a quiet girl sitting next to her. "Abbie, tell everybody your good news."

The girl smiled, her blue eyes flickering downward. "It ain't nothing."

"Oh, yes it is," Loretha prodded her. "Tell them."

"I got a job," she said, her shoulders slumped. "I'ma be working at the dry cleaners on Washington Street."

"You must be crazy," Carmen said, turning up her nose. "You gon' be stuck in a dry cleaners pressing clothes in all that heat. What they payin' you, minimum wage? You can't make no real money doin' that."

Abbie slid further down in her chair. One of the other girls rushed to her defense.

"I'm happy for you, girl," Rhonda said. She pointed her fork at Carmen. "Ain't like you making no money. Every dime you get turning tricks goes to your pimp. How much money you got in your purse right now?"

Carmen's lip tightened, but she didn't respond.

"Zero," Rhonda said, forming the number with her thumb and index finger. "So don't be dissin' nobody else. We tryin' to get out of the life and we don't need no haters up in here."

"I don't even wanna be here." Carmen pushed her chair back from the table with a loud screech.

Before Loretha could intervene, she was out of the kitchen and bounding up the stairs, two at a time.

CHAPTER 29

Day Two: 9:05 a.m.

Dre decided not to share the information he'd learned about Jaden's nonexistence with Donna.

Using his key to enter his sister's house, he was stunned at how uncomfortably dark and quiet it was. It had never been like this when Brianna was around.

Dre found Donna in the den, curled up on the couch, staring at a muted TV screen. He stood there for a few seconds staring down at her, feeling completely inept for not being able to take away her pain.

Donna must have sensed his presence because she suddenly shot to her feet. "Where's my baby? Did you find her?"

Dre took her by the shoulders and pulled her into his arms. "No, sis, but I will."

Donna started to sob into his chest, her body convulsing so hard he had to hold on tight to keep her from falling to the floor.

His mother rushed into the room, momentarily paralyzed by what she saw.

"What happened? Oh my Jesus!" she wailed. "Is Brianna dead? Please, Jesus, please! Don't tell me Brianna's dead!"

"Mama, mama!" Dre said, "you gotta calm down. No, Brianna is not dead."

He spoke the words slowly and firmly as if he was trying to make himself believe them. Then he threw an arm around his mother and pulled both of them into a tight circle, hoping to quell their weeping.

Dre refused to let himself cry. He had work to do. He couldn't afford to spare even an ounce of emotional energy for anything except finding Brianna.

* * *

Since Donna's place was only a few minutes from Long Beach Boulevard, Dre headed over there hoping to luck up and spot Loretha Johnson. From what he'd heard, you could find girls walking the track day or night.

So far, his caffeine overdose was doing its job. Dre had to force his mind not to think about what could be happening to Brianna. Those images were much too painful. He loved that little girl and realized as he sat at a stoplight that he'd never once told her that.

He hit a speed dial button on his smartphone.

Sheila, his one-night stand who had turned into a lifetime migraine, answered the phone.

"Put Little Dre on the phone," Dre said.

"You can't say hi to nobody?"

"Hi, Sheila. Now give Little Dre the phone."

"He can't talk right now. He 'bout to be late for school."

"He should already be at school. Put him on the phone!"

"Don't be talking to me like that! I don't know who you think you are. And he ain't late. They have a half day today. You just better have my check on time."

He could hear Sheila cussing him out in the background. His son picked up seconds later.

"Hey, little man, you doing okay?"

"Yeah."

"You doing good in school?"

"Yeah."

Dre paused as his words got caught in his throat. "You know I love you, right?"

"Dang, Dad. Why you being weird?"

Dre laughed. "I just wanted you to know that I love you, okay."

"Yeah, okay. I gotta leave for school now."

His son was ten years old and Dre had never told him that he loved him until today. Going forward, he would change that. He'd never told Brianna that he loved her either. When he got her back, he would change that too.

He'd just made a right onto Long Beach Boulevard when he noticed the first girl. She was dressed in shorts, a sports bra and stilettos. On the opposite side of the street, he spotted another girl, just as scantily dressed. For years, this short strip in Compton had a rep as the place to pick up black prostitutes. But these weren't women. They weren't even teenagers. These girls were babies.

He pulled over and parked in front of a laundromat. By that time, he spotted two other girls, just as young.

Where were the police?

He watched as a black man in a silver-blue BMW slowed to a stop on the opposite side of the street. One of the girls Dre had been watching scampered up to the man's car.

Just then, Dre heard a light tap on his own passenger window, which made him flinch.

The young girl in the shorts he'd seen seconds earlier was waving at him to roll down the window.

What the—!

The girl looked even younger up close. She couldn't be any older than eleven or twelve.

Dre hit a button rolling down the window.

"Hey, baby, you looking for a date?" The girl tried, but failed to make her high-pitched voice sound sexy.

Something inside him wanted to cry. All he could see in this girl was Brianna's face.

Was this what Shep had her doing?

"C'mon, baby. Don't be afraid of me," the girl purred. "I give good dates." She wiggled her brows in a manner that she probably thought was seductive. She actually looked like a cartoon character.

"How old are you?" Dre shouted. "And where the hell are your parents?"

The girl jumped back, stumbling on her high heels.

"I ain't got no parents," she shouted back at him. "You must have a problem. I ain't got time for this."

He watched her strut away, then turned back to the man in the BMW across the street. The girl Dre had been watching a second ago was climbing into the man's car.

As they pulled off, Dre started his engine. He did a U-turn in the middle of the street and followed them. He couldn't understand how this could be going on in broad daylight. A sheriff's substation was only a few blocks away.

Dre hung back and watched as the car parked behind Rite-Aid, next to a large trash dumpster. He parked in front of the store and hopped out.

As he approached the BMW, he could see the young girl's head bobbing up and down in the man's lap.

Dre banged on the window with his fist. "What the hell are you doin'?"

The man's eyes flashed panic. He was dressed in a monogrammed shirt and purple tie. He grabbed the girl by her long braids and hurled her away. She banged her head against the passenger window and cursed.

"Uh...uh, Officer, I...I...Please don't arrest me!" the man blubbered as he zipped up his fly. "My wife will kill me!"

The man apparently thought he was an undercover cop.

"You friggin' pedophile!" Dre yelled. "That girl is a child."

"She told me she was eighteen! Please don't arrest me!"

The girl was already out of the car running as best she could on five-inch heels.

"Hey!" Dre called after her. "Hold up!"

He easily caught up with her as the BMW raced off.

"Why are you out here doing this?" he said, roughly grabbing her by the arm. "How old are you?"

"Get your hands offa me. You a cop?"

"No, I'm not. But I should take your ass to jail anyway."

"Leave me alone," she screeched, struggling to pull away. "My daddy's gonna kick your ass."

"Does your daddy know you're out here?"

"My daddy's the one who put me out here. You gon' be in trouble when he come pick me up."

It suddenly hit Dre that the child was referring to her pimp as her *daddy*.

"Let me go!"

He released her arm and she took off running. Dre, however, just stood there. Stunned and dizzy with anger.

He wasn't sure how many times his smartphone had rang before he finally pulled it from his pocket and checked the caller ID. Angela had been calling him all morning. He couldn't deal with her constant requests for updates right now. He shoved the smartphone back into his pocket and started walking toward his car.

A few seconds later, he heard a buzz that told him he had a text.

He checked the screen of his smartphone. It was Angela again. He read her text, then held the smartphone up closer to read it a second time because he couldn't believe what he was seeing.

Angela: i know where b is. call me!!!

What? How? Dre's hand trembled as he hit the call back button.

The phone barely rang before he heard Angela's voice.

"I know where Brianna is!"

"What? How?"

"I called a friend who's an FBI agent. He pinged Brianna's iPhone and gave me the location. She has to be with the phone!"

"Where is it?"

"At a house on Sixty-seventh Street," Angela said. She gave him the address. "I just looked it up on Google Maps. It's off Normandie, between Florence and Gage."

That wasn't far from where they'd looked before. Dre was already starting up the car. "I'm going straight there."

"Do you want me to call the police?"

"Hell no."

"You can't go there by yourself."

"I'm not going by myself. I'll have my cousin meet me there."

He zipped down Long Beach Boulevard toward the Freeway. The muscles along his neck constricted into knots.

"What do you need me to do?" Angela asked.

"Pray," Dre said quietly. "I need you to pray that I find her."

CHAPTER **30**

Day Two: 9:30 a.m.

"**E**verybody ready to get started?"
Judge Katie Spratt entered her courtroom from a side door and took a seat in the loose circle of chairs placed in the middle of her courtroom. She was dressed in slacks and a blouse with orange, pink and yellow flowers.

"We have fifteen cases to review, so let's get started."

The judge was famous for her warm smile and friendly demeanor. After seeing far too many girls appearing in her court on solicitation charges, she became one of the moving forces behind STAR court and helped write the state grant that funded the program.

As one of the defense lawyers, Angela took a seat outside the circle. She was a ball of nerves after the call she'd just made to Dre. It was going to be a long day in court, which would help keep her mind off Brianna. There were a few arraignments on calendar today, but mostly progress reports before the judge.

Every Tuesday, Judge Spratt held STAR Court. Prior to a girl's appearance before the judge, a representative from the various agencies who were part of her support team discussed her progress since the last court date.

Seated in the circle with the judge were four social workers, three probation officers, two counselors and three women from Saving Innocence. The prosecutor and defense counsel typically sat on the perimeter of the circle.

The judge took a powder-blue file from a thick stack and opened it. "Let's start with Anya Garcia. How's she doing?"

The girl's social worker fielded the question. "She got into some trouble at school last week. When she signed in for detention, she wrote another student's name down. So she was suspended for three days."

"Three days?" the judge said with a wry smile. "That sounds like a bit much."

The social worker shrugged. "Other than that, she's doing fine. No contact with her pimp that we know of."

"Let's count that as a victory," Judge Spratt said. She picked up another file. "Precious Norwood. How's she doing?"

"So-so," Diana, one of the probation officers, volunteered. "I saw her last week. She hates the facility she's in and wants to go home. *Home* meaning back to her pimp."

That news was met with a long, collective sigh.

Marcel, Precious' social worker, held up a finger. "I got a call from one of her teachers yesterday. Precious used the phone of a friend at school to contact her pimp." Her lips pursed in frustration.

"I'll definitely have to have a talk with her about that," Judge Spratt said, making a note in her file.

"Her mother is her biggest problem," Marcel continued. "She came to visit her a few days ago. They got into a loud argument. Looks like she's still using."

The judge shook her head. "Let's see if we can get the mother in a drug treatment program. Is her father going to be in court today?"

"He said he would be," Marcel said.

"Great. He seems fairly responsible. I'd like to get her back home with him if we can."

"We've done an assessment of the father's home and it's suitable for her to return there. The stepmother, however, is worried about Precious being a bad influence on her three daughters. I get the impression that she'd prefer not to have Precious back home."

It took another hour to review the status of the rest of the girls. The judge called for a short break. The chairs were rearranged into two rows along the back wall to make space for family members to sit once the judge started hearing cases.

Judge Spratt returned, dressed in her black robe now, and took the bench. A court reporter sat below her.

"We have a couple of arraignments to get out of the way first," the judge began.

She called the first case and the bailiff ushered Angela's client, Jolita, into the courtroom. She sat in a chair next to Angela.

The judge directed her attention to Jolita. "Young lady, you've been charged with Penal Code Section 647b, soliciting prostitution. Has your attorney explained to you what that means?"

"Yes."

"Counsel, do you waive formal reading of the petition and statement of rights and enter a denial on behalf of your client?"

"Yes," Angela replied. She glanced down at a file in front of her. "Your Honor, I'd like to request that Jolita be placed in the STAR program. I've explained to Jolita what that means and she understands everything she'll have to do."

"Is that true?" the judge asked gently. "Do you understand what the STAR program requires?"

"Uh, yeah," Jolita said, her voice barely audible.

"Okay, then, tell me what you know about the program?"

Jolita's eyes darted up at Angela. "Um…I have to go to school and get counseling and talk to my probation officer on time and stuff like that."

"And you have to make good grades in school. Can you do that?"

"Yeah."

"Your Honor," Angela said, "I'd also like to request a suitable placement for Jolita. There's currently no family member who can meet DCFS requirements."

The judge looked over at the probation officer assigned to her courtroom. "What do we have available?"

"We can probably get her into Diamondale," she said.

"Is that a nice place?" Jolita whispered to Angela.

Angela smiled and nodded.

Judge Spratt turned back to Jolita. "I want you to understand that it's a privilege to be part of the STAR program. You'll have to abide by all of our rules. You can't have any contact with your friend Nay-Nay Green or her brother Ronny Green. Do you understand that?"

Jolita poked out her lips. "They're my friends. Why can't I talk to them?"

"Because your friend and her brother aren't good influences for you. If I learn that you've been to their house, talking to them on the phone or even texting them, you won't be able to continue in the program. Do you understand?"

Jolita rolled her eyes. "Yeah, okay."

"I don't allow girls in my courtroom to give me attitude." Judge Spratt's tone went from gentle to firm.

Jolita's eyes fell to the table.

The judge shuffled through some papers in front of her. "I have a report here that says you used to make pretty good grades in school."

"Yep," Jolita said, lighting up a bit. "But that was before my mama left with her boyfriend and my grandmamma got on drugs."

Jolita's matter-of-fact explanation for her bad grades set off a chain of head shaking.

"Well, I want you to start making good grades again. Your probation officer is going to give me a report from each one of your teachers."

"Okay."

The judge turned her attention back to Angela. "I'll see you and your client back in ten days for the pre-plea report."

"Thank you, Your Honor."

Jolita's probation officer had to prepare a report stating whether it was in her best interest to remain detained in a group facility. At her next court appearance, Angela would try to get the charges dismissed or reduced. If she was unsuccessful, Jolita would go to trial.

The judge called another case and a different attorney stepped up to the defense table with his young client.

Angela used the short break before her next case was called to step into the hallway to check her messages. No voicemail or text message from Dre. He should have made it to the address she'd given him by now. Why hadn't he called to let her know that he'd found Brianna?

Angela fired off a short text and prayed for some good news.

CHAPTER 31

Day Two: 10:30 a.m.

Dre spotted the yellow house the second they turned onto 67th Street. His mind was now racing as fast as his heart was pumping. The house was exactly as Leon the crack head had described it. High iron gates surrounded the home and thick shrubbery lined the front like well-trained bodyguards.

He parked his Jetta half a block away and was relieved to see Apache pulling up behind him.

His cousin hopped out of his Benz and ran up to Dre's car. "This is it, man!" he yelled in excitement. "We 'bout to go get little shorty."

"Hold up," Dre said, climbing out. "We need to have a plan. We don't know what we're going to find inside."

Apache pulled his Glock from his waistband and waved it in the air. "I got my plan right here, cuz. Let's do this!"

"Put that thing away!"

Dre's eyes zipped up and down the street. He wanted to rescue Brianna, but he preferred to do it without facing an assault charge or a murder rap in the process. He wasn't worried about what they'd done to Leon coming back on them. Leon and his two cronies were probably still terrorized from Apache's threat. He just hoped they'd gotten him to the hospital before he bled to death.

He looked Apache squarely in the eyes. "Man, listen to me. I only want you to use that thing for self-defense. Don't shoot first."

Apache smirked, then laughed. "Yeah, okay."

Dre figured there had to be a couple of dudes guarding the girls and he assumed they'd be armed. But he had enough adrenalin built up to take them on with his bare hands. He reminded himself that they were dealing with kidnappers, not killers. Still, it was possible that something could go wrong once they got inside the house. If he was able to safely deliver Brianna back to his sister, he would pay the cost. No matter what that was.

"We're going to hop the fence," Dre said, "then go around to the back of the house. Follow my lead."

"I'm with you, cuz."

The two headed in the direction of the house, their steps unrushed. They both easily scaled the fence and walked in tandem down a wide driveway.

"Let's check the garage first," Dre said, drawing Apache away from a back door that appeared to lead into the house.

He grabbed the handle and tried to pull the garage door upward, but it wouldn't budge. He figured it must have been controlled by remote. He spotted a side door and opened it. The garage was dark and musty. Dre spotted rope, soiled sheets and a pile of discarded clothes. Something caught his eye.

Dre stepped further inside and held up one of the items of clothing. His throat went completely dry. It was a Lakers tank top. The one he'd bought for Brianna. He was sure of it.

"This is the right place," Dre said, growing both excited and anxious. "This is the place."

He stuffed the shirt into his back pocket. "Let's head inside."

Dre walked over to a small window to the left of the back door. The window was blacked out, but a small section of the glass was missing near the bottom. He had to stand on his tiptoes to see inside. He could make out a messy kitchen, but nobody was in it.

Apache examined the wrought iron door. "We ain't gettin' in here without making a whole lot of ruckus. This place is locked down tighter than a prison."

Dre stepped away from the window and grabbed the knob of the door, prepared to rip it off with the sheer strength of his anger. To his surprise, the knob turned and it creaked open, revealing another door. This one made of wood.

"Looks like somebody got sloppy," Apache said with a smile.

Dre reached for the knob of the inside door, but it was locked.

"No biggie," Apache said, pushing him aside. He pulled a long screwdriver from his back pocket and stuck it into the lock. In seconds, a metal part popped out and the door knob turned easily.

Apache looked over his shoulder, smiling. "I got skills."

Dre eased the door open, then waited. They'd been as quiet as possible, but Dre was surprised that they hadn't alerted anyone inside. If they were running the kind of human trafficking operation Coop had described, they probably had cameras posted, though Dre had not spotted any. He feared they could be walking into a trap.

Apache tried to walk past him, but Dre grabbed him by the shoulder.

"Hold up."

They both stood still, just inside a short hallway that housed a washer and dryer, listening for the sound of movement. Dre took a few more steps and found himself in a kitchen. The sink was piled with dishes. On the counter next to the refrigerator, he spotted discarded paper plates with bones and wadded-up napkins. Someone had recently had a meal there.

Apache was rocking from heel to toe, his fingers caressing the Glock. "Man, let's bum rush 'em."

"No," Dre said gruffly. "Just stay back and follow my lead."

Though it was mid-morning, with all the windows covered, the house was nighttime dark inside.

They heard what sounded like the slap of a window shade. Both men froze in place. They stayed that way for several seconds before proceeding out of the kitchen, past a small den and down a dark hallway.

Dre spotted a door on his left and stepped inside. He flicked on a light switch. The room held a bed and dresser, but no other furniture. He understood now why the place was so dark. No light seeped into the house because the windowpanes had been painted black.

Where the hell is she?

Dre backed out of the room and spotted another door on the right. This one had three deadbolts, but no doorknob.

He pushed the door open and what he saw sickened him. He spotted a puddle of dried blood near a window. A soiled mattress took up most of the room. The scarred hardwood floor held the scent of urine, feces and body odor. Dre covered his nose with his forearm.

Dre stormed out of the room, no longer concerned about being quiet. He ran down the hallway, flinging doors open, and kicking them in if they were locked. He found a bathroom, and two other small rooms. He tore through every inch of the place. But there was no sign of Brianna or anyone else.

He wailed and punched the wall, sending plaster flying in all directions. In seconds, his fist swelled, sending a throb of pain up his arm. But it was no comparison to the pain twisting in his gut.

Brianna had been here. The Lakers shirt he had tucked in his pocket proved that.

But where was she now?

CHAPTER 32

Day Two: 11:15 a.m.

Shep relaxed on his front balcony in a cushy patio chair, sipping a concoction of kale, celery and carrot juice that he made himself. He found the images on the screen of his iPad quite entertaining. He tapped a button, rewinding the video and watched the entire sequence for the third time.

Initially, he'd been amused as he watched Dre and his long-haired sidekick tear through the house on 67th Street. His amusement had slowly simmered into anger, but he successfully restrained it.

Shep had installed cameras all over the house to keep an eye on his girls as well as the people he paid to watch them. The cameras had never been of much use until now.

This Dre cat had some big balls, Shep thought. He still couldn't believe the way Andre Thomas was disrespecting him.

Shep was just glad he'd made the decision to move the girls out of the house only minutes before Brianna's uncle had broken in. Shep had a sixth sense which often alerted him when trouble loomed. He'd been successful in the trafficking game not just because he was smart, but because he had an instinct that told him what and what not to do. He never panicked when faced with a crisis. You didn't have to when you had the kind of intellect he possessed.

He set his iPad on a side table and positioned himself more erect in the chair.

So hum, he repeated mentally. *So hum.*

Closing his eyes and drawing in a deep breath through his nostrils, he allowed the air to slowly escape through his mouth. He did this non-stop for thirty minutes.

After finishing his meditation, he walked inside, retrieved his journal and reviewed the quote he'd written down at six that morning: *"Our greatest glory is not in never falling, but in rising every time we fall." –Confucius.*

Yes, he told himself, he would handle this situation. He found his smartphone and speed-dialed Clint.

"Hey," Clint said gruffly.

"You still have the girl tucked away?"

"Yeah."

"Keep a close eye on her. She's precious cargo. You break her in?'

"Uh, yeah." Clint didn't offer any details.

"So how was it?"

His response was slow in coming. "It got a little rough. She wouldn't cooperate. Her face is a little swollen, but it'll heal."

Shep sat up. "How many times do I have to tell you?" he said sternly. "Don't hit my girls in the face. I don't sell damaged goods."

"She bit me," Clint explained. "I just reacted. She'll heal."

Shep was about to continue the scolding, but gave it some thought. It would be better to send Brianna back with both mental and physical scars.

"I think it's time for me to make contact with Businessman," Shep said. "Set up a meeting."

There was no response from the other end of the line.

"Is that a wise move?"

"Everything I do is a wise move."

"This dude ain't no rookie. He knows the streets."

"And so do I. It's one thing to go around town disrespecting me, but this guy had the audacity to come onto my property uninvited."

"What?"

"I'm watching the video right now. He broke into the house on Sixty-seventh about thirty minutes ago."

Shep figured that Clint was probably bracing himself for a lecture. After all, Clint should've been able to control this situation. But Shep had more important matters to attend to first.

"Contact Businessman and tell him I want a meeting with him at City Stars. And tell him to come alone."

"He's not going to do that."

"He will if he wants that girl back."

CHAPTER 33

Day Two: 12:10 p.m.

Brianna awoke to the sound of laughter. It took her eyes almost a full minute to come into focus. Every inch of her body ached and she was woozy with hunger pains. She glanced at her surroundings and nothing looked familiar.

She was no longer on a mattress in a cold, dark room. This place looked like an actual bedroom. She was sprawled on a twin bed now. There was another bed across the room. Piles of clothes littered the floor. A boxy, older-model TV sat on a dresser at the foot of the bed.

"Hey, sleepyhead. 'Bout time you woke up."

A face she didn't recognize was peering down at her.

"What's your name?" the girl asked. She was wearing so much makeup she looked like a brown-skinned clown.

"Brianna," she said, realizing that it hurt to talk. Her throat felt like it was on fire.

"I'm Kym and you already met Tameka." Kym pointed toward a girl standing in the doorway. She hadn't been there a second ago. Or had she?

"You must'a really messed up bad, cuz you got hit in the face. They don't never hit us in the face. It's gonna take a whole lot of makeup to cover up them bruises."

Brianna pressed her hand to her face and winced. Even the lightest touch fired sharp jabs of pain in all directions. She remembered now. Clint had beaten her up. He had stopped when she'd faked an asthma attack. She had no recollection of how she got to this room though. They must have drugged her again.

"You have to help me get out of here." Brianna began to cry. "I don't belong here."

Both of the girls laughed. "Don't worry you'll get used to it. You're in the life now, girl. So just deal with it."

"What are you talking about? What life?"

"Just wait," Kym said. "After a while, you won't even miss the square world."

Brianna felt like these girls were talking in code. She managed to sit up, but did not have full control of her body and fell back onto the bed. She also did not remember changing into the cut-off shorts and bra-like top that she was wearing now.

"Freda gave you a shot," Kym said. "Enjoy the high cuz it'll wear off soon."

"Where's Kaylee?"

"She was here a while ago, but she left to go on a date. She's working tonight."

Brianna shivered at the thought of Kaylee having sex with some stranger.

"My mama's looking for me," Brianna cried. "I have to get out of here."

Tameka laughed. "Your mama ain't lookin' for you, girl. She's probably in bed with her boyfriend right now, not even thinking about you."

"My mother doesn't have a boyfriend," Brianna shot back.

"So she's gay?" Kym asked.

"No!"

"Don't try to act like you're all goody-two-shoes," Kym said. "What we do ain't no big deal. Clint and Freda buy us lots of stuff." She stuck out her arm. "Look at my new bracelet. On Saturday, we're going to get our nails done. If you act right, they might let you come too."

"I don't need nobody to buy me nothing!" Brianna shouted. "I just wanna go home!"

"You really don't get it," Tameka said. "They ain't lettin' you go home." Her tight leather skirt barely covered her privates. Her thin top was stretched tight over her protruding belly.

"I have to get to work." Tameka yawned. "I got the lunch crowd today."

"Take me with you!" Brianna begged.

"You can't do the lunch crowd yet," Tameka said gently. "You gotta pay your dues first."

Tameka bounded out of the room.

Brianna looked all around. "Where are we?"

"Don't matter," Kym said. "You ain't goin' nowhere."

"If it don't matter, then tell me. Where are we?"

"Somewhere in the San Fernando Valley," Kym said. "That's all I know. From the backyard, you can see the mountains. You need to be glad you ain't in the hood no more. If you don't act right, they might take you back there. It's way nicer here."

"Why do you stay here? Why don't you run away?"

"And go where? This is way better than the projects. I hate Nickerson Gardens."

"Don't you miss your family?"

"Hell naw. And they don't miss me. My mama's too busy getting high and I got tired of all her boyfriends trying to have sex with me. This is my family. I have a daddy now and a lot of wives-in-law. Everybody in here is tight. It's all good."

Brianna had no idea what a wife-in-law was. "But they make you have sex with men. How can you do that?"

"To get paid." Kym looked at Brianna with her face in a scrunch. "It's just sex. You can make more money in one night doing what we do than you can make in two weeks slaving at Wal-Mart. You'll see."

Brianna had to get this girl to understand that she would never *see*. "I'm not doing that!"

"You should've never run away from home then," Kym said.

"I didn't run away. They kidnapped me!" Brianna began to cry again. "I thought I was going to meet Jaden."

Kym slapped her thigh and started laughing. "You one of them girls that got scammed. I can't believe you fell for that. You stupid."

Just then, Freda stepped into the room.

"Good to see you're awake. Hopefully, that beatin' Clint gave you will make you a little more cooperative. You can't go around biting and scratching people."

Brianna eyed the woman. If she got close enough, she would claw her face again.

"We're putting you to work tomorrow," Freda said. "So get ready."

CHAPTER 34

Day Two: 1:10 p.m.

Bonnie Flanagan watched the clock on the wall of her classroom like it might self-destruct any second. When the bell finally rang signaling the end of the period, she charged straight for the administration office. She walked right past the school secretary and barged into the principal's office without bothering to knock.

"Did you hear about Brianna Walker?" she asked, wringing her hands. "Her uncle came by this morning. She's missing. All the kids are talking about it. It's happening again."

In her early fifties, Bonnie looked good for her age but had the body of a borderline anorexic. One of a handful of white teachers at Maverick Middle School, Bonnie considered teaching a calling. She cared about her students as if she'd birthed them herself.

Manuel Ortiz took his time swiveling his chair around to face her. Most teachers were afraid of Mr. Ortiz, with his sunbaked, pock-marked skin and badly receding hairline. But Bonnie not only had close to thirty years of teaching under her belt, she had home-grown bravado acquired on the streets of South Boston. There was nothing the principal could do to her and if he did try something, she'd sue his fat butt.

"Please don't tell me you're back in here with that crazy theory of yours again."

"Brianna would make the fourth girl from this school to go missing in the last eighteen months." Bonnie's aqua-blue eyes were near tears. "I don't understand why you're ignoring it."

"I'm ignoring it because there's no connection. I heard some of the kids talking about it this morning. Brianna Walker supposedly ran off with some boy on Facebook. I have to say, though, I *am* a little surprised. I pegged her for a good girl."

"She *is* a good girl. We need to contact the police. For some reason they haven't made the connection. Somebody's snatching our girls."

"Like I told you the last time you came in here with this nonsense, I'm not going to the police and neither are you. And I hope you didn't mention your unsubstantiated theory to Brianna's uncle. Did you?"

Bonnie grimaced, then slowly shook her head. She had wanted to share the information with Brianna's uncle, but feared Ortiz's wrath.

"Do you know how many schools in Compton have the honor of being a California Distinguished School? Just one. Maverick Middle School. My school. We don't need the bad publicity."

"Oh, I get it. It's all about you. You're looking for your next promotion."

Everyone knew that Ortiz was dying to be Superintendent. There were rumors that he'd been accused of inappropriate contact with a tenth grader when he was an assistant principal at Centennial High School. Bonnie doubted the stories. There was no way he'd continue to be so affectionate with the students if he'd gone through that kind of ordeal. But then again, Ortiz was arrogant enough to think that he was untouchable.

"It's not about me," Ortiz huffed. "It's about the students. And they don't need this kind of bad press. Not when you have absolutely no facts to go on."

"Well, we should at least let Brianna's mother know about the other girls."

Ortiz leaned in and pointed a fat finger across the desk. "You're not talking to anybody. Do you understand?"

Bonnie wasn't crazy. There was a connection. There had to be. She'd taught three of the four girls. They were all smart and well-behaved. Girls like that didn't run off.

Bonnie left the principal's office and walked across the hall to see if the assistant principal was in. She again entered without knocking.

"Sometimes, I want to choke that fat pig," she said, flopping into a chair in front of Richard Wainright's desk.

"And good morning to you too," he said with a curious smile. A slender man with lush black hair, he appeared unusually tall even from a sitting position. "What did our illustrious principal do to piss you off today?"

Richard Wainright was Ortiz's second in command. The teachers liked him because he never took sides. He stayed out of any political mess and you could always count on him to do the right thing where the kids were concerned.

"He still refuses to tell the police about those other missing girls," Bonnie said. "We should've told Brianna's uncle about them."

Wainright closed a folder and set it aside. "No, we shouldn't have."

He had heard Bonnie's theory before and, like Ortiz, discounted it.

"We have absolutely no evidence to support a link between those cases," Wainright said. "Why upset the family like that? For all we know, Brianna may have actually run off. It's hard to know what these kids are doing on the Internet."

"Did you hear anything her uncle said? There is no *boy*. It was probably some sexual predator."

Wainright tugged at his expensive tie. He always dressed as if he was on his way to some important social affair. Today, he was wearing a stylish navy-blue three-piece. All the other teachers assumed that Wainright had family money. Only Bonnie knew the truth. Wainright had confided in her that he had his broker's license and regularly sold real estate on the side.

"Four girls have gone missing in eighteen months," Bonnie pressed. "Somebody's kidnapping our girls."

"But what *evidence* do you have that they've been kidnapped?"

"I don't have any evidence," Bonnie snapped. "I just have a feeling."

Wainright's forehead creased. "And that's what you told Ortiz?"

"Yes, and he ordered me not to contact the police or Brianna's family."

"C'mon, Bonnie. We just got our rating as a Distinguished School. We don't need this kind of publicity."

"You sound just like him," Bonnie sniffed. "I don't understand why you're so afraid of him."

Wainright bristled. "I'm not afraid of him. I just find it more productive to stay on his good side. I like it here. I've seen Ortiz ship people out of here for looking at him the wrong way. You might want to think about that."

"I thought you, of all people, cared about our students. We're obligated by law to report any suspicion of harm to a child."

"That's not fair," Wainright sputtered. "You know I care about our kids just as much as you do. If you had some evidence to support this gut feeling of yours, I'd call the police myself."

Bonnie's shoulders drooped. She wasn't crazy. And she didn't care what Ortiz, Wainright, or anybody else had to say.

Somebody was kidnapping their girls.

CHAPTER 35

Day Two: 6:35 p.m.

Since getting word of Brianna's disappearance, Dre had been surviving on caffeine as his primary source of energy and he had a visible case of the shakes to prove it.

Following the failed rescue on 67th Street, Dre had parted ways with Apache, but told him to remain on standby. He needed some time alone to contemplate his next move. He would find out if Angela knew how to get in contact with Loretha Johnson. Maybe one of Angela's clients had stayed at Loretha's home. He'd forgotten to ask her when they'd talked earlier. It was getting harder and harder for him to think straight.

Dre had expected to have heard from The Shepherd by now. Obviously calling him out all over town had not been enough to smoke him out.

Sitting in his Jetta on Adams in front of The Cork, his favorite neighborhood hangout, Dre leaned his head back against the headrest. For the first time since this ordeal had begun, he took a moment to pray in earnest. He'd done some bad things in his life, so he had some nerve asking for God's help. But he swore to the Big Man that if he got Brianna back safe, he wouldn't even jaywalk.

He climbed out of the car and headed into the darkened restaurant and bar.

"What's up, my brother?" The burly bouncer waved him through without a pat down. "You look like crap. You okay?"

Dre hadn't had a bath or shaved since learning of Brianna's disappearance and didn't want to know what he looked like.

"Yeah, I'm fine."

He stepped inside and took a seat at the bar. The soft jazz calmed him. While he hoped to hear from Shep soon, his next move was to focus on finding Loretha Johnson. He'd head back to the track in Compton later tonight to look for her.

Dottie eyed him from the other side of the bar. "You okay?"

Dre fidgeted with his hands. "Nope."

Dottie was barely five-feet and smiled more than anyone Dre had ever met. Their friendship went all the way back to high school.

"Can I help?"

"I wish you could," he said. "For now, how about some red beans 'n rice?"

Dottie left to place his order and returned with a Pepsi without Dre having to ask for it.

"You wanna talk about it?"

He'd almost gotten with Dottie once, a long, long time ago. But he came to his senses and decided that he didn't need to mess up a good friendship.

"Somebody snatched my niece, Brianna. Some dude who considers himself a pimp. He's trafficking little girls like they're crack." Dre paused. "I'm going to get her back and then I'm going to kill him."

Dottie covered her mouth, then dropped her eyes. Something in her face conveyed more than shock.

"You know something?" Dre asked.

"Who's the pimp?" she asked softly.

"Rodney Merriweather. They call him The Shepherd."

Dottie closed her eyes then slowly swung her head from left to right. "That's bad news. Really bad news."

Dre sat up straighter on his stool. "You know him?"

"Only from what I've heard from people sitting where you are. He's taken the pimping game to a whole new level. He's heartless."

"You know where I can find him?"

She shook her head. "I hear he's very secretive. Some of the people closest to him don't even know where he lives."

Another waitress set a plate in front of him. Dre scooped a spoonful of rice into his mouth.

"I'm looking for this woman he used to pimp," Dre said, talking and chewing. "I'm hoping she might have some useful information. Her name's Loretha Johnson. You heard of her?"

Dottie's face brightened. "Yeah. She runs Harmony House. My church, West Angeles, donates food and clothing to her place."

Dre stopped chewing and set down his fork. "You know where the house is?"

"You can't go there. It's like a safe house. Nobody's supposed to even know that the girls stay there. If you show up, they'll think you're up to no good. Loretha don't play."

"Just tell me where it is. I really need to speak to her."

Dottie stuck her hands into the pockets of her jeans and waited several beats. "It's not far from here. In Lafayette Square. It's one of those big old houses with wood paneling and tons of bedrooms. I think up to fourteen girls live there at a time."

"You have the address?"

"I told you. You can't go there."

"I don't plan to. I just want to talk to Loretha. I'll wait until she leaves and talk to her away from the house. I promise. So do you have the address?"

Dottie looked off. "No," she said uneasily. "But I can probably get it from one of my church members. How about if I just get you Loretha's telephone number instead?"

"How about if you get me her number *and* her address? I promise you, I'll call first."

Dottie still appeared hesitant.

Dre leaned in over the bar. "Please. She may be my best shot at finding my niece."

CHAPTER 36

Day Two: 7:15 p.m.

Address in hand, Dre left The Cork and, contrary to his promise to Dottie, he drove straight to Lafayette Square. He had called Loretha's number three times, but his calls went straight to voicemail.

Dre had been floored when he entered the four-square-block enclave. He was familiar with Baldwin Hills, Ladera Heights and View Park, where a lot of blacks with cash lived. But the stately homes in Lafayette Square rivaled those in Beverly Hills. The only downside was having to drive through a rundown neighborhood to get there.

There was only one street leading into and out of Lafayette Square. All of them dead-ended so it was impossible to circle the block. After locating Harmony House, he parked half a block away and turned off the engine.

Dre noticed someone peek from behind a curtain at a house across the street. It was after seven o'clock and just beginning to get dark. The people inside probably figured he was up to no- good. He hoped they didn't call the police.

From what he'd been told, Loretha walked the track three or four nights a week in search of runaways and girls who wanted to get away from their pimps. He hoped to spot her leave the house tonight. If she did, he planned to follow her.

Dre had nodded off when his own snoring woke him up. It was close to eight o'clock now. He couldn't sit here all night. He fired up the engine and drove the car several feet, stopping directly across from the address Dottie had given him.

He got out and crossed the street. He was surprised that the front gate wasn't locked. He headed up the short walkway, mentally rehearsing what he would say.

My name is Andre Thomas. I need to talk to you about The Shepherd. He kidnapped my niece.

Dre stepped onto the wide porch and rang the doorbell. He was certain he heard movement inside. Then he saw the curtain move ever so slightly.

"I need to talk to Loretha Johnson," he yelled through the door. "I'm trying to find my niece. She was kidnapped by The Shepherd. This is for real. I don't mean anybody any harm. I—"

"Don't move!" Dre felt the cold steel of a gun pressed to the back of his head. "Put your hands where I can see them."

Dre slowly raised his hands in the air.

From behind, someone roughly patted him down.

"I don't have a gun. I just wanted to—"

"This is a private home and you're not welcome here. You're going to turn around and leave."

"I'm looking for Loretha Johnson."

"*I'm* Loretha Johnson. I don't know you and I don't want to know you. I just want you to get the hell off my property."

Dre made a move to turn around.

Loretha slammed the butt of the gun against his head, which halted his movement.

"Ow!"

"I asked you to leave."

"My niece, Brianna—"

"Do you think I'm stupid? I saw you parked up the street. One of my neighbors called me because she thought you might be trouble. I don't like pimps showing up on my doorstep trying to take my girls. If I blow your brains out all over this porch, I won't spend a day in jail because you're trespassing. And just so you know, I'd personally like to blow away you and every other pimp on the planet. So if I were you, I wouldn't say another word. I would just leave."

"But—"

Dre heard the gun cock.

"Get off my property!"

Dottie had been right. He should not have come to the house. The woman thought he was a pimp. If he wasn't so shaken from having a gun jammed into his head, he might laugh.

He turned and headed back down the walkway without even getting a look at the feisty Loretha Johnson.

When he reached his car, he finally gazed back at the house, but the porch was empty.

* * *

Dre stood on Angela's doorstep, ready to crumble.

"Oh my goodness," she said, upon opening the door.

Angela took in his wrinkled clothes, stubbled face and gloomy demeanor. His eyes were sunken and shrouded by dark patches and he smelled. He also seemed unsteady on his feet, but Angela did not detect the smell of alcohol.

Angela reached out and hugged him, pulling him inside. "I've been so worried about you."

She took him by the arm and led him into the living room. Dre flopped onto the couch as if he'd lost control of his motor functions.

"Was Brianna at the house? Did you find her?" Angela sat down next to him, then reached up to turn on the lamp sitting on an end table.

Dre finally spoke. "Don't."

"Don't what?" Angela asked.

"Don't turn on the light."

She sat back down and threw her arms around him. Dre sagged into her. He made no sound or movement, but when she felt the wetness against her neck, she knew he was crying.

Angela had no idea how long she'd held him, but at some point, Dre simply started talking.

"Bree wasn't at the house on Sixty-seventh. They must've moved her. I've done everything I can think of, but I can't find her." His voice quivered with emotion and he continued talking in a ramble of disjointed sentences.

"I can't face my sister again if I don't get her back. My mother says she's losing it. I didn't know all this perverted crap was going on. I thought I found this woman who could help me get her back, but she put a gun to my head. Loretha Johnson was my best bet, but she wouldn't even talk to me and—"

"Loretha Johnson? From Harmony House?"

Dre pulled away from her. "You know her?"

Angela turned on the light. "The Black Women Lawyers Association of L.A. gave her an award for her work on behalf of sexually exploited children. We also deliver baskets to the girls every Christmas. I'm approved to be a Harmony House mentor, but could never find the time to do it. Please tell me you didn't go over there."

Dre lowered his head and wiped his palm down his face. He winced, having forgotten about his bruised knuckles, as well as the sore spot where Loretha had slugged him.

Angela took in his swollen knuckles and gasped. "What happened to your hand?"

"I had a little encounter with a wall," he said, not wanting to talk about it. "I was hoping Loretha could lead me to The Shepherd. But she thought I was a pimp. Can you believe that?"

"Yes," Angela said, trying not to sound as if she was scolding him. "You're a stranger. She has to protect her girls. Why do you want to speak to her?"

"The scum who took Brianna used to be her pimp. I figured she could help me get to him."

Angela was quiet for a moment.

"I could probably arrange a meeting with her. She'll talk to you if she knows you're legit. If I'm with you, she'll be more comfortable. I'll call her now. Maybe we can meet her someplace. That woman works twenty-four-seven. I don't think she ever sleeps."

Angela got up, found her smartphone on the kitchen counter and started scrolling through her contacts. Before she could find Loretha's number, Dre's smartphone rang.

He pulled it from his pocket and clicked it on. "Yeah?"

Angela watched Dre's face go from slack-jawed to tight-faced. His right knee began to bounce up and down. She prayed he wasn't hearing bad news about Brianna. For the next several seconds, all Dre did was listen.

"I'll be there," he finally said, then hung up.

Angela rejoined him on the couch. "What's going on? Who was that?"

Dre exhaled long and hard. "One of The Shepherd's flunkies." He slowly got to his feet. "I gotta go."

"Go where?"

"To meet The Shepherd."

CHAPTER 37

Day Two: 7:20 p.m.

Freda entered the room where she found Brianna on her knees begging Kym to help her escape.

"That ain't gonna happen," Freda said, then turned to Kym. "I need to talk to Brianna alone."

"No prob. Enjoy your first lesson," Kym said to Brianna with a wink.

Freda bent over in front of the TV and slid a disk into a DVD player.

She sat down on the bed opposite Brianna. "I want you to watch this because this is what you're going to do."

"I'm not doing nothing and you can't make me!"

"Oh, yes I can," Freda said with a sullen smile. "We'll give you a little cocktail to get you all loosened up. This is a video of Shantel. She's one of Shep's top moneymakers because she knows how to treat her clients."

Brianna wanted to turn away from the television screen, but at the same time her eyes were drawn to it.

The girl on the video didn't look like the same Shantel that Brianna had met. She was now wearing a pile of makeup and a short curly wig. She was dressed in traditional hooker ware: stilettos, short skirt and a bust-enhancing top.

It was obvious that Shantel was in a cheap motel room. Everything in the room—the lopsided bed, the scarred end tables, the cheap headboard—looked worn out, like the furniture at the second-hand stores her grandmother liked to visit. Brianna had never stayed in a motel or a hotel for that matter, but she'd seen enough TV to recognize it as the kind of place where criminals on the run hid out.

On the video, there was a knock on the door and Shantel walked over to open it. There was a stiff smile on her face but Brianna could see the nervousness underneath it. Or maybe it was fear.

A large man, a large ugly white man stepped into the room.

"You don't have to worry about nothing crazy going down," Freda said, as calmly as if she was giving Brianna a makeup lesson. "One of Shep's guys won't be far away and he has a key to the room. All you have to do is yell and he'll come running."

"What kind of date do you want tonight, sweetie?" Shantel asked in a sultry voice.

"I need a blow job to get me going," the man said, drooling. *"Then, I want it missionary style."*

Shantel stuck out her hand. *"That'll be fifty, plus another one-fifty."*

She took the bills, tucked them under the mattress, then stripped off her clothes, revealing a scrawny body. Her flat breasts looked like two biscuits that failed to rise.

"You have a sweet face, Daddy," she said, walking up to the man and stroking his cheek.

"See," Freda said, pointing at the screen. "That's why Shantel gets so many repeat clients. She's extra nice. She knows that man is hideous."

Shantel climbed into bed and waited as the man disrobed. Thick, black hair covered his chest, making him look more animal than human. His private part hung from his flabby body like a long, limp hotlink.

The man joined her in bed and Shantel bent to take him into her mouth. The man moaned as if he was in pain.

"Okay, okay," he said, stopping her after only a few seconds, now that he'd sprang to life. *"I'm ready now."*

He slipped on a condom, then laid Shantel on her back and pounced on top of her. Brianna covered her mouth with both hands, certain that she was going to throw up. There was no way she could do that.

"Give it to me, Daddy," Shantel called out in a monotone voice. *"Give it to me, Daddy. You the best."*

Brianna focused on Shantel's dead eyes as they stared up at the ceiling.

After just a couple of minutes, the man heaved himself into Shantel three, maybe four more times, yelled out and was suddenly still.

"Okay, Daddy, party's over. You have to get up so Mommy can breathe."

The man rolled over to the other side of the bed and Shantel hopped up and started putting on her clothes. *"Okay, Daddy, time to go."*

"That's another thing Shantel is good at," Freda said, beaming like a proud mother. "She knows how to get 'em in and out."

Shantel watched the man dress, then opened the door for him. Seconds later, there was another knock and a different man entered the room. This one was an older black man with gray hair.

"Nice," the man said, grinning.

"Shantel has some real stamina," Freda said. "That girl can do fifteen, twenty johns a night, no problem."

Brianna tried to hold it in, but couldn't. She leaned over the side of the bed and vomited all over the floor.

Freda jumped out of the way.

"You stupid slut! You're going to clean that up. And you better not do that tomorrow."

Brianna didn't respond. They couldn't make her have sex with some strange man. She wouldn't do it. She would rather die.

CHAPTER 38

Day Two: 7:30 p.m.

Dre sat quietly in his car a block away from City Stars, listening to some soft jazz. He was trying to get his emotions under control. When he walked into City Stars and came face-to-face with The Shepherd, he needed to be calm and rationale. It would be a bad move to just start pounding the dude's face in.

The Shepherd would probably be surrounded by bodyguards, which was why he'd insisted that Dre come alone. On the phone, Dre had agreed to do so, but he had no intention of keeping his word.

His first call after leaving Angela's place had been to Apache. He quickly explained what was about to go down. He wanted Apache to get to City Stars ahead of him and pretend to be a customer. The club had metal detectors, so there was no way Apache would be allowed inside with his Glock. But his cousin didn't really need a weapon to be deadly. He'd earned the name Apache, not only because of his physical appearance, but also because of his resourceful nature. He could be more dangerous with his bare hands than with a gun and a bullet.

Next, he called his childhood buddy, Mossy. Mossy was an analytical thinker who would never fly off the handle like Apache. He was the man Dre relied upon when he needed both muscle and street smarts. Despite what Dre had been told, when he walked into City Stars, Mossy would be at his side.

Dre tossed back his third shot of 5-Hour Energy. He already felt antsy and needed food, not more caffeine. But he still didn't have much of an appetite. He wished he'd taken the time to finish his red beans 'n rice at The Cork.

He gazed down the street and could see one of the bouncers standing out front talking to two other dudes. He was about to call Mossy when there was a knock on the front passenger window.

Dre jumped so high his head nearly hit the ceiling.

"Sorry, man," Mossy said, getting into the car. "I should've figured you'd be on edge. Frankly, I don't know how you're managing to even think straight. If these dudes had my baby, I'd be stone crazy."

Mossy and his long-time girlfriend had a twelve-year-old daughter.

Dre didn't want to tell him that he *was* crazy. Somehow, he'd managed to keep crazy on temporary lockdown.

"So what's the plan?" Mossy asked.

"They wanted me to come alone, so I know they're going to give me some flack when I show up with you. But we'll deal with that when we have to. Apache's already inside."

"Man, why'd you call that fool? He'll end up getting both of us killed."

Dre smiled. "They're not gonna let him in there with a piece. So we're good."

Mossy shook his head. He'd been privy to some of Apache's prior exploits and considered him a loose cannon. "If you say so."

"This Shepherd dude has a real ego," Dre said. "I figure I must have pissed him off by going around town calling him out. I suspect he'll send me through some hoops before giving Brianna back."

"Are you sure he's really got her?"

Dre reached behind him and grabbed Brianna's top from the backseat. "I found this at the house we searched on Sixty-seventh Street. It's definitely hers. I bought it for her." Saying those words out loud seemed to heighten his pain.

"You really think he's going to give her back?"

"He'll have to," Dre said. "Or I'll kill him."

Mossy looked him in the eye.

"In fact, I'm still going to kill him *after* I get her back."

They exited the car and walked toward the club.

They were several yards away when the bouncer lowered his chin and said something into the headset he was wearing. Dre recognized him as one of the bouncers who'd thrown him out the night before. He was probably letting The Shepherd know that he had not arrived alone.

Dre attempted to walk past him into the club.

"Hold up. The cover charge is ten bucks."

"We didn't come to watch the show."

The bouncer shrugged.

Dre pulled twenty bucks from his wallet and flung it at him. The man caught the bill in mid-air, but did not step aside.

"You're supposed to be solo," he said.

Dre's jaw tightened. "Tell your boss I'm not coming in alone. We're not strapped so what's he afraid of?"

The man turned away and spoke into his headset again.

A minute later, the man took his time patting both of them down, then lifted the rope and led the way inside.

Dre spotted Apache standing near the edge of the stage, tossing bills as a topless stripper shook her breasts in his face. He didn't even notice them.

"Don't say a word," Dre muttered.

The bouncer passed them off to another larger dude with *Security* stenciled across his black T-shirt.

"Follow me," the second man said.

He led them to one of the private high-roller booths in the back of the club. Three steps led up to the elevated area that looked out over the stage. A circular, red velvet couch took up most of the booth. A black lacquer table stretched from one end of the couch to the other. Clint sat smiling in the booth, his arms extended along the back of the couch, dark shades resting on his nose. Another bouncer stood at the bottom of the steps.

Dre felt a rash of heat rise up his neck. He wanted to choke the smile off Clint's face.

Mossy must have sensed that he was close to losing it. "Hold it together, man. We gotta get Brianna back first."

Dre climbed the short steps and settled into the booth facing Clint. When Mossy attempted to follow him, the bouncer held out his arm, blocking him. So Mossy remained outside the booth, face-to-face with the bouncer.

Clint made a show of lifting his cocktail glass, then took a sip. "What you drinkin', bruh?"

"Nothin'," Dre said. "Where's The Shepherd?"

"You're turning down a free drink?"

"I don't drink. Now answer my question." Dre kept his hands underneath the table. He was shaking with rage and didn't want Clint to mistake his physical response for fear.

Clint pointed a skinny finger at the stage. "Check out Katrina. She's one of my newest hires. She's still a little green, but it don't matter when you're as fine as she is."

Dre glanced over at Katrina as she awkwardly danced around the pole. Her moves were slow and uncertain, as if she was waiting for someone to give her directions. Half a dozen men stood near the stage, hurling cheers and bills her way. Apache was right in the middle of them, grinning like he was about to get laid.

"You know what I came here for," Dre said, his focus back on Clint. "Where's The Shepherd?"

"I'm calling the shots on this. Let me tell you what we—"

"I only want to talk to The Shepherd. So where is he?"

"You'll meet him soon enough."

"I want to meet him now."

"If I were you, I'd calm down. You're not in a position to be calling the shots. Not if you want your niece back."

Dre's right knee began to bounce up and down and he couldn't make it stop.

"So where were we?" Clint asked.

"Why don't we just cut to the chase," Mossy said. "How do we get the kid back?"

Clint lifted his shades and peered down at Mossy. "And who are you?"

"Family," Mossy said.

Clint redirected his attention to Dre. "The Shepherd has some terms you need to accept."

"I'm listening," Dre said.

"Shep wants to explain them himself." Clint picked up an iPad from the couch. "He had a prior commitment tonight. So we're hooking up with him on FaceTime."

"So he's a punk?" Dre said, his whole body blazing with anger. "Too scared to face me?"

Clint stopped fiddling with the iPad and gave Dre an ominous glare.

"I'ma give you a little helpful advice," he said. "Once we connect with Shep, you need to show your respect. If you don't, you might never see that girl again."

CHAPTER 39

Day Two: 7:50 p.m.

Since learning of Brianna Walker's disappearance, Bonnie could barely put one foot in front of the other. She kept imagining all the horrific things that could be happening to her. The girl's mother had to be going absolutely crazy.

Before leaving school, she'd looked up Brianna's file and had written down her home address. Although Brianna's uncle had given her his number as well as his sister's number, Bonnie felt it would be cruel to deliver this information over the telephone.

That was the reason she was headed to Brianna's house at almost eight o'clock at night.

Bonnie watched all the reality crime shows. *The First 48* was her favorite. So she knew that cases that weren't cracked within the first few hours became more difficult to solve with each passing hour. She couldn't remain silent a minute longer and was mad at herself for not having the guts to tell Brianna's uncle about the other missing girls earlier that morning.

At least she'd finally gotten up the nerve to call the police. After being bounced around, she landed the ear of a detective who was familiar with the case. But once he heard that she wasn't a family member and that she didn't have any evidence to back up her suspicions, he rushed her off the phone.

Bonnie parked her Ford Escort in front of the modest home on Magnolia Street. Locking her car door, she marched up the driveway and rang the doorbell. When no one answered, she knocked softly on the door. Again, no response. Just as she was about to knock again, the door opened, but just a crack.

A gray-haired woman peered out at her.

"Yes?" the woman said. "Can I help you?"

"Is Ms. Walker home? I'm Bonnie Flanagan, Brianna's teacher. I just wanted to know how she was doing and whether she's heard anything about Brianna."

"Not a word," the woman said, opening the door wider, but not asking her in. "And Donna's not doing too good. She's not even here. She constantly walks the streets putting up posters and asking people if they've seen Brianna. She's out there with my son Anthony now. I'm scared she's losing her mind. And I've been praying to Jesus that I don't lose mine."

The anguish that plagued the woman's face gave Bonnie a chill.

"Is Brianna's uncle here?"

The woman shook her head.

Bonnie hesitated, uncertain about whether she should tell this woman what she knew.

"Well, please tell them I came by." She opened her purse. "Could you give them my number?"

The woman took Bonnie's business card.

"Why don't you head on up to the shopping center at Rosecrans and Central. You might find Donna down there putting up posters of Brianna. I've told her that she's just gotta have faith. Jesus will bring Brianna home."

Bonnie left and drove north on Wilmington Avenue, then made a left onto Rosecrans Boulevard, hoping to spot Donna. As soon as she pulled into the shopping center parking lot, she saw her.

Donna Walker was wearing jeans and a light sweater. She was standing at the bus stop, taping a poster to the side of a Plexiglas enclosure. Bonnie saw a man across the street doing the same thing.

She parked a few yards away near a Chinese takeout restaurant. Before getting out of the car, she cautiously checked her surroundings.

"Mrs. Walker?" Bonnie said softly as she approached.

Donna whirled around, apparently startled to hear her name being called.

"I'm Brianna's English teacher. I remember you from the last parent-teacher conference."

When she got closer, Bonnie could see that the poster had a color photograph of Brianna above the words, *Help me find my missing daughter.* It listed Brianna's name and a phone number.

Donna rushed up to her, invading her personal space. "Have you heard something?"

"No," Bonnie said. "Not about Brianna. But I do have some information to share with you."

Donna's eyes expanded.

What Bonnie was about to do would make life rough for her at work. Once Donna heard this information, she'd probably run straight to the police. Manuel Ortiz wouldn't like it that she had disobeyed his direct order. But Bonnie couldn't live with herself if she didn't do everything in her power to bring Brianna home. Once the police started connecting the dots regarding the other missing girls, it might lead to something helpful.

She paused to take a breath.

"Your daughter isn't the first student at Maverick Middle School who recently disappeared," Bonnie said, resting her hand on Donna's forearm. "She's the fourth."

CHAPTER 40

Day Two: 8:05 p.m.

Dre and Clint remained locked in a silent standoff.

"Look, man," Clint finally said, as if he was doing him a favor, "I know my boss. I'm just trying to help you out. When I hit this button and connect you with Shep, if you keep talking all that ying, yang, all bets are off."

Dre couldn't remember the last time he'd been faced with such a difficult task. He wasn't a violent person. Despite more than a decade of dealing drugs, he'd never had reason to want to kill anyone. But remaining in his seat right now, facing the man who knew his niece's whereabouts was tough.

"We didn't come here to chitchat with you," Mossy said, speaking for him. "Let's do this."

Clint set the iPad on its side, landscape style, then pushed it further away so they could both see the screen. He tapped a few buttons and in seconds a face appeared.

The Shepherd was nothing like Dre had expected. He was clean-shaven, with no distinguishing features except for a faint scar above his left eyebrow. Dre couldn't tell whether he was tall or short. He couldn't have been more average-looking.

"Thanks for dropping by," Shep began. "So what can I do for you?"

Dre's right knee began to bounce again and he could not make it stop. *Keep it together,* he told himself.

"You know why I'm here," Dre said. "Where is she?"

"Safe and sound," Shep said.

"Where?"

"With me."

"I want her back."

"Okay." Shep yawned as if he was bored. "What are you prepared to pay?"

"Pay? You must be out of your mind," Dre seethed.

"Temper, temper," Shep said. "I'm a businessman and I'm here to conduct business. I need a return on my investment."

Dre looked at Clint, then at the bouncer, who took a step closer to the stairs as if signaling him not to do anything stupid. Dre noticed that a second bouncer had appeared.

"What investment?" Mossy asked. "You kidnapped her."

"I've already put in time and money. If you want her back, it's going to cost you twenty-five grand."

Dre made eye contact with Mossy.

Hold it together, Dre told himself.

"I ain't got twenty-five grand," he said.

"Yes, you do," Shep said from the screen of the iPad. "I understand that you were a pretty successful drug dealer, Businessman. Wasn't that your name on the street?"

"You must be crazy," Mossy said. "You really don't wanna mess with us."

Clint turned the iPad around, so that The Shepherd could see Mossy.

Shep laughed. "So you're threatening me?"

"Yes," Dre and Mossy said simultaneously. "We are."

"I don't think you have anything to threaten me with. You ain't going to the police because once they look up your sheet, they might just arrest you. So if you want your niece back, you need to figure out a way to come up with some cash. And if you *are* stupid enough to go to the cops, you'll never see that little girl again. I promise you that."

"How do I even know you have her?" Dre asked.

"Tell you what, give me a call when you get my money together and I'll email you a picture. Will that work?"

Neither Dre nor Mossy responded.

"So how much time do you need to get my money. Two days? A week? The longer you take, the more johns she'll have to service."

In an instant, Dre grabbed Clint's glass and pounded it into the iPad, shattering the screen. By the time he reached for Clint's neck, one of the bodyguards had dived across the table and pressed a gun to his head. Dre stiffened.

The other bouncer had Mossy's arms locked behind his back and was tugging him toward the rear of the club.

With the music so loud and everybody's focus on a different girl who'd taken the stage, no one seemed to notice the commotion. Not even Apache.

"Get the hell outta my establishment," Clint said, jumping out of the booth.

"I'ma get Brianna back," Dre yelled over his shoulder as the bouncer forced him out of the booth and in the same direction that Mossy had been taken. "And after I do, I'm comin' back for your ass!"

* * *

Dre and Mossy were hustled past the men's room toward an emergency exit door. The two goons kicked the door open and hurled them into the alley.

Mossy got to his feet and dusted himself off, noticing a big tear in the knee of his slacks. Dre landed on his hands and was bleeding from a piece of glass. He pressed his thumb against the cut in an effort to stop the bleeding.

Dre slowly got to his feet. His body was so consumed with anger he could barely steady himself enough to walk.

Neither man spoke as they walked down the alley.

"We're going to get her back," Mossy said finally. "But these are some cold-ass cats."

"If we can't get to The Shepherd," Dre said quietly, "then I wanna take Clint down. Make him talk. He knows where Brianna is. We can get Shep's ass later."

Mossy thought for a moment. "That might not be a bad idea. But we're going to need some manpower to pull that off. And not your crazy-ass cousin."

This was the first time he'd thought about Apache since they'd walked into the club. He was probably inside getting a lap dance now.

"I need you to get some guys together," Dre said. "Call Gus, Terrell and Bobby and tell 'em the deal. I'll call my brother too. Have 'em meet me at my place."

Dre pulled out his smartphone to call Apache, but it rang just as he was about to dial. The caller ID flashed Angela's name. He didn't want to deal with her right now, but answered her call anyway.

"You okay?" she asked.

"Yeah."

"Did you meet with The Shepherd?"

"Naw. Just one of his guys."

"So did you find out any more information about Brianna?"

Dre couldn't tell Angela what he was about to do. She wouldn't understand.

"No," Dre lied.

"I'm sorry."

"Me too."

They both held on to the silence for a few seconds.

"I just spoke to Loretha," Angela continued. "She's willing to talk to you."

That news gave Dre a lift he desperately needed.

"She's sorry about putting that gun to your head, but she thought you were a pimp coming after one of her girls. She suggested that we meet at the Denny's on Sepulveda. She can meet us in a couple of hours. "

"A couple of hours? I don't have that kind of time."

"The woman who helps her out at Harmony House won't be home for a while," Angela explained. "She can't leave the girls there alone. Why don't you come over here until then. Have you even had any sleep since this all started?"

"I can't sleep," Dre said. "Not until I find Brianna."

Dre hung up and told Mossy about his plans to meet with Loretha.

"I'm heading over to Angela's," Dre said, tossing Mossy the key to his apartment. "Call Apache and tell him what went down. Then I need you to round up the guys for a meeting at my place."

CHAPTER 41

Day Two: 9:45 p.m.

After making Brianna clean up the mess she'd made by puking all over the floor, Freda stormed out of the room. She'd returned two hours later and was still in the midst of her lecture.

"You're making this harder than it has to be!" Freda said, disgusted. "It ain't that bad. You know how many tricks I turned in my day?"

Brianna pressed her face into the mattress and sobbed. She was so afraid, but she would not let this evil woman know it. Her Uncle Dre was going to find her. She was sure of that.

"I told you, I'm not being no hooker and you can't make me be one."

Freda scowled at her. "Before you start professing what you will and will not do, you need to understand something. If you don't start cooperating, your mother is going to get the same kind of beat down Clint gave you. Do you understand?"

"You can't do anything to my mother!" Brianna yelled. "My uncle will kill you!"

"You don't think so?" She crossed the room and retrieved a large leather bag from the bed and started fishing around in it. "I have another video for you to watch."

Freda pulled out her smartphone, hit several buttons and held it up for Brianna to see.

"Pay close attention, little girl. I think there's somebody on this video you might recognize."

The video was taken outdoors, during daylight hours. Brianna's face went numb when she saw her mother leaving their house. *They were watching her mother!*

Brianna felt something press hard against her chest and she could barely breathe.

The camera moved in closer. Her mother looked so sad. As sad as Brianna felt right now. Brianna was certain she was about to throw up again.

The camera followed her mother as she walked up Magnolia Street, past her friend Sydney's house. She had a bag hung over her shoulder and she was holding it tight. When Donna got to the end of the block, she walked over to a thick telephone pole. She reached into the bag and pulled out a piece of paper and stapled it to the pole.

There was suddenly sound.

"Ma'am, did you lose your pet?" Brianna couldn't see the male voice speaking to her mother and she had no idea where the camera was.

Donna turned around and Brianna saw her mother's sad eyes again. Brianna was so sorry that she had disobeyed her mother and gone onto Facebook. She'd always thought her mother was paranoid when she talked about child predators on the Internet. But her mother had been right. If only she had listened to her mother, she'd be home right now.

"Somebody took my baby," Donna sniveled.

The camera moved closer and zeroed in on the poster. It showed Brianna's most recent school picture.

Tears streamed down Brianna's cheeks now.

"Ma'am, that's a shame," the male voice said. *"Give me one of those posters. I'll take a picture of it and have my son put it on his Facebook page."*

Donna gladly handed him one. *"I'd really appreciate that,"* she said weakly.

Her mother seemed to be in a trance. Without saying good-bye, she crossed the street and began taping another poster to another telephone pole. The camera followed her for a while longer as she walked down the street, stopping to put Brianna's picture on a gate, a bus bench, even a city trash can.

Freda shut off the smartphone.

"One of Shep's guys took that video," she said. "He was the one talking to your mother."

Brianna felt like she was about to have a real asthma attack.

"You see how close he got to your mother? He could've snatched her off the street easier than we snatched you. If you don't start acting right, the next time we follow her, she's going to get a beating worse than the one you got. I'll show you that on tape too."

"Why are you doing this?" Brianna cried. "You're evil!"

"Don't take it personal. This is all about the money. We're counting on you to make us a whole lot of it."

Brianna could not let them hurt her mother. "If I do what you want me to do, can I go home?"

"We'll see," Freda said with a wink. "But if you don't do what we tell you to do, you won't have a mama to go home to."

CHAPTER 42

Day Two: 11:05 p.m.

Dre and Angela had been sitting in a booth at Denny's for about fifteen minutes.

"You sure she's coming?" His eyes had been pinned on the entrance from the second they'd arrived.

"She's coming," Angela said. "Just relax. She probably had an emergency with one of her girls. If she's not here in a few more minutes, I'll call her."

Dre took a bite of the hamburger he'd ordered. He still had no appetite, but knew he needed to get something into his system besides caffeine.

His eyes darted back to the door. "Is that her?"

A petite woman with dreadlocks had just entered the restaurant. She was wearing jeans and a heavy military-type jacket. Angela held up a hand, waving her over.

Dre couldn't stop staring. He was both surprised and embarrassed that a woman no taller than Brianna had gotten the jump on him. He could tell that Loretha Johnson had been a very attractive woman in her day. He pegged her to be in her early thirties, but she had a frayed look about her. The streets had definitely taken their toll. It wasn't just the crow's feet or the coarseness of her skin. It was as if a bubble of exhaustion encased her.

Loretha eased into the booth, placing Dre in the middle.

She smiled sheepishly. "Sorry about our little confrontation. I'm like a mother bear when it comes to my girls."

"No prob," Dre said. "I'm just glad that gun didn't go off."

"I know how to handle a weapon," Loretha said confidently. "The only way it would've gone off is if you'd tried something. I definitely would've shot you."

She turned to Angela. "I'm not supposed to have a gun in the house with the girls, but I've had a couple of pimps come knocking before and I refuse to go unprotected." She smiled. "So, I won't mention that little incident again if you don't."

"No problem," Angela said. "That's enough talk about guns. We have a problem and we hope you can help."

After a waitress poured Loretha a cup of coffee, Dre began by telling her everything that had happened to date. He stopped short of mentioning his virtual meeting with The Shepherd, fearing that information would upset Angela.

"I feel like I'm trapped in a nightmare that won't end," he said.

Loretha sighed heavily. "You are. What's going on out there in the streets today is nothing like it was in my day. The girls are getting younger and younger. And now that the gangs are in on it, it's big business."

"But how can they be bold enough to just snatch a kid off the street and turn her out without fearing that her family'll come looking for her?" Dre asked.

"The girls they typically target don't have much of a family in the first place. How many times have you seen news coverage about a missing brown or black girl from Compton or Watts on TV? Our kids don't get media coverage when they go missing. These girls are society's throwaways. But I have to say that I am seeing cases where they're snatching girls from nice neighborhoods who don't fit this profile. The so-called guerilla pimps are getting bolder because the risks of getting caught are low and the financial rewards are extremely high. And then you have the romeo pimps who don't have to snatch them. It's easy for an impressive-looking guy all dressed up in jewelry and fancy clothes to gain a girl's trust."

"I can understand how a girl might be initially lured in," Dre said, "but why don't they just run away?"

"It's not that simple. First, the pimp keeps really close tabs on them. And by the time a pimp puts a girl on the street, she's so traumatized and brainwashed that she'll do whatever she's told to do out of fear. They're beaten or threatened with death or the death of someone close to them. The girls I see show the same signs of Post-Traumatic Stress Disorder as the soldiers coming back from Iraq and Afghanistan. The only difference is they never get treated for it."

Loretha was growing animated, pointing her finger as she spoke.

"And you have to remember that we're talking about children. The youngest one I've seen was nine. The first few times they have sex with a john is bad, but after being raped day after day, they become numb to it. You ever heard of the Stockholm Syndrome? That's where hostages begin to bond with their captors. Well, it's real."

Angela saw alarm in Dre's face and knew he was imagining this happening to his niece. She could feel his leg bouncing up and down underneath the table. She wanted to stop Loretha. To tell her that they'd heard enough.

"It's like a rat who realizes that he's trapped. He finally stops trying to escape, even after the gate's been opened. Those three girls who were kidnapped by that psycho in Cleveland a while back were there for over ten years before one of them tried to escape. The psychological beat down these girls experience is way worse than the physical one. Bruises eventually heal. It can take years to heal your soul."

Loretha poured cream and sugar into her coffee.

"Frankly, many girls don't leave because they're too embarrassed to return home. And even if she could leave, where is she going to go? Her family didn't want her in the first place and there aren't nearly enough facilities like mine to house them.

"Her pimp, however, promises to always take care of her. In the beginning, he romances her, tells her he loves her and praises her for all the money she's making him. For many of these girls, it's the first time they've *ever* been praised by *anybody*. So they begin to feel okay about what they're doing. Then a month or two, or four or five later, there's a new girl, a younger girl, who's demanding the pimp's time and attention. He now uses beatings, not praise, to control her. She either makes him money or she gets beat up. And every dime she makes goes to her pimp. It's slavery."

Loretha paused. "That's basically my story, but it's being repeated over and over and over again all over the country and even around the world."

Dre picked up his hamburger, then put it back down. He wasn't sure how to respectfully ask his next question. "How long ago were you—uh, when did you leave The Shepherd?"

Loretha grimaced. "A little over five years ago. I was no longer working the streets when I left. Shep hadn't taken his operation online yet. I was the one—" She paused as her eyes moistened. "I was the one who lured girls in for him. They were much more likely to trust a woman."

Angela squeezed Loretha's forearm. "How old were you when you first met him?"

She laughed softly. "Sixteen and as grown as hell."

"So you were a teen prostitute?" Dre asked.

Loretha nearly bared her teeth. "There's no such thing as a *teen prostitute*," she snapped. "They're children. Sexually exploited children."

Dre held up both hands, palms out. "I'm sorry. I didn't mean to—"

"No, no, I'm sorry," Loretha said, slumping against the booth and cupping her forehead. "But that's another term that really pisses me off. If a teacher is caught sleeping with a fifteen-year-old student—a student who claims she's *in love*—she's an abuse victim. But if a grown-ass man picks up a child off the street and pays her for sex, she's a prostitute. There's an adult taking advantage of a child in both situations.

"In the school scenario, the child gets counseling," Loretha continued. "In my world, the child goes to jail. The teacher might spend years in prison, but the john will get nothing more than a slap on the wrist, if he's even caught, that is. Let's not talk about the pimp because he rarely faces any jail time. In both cases, children are being sexually exploited. The only difference is the exchange of money. That shouldn't make a difference."

Dre took in what she was saying. "I guess I never thought about it like that."

Loretha sucked in air and took a moment to collect herself. "When Shep got his hands on me, I was fresh off the bus from Cleveland. I was certain I was going be the next big female rapper. Queen Loretha." She laughed. "I had saved up forty-two hundred dollars from babysitting, braiding hair and my job at the mall. I thought it would last me until I signed my record deal.

"One of Shep's guys zeroed in on me ten minutes after I stepped off the Greyhound bus. I probably had *lost little girl* stamped across my forehead. He fed me, gave me a place to stay and promised to hook me up with one of his record producer friends. I was so naive."

"And they put you on the street, just like that?" Angela asked.

"Nope. They groomed me. At first, I was Shep's girlfriend. Treated like royalty. Always praised for my body. The first thing he did was put me on the pole at City Stars. I actually enjoyed the dancing and having men throw money at me. And by the way, ninety percent of the women in the sex industry have a history of sexual abuse. I was no different. In no time, I went from lap dancing to private dancing. After that, hitting the track and turning my first trick didn't seem like that big of a deal. Shep constantly told me I was special. He ultimately took me off the streets and saved me for his high rollers. I was making upwards of five grand a week. Except I was making it for him, not me."

Dre thought about Katrina and wondered if she'd end up following that same path.

"What can you tell us about The Shepherd?" Dre asked.

Loretha shrugged. "Shep is a businessman first and a pimp second, which is why he's never spent a day in jail. He thinks of himself as some supreme being. In his mind, he's like a David Koresh or a Jim Jones."

"Hold up," Dre said. "This cat sounds delusional."

Loretha laughed. "I didn't realize it at the time, but I think he is. Has an ego the size of a mountain. There're two things he covets: power and money. He demands respect and will be offended by the most harmless slight. Like someone walking into a room and failing to acknowledge him. And no matter how much money he makes, he'll never have enough of it."

"Is the business really that lucrative?" Angela asked.

"He's made millions of dollars over the years."

Angela's face contorted. "Millions?"

"Millions," Loretha repeated. "He's got a lot of girls, and not just here in California."

"Is he violent?" Angela asked.

"He never laid a hand on me and I never saw him get violent with any of the other girls. But there were rumors that he'd paid others to kill for him. Frankly, I think he put those rumors out there so people would fear him. He's basically a punk at heart who's hiding behind this illusion of power that he's created in his head."

Dre folded his hands and set them on the table. This was all very interesting, but there was really only one thing he wanted to know. "Where do you think he might be holding Brianna?"

"Finding your niece is going to be hard," Loretha said. "His girls never stay in one place very long. He has several properties in L.A. and I hear he now owns a couple of rundown motels in the Valley."

"We should go online and search for properties in his name," Angela said.

"That'll be a waste of time. Shep has so many shell corporations, you'll never find anything that's directly tied to him."

"Where does he send the girls to…" Dre had a hard time coming up with the right words. "Do what they do?"

"I hear he runs most of his operation online now. The guys make appointments online and go to his motels for their *dates*. He may have a few girls on the tracks in the Hollywood area, but he only puts them on the street to punish them for some infraction, like being too sick to turn a trick."

Loretha lowered her head and rubbed the back of her neck.

"How'd you break away?" Angela asked.

"Shep eventually got me strung out on heroin. He never touched the stuff himself, but he used drugs to control others. I was just worn out. I couldn't take it anymore. I also started to feel guilty about the girls I was bringing into the fold. One in particular."

A heavy silence settled over the booth. Neither Angela nor Dre said a word, willing to let Loretha reveal her story at her own pace.

"There was this long-time client we called Demonic. Guy in his fifties. Professional man. Looked like somebody's grandfather. He liked getting a little rough with the girls. He paid big for this privilege. Shep charged him three grand for an hour with a girl. He only let him have girls who mouthed off."

Loretha stopped to take a sip of her coffee, then continued.

"Rena was seventeen. Back then, Shep didn't mess with the really young ones. She was raised in the foster care system and had been in and out of trouble. One of Shep's guys found her at a park. The girl had a strong personality, always talking back. To teach her a lesson, Shep gave her to Demonic. When she came back later that night, she was all bloody and beaten to a pulp. Rena told me that Demonic punched her in the face and sodomized her with a broomstick. He also used a lighter to burn her breasts and groin. She had blisters everywhere. I swear he'd never done anything that sick to any of the other girls."

Loretha wiped a tear from the corner of her eye.

"Rena was never the same after that. A week later, she ran off. After I got my life together, I started looking for her. I only found her several months ago, pushing a grocery cart up Figueroa. She lives underneath the freeway. I brought her to Harmony House once, but she disappeared within a couple of days. One of my social worker friends tried to help her too, but Rena would always go right back to the street."

Angela reached out and placed a hand on top of Loretha's.

"After Rena told me what Demonic had done to her that night, I was never the same either. *I* let that happen to her. My addiction was no excuse. A few days later, Shep sent me out to the mall to recruit some new girls. But I couldn't get the image of Rena out of my head. It was a Sunday morning and there was a church right across the street from the mall. Something drew me inside. When I stepped in there, I swear that minister was preaching a message for me and nobody else. When I finally gathered the courage to walk down the aisle to join the church, I was crying so hard, I could barely stand. They took me to a women's shelter and the rest is history."

"Shep never came looking for you?" Angela asked. "You're basically trying to put him out of business."

"Let's just say we have a gentleman's agreement. I have enough information to send him away for a very long time."

"Then why don't you then?" Dre asked, his tone critical.

Loretha's gaze fell to the table. "Because I'd be in jail right along with him. I can't make excuses for the horrible things I did. That's why I work so hard now to save every girl I can find. I want to get to them before some pimp turns them into the kind of person I used to be."

She paused. "But don't worry. Shep's eventually going to get everything he deserves." Loretha's words sounded more like a prediction than a statement.

Though little of what she'd heard was news to her, Angela felt saddened.

"I want to help," she said in a determined voice. "I completed your training program and got certified late last year, but I never made the time to volunteer. I need to do more than just represent these girls in court. I want to help them get out of the life."

Loretha hung her head. "I hate that term. *The life*. Makes it sound as if it's something glamorous or special. It's no life at all."

When embarrassment clouded Angela's face, Loretha reached out and patted Angela's hand.

"I'm sorry. I don't mean to be so touchy. I'd love it if you could come speak to our girls and maybe even mentor some of them. They really need to see someone who looks like them making it in the world."

"I could probably get some of my friends from Black Women Lawyers and California Women Lawyers to be mentors too. Maybe I could even set up a formal mentoring program for you."

"Excellent."

Loretha turned to Dre.

"If you want to get to Shep, you have to get to one of the guys closest to him. They're not all that bright. Clint Winbush is his main gopher."

"I've met him," Dre said.

She smiled. "If a cop ever got him in an interrogation room, he'd start wailing like a baby in two seconds flat. If anybody knows where Brianna's being held. He does."

All three of them appeared exhausted by their dire discussion.

"You need to do everything you can to find your niece," Loretha said. "Fast. She's only been with Shep a couple of days, so he probably hasn't put her out there yet. But it won't be long before he does."

DAY THREE MISSING

"Human trafficking is a low-risk, high-profit business—an estimated $32 billion-a-year global industry that has recently attracted the participation of increasingly sophisticated, organized criminal gangs. Domestic street gangs set aside traditional rivalries to set up commercial sex rings and maximize profits from the sale of young women."

—*The State of Human Trafficking in California,*
California Department of Justice

CHAPTER 43

Day Three: 9:45 a.m.

Not long after their meeting with Loretha, Dre received a frantic call from his sister. She was talking a mile a minute, making it difficult for him to comprehend what she was saying. When he finally did understand, he couldn't believe it.

Three other girls from Brianna's school had disappeared in the last eighteen months.

What in the hell was going on?

Dre had immediately rushed back to his sister's house in Compton and spent much of the night trying to calm her down. The next morning, they made multiple calls to the police as well as city hall, but no one seemed to be taking their concerns seriously. Dre finally decided that they needed to speak to Brianna's principal. Donna had promised Bonnie Flanagan not to disclose how she'd learned about the other girls.

They were now sitting in the parking lot just west of the school's main office.

"Let me do the talking when we get inside, okay?" Dre said.

If Donna started crying, they'd get nothing accomplished. She looked a mess. Her hair was barely combed and her eyes were so swollen they bulged from her face. He rubbed his scratchy chin and silently acknowledged that he wasn't a pretty sight either.

Dre climbed out of the car, then walked around to open the passenger door and helped his sister out.

She looked up at him with a weak smile. "You never did that before."

He simply smiled back, placed his arm around her shoulders and led her into the school.

They signed in and told the receptionist that they wanted to see the principal.

"Do you have an appointment?"

"No," Dre said. "But it's pretty important."

The woman started to give them attitude, but must have taken in their sad demeanors. She glanced down at their names.

"Oh," she said, putting a hand to her mouth. "You must be Brianna's mother and father."

"Mother and uncle," Dre corrected her. "Her father's deceased."

"Mr. Ortiz is in a meeting with our assistant principal, but I'll see if he has a few minutes."

The woman disappeared down a hallway.

A short while later, a chubby man in a suit that fit too snugly around the middle sloshed down the hallway.

He extended a hand long before he reached them.

"I'm Manuel Ortiz. I'm so sorry to hear about Brianna. Let me show you to my office."

Dre and Donna followed him back down the hallway and into his office. He introduced them to the assistant principal, Richard Wainright, who remained standing after they were seated. Dre made no mention of their earlier meeting. Frankly, he was pissed off that Bonnie and Wainright hadn't told him about the other missing girls on his prior visit. According to what Bonnie told Donna, Ortiz had forbade disclosure of the information. Dre wanted to know why.

"Brianna is one of our brightest students," Ortiz said. "Her disappearance is so tragic."

"Yeah," Dre said awkwardly. "We're hoping you can help us with some information."

"What kind of information?"

"We understand that three other girls from this school have also disappeared."

The principal's easygoing manner faded away. He hurled a look at Wainright. "And where did you hear that?"

"Does it matter?" Dre said.

"Yes, it does?"

"Well, we're not at liberty to say."

The escalating tension seemed to unnerve Wainright. He rubbed his hands together.

"That's fine," Ortiz said. "I think I already know who told you. You need to know that Bonnie Flanagan has a very vivid imagination."

"So there haven't been any missing girls?" Dre pressed.

"I have close to eight hundred students at this school," Ortiz said. "Some officially check out, others never show back up. There's no concrete evidence that any of my students have met with foul play."

"But what about those three girls?" He looked down at the paper Donna had given him. "Leticia Gonzales, Imani Jackson and Jasmine Smith. Did they disappear?"

"I don't think *disappear* is the right word. Are they no longer students here? Yes."

"What happened to them?"

"I don't know the full story and even if I did, I couldn't tell you because that information is confidential."

"Fine," Dre said. "I'll contact their families myself. Just give me their addresses and telephone numbers?"

Ortiz scratched his head. "I'm not able to do that."

"Why not?"

"That information is also confidential. So I can't do that either. Not without the family's permission."

"Okay, then." Dre pulled out one of his business cards and placed it on the desk. "I'd appreciate it if you could contact each of the girls' families, pass along my number and ask them to give me a call."

Ortiz rubbed his forehead. "Uh…we really can't get involved in this. We just don't need this kind of attention focused on our school right now. Have you contacted the police?"

"Yeah," Dre said. "They're not much help, which is why we're here talking to you instead of them."

"I'm really sorry that Ms. Flanagan took it upon herself to get you all riled up. We have no reason to think that there's a connection between any of these girls."

"Do you know that for sure?"

"Well, I just think that..." His voice trailed off. "Ms. Flanagan is a good teacher, but she's also a bit of a busybody. I wouldn't put much stock into anything she told you."

"We won't know for sure that there isn't a connection until somebody looks into it and I'd like to do that."

There was a gentle knock on the door. The receptionist who'd greeted them earlier stuck her head into the room.

"Mr. Ortiz, you better get going. You're going to be late for your meeting."

He glanced at his watch and stood up. "I'm sorry, but I have to cut this short. I have a meeting in the Valley and I'll need to leave right now if I'm going to make it on time."

Donna started to sniffle. "I don't understand why you don't want to help us find my baby."

Ortiz tugged at his tie and picked up a folder from his desk. "We're all praying for Brianna's safe return. I wish there was something more I could do for you, but I can't. I have to run. Mr. Wainright will show you out."

"I'm really sorry," Wainright said apologetically, after the principal left.

"You told me you wanted to help," Dre challenged him. "Can you get us telephone numbers for those girls' families without the principal knowing about it. We won't tell anybody how we got 'em."

Wainright glanced at the open door, then walked over to close it.

He paused for a long moment as if he was weighing the impact of what Dre was asking him to do might have on his career.

"Give me those names," he said, just above a whisper. "I'll contact the families myself and see what I can find out."

CHAPTER 44

Day Three: 10:00 a.m.

Angela stepped onto the porch of Harmony House and happily knocked on the door.

"Wow," Loretha said, welcoming her inside. "I didn't expect you to show up this soon."

Angela smiled. "My calendar was completely open this morning. So I figured why wait."

"Let me give you a quick tour of the house. We've made lots of changes since the last time you were here. We have a GED program for the girls now."

She walked Angela over to a small area of the living room that had been sectioned off with a room divider. "We have two teachers from Crenshaw High who come over twice a week to help the girls prepare for the exam. And this is where we have our group counseling sessions." She pointed to the far side of the living room.

"Most of the girls are at school or work right now," Loretha explained. "We have a new girl who came in last night."

They walked down a long hallway into a large wood-paneled room where a young Latina was watching television.

"This is Carmen," Loretha said.

Carmen looked Angela up and down. "You my new social worker?" the girl asked, loudly smacking on gum.

"No," Loretha said, "she's going to organize a mentoring program for us."

"You look like a social worker," the girl said. "Or a lawyer."

Loretha smiled and backed out of the room. "It might be a good idea to dress down next time. Jeans are fine. Less intimidating for the girls."

Angela looked down at her black suit, embarrassed that she hadn't realized that.

"Let me show you our bedrooms. They're—"

Loretha's smartphone rang.

Angela watched Loretha's face and could tell that she wasn't receiving good news.

"Just hold on," Loretha said into the phone. "I'll be right there."

Loretha started moving toward the door. "Anamaria!"

A pretty Latina bounced into the room.

"I just got a rescue call," Loretha said to the woman. "Keep an eye on Carmen in there."

She turned to Angela. "You wanna come?"

Loretha hit the streets like a race car driver, darting in and out of traffic. If a traffic light took more than a few seconds to change, she pounded the steering wheel and cursed.

Loretha explained that they were going to pick up a girl Loretha had approached on the track in Compton a couple of nights ago.

"It's hard to get the girls to just walk away. They're scared and they have no idea how they're going to make it without their pimp. I tell them I can help, but they don't believe me. So the best I can do is give them my card and tell them to call me if they need help—day or night."

"So she called you?"

"Yeah. Said her *daddy* beat her up cuz a john ran off without paying after getting a blow job."

"How is that her fault?" Angela asked.

"Don't try to apply logic to something that's completely illogical."

"How often do you get calls like this?"

"Lately, about three times a month. I wish it was more often. Every time I get one of these calls, it means I have another shot at saving a child."

"So is this how most of the girls come to Harmony House?"

"About three-fourths of my girls come to me through a social worker or referral from the court system. The rest call me after they've been beaten half to death."

"They must feel relieved to get away from their pimps."

"For a while," Loretha said. "Then they start to miss him and want to go back. You ever break up with a guy who was a complete asshole, but three weeks later, you wanted him back. It's the same thing."

"Yeah, but he wasn't beating me."

"It's like a domestic violence victim who refuses to testify against her husband or boyfriend. It doesn't seem so bad once a few days have passed."

Angela recalled her mixed emotions when her ex had been stalking her. Her family didn't understand her reluctance to get the police involved. Angela hadn't wanted him in jail. She just wanted to be left alone.

"Do many of the girls go back to their pimps?" she asked.

Loretha laughed loudly. "Oh, about ninety percent. It can take three or four cycles, or even more, before they begin to get it. To understand that nothing's going to change. The younger the girl is when she's first exploited, the harder it is for her to break away."

"I thought my job was tough defending the girls in court," Angela replied. "How do you do this day after day after day?"

"I *have* to do it," Loretha said. "I owe it to them. I consider it my penance. And when I have a victory, it's all worth it. My assistant, Anamaria, is my biggest and best success story. Her first abuser was her father. After she told one of her teachers what her father was doing to her every night, she was placed in a foster home. There, her seventeen-year-old foster brother raped her. Repeatedly. She was eight. Her pimp got her at the age of twelve when she ran away from her third foster home. Her pimp was the first person in her life to show her any real affection. If you can call it that."

"Her mother never came back for her?"

"Her father was the sole breadwinner. When he went to jail, her mother never forgave Anamaria for breaking up the family. The entire time she was in foster care, her mother never came to see her. Not once in four years."

This was so depressing that Angela wanted to cry. She'd been so excited about helping out at Harmony House. But now she wondered if she had the emotional stamina to handle it.

Loretha pulled to a stop in front of a laundromat that appeared to be empty. She looked up and down the street.

"Get behind the wheel," she said, dashing out of the car. "And keep the engine running."

Loretha dashed inside and less than a minute later, she walked out cradling a young black girl. She hustled her into the backseat and climbed in alongside her.

"Hit the door locks!" Loretha yelled. "Let's go. We gotta get her out of here before her pimp comes."

Unfamiliar with the car, Angela fumbled to find the door locks. She finally took off into traffic with a lurch and a screech.

Loretha pressed the girl's head into her lap. "You're safe now, Peaches," Loretha said in a soothing voice.

"We should call the police," Angela said.

"I will," Loretha said. "As soon as we get her out of here."

Angela glanced at the sobbing girl in the rear-view mirror. One side of her face was bruised and bloody.

"Don't worry, baby, it's going to be all right," Loretha said, softly stroking the girl's hair. "You're safe now."

CHAPTER 45

Day Three: 10:30 a.m.

Brianna stared at the clothes spread out on the bed. Freda had ordered her to put them on, but Brianna didn't want to touch them, much less wear them. It wasn't just that they were slutty-looking. Based on the smell, they'd recently been worn by somebody else.

The door flew open and Freda charged into the room.

"I told you to get dressed!" she shouted at Brianna. "We gotta go. Do you want me to make a call and have somebody pick up your mother?"

Brianna lowered her eyes and slowly shook her head.

"Okay, then. Get dressed. Now!"

Freda stood there, hands on her hips and waited.

Brianna shimmied out of the shorts they'd given her and picked up the skirt. It was no bigger than a hand towel.

She reached for the top, but Freda stopped her. "Take off your panties. You won't need underwear around here."

The tears began to flow as Brianna eased out of her panties. The top she was supposed to wear looked like a sequined bra. Her breasts weren't big enough to fill the cups.

"Here." Freda shoved some pads at her.

Brianna didn't reach for them because she had no idea what they were.

Freda huffed loudly, then pulled her by the arm and stuffed the pads down her top. Then she took Brianna roughly by the chin and patted her face with foundation, laying it on thick to cover her bruises.

"Ow!" Brianna winced, still sore from Clint's punches.

Freda ignored her pain. She painted her lips with an apple-red lipstick and coated her top lids with fuchsia eyeliner and brushed her lashes with mascara.

Brianna had always wanted to wear makeup, but her mother insisted that she wait until her sixteenth birthday. Now she didn't care if she never did.

"You sure bruise easy," Freda said, stepping back to admire her handiwork. "Now we gotta do something with that wild-ass hair of yours."

She roughly raked a comb through Brianna's hair, then brushed it back and pulled it into a bun on top of her head. "The fellas are gonna love you. You might be able to give Shantel some real competition."

Freda pointed to a pair of high-heeled shoes. "Those are for you. You can fit a seven, can't you?"

Brianna didn't respond. She just robotically stepped into the shoes. She'd wanted to wear high heels too. These were a size too big and way too steep. When she took a few steps, it felt like the ground was moving.

Freda shoved a glass in her face. "Here, drink this."

Brianna could smell the strong scent of alcohol. She felt so weary and defeated that she simply closed her eyes and chugged it down. The hot liquid burned her throat, but she didn't object or cry out.

"We're taking it easy on you since it's your first time. We're only setting you up with blow jobs for now. Don't worry about being perfect. They'll like whatever you do."

* * *

Clint and Brianna pulled up in front of a shabby motel. Brianna felt like she wasn't in her own body and her mind kept wandering off. She wished the alcohol would make her go to sleep. Then she could just wake up when it was over.

Though it was hard for her to think, Brianna had come up with a plan. When she was alone with her client, she would tell him that she was only thirteen and beg him to help her escape. She suddenly felt hopeful.

Clint walked her to a room on the first level. "If you're planning on doing anything stupid, think about your mother. If you mess up, I'm personally going to rape her myself."

And my Uncle Dre will kill you, she thought.

The room looked as raunchy as the one on the video of Shantel.

"Just have a seat," Clint said, backing out of the door. "Your client will be here in a minute."

Brianna sat down on the edge of the bed, facing the door. Whatever it was that Freda had made her drink was finally kicking in. She felt like she could float away. At least she wouldn't have to have sex with the man, just a blow job. She would close her eyes and do what she needed to do to protect her mother. She owed her that after disobeying her. And anyway, she was going to beg the man to help her escape. He probably would once he'd heard how they'd kidnapped her.

I can do this, she told herself.

When the door opened, a short Latino man entered, followed by Clint.

"Treat this dude right," Clint said. "He's a good client." He backed out of the room and closed the door.

"Muy bonita!" the man exclaimed. He reached out to squeeze her breast, but she jerked away.

"They told me this is your first time." His face dripped with lust. "I love virgins! I pay triple para tu."

Brianna gasped.

In order to save her mother, she had prepared herself to give the man a blow job. But Freda had obviously lied to her. She would not give up her virginity to this sicko.

"You have to help me!" Brianna cried out in a hush, fearful that Clint was outside listening. "I'm only thirteen years old. They kidnapped me. Please, can you call my mother and tell her where I am?"

The man laughed. "Yes, senorita. I be glad to do that. Soon as we get done."

The man unzipped his pants and stepped out of them. He wasn't wearing any underwear. Brianna stared at the revolting object that sprang out from a mound of wiry, black hair.

A nasty boy at school had sexted his penis to her. But Brianna had never seen one in real life before.

She started to sob. "Please don't…I can't…Please."

"I won't hurt you, senorita. Open your legs. I'll be bery, bery gentle."

He reached out and ripped off her top. The padding fell to the floor.

Brianna crossed her arms, covering her breasts.

He laughed. "Poquito chi chis! I like!" He took a step closer.

"Wait!" Brianna held up a hand. "I'll—I'll give you a blow job. She dropped to her knees as she'd seen Shantel do in the video."

The man's smile widened. "Okay, okay. Bueno, bueno!"

With all the bravado she could muster, Brianna took him into her hands. He felt warm and slimy and smelled of cigarettes. Thinking only of her mother, she closed her eyes and guided him toward her lips.

The second he shoved himself into her mouth, Brianna gagged and reflexively clinched her teeth. She froze, unable to move.

The man screamed so loud, the furniture started to rattle. It took several seconds before Clint burst into the room.

"What's goin' on in here?" he yelled.

He tried to pry Brianna's mouth loose while the man shouted in Spanish.

Brianna heard all the yelling, but couldn't react. She was quivering and sweating, stuck in a trance-like state.

The last thing she remembered was Clint's fist coming straight for her face.

CHAPTER 46

Day Three: 10:50 a.m.

Dre and the seven men crowded into the living room of his apartment off Slauson and LaBrea had spent the last two hours crafting a plan to get Brianna back.

After the trip to Brianna's school, Dre had called Clint and agreed to pay the twenty-five grand. Actually, he had no problem doing that if it guaranteed Brianna's safe return. He could exact his revenge later. But Dre wasn't stupid enough to take Clint or The Shepherd at their word. Men who snatched little girls off the street and forced them into prostitution, couldn't be trusted. Therefore, Dre had to do things his way.

"I say let's just walk into the club with guns blazing," Apache suggested. "That'll send a message quick."

Dre massaged his forehead. "Whatever we do, we need to be smart about it. This dude Clint is weak. If we get him alone, he'll break."

"Most definitely," Mossy agreed.

Gus, Dre's former cellmate, asked a question. "So what you wanna do? Snatch the guy and make him talk?"

"Yeah," Dre said. "That's the plan."

Terrell and Bobby, guys from Dre's old neighborhood, nodded their agreement.

"That'll definitely get their attention," Bobby said.

D'wan, a buddy of Mossy's, held up his hand. "Wouldn't it be easier to follow the dude home and grab him there?"

"Probably," Dre said. "But I'm tryin' to send a message. I want to do this on The Shepherd's turf."

"Hold on a minute, everybody," Dre's brother Anthony was leaning against the wall, taking it all in. "We can't do anything illegal."

Everybody stared at him in disbelief. Out of respect for Dre, they held their tongues and waited for him to respond.

"What we're about to do definitely ain't legal," Dre said to his brother. "I told you before you came over here, I got this. You've always been squeaky clean. If you wanna stay that way, you should leave now so if this blows back on us, you won't be a part of it."

Anthony scratched his forehead. "I want to help get Brianna back too, but…"

Dre walked over to his brother and threw an arm around his shoulders. "I know that. But you don't need to be here. Just go home. I'll call you as soon as we get Bree back."

Anthony shrugged. "Well, if y'all don't really need me…"

Apache mumbled something indecipherable as Dre escorted his brother to the door.

"Don't worry about it. We'll handle it."

They could all see that Anthony was eager to leave. His face relaxed the second Dre opened the door, freeing him.

"Man, Anthony is weak!" Apache said as soon as he was gone. "He was always the first one to run from a fight even when we were kids."

Dre stopped Apache with a hard look.

"Don't say another word. He's still my brother. I'm not blamin' him for wanting to stay on the up-and-up. Anybody else here got a problem with what we're planning to do?"

Dre took his time sweeping his eyes around the room, making eye contact with the remaining six men. The looks he got back were sure and strong.

"Terrell and Bobby, I want you to head over there a little later and case the joint. If Mossy or I try to do it, they'll recognize us. In the back near the men's room, there's an emergency exit door. When the time is right, I want you to grab Clint and shove him out into the alley. Maybe you can catch him coming out of the men's room."

"Won't the alarm go off when that door opens?" Bobby asked.

"It didn't when they threw us out of it," Mossy said. "Messed up a perfectly good pair of pants."

"I'll be driving Mossy's van, waiting for you in the alley with the engine running," Dre said. "What I don't know is whether one of the bouncers will be guarding that door. I doubt it. But that's what I need you to tell us. Text me when you find out."

"We got you," Terrell said.

"Okay, then. Gus and D'wan, you're going to drop in much later. I want everything to go down around one-thirty in the morning. The club will still be pretty crowded then. I need you to start a fight. While the bouncers focus all their attention on breaking up the fight, Terrell and Bobby can grab Clint."

"Got it," D'wan said.

Dre looked at his watch.

"Mossy, I need you to check out the abandoned warehouse where we're taking him. It's in Gardena on Maple off Alondra. A dealer I know used to operate out of there. Most of the neighboring buildings are empty too. But I want you to make sure. I need you to be there to open the doors for us. Also, check for any surveillance cameras in the area."

"Sounds like you've given a lot of thought to this," Terrell said.

"I have," Dre replied.

"What about me?" Apache asked.

"You'll be in Mossy's van with me."

"Aw man! I wanna see some action."

"You'll see plenty of action. I'm gonna let you make him talk."

That put a big smile on Apache's face. He whipped something out of his back pocket and waved it in the air. "This little gadget right here," he said, holding up a stun gun, "can make a mute man speak."

Mossy frowned and scratched the back of his neck. If he had his way, Apache wouldn't even be in the room.

"I don't want to rain on this parade," Gus said, "but we gotta consider the fact that grabbing this dude could put your niece in even more danger."

Dre had already considered that. He prayed that Loretha was right. That the rumors of The Shepherd ordering others to kill for him were just that.

"I have to take that risk," Dre said. "After we do something as brazen as walking into his club and snatching his boy, he's gonna understand that we mean business."

"Are you one hundred percent sure that he really has your niece?" Gus asked.

"He's supposed to be sending me a picture. He thinks he's about to get twenty-five grand, so I'm sure he will."

"So instead of the money, you're gonna try to trade Clint for Brianna?"

Dre shook his head.

"Naw. From what I hear, this dude doesn't care about anybody but himself. He'd sacrifice Clint the same way he would one of the girls he's pimpin'. I want Clint for two reasons. One, I think we can get his weak ass to tell us where Brianna is. And two, if The Shepherd thinks we've gotten Clint to spill the beans about his operation, that gives us a whole lot more leverage than twenty-five grand."

CHAPTER 47

Day Three: 11:15 a.m.

Clint yelled a string of expletives as he dragged Brianna out of the motel room and hurled her into the backseat of his Escalade.

"You stupid little bitch!" He climbed into the driver's seat and glanced back over his shoulder. "You need to get with the program!"

Brianna cowered on the floor, mentally blocking out his tirade.

She tried to remember what had happened before Clint punched her in the face. She did remember having her teeth clamped tightly around the man's penis. She must have briefly passed out. When she woke up, she saw the man hopping around the room as if his feet were on fire.

Brianna knew that she would get another beating when they got back to the house. She was scared but also a little numb. Maybe Freda would give her another drink. That made everything a little easier to handle.

The car finally came to a stop inside a dark garage. Brianna had no idea where the house was located. Clint had made her cover her head with a black pillowcase during both legs of the trip. A door in the garage led directly into the kitchen. Because she'd been forced to lie on the floor in the backseat, it was impossible to signal anyone for help.

Clint hopped out and opened the back door of the SUV. Snatching her by the arms, he started lugging her toward the back door of the house. One of her four-inch pumps flew off and hit Clint in the groin.

He bent over and winced.

Still a little high, Brianna giggled.

"I bet you won't be laughin' when I get your ass inside!" Clint yelled.

Freda met them at the door. "How'd she do?"

"This little girl is nuts. I don't know why Shep even wants to fool with her. She nearly bit that dude's dick off."

Clint powered past Freda, dragging Brianna behind him.

"What are you gonna do?" Freda asked, following after them.

"I'ma kick her ass until she gets the message."

"Don't mess up her face again," Freda warned.

Clint yanked her down the hallway and into one of the bedrooms, with Freda following after them. When he hurled her onto the bed, Brianna's shoulder hit the wall. She yelped like a wounded puppy. Clint left the room and returned seconds later with an extension cord.

The prospect of another beating snapped Brianna out of her drunken haze. She hopped off the bed and cowered in a corner of the room.

Freda jumped in front of Clint, shielding Brianna.

"Hold up, Clint. You're too upset. You need to calm down. You can do this later."

"No, I need to do this now. Get out of my way."

"Shep just called," Freda said. "He needs you to call him back right away."

"He can wait."

Freda didn't move. "No, he can't."

Clint was breathing hard, his chest heaving up and down. Beads of sweat trickled down the side of his face.

The standoff lasted several seconds, then suddenly, as if he was out of energy, Clint stomped off.

Freda turned to Brianna, who was balled up in the fetal position, massaging her shoulder, too shell-shocked to cry.

"You owe me, little girl," she said, wagging her finger at Brianna. "I only stopped him because I knew he was mad enough to kill you."

CHAPTER 48

Day Three: 11:30 a.m.

Angela sat in Harmony House's Trust room on the twin bed opposite a sleeping Peaches.

Sitting there, Angela acknowledged for the first time that she'd built a professional wall between herself and her juvenile clients. She represented girls like Peaches every day. She was no different from Shenae or Jolita or any of her other clients. Angela had always been willing to go to the mat for them on the legal front, but when she walked out of the courtroom, she filed them away with the rest of her cases, refusing to let their tragic lives intersect with hers.

She had an excellent excuse. Becoming personally involved with a client would be unprofessional. Any good lawyer would agree. That didn't mean, however, that she couldn't do something to help those girls who weren't her clients.

Over hot chocolate and donuts, Peaches had shared her story. She began in an emotionless, matter-of-fact fashion, as if there had been no pain. But soon, cracks in her stony demeanor unveiled a battle-weary little girl. The child's story burned a hole through Angela's heart.

Peaches had been living the life of a normal little girl in nearby Inglewood when her father was killed by a drunk driver two days before Thanksgiving the year she turned eleven. Her mother sank into a dark depression and three months later, took her own life. Peaches and her ten-year-old brother were passed around from one relative to another, each one resenting the burden they posed on already-tight resources.

Somehow, Peaches weathered these difficulties and did well in school. While walking home alone one day—she had never managed to make many friends—four boys from the neighborhood jumped her in an alley, pulling a train on her. The traumatized child ran home to an aunt who blamed her for *being fast*. Her grades started to plummet and she became combative toward her aunt, who eventually put her in foster care. That was where she met her twenty-four-year-old *boyfriend*, Gerald. A pimp with a long history of targeting emotionally scarred young girls, he promised to marry Peaches and she readily ran away with him. Within two months, he'd put her on the street, forcing her into submission with verbal and physical threats, tempered by occasional acts of kindness.

"He used to take me to the Red Lobster," Peaches had proudly announced, as if she was referring to a five-star restaurant.

Gazing across the room at this sleeping child, Angela declared to herself that this one little girl would be hers to save. She closed her eyes and prayed for Peaches. Then prayed yet again that Dre found Brianna before she could be sucked into this sick world.

Peaches finally began to stir. She sat up against the headboard and rubbed her eyes. She winced in pain at her own touch, having forgotten about her bruised face.

"Why you starin' at me like that?" Her words came out garbled due to her busted lip.

"I'm sorry," Angela said, turning away. "I didn't mean to stare. Do you want something to eat?"

She puckered her lips. "Look, I don't need you crowding me. I can take care of myself."

Angela had already been prepped by Loretha as well as by her own experience with sexually trafficked girls. In the beginning, they carried mountain-sized chips on their shoulders. Their way of protecting themselves from further hurt and disappointment. It would take time to tear down her wall of distrust.

"Okay then." Angela got up and started toward the door. "Just let me know if you get hungry."

She had stepped into the hallway and was about to close the door when she heard Peaches' distorted voice.

"So what they got to eat?"

Angela held her smile inside and reentered the room. "Let's go downstairs and find out."

In the brightly colored, lime-green kitchen, Angela found chips and tuna salad and made a sandwich for both of them. The other girls were in a group session at the moment. Peaches would join them tomorrow, after an orientation with Anamaria.

They sat on stools at an island in the middle of the kitchen. Five minutes passed without a word between them.

"I don't need you to feel sorry for me," Peaches said between chews.

"Who said I'm feeling sorry for you? Just because I made you a sandwich doesn't mean I feel sorry for you."

"Well, I just wanted you to know. Don't nobody force me to do what I do. I make my own decisions."

"Okay."

They continued to eat in silence. There was so much Angela wanted to say and do for this child. But she knew too much enthusiasm too fast would be met with rejection.

"You lucky," Peaches said after a while, her eyes on Angela's hair. "You got good hair."

Angela laughed. "Yep, I do have good hair. And so do you."

Peaches' face scrunched up like a balled-up piece of paper. "No, I don't. My hair is way too nappy." The girl's dark brown hair was a mass of thick, shapeless strands pulled back behind her ears.

"Your hair's not nappy," Angela said. "It's actually curly."

"You trippin'."

Angela reached across the table and felt the texture of Peaches' hair. "I bet I could show you how to make your hair look like mine."

"I bet you can't."

Angela stuck out her hand. "Okay, then, it's a bet."

Peaches clutched Angela's hand. "So what we bettin'?"

Angela thought for a moment. "If you win, I'll take you to see a movie, provided it's okay with Loretha. If I win, then I'll take you to see a movie."

That made Peaches crack up. "Okay. That's a good bet."

Angela took the last bite of her sandwich and stood up.

"You leavin'?" Peaches asked, almost wistful.

"Yep." Angela tossed her paper plate into the trash can near the side door. "Have to go to a meeting. I'll be back this afternoon."

"So when you gonna do my hair?"

Angela silently cheered. She was making a connection.

She pulled a small plastic container from her purse. "Here's the gel I use. I'll have Loretha show you a YouTube video. It'll teach you how to use it. I want you to give it a try first."

Peaches opened the container and took a whiff. "This smells good. But I'm tellin' you, my hair is really, really nappy. My Aunt Gina used to call me beady bead."

"Just give it a try. I think you're going to be surprised."

"Don't forget about our bet."

"I won't."

Angela walked around the table and gave Peaches a hug. She stiffened, as if she was uncomfortable with being touched. After a second or so, Peaches politely squirmed free.

Angela placed the strap of her purse over her shoulder. "Okay, see you later."

"You comin' back today, right?"

This time, Angela didn't suppress her smile. "Right."

CHAPTER 49

Day Three: 12:10 p.m.

"I really think you should give this some more thought," Wainright pleaded. "This isn't going to go down well."

What Ortiz was directing him to do was nothing short of retaliation and he wanted no part of it. Unfortunately, it was his job to carry out all the unpleasant tasks the principal was too much of a coward to do himself.

"I didn't ask for your opinion," Ortiz ranted. "Just do it. Bonnie Flanagan disobeyed a direct order and she needs to be taught a lesson."

Wainright left the principal's office, shoulders slumped. He had his instructions, and if nothing else, he was a soldier who knew how to follow orders. He checked the teachers' schedules to confirm the time of Bonnie Flanagan's free period.

Bonnie was cleaning the whiteboard when he entered her classroom. He closed the door behind him.

"How's it going?" Wainright asked.

"Hey, Rich."

She sounded as if she was glad to see him. That would soon change.

"I have some good news and some bad news," he began.

Ortiz had come up with a legitimate educational reason for his decision, but Wainright knew Bonnie wouldn't buy it.

Bonnie stepped over to her desk. "I'll take the good news first."

"Your Honors students performed exceptionally well on the last round of state testing. Your students ranked the highest in the school and the district. Your teaching strategies have produced some phenomenal results. Ortiz is very impressed with what you've achieved."

"Thanks," Bonnie said, sounding wary about the other half of his message. "So what's the bad news?"

"We'd like to try out your teaching strategies on some of our lower-performing students. So Mr. Ortiz has decided to do some mid-year juggling of classes. Ms. Williams started maternity leave last week, so you're being reassigned to teach her classes. Effective tomorrow."

"Tomorrow! You have to be kidding!" Bonnie locked her arms across her chest. "Those are the most unruly students in the school. And what happens to my students? I have three Honors classes."

"A sub will take over your classes using the teaching strategies you've developed."

"Not on your life! How can you—" She froze as if a light bulb had just clicked on in her head. "This is retaliation," she said, slowly. "Mr. Ortiz found out that I spoke to Brianna Walker's mother. That's why he's doing this."

Ortiz had, of course, instructed Wainright not to mention the visit he'd had from Brianna's mother and uncle. It was Ortiz's position that this was an administrative decision with no connection at all to that visit. As weak as it was, that was the principal's story and Wainright was sticking to it.

"It has absolutely nothing to do with that."

"So he knows?"

Wainright didn't answer.

Bonnie picked up a cloth and started polishing the whiteboard with enough force to unhinge it. "Did Brianna's mother call him?" She looked at him over her shoulder.

"Actually, she came to the school along with Brianna's uncle and met with both of us."

"So what did Ortiz do? Tell them I was some kind of lunatic?"

"No. But he made it clear that we didn't think there was a connection between Brianna's disappearance and those other students."

"He doesn't know that. Not for sure. And neither do you."

"Well, actually we do."

"What are you talking about?"

"Please keep this to yourself," Wainright said. "I made some calls to the other girls' families this morning. Ortiz instructed me not to disclose what I found out to anyone else because of the girls' privacy rights."

Bonnie darted over to him. "What did they tell you?"

Wainright went on to explain that Leticia Gonzales had indeed disappeared, but at the hands of her mother. Leticia's parents were locked in a contentious divorce and her mother feared losing custody. Her family suspected that Leticia and her mother were in hiding some-where in Mexico.

Imani Jackson had run away from home. She returned months later and was sent to Birmingham to live with her grandmother. Jasmine Smith had run away from an abusive family situation. Months later, she was found living with an older boyfriend and put into foster care.

Bonnie slumped down on her desk. The information left her stunned.

"Oh my goodness." She pressed a palm to her cheek. "I have Brianna's mother thinking her daughter's been snatched by some kid-napping ring."

"That wouldn't be the case if you had followed Ortiz's directions. But don't worry about it. Ortiz doesn't know it, but I called Brianna's mother and shared what I found out."

Bonnie accepted the scolding because she deserved it. "Well, I'm glad I was wrong."

Wainright smiled. "Me too."

Bonnie put her hands on her hips and stood up. "Regardless, that does not give Ortiz the right to retaliate against me."

"Look, Bonnie—"

"I'm not giving up my Honors classes," she said firmly. "If we need to take this to the teacher's union, I will."

"C'mon, Bonnie. There's no need to go there."

"If you expect me to give up my cream-of-the-crop students for Ms. Williams' little demons, there most definitely is."

CHAPTER 50

Day Three: 12:30 p.m.

Mossy, Apache, Gus and D'wan were now sitting around the kitchen table, as Dre finished a telephone call.

"That was Terrell," Dre said hanging up. "He and Bobby have been scoping things out. They only have two bouncers during the day, instead of the four they have at night. The club is packed right now with the lunch crowd. Terrell said both of the bouncers are walking around socializing with the girls. One of them was getting a lap dance."

"Sounds like a pretty lax operation," Mossy said. "I hope it's like that tonight too."

"Me too," Dre said.

"And if it don't go down like it's supposed to," Apache said, "we should wait until Clint is ready to leave and shoot him in the foot."

Mossy gave Dre a look that mirrored what he'd been saying all along. *Your knucklehead cousin is going to get us all killed.*

"It ain't goin' down like that," Dre groaned. "We need to use our heads. This is a chess game. And we've got the queen."

"Queen?" Apache said. "I'd rather have the king."

Mossy chuckled. "See what I'm talkin' 'bout?"

Apache looked from Mossy to Dre. "What?"

"Never mind." Dre grabbed a pad and scanned the notes he'd written down earlier.

"I just can't wait until we get the dude," Apache said, waving his stun gun in the air. "After I give him a jolt of the right motivation, he'll be chirping like a sparrow."

"Have they sent you that picture yet?" Gus asked.

"Naw," Dre said.

"Maybe they don't really have her."

That thought pained him. If they didn't have Brianna, Dre wouldn't know where to begin searching for her.

Dre cracked his knuckles. "He's supposed to send me a picture before we agree to a location to do the exchange. I'm not going to make a move until I see it."

"I don't mean to be negative or nothing," Gus said, "but if this don't work, you gonna pay the money?"

Dre felt confident that his plan would not fail. "If that's the only way to get her back, hell yeah."

"You actually got that kind of cash sitting around, cuz?" Apache asked.

"Yep." Dre pointed at a duffle bag on the floor near the door.

Apache walked over to the bag, unzipped it and peered inside.

"Wowza! I ain't never seen this much cash before. I can't believe you gave up slingin' drugs behind some broad."

"Sit your ass down," Dre said. "You're making me nervous."

"These are some cold dudes," D'wan said. "I don't understand how they think they can just snatch somebody's kid off the street and turn her out."

Dre shook his head. "Apparently, they're doing a lot of it and nobody's stoppin' 'em. Until now."

A quick buzz from Dre's smartphone signaled a new text message. It was from an unknown sender. Dre snatched it from the table. "This might be it."

The guys crowded around him as Dre braced himself for what he was about to see. He paused a few seconds before clicking on the link.

Once he did, instead of a photograph, a video began to play.

From the very first frame, Dre felt bile rising in his throat. As his fingers gripped the edge of the table, he fought the urge to hurl the device across the room. Seconds later, he shot up from his seat, dashing for the trash can. He didn't make it in time and vomited on the floor.

Mossy held up a hand and took a step back. "Goddamn!"

Each man who looked at the video uttered his own expression of shock.

The short portion of the video Dre watched showed Brianna being repeatedly punched. She was naked, coiled up in the fetal position, with bruises all over her body, crying.

"These sick freaks are goin' to hell," Apache said. "I'ma personally show 'em the way."

CHAPTER 51

Day Three: 1:00 p.m.

Loretha walked into the empty conference room carrying a large duffle bag containing a stack of handouts. A big part of Loretha's work involved helping those involved in administering social services understand the tragedy of sexually exploited children.

She gave quarterly presentations to social workers, teachers and school staff, counselors and police officers. They were on the front lines and had the ability to reach a child before she became the prey of a pimp.

Loretha placed pamphlets about Harmony House in front of each seat around the U-shaped conference table. The first two attendees walked into the room and greeted her.

"Good morning," Loretha said. "Thanks for coming."

"I just wish you didn't have to come talk to us about this," one woman said. "Instead of getting better, the problem seems to be getting worse."

That was so true. The number of children entering the sex trade was climbing at an alarming rate. Rescuing them was often a futile effort because there weren't enough foster homes, group homes or juvenile facilities to house them once they'd escape from their pimps.

In another ten minutes, the conference room was full.

"Thanks for coming, everybody," Loretha began. "You should feel free to call me whenever you have an emergency placement. And if I have an empty bed, it's yours."

"One of the things I wanted to alert you about is a new method pimps are using to recruit girls. They're using other minors to entice new girls into the sex industry."

"They've always done that," one woman said.

Loretha smiled. "Not like they're doing it now. We've come across several cases where the pimp puts a girl on the track specifically so that she can get arrested and sent to a group home. Once she's there, it's her job to convince the most vulnerable girls to run away with her. The pimp pays the girl for every recruit she attracts and it places her at a higher level with the pimp. She's also rewarded by no longer having to walk the track."

"Good Lord!" said one of the women.

"It's turning out to be a pretty effective recruiting tool."

The room went silent and Loretha didn't speak for a few moments, giving them time to swallow this information.

"We're also seeing the creation of a trafficking circuit between L.A. and Oakland. One gang will kidnap a girl in L.A. and trade her for a girl snatched by a gang in Oakland. They're even shipping girls down South to cities like Atlanta and Birmingham. Taking a girl out of state more effectively cuts her off from everyone she knows."

"Are you saying different gangs are actually working together?" one woman asked.

"That's exactly what I'm saying."

"And don't make the mistake of thinking that this can't happen in your neighborhood. These guys are getting bolder and bolder. They're snatching girls wherever they can find them, not just black and brown girls in the inner city. They're even infiltrating schools in middle and upper-middle class neighborhoods."

When the session ended sixty minutes later, Loretha hurriedly packed her things and rushed to her car. After driving about twenty minutes, Loretha parked near a freeway overpass, grabbed two plastic grocery bags from the front seat and exited the car. The bags held sandwiches, packaged food items, vitamins, a few toiletries and clothes. She walked several feet, then climbed a short incline underneath the freeway.

She passed two homeless men nodding off. One of the men's eyes shot open and he growled at her.

"Leave me the hell alone!"

Loretha knew that she had to appear fearless. If they sensed that she was afraid, they'd be on her. But she didn't have to pretend. She didn't know why but she wasn't afraid.

Loretha culled through the thick foliage until she spotted a familiar grocery cart tied with red ribbons and brimming with junk.

Good. Rena was still here. She was never too far from her cart.

"Rena," Loretha called out softly. "Are you here?"

Loretha heard a gentle rustling of the foliage and Rena stuck her head out of a large cardboard box. The woman wore a tattered hoodie that had originally been gray, but was now sooty black. Her face was ashen and her hair matted and bald in patches. The whites of her eyes were yellow.

"I brought you some stuff," Loretha said, extending the bags in front of her with both hands.

Rena crawled forward on her hands and knees. She took the bag without standing up, then backed into her hiding place.

"You doing okay?" Loretha asked.

Rena nodded in quick successive movements as if she could not control her head.

Loretha had been delivering regular care packages to Rena for several months. She'd never once spoken.

"Okay, good. If you ever wanna come inside, I've got a room for you," Loretha said. "My card with my number and address is inside the bag."

She'd been repeating that offer for months with no response whatsoever from Rena. Loretha knew she would never take her up on it. She wasn't even sure the woman understood her. Rena, who'd been beautiful and sexy and vibrant, had literally lost her mind after that single night with Demonic. What else could explain her desire to live on the street, pushing a grocery cart around for most of the day?

Too many times to count, Loretha had asked God to bring her back, but she no longer had any faith in that prayer.

Rena tore into the large bag of barbecue potato chips. Loretha knew from the old days that she loved them.

"I have to go, now," Loretha said, swatting at a spider crawling up her arm. "I want you to call me if you need me."

No response from Rena.

As Loretha backed down the hill, trying not to slide down to the street, she thought she heard something that sounded like words. Loretha turned back to Rena.

"Did you say something?" Loretha asked.

"Thank you," Rena said hoarsely, flashing a toothless smile.

Joy filled Loretha up from the inside out. Maybe the Rena she'd known was still in there somewhere. She had to restrain herself from running over to hug the woman. That would only frighten her.

"You're welcome," Loretha said, her smile so wide it hurt. "You're so very welcome."

CHAPTER 52

Day Three: 3:30 p.m.

Angela stepped into the foyer of Harmony House and greeted Loretha with a hug.

"Is Peaches ready?"

Angela was pumped about her new role as Peaches' mentor. She had a special evening planned for the girl.

"She'll be down in a minute." Loretha had an uncertain look on her face. "We need to talk first."

Angela followed Loretha into her office where they sat down on a couch across from Loretha's desk. "Is something wrong?"

"First, I want you to know that you're about the *only* person I'd let one of my girls go on an outing with this soon. And second, I need to make sure you know what you're getting yourself into."

Angela rolled her eyes. "I deal with these girls every day."

"You deal with them as their lawyer, not as part of their lives. My girls are very fragile. Everybody in Peaches' life who was supposed to protect her, let her down. Her parents left her when they died, her aunt verbally and emotionally abused her, her pimp beat her up. If you're going to be a part of her life, you need to be there for the long haul. Through the good and the bad. And there's going to be some bad. A lot of it."

"I understand that. I'm committed. For the long haul."

Loretha's eyebrows arched with skepticism. "There're going to be times when Peaches doesn't act like a happy inquisitive child. She's going to be a foul-mouthed half-woman. The connection to her pimp hasn't been broken yet. She may—no, she probably will—go back to him at some point. And we have to be there for her when she returns to him a second time or a third time or more."

"I understand," Angela said. "But Peaches isn't going back."

Loretha gave her a cynical look.

"I'm going to be the one who helps this girl see that life can be different and that she has other options," Angela promised.

"I'm going to hold you to that. The real reason I'm allowing this is to take her mind off the hearing tomorrow. It's a scary thing to have to testify against your pimp. You'll be there, right?"

"Wouldn't miss it."

Peaches bounded down the stairs in jeans and a T-shirt. Her bruises were covered with makeup. She was proudly sporting her new natural curls.

"How you like me now!" She did a model's twirl. "My hair is crack-alackin' like a mug!"

Loretha turned to Angela and laughed. "I assume crackalackin' is a good thing, but maybe you should translate for me."

"Y'all is so lame," Peaches said. "I had no idea I could get my hair curly like this. I'ma be looking diva-licious in court tomorrow."

Loretha and Angela exchanged glances. They both knew Peaches wouldn't be this excited when she actually had to confront her pimp.

"We're going to see the new *Shrek* movie," Peaches beamed. "At the Magic Johnson Theater."

During the drive to the Crenshaw Plaza, nothing Angela did could make Peaches open up. So she decided not to push it. Loretha had warned her that it would take some time to build a true bond with the girl. Once the movie started, Peaches laughed loudly while munching on popcorn and Milk Duds. Later, at TGI Friday's she finally began to talk in more than one-word sentences, but turned somber again once they'd finished dessert.

"What's the matter?" Angela asked.

She shrugged. "When I do regular stuff like this, that's when I really miss my mama and daddy."

"That's completely normal. My grandmother died a few years ago and I miss her too."

"I wonder how my little brother's doing?"

"When's the last time you saw him?"

Peaches wiped sweat from her water glass with her index finger. "When I ran away with Gerald."

"You haven't talked to him during all this time?"

"Nope. Gerald wouldn't let me." Peaches paused. "Can you take me to see him? He stays with my Aunt Gina now. They still live in our old house by the cemetery in Inglewood. It's not that far from here."

Angela could only imagine the happy memories the house held for her. Maybe a return visit would be a good thing.

"I'll need to clear that with Loretha first."

"Okay. Can you call her?"

Angela took out her smartphone and tried to reach Loretha, but she didn't pick up.

"We don't have to stay long," Peaches begged. "I just want to say hi to my little brother. We haven't seen each other in three years."

Angela reasoned that it couldn't be a bad thing for Peaches to connect with the one person in the world she truly cared about.

"Okay," Angela finally said. "But we're not going to stay long."

Following Peaches' directions, Angela drove the short distance to Regent Circle in Inglewood. She was surprised by the large, impressive homes on the quiet street lined with eucalyptus trees. Angela had expected to find a much different neighborhood, economically speaking. These homes had to be in the half-million-dollar range.

"It looks just the same as I remember," Peaches gushed. "My daddy used to have us out here sweeping the driveway and cutting the grass every Saturday. I helped my daddy plant those bushes over there."

Peaches still hadn't made a move to get out of the car.

"If you've changed your mind, that's fine," Angela said gently.

"No, I still wanna go. I just wanted to look at the house."

Peaches finally pushed the car door open and they walked together toward the front door. She timidly pressed the doorbell.

"Who is it?" a woman's melodic voice called out.

Peaches wrung her hands. "It's Peaches." Her voice was much smaller now.

Seconds later, the door opened and a woman dressed in a gray pantsuit peered at them through a screen door. She was tall and thick with stiff-looking hair that was obviously a weave. Angela could see the family resemblance. The wide cheekbones, the long neck, the full lips.

"Peaches? Is that really you?" The woman leaned out of the door and pulled Peaches into a bear hug. "Girl, let me look at you! You're about as tall as I am! You look just like your mama!"

Angela introduced herself to Aunt Gina and explained that they had just dropped by to say hello.

"So you're wearin' your hair natural now," Aunt Gina said, reaching out to touch it.

Peaches looked down at her hands.

"It looks nice on her, doesn't it?" Angela said.

"I'm not into all that nappy hair stuff," Aunt Gina said, turning up her nose. Her hair looked as if she'd snatched it off a store mannequin. "As far as I'm concerned, nappy hair needs a perm or a straightening comb."

Angela glanced over at Peaches. The happy kid she'd bonded with all afternoon was about to retreat into her shell.

"Is Damon here?" Peaches asked, never directly looking at her aunt.

"Yep. His lazy butt is in the backyard cutting the grass." The woman walked into the kitchen and opened a back door. "Damon, you got some company," she yelled.

Aunt Gina waited a beat and was about to call out again, when a lanky teenager lumbered into the kitchen. When his eyes landed on Peaches, they lit up.

"Hey, sis!" he said, running over to embrace her.

Peaches took a step back to get a better look at him.

"How did you get taller than me?" Peaches playfully punched him in the shoulder, then hugged him again.

Damon laughed.

"That boy is only fourteen years old and he's already eating me out of house and home." Aunt Gina smiled and tucked a swatch of her weave behind her right ear. "I hope you're not trying to move back in here. We barely have enough room as it is. I'm working at L.A. Unified now. But my check can only go so far."

Peaches looked down at the floor. "I ain't trying to come back."

"So where you stayin'?" Damon asked. "We have to hang out sometime." His voice had that too-deep baritone of a teenage boy on his way to becoming a man.

"Uh...I live with a family in L.A."

"Where in L.A.?" Aunt Gina asked.

"Near Crenshaw and Washington," Angela said.

"Crenshaw and Washington? Is it safe over there?"

Probably safer than being here with you," Angela wanted to say.

"Damon, you need to finish getting that backyard done. Then I want you to sweep out the garage, mop the kitchen floor and clean the bathroom. And ladies, I hate to be rude, but I was on my way to a meeting at the church."

Damon was hesitant to leave. "Will you call me?"

"I will," Peaches promised. She hugged him again. "What's your phone number?"

"I'll give it to you," Aunt Gina said before Damon could respond. "You need to get back to your chores."

Damon reluctantly backed out of the room.

Angela threw her arm around Peaches' shoulders. This time, Peaches didn't flinch or pull away. "I guess we'll be going then," Angela said.

Aunt Gina darted across the room and opened the door. "Thanks for dropping by."

They stepped across the threshold onto the porch and Aunt Gina followed them outside

Peaches finally made eye contact with her aunt for more than a split second. "Uh...can you give me Damon's number?"

Aunt Gina scratched the back of her weave. "I don't really know how to say this, but I don't think it's a good idea for you to be in contact with Damon."

Heat stung Angela's cheeks. "Why not?"

"I know what you been doing," Aunt Gina said, lowering her voice to a sinister level. "One of my church members said she saw you out on Long Beach Boulevard in Compton prostituting yourself. I was so embarrassed I didn't know what to do. Is it true?"

Peaches turned away, her eyes saturated with shame.

"No, it's not," Angela said, before Peaches could respond.

Angela wanted to yell what Loretha had told them over breakfast at Denny's. *Peaches is not a prostitute. She's a sexually exploited child.* But she knew this callous woman wouldn't get it.

"Let's go." Angela protectively wrapped her arm around Peaches as Aunt Gina trailed after them down the driveway.

"Sister Miller told me she saw it with her own eyes. My brother would turn over in his grave if he knew his only daughter was out there turning tricks."

Angela wanted to cover Peaches' ears. She also wanted to punch Aunt Gina in the mouth.

"Go to the car," Angela told Peaches in a stern voice.

Peaches obediently ran off.

Angela turned back to Aunt Gina. "Maybe Peaches wouldn't be in the situation she's in if she'd gotten some support from you rather than criticism after she was gang raped."

Aunt Gina pressed her hand flat against her chest. "Don't you dare try to blame that girl's bad choices on me! Peaches was always fast. I pray for that child every day."

"You need to pray for your damn self!"

Aunt Gina recoiled, her back hunching like a snake ready to strike. "How dare you talk to me like that. You don't even—"

"Hypocrites like you make me sick!"

Angela stalked down the driveway.

"You okay?" she asked, back in the car with Peaches.

The girl responded with a curt nod.

As Angela pulled away from the curb, she felt like kicking herself. They'd had a great day. Peaches had started opening up to her. No telling what kind of damage this visit had done.

"What kinda music you like?" Peaches asked five minutes later. She was smiling again, having buried her hurt, covering it up with a thick pretend shield.

"R&B and gospel. What about you?"

"I *like* everything, but I *love* me some Rihanna." She gave the radio knob a spin, stopping when she came to a Kanye West song.

It didn't seem right to just ignore her aunt's cruelness.

"Peaches, your aunt was wrong to—"

"It don't matter," Peaches said cutting her off. "Like Gerald told me, I don't need no family anyway."

CHAPTER 53

Day Three: 9:30 p.m.

Brianna lay in bed determined to plot her way out of this bad dream. Maybe she should fake another asthma attack. One so bad they had to rush her to the hospital. But she didn't trust these evil people. If they thought she was really sick, they would probably just let her die.

She wondered when Kaylee was coming back. She had only talked to her once since coming to the new house. Poor Kaylee was no doubt doing everything they told her to do. Brianna could tell that Kaylee wasn't strong like she was. Probably because she wasn't raised in the church.

Brianna refused to stop believing that her Uncle Dre was coming to get her. She'd once overheard her mother and grandmother talking about her uncle being in prison. He would probably get some of his prison friends to help him rescue her. When they busted into the house, she wanted them to shoot both Clint and Freda right in the heart. She didn't care if thinking like that wasn't being a good Christian. Like her grandmamma always said, some people just got the devil in 'em.

There was a hard knock on the door, then it flung open. "You hungry, girl?"

Shantel stepped into the room. As far as Brianna was concerned, she was just a mini version of Freda. Her Uncle Dre should shoot her too. She flashed back to Shantel having sex with that nasty man and wanted to throw up. She really wanted to tell Shantel to get the hell away from her, but she was so hungry. Maybe if she ate some food, she could think better.

"Yeah," Brianna said, sitting up.

"Then c'mon. This ain't no restaurant. Ain't nobody gonna serve you."

Brianna stood up. She'd forgotten that she was still wearing the short skirt they made her put on for her *date*. She wished she had something to cover up her legs. The house was so cold.

This was the first time she'd been let out of the bedroom, except for going to the bathroom. Kym was right. This place really was much nicer than the other house. The couches and furniture appeared to be new. The kitchen was well-kept. But just like the other place, the windows were blacked out. She spotted containers of Chinese takeout on the table.

"The paper plates are over there," Shantel said, sitting down.

Brianna took a seat across from her and dished out some fried rice onto a plate. She tried to chew but her jaw was too sore.

Shantel got up from the table and poured an amber liquid into a short glass.

"Here," she said. "This will make you feel better."

Brianna took a whiff and knew it was alcohol. "I'm not drinking that."

"Fine. I was just tryin' to help you feel better. I don't care if your face never stops hurtin'."

"I wanna go home," Brianna pleaded.

"I already told you, you're not going nowhere. I didn't want to be here at first either. But this is better than being at a lot of places. At least we get to go shopping sometimes and eat what we want."

Shopping? Maybe that was her way out. If they took her to a mall, she could scream and yell and get somebody to rescue her.

"I wanna go shopping," Brianna said.

"You can't go shopping unless you start going on some dates first and make some money. They ain't takin' care of you for free."

"I told you I'm not going on no date!" Brianna exploded. "And stop calling it a date. You're a prostitute. You can be one if you want to, but I'm never gonna be one!"

"Go back to your room!" Shantel yelled, snatching Brianna's plate of fried rice from the table. "Freda told me to be nice to you and try to get you to act right. But you crazy!"

"You're the crazy one if you think you can just kidnap somebody off the street. You're going to jail."

"You don't get it," Shantel spat, "nobody don't care about ho's. That's what I am and that's what you're gonna be too. You know how many girls Shep has kidnapped? Tons of them. And nobody has ever come lookin' for 'em because nobody cares about 'em. Even if the police pick us up, we can turn around and go right back to Shep. And because we're juveniles the most we can get is six months. And that ain't no time."

"Why do you wanna do this?" Brianna cried. "Why don't you just get a job?"

"I can make more money in one day on the Internet than I can make in two weeks working a square job. So as far as I'm concerned, I'm just a smart businesswoman."

Brianna stood up and swept the containers of food onto the floor.

"You must'a lost your mind," Shantel screamed. She swung at Brianna, but Brianna saw the punch coming, grabbed Shantel's arm and hurled her to the floor.

Brianna dashed for the kitchen door. To her surprise it opened easily. But on the other side, there was another door, a heavy metal one with two deadbolt locks. She tugged on the door, but it wouldn't budge.

Shantel yelled from the floor. "I already told you, you can't get out of here. Why you so hardheaded?"

"You have to let me go!" Brianna screamed. "If you let me go, my mother will pay you. I swear."

"I don't need your money," Shantel said. "I'm a businesswoman."

"You're not a businesswoman!" Brianna fired back. "Where's your house and your car, Ms. Businesswoman? You can't even leave the house when you want. You're just a slave, but you're too stupid to know it."

"You just wait until Freda get back and I tell her how you been actin'," Shantel shouted at her. "I hope they give you to Demonic. And if they do, you're gonna wish you was dead."

DAY FOUR MISSING

"Once a 'Romeo Pimp' has gained a victim's trust, he systematically breaks down her resistance, support systems, and self-esteem. Victims are coerced into submission through gang rape, confinement, beatings, torture, cutting, tattooing, burning, branding, being deprived of basic needs, and threats of murder."

—*The State of Human Trafficking in California*
California Department of Justice

CHAPTER 54

Day Four: 1:30 a.m.

I t was thirty minutes before closing time at City Stars and Dre was more nervous than he'd ever been in his life.

He was sitting behind the wheel of Mossy's van, parked half a block away from the club. Apache was in the back section of the van. Bobby and Terrell were holding it down inside, while Mossy was waiting for them at the spot where they planned to take Clint after kidnapping him.

"Man, we need to get this show on the road," Apache said from the back of the van. "After that sick-ass video of little shorty, I think we should just fire on the place and ask questions later."

"Please shut up." Dre was finding it hard to sit still.

Apache abided by Dre's request for all of thirty seconds. "How much longer we gotta wait?"

Dre ignored him. D'wan and Gus should have been there by now. If they didn't get there soon, the club would be closed. *Where the hell were they?*

Dre fired off a text to Gus.

Dre: u comin?

Gus: almst thre

Five minutes later, he watched Gus park his Tundra and walk into City Stars. D'wan pulled up on his Harley a short time later.

"It's about time," Dre said to himself.

He drove the van to the mouth of the alley behind the club. It was all out of his control now. He prayed everything went down the way they'd planned.

For the next eighteen minutes, Apache and Dre waited in silence. Dre's fingers alternately tightened and released around the steering wheel. *What was taking so long?*

Then Apache started humming and tapping out a beat on the back of Dre's seat. "Can we get some music or something?" he asked.

"Will you please shut up?" Dre replied, more than annoyed. "We need to be alert so—"

The buzz of his smartphone stopped him mid-sentence. He picked it up and read the text.

Gus: bout 2 go down

"It's time!" Dre started up the van. "Open the door!"

Apache did as instructed as the van crawled down the alley. Dre stopped just past the back door of the club, engine running.

"I don't know why you didn't let me go inside where the action is," Apache complained.

"Shut up!" Dre snapped. "When we get this fool, you're going to get plenty of action. Just be ready to slam that door shut as soon as everybody jumps in."

Exactly five minutes later, Bobby and Terrell busted through the back door of the club and into the alley. They tossed a squirming Clint into the van and hopped in with him.

Dre hit the gas before Apache had time to close the door.

CHAPTER 55

Day Four: 1:45 a.m.

Brianna was rolled into a ball on the bed, listening to Kym and Tameka joke about the johns they'd serviced that night. She could barely keep her eyes open, but was too afraid of what might happen to her if she let herself fall asleep.

"The first guy smelled like puke," Tameka complained, twisting her lips. "I couldn't wait until he was done."

Kym laughed. "You lucky he only lasted two minutes."

Tameka joined in the laughter. "More like a minute and thirty seconds."

"Hey, peeps!" Brianna heard a man calling out from kitchen. "Anybody awake up in this mug? Daddy's home!"

"Yuck!" Kym grabbed her clothes from the bed. "I hate him." She dashed out of the room and down the hallway."

Brianna hopped off the bed, frightened by the ashen look on Tameka's face.

"What's the matter? Who's that?" Brianna asked.

"It's Darnell," Tameka whispered. "He's ugly and stinky and got rotten teeth. He works for The Shepherd. He thinks he can just come up in here and have sex with us anytime he wants. Freda already told him about that. But she ain't here."

Tameka looked around the room as if she was searching for a place to hide. She dashed into the closet and closed the door.

Before Brianna could follow her, a man burst into the room.

"Where's everybody at? Is this any way to welcome Darnell home?"

A man with the face of a canine stared hungrily at Brianna. His hair was uncombed and he smelled like he lived on the streets. Brianna wanted to run, but her body was suddenly immobilized.

"You must be the new girl," Darnell said, stepping further into the room. "Come over here so Daddy can get a look at you."

Brianna started to tremble. The fact that Kym and Tameka were scared of what this man might do made Brianna doubly terrified.

"I said come here!" Darnell shouted.

Brianna still didn't move.

Darnell stepped closer and held both of her arms up high. He turned her around and started running his hands all over her rear end. Brianna tried to pull away, repulsed by the man's touch.

"Whoooo weeeee! This is some real tender meat right here," he said, slapping her on the rear end. "Daddy can't wait to test drive you."

Brianna finally squirmed free, but had now backed herself against the wall. "Leave me alone!"

"Darnell's been on the road for eight long hours and this is how you gonna treat him? I brought some new girls down from Oakland. Had to pull off the road to test out a couple of 'em. But none of 'em was as fine as you. I bet you still a virgin. Well, Darnell gonna do you a favor and break you in. Take off your clothes. Let me see what you workin' with."

Brianna was certain she was about to puke. "Get the hell away from me!"

He frowned. "That ain't no kinda way to talk to Daddy." Darnell grabbed Brianna's thin top and ripped it off. "Dang! You ain't got no titties, girl."

"Get away from me!" Brianna bent at the waist, crisscrossing her arms to cover her breasts. "Please leave me alone!"

"I like it when they beg," Darnell said, laughing and rubbing his groin. "We gonna have us a good time. What's your name?"

Brianna had her eyes on the open door and wondered if she could make it past him before he caught her. But then what would she do? Maybe she could get to the kitchen and grab a knife from the drawer.

As if he'd been reading her mind, Darnell took a few steps backward, slamming the door shut without even looking behind him.

"I asked you your name, little girl. Don't make me get ugly." His tone had gone from playful to gruff.

"Bree...Brianna." She took a sideways step. Darnell did the same.

Brianna was having trouble breathing again, and this time, it wasn't an act.

Darnell started unbuckling his belt.

"Well, Brianna, you and me 'bout to have a little private party."

CHAPTER 56

Day Four: 2:00 a.m.

"I don't see anybody coming," Dre said, checking the rearview mirror as he sped down the alley.

He made a sharp right, then a series of turns that he'd mapped out in his head the day before.

"That's because they probably don't even know he's gone yet," Terrell said with a laugh. "The minute Clint walked out of the men's room, I gave the signal and Gus and D'wan pretended to punch each other out. All the bouncers ran over there, while I clocked the dude and stuck a sock in his mouth to keep him from screaming as we carted him out the back door. Your plan worked like a charm, bruh."

Clint was tied up on the floor of the van. He stopped squirming after Apache punched him in the face and he passed out.

Dre felt ecstatic about how smoothly everything had gone down. But he also knew his plan could put Brianna in further danger. Dre wished he could've kidnapped someone who meant as much to The Shepherd as Brianna meant to him. But there appeared to be no one like that in his life.

It took less than twenty minutes to reach the abandoned warehouse in Gardena where Dre had arranged to take Clint. The van rolled into a humongous building that looked like something out of a James Bond movie. Cold, dark and isolated.

Mossy walked up to the van. "You were supposed to call me and let me know everything went down according to plan. I've been sweatin' bullets."

"Sorry, man." Dre slapped his friend on the shoulder. "I got so excited I forgot all about calling you."

"I just wish I could've been the one to grab dude," Apache moaned.

Bobby and Terrell retrieved Clint from the back of the van and dumped him on the ground in front of the van. The bright headlights from Mossy's van and Dre's Jetta were their only source of light in the expansive warehouse.

Dre opened a bottle of water and doused Clint, who slowly began to wake up. He squinted at the bright lights, then took in the five men staring down at him. His eyes landed on Dre last. The distress in them pleased Dre immensely.

Bobby and Terrell lifted Clint from the ground and set him in a rusted-out chair in front of Dre. His feet were bound and his hands were tied behind his back.

"Hey, Mr. Big Shot," Dre said.

Clint started to whimper.

"We're going to show you what it feels like to be kidnapped and beaten up," he said.

Clint's whimpers quickly grew into sobs. A string of saliva stretched from his lower lip to his white silk shirt.

"We need some information," Dre said. "My cousin here is going to show you what's gonna happen every time you fail to answer one of my questions."

Dre stuffed a towel deep into Clint's mouth, then gave Apache a nod. His cousin stepped forward and happily zapped Clint in the groin with his stun gun.

Clint howled and writhed, tumbling from the chair onto the dusty concrete floor.

"That's just a sample of things to come," Dre said.

Bobby and Terrell picked him up and placed him back in the chair. Clint doubled over in pain.

Dre jerked the towel from his mouth and waited while Clint vomited all over himself.

"Where's my niece?" he demanded.

"I don't know," Clint bawled. "I swear."

Dre turned to Apache. "Go for it."

His cousin rushed forward and zapped him in the nuts a second time.

Clint's screams would've penetrated the walls if they hadn't been in a soundproof building.

"You're the one calling the shots here," Dre said. "We can do this all night long if you want. Too many zaps could actually kill you."

He gave the signal and Apache moved toward Clint for a third time.

"No, no! Okay, okay! She's at one of Shep's houses in the Valley. It's on Wardlow."

"Aw man!" Apache punched Clint hard in the chest. "I can't believe you punked out that quick. I only got to zap you two times."

Mossy shook his head and gave Dre another I-told-you-he-was-crazy look.

Dre stepped closer to him. "What's the address?"

"273 Wardlow Circle."

"Who's at the house?"

"Just Freda and a few of the girls," Clint cried. "She's in charge of watching them."

Bewilderment flooded Bobby's face. "Ya'll got women helping y'all?"

Dre turned to Mossy. "Check the address."

Mossy grabbed his iPad from the van and tapped in the address on Google maps, then showed the screen to Dre.

"Describe the house?" Dre said. "I want to make sure you're not jerking me around."

Clint sputtered out his words between sobs. "It's beige, two big windows in front. There's a six-foot gate around the entire house."

"That's it," Mossy said.

"Where does The Shepherd live?"

"I don't know!"

Dre pointed at Apache. But before Apache could zap him again, the information spilled out of Clint.

"He lives in Newport Beach."

"What's the address?"

"I don't know it by heart. I swear I don't!"

"Apache!" Dre called out.

"The house is on Ocean Boulevard. The address is in my phone!" Clint cried out. "In my pocket!"

"Man, you're a little sissy!" Apache slapped him upside the head, then pulled the phone from his pocket and tossed it to Dre.

"Look it up," Dre said, passing the phone to Mossy.

"I need the address to every single house where The Shepherd keeps girls."

Clint hung his head. "It's in my phone too. Under *locations*."

They waited as Mossy checked. "Yep, here it is right here."

Dre started moving toward his car. "Let's go, everybody. Apache, you stay here with him."

Apache was salivating. "Hey, dude, you and me gonna have big fun tonight."

"Please, please! Don't leave me here with him!" Clint screamed. "Please! He's crazy! He'll kill me!"

Dre took two steps back, grabbed the stun gun from Apache's hand and also snatched the Glock from his waistband.

"Don't touch him. Just watch him. See if you can find out some more information about The Shepherd's operation."

Apache looked as if he was about to cry. "Y'all can't leave me here with no heat!"

Dre ignored him. He was just about to walk past Clint again, but something stopped him. He stared down at Clint's left hand for several long seconds. Then he reared back and punched him in the face so hard he flew off the chair and crashed to the ground. In a wild flurry of movement, Dre started kicking him in the ribs, then stomped repeatedly on his head.

After a few seconds, Mossy grabbed Dre by the arm and dragged him away. "Yo', man, we just tryin' to get your niece back. We don't need no murder wrap."

Clint lay on the floor moaning.

"He was the one—" Dre tried to speak, but he was so worked up he had trouble getting the words out. "He was the one beating up Brianna on that video."

Mossy was still holding on to Dre. "How do you know that?"

He pointed down at Clint's hand. "I saw that diamond pinky ring he's wearing on the video. I'll never forget it."

Dre's right hand throbbed with pain. As good as it felt to beat the punk down, he was glad that Mossy had stopped him.

If he hadn't, Clint might've ended up dead.

CHAPTER 57

Day Four: 2:05 a.m.

Brianna closed her eyes and prayed. *Dear Jesus, please help me!*
She heard the clink of Darnell's belt buckle hit the floor. She refused to open her eyes.

Jesus, please! Jesus, please! Jesus, please!

"Open your eyes, girl," Darnell taunted. "Don't you wanna see the nice big package Daddy brought for you!"

The door suddenly burst open.

"How many times do I have to tell you to leave my girls alone?" Freda yelled at the top of her lungs. "Get the hell out of here!"

Darnell scowled at Freda, then at Brianna. "I was just having a little fun with the girl," he said.

"And I've told you a million times not to touch my girls."

He took his time stepping back into his pants as if he wanted Freda to admire his equipment.

"Hurry up and put your pants on. Don't nobody want to see that," she snarled. "You're disgusting."

Darnell laughed, still moving in slow motion.

"Did you drop off the girls from Oakland?"

"Yeah."

"How many?"

"Seven."

"I'm going to ask every last one of 'em if you touched them and if you did, I'm tellin' Shep."

Darnell's playful expression disappeared. "Don't do that, okay? I didn't mean nothin'. I was just playing around."

"Just get out. You're supposed to be transporting girls over to the motel anyway. And I better not hear that you tried to mess with 'em."

Neither Tameka nor Kym came out of hiding until they'd heard Darnell leave the house.

"I hate him!" Kym said running up to Freda. "He always be botherin' us."

"I'm sorry, y'all," Freda said. "I'll make sure he never comes back here again unless I'm here."

Freda's smartphone rang and she pulled it from her purse.

Brianna was still hugging herself to cover her exposed breasts.

"You're kidding! Oh my God!" Freda covered her mouth with her free hand.

Brianna, Kym and Tameka stared up at Freda as she continued the conversation, wondering what horrible news she was receiving. Her eyes seemed to bear down on Brianna as if she had done something wrong.

"Clint told you we needed to give that girl back," Freda said into the smartphone. "She ain't worth it."

Brianna's pulse began to pick up speed. Was she about to go home?

"I'm not disrespecting you," Freda said. "I just—"

Freda paused, then rolled her eyes as she continued to listen. "Okay, okay."

She hung up and stepped up to Brianna. "You've been nothing but trouble from the minute you got here," she said, pointing a finger inches from Brianna's nose. "Put on some clothes!"

Brianna didn't know what to say, so she didn't say anything. The woman must be nuts. She didn't want to be there in the first place.

Brianna picked up a T-shirt from a pile of clothes on the floor.

Freda grabbed her by the arm. "Come on, you've got to go. Tameka, you're comin' with us."

"I'm going home?" Brianna asked, hopefully.

"You wish," Freda said, dragging her barefoot down the hallway. "I'm hiding you out in one of the other houses. Your uncle had the nerve to kidnap Clint. Shep is really pissed off now. No tellin' what he's gonna do to you."

Day Four: 7:45 a.m.

Bonnie finally faced the fact that for the time being there was little she could do about having her honors classes stripped away. She'd filed a grievance with the teacher's union, but it could take weeks before a union rep even contacted her to follow up.

She was in the courtyard, watching students make their way to class when she spotted Ortiz surrounded by a group of eighth-grade girls. One of them had her arm linked through his. He reached out to hug another one.

Bonnie's lips twisted in disapproval. In this day and age when teachers feared false allegations of abuse from both male and female students, the principal's behavior just didn't make sense. Perhaps those rumors about Ortiz and a student at his prior school were really true. Bonnie hurried by, hoping he didn't notice her.

"I got a copy of that grievance you filed," he said, catching up with her.

"Good." She did not bother slowing down.

"It's a waste of time."

"We'll see."

"Good morning, Mr. Ortiz," Tanya, the head of the Pep Squad sauntered by in a skirt that barely covered her bulbous butt.

Ortiz turned away from Bonnie and waved. He gave the girl a lustful, lingering look that stopped Bonnie in her tracks. Watching Ortiz's hungry eyes following Tanya as she bounced around the courtyard sickened her.

"You're a complete disgrace to the teaching profession," she hissed under her breath.

Bonnie continued on to her classroom, seething over what she had just witnessed. When she entered the building, she spotted Wainright approaching her from the far end of the hallway.

"You're looking pretty spiffy for your first day with your new students." Wainright gave her a warm smile. "That dress looks like it came right off the page of some fashion magazine."

"Don't try to butter me up," Bonnie growled.

"C'mon, Bonnie. Don't take it out on me. You know I would've changed things if I could have."

"Yeah, sure."

Wainright followed her into her classroom. "Look, we've been friends for a long time. I just want to make sure this hasn't changed anything between us."

She sighed. "I know you were just following orders. I'm not mad at you. But I could strangle Ortiz."

"Just hang in there. I have a feeling you're going to do some amazing things with these students."

"We'll see." She locked her purse inside the desk drawer, then looked around the room. "Look at this place. The walls are completely bare. This room should have been decorated long before the school year started."

"I'm sure you'll have it in shape in no time."

Bonnie merely huffed.

Wainright was about to leave when Bonnie stopped him.

"Can I ask you something?" she said, walking around her desk. "I heard a rumor that Ortiz was accused of inappropriate conduct with a student when he was at Centennial. Do you know anything about that?"

"Please don't try to recruit me to be a soldier in your war against Ortiz."

"I'm not trying to get you involved. I'm just wondering if you heard that rumor."

"Yes, I've heard it, but I have no idea whether it's true or not. Why are you even bringing it up?"

Bonnie hesitated. She didn't know how much she should share with Wainright. He noticed her hesitation.

"C'mon, you can talk to me."

"I just don't like the lustful way he looks at some of the female students," she admitted. "Always giving them hugs."

Wainright peeked over his shoulder as if to confirm that they were alone. "I've seen that too. I have no idea why he does that."

"I knew I wasn't crazy!"

He held up both palms. "Hold on now. I've never actually seen him behave inappropriately with a student. So let's not get any rumors started."

"I'm not starting any rumors. It's just good to know that I'm not imagining things."

"I better get going," Wainright said, obviously uncomfortable with the topic.

Bonnie took a seat at her desk. She was not going to start any rumors about Ortiz, but she certainly planned to keep a close eye on him. Since he'd blatantly retaliated against her, she'd find her own legitimate way to retaliate right back.

If she got even an inkling that the arrogant, self-righteous Manuel Ortiz was involved with a student, she wasn't going to waste her time reporting him to the school district or her union rep.

She was going straight to the police.

CHAPTER 59

Day Four: 8:30 a.m.

As Loretha and Angela had feared, Peaches' brave front about testifying against her pimp crumbled the second she laid eyes on the courthouse.

The two women cradled her in the hallway outside the courtroom.

"Y'all don't understand," she said through tears. "He'll kill me."

"No, he won't," Loretha said, holding her close. "If you testify, he's going to jail."

"Not for long. He got a good lawyer. He always gets out."

"The charges against pimps are tougher now. If he's convicted, it will be years before he's back on the street."

"He got friends," Peaches cried. "He can put a hit out on me from prison."

The courtroom door opened and a smiling young prosecutor stuck her head out. She noticed Peaches' tears and her smile faltered.

"Is she okay? She isn't backing out, is she?" Cindy Bachman asked, hurrying over. She was a chubby woman with woolly auburn hair.

"She'll be fine," Loretha said. "Just give us a minute."

"If she doesn't testify, I don't have a case."

"We know that," Loretha snapped. "Just give us a minute."

Cindy threw up her hands. "This guy is a scumbag. I can't convict him without her testimony."

Loretha glanced down the hallway and muttered something under her breath that Angela didn't quite hear. Loretha suddenly angled her body as if to physically shield Peaches.

"Hey, Peaches."

A short black man accompanied by a lanky, balding white man, greeted Peaches as he headed into the courtroom.

"That's Gerald," Loretha said with a sneer.

Gerald Renthroe looked nothing like a pimp. At least not the pimps depicted on TV and in the movies. He was barely five-three with the build of an elf. His navy-blue suit and red-and-white tie was stylish enough that someone might mistake him for a midget lawyer.

"Did you see the way he looked at me?" Peaches screeched. "He's gonna kill me. I can't do it! I can't do it!"

"Oh, this is just great," Cindy said.

Angela glared at the prosecutor "You know, it might help if you showed a little compassion."

"I'm sorry." She placed a hand on Peaches' shoulder. "I know you can do it, Peaches. Just answer my questions the way we practiced, okay?"

"We can't force you to testify," Loretha said. "It's your decision. What do you wanna do?"

"If I testify, will he go to jail today?"

Loretha glanced at Cindy. This was only a preliminary hearing to decide if there was enough evidence to charge Gerald. The actual trial would be months away. Gerald was currently out on bail. He would walk out of the courtroom today and remain on the streets for months.

"The judge probably won't put him in jail today," Cindy said softly, "but if you don't testify, the charges will be dropped."

Peaches took a long time to think about her options. "I can do it," she finally said, wiping her eyes with the back of her hand. "When I remember how he punched me in my face and busted my lip I know I have to do it."

Cindy's face brightened as she started walking toward the courtroom. "I'm going inside and let the judge know we're ready to proceed."

Peaches stared up at Angela. "Would you testify if you was me?"

Angela hugged her. "I'd be scared just like you are. But, yeah, I would."

It was another ten minutes before the courtroom door opened and Cindy beckoned them inside.

Angela and Loretha walked a shaky Peaches down the center aisle of the courtroom. Since this was a preliminary hearing, there was no jury present. Only the judge would decide if the prosecutor had enough evidence to proceed with a trial against Gerald.

"Go on up and take a seat in the witness box," Loretha urged her.

The prosecutor smiled warmly at Peaches.

"Swear the witness in," Judge Rene Blaine instructed.

The clerk stood. "Do you solemnly affirm that the testimony you are about to give in the case now pending before this court shall be the truth, the whole truth and nothing but the truth?"

Peaches looked around as if she was confused.

The judge peered down at Peaches from her perch. "Young lady, did you understand?"

"Yes. I'ma tell the truth."

Peaches did as they had told her and kept her gaze directly on Cindy and not on Gerald.

"Please state and spell your name for the record," the clerk stated.

"Priscilla, but they call me Peaches." She quickly spelled her name. "They told me I can't say my last name cuz I'm a juvenile."

"Ms. Bachman," Judge Blaine said, "you may proceed."

Cindy stepped forward. "Is it okay if I call you Peaches?"

"Yep."

"And how old are you, Peaches?"

"Fifteen."

"And where do you reside?"

"In Los Angeles County. They told me I can't say where I really stay cuz it's a safe place for gettin' out of the life."

"Do you know the defendant Gerald Renthroe?"

Peaches shuddered, then nodded her head.

"You'll have to speak out loud so the court reporter can take down your words," Cindy said.

"Okay."

"So do you know the defendant?" Cindy repeated.

"Yes."

"And how do you know him?" Peaches stole a quick glance at Gerald, then at Loretha and Angela sitting in the galley.

"Uh...he was my boyfriend."

Loretha grabbed Angela's hand. They had rehearsed this with Peaches over and over again last night. That was not the answer she was supposed to give. She was supposed to say that Gerald was her pimp.

The prosecutor looked down at some papers on the table in front of her.

"Isn't it true that he's also your pimp?"

Peaches hitched her right shoulder. "Um...I don't know."

Cindy glanced back at Loretha. She had personally called the prosecutor's office and pressured them to file charges against Gerald.

"Did Mr. Renthroe punch you in the eye and give you that cut on your lip?"

Peaches absently touched her face. This time, her eyes darted toward Gerald and stayed there. She did not respond for a long, long time.

Loretha was squeezing Angela's hand so hard it hurt.

"I don't remember," Peaches finally said.

Gerald leaned over to say something to his attorney. Angela could see that he was smiling.

Cindy ran her hand through her hair. "Your Honor, may I approach?"

Gerald's attorney followed the prosecutor to the bench. Angela knew what was about to happen and it made her want to scream. The sidebar was over in a minute or so.

The two lawyers returned to their respective tables while the judge scribbled something on the paper in front of her.

"Young lady, you can step down," she said to Peaches. "Case number CV-9838, *The People vs. Gerald Renthroe,* is hereby dismissed."

CHAPTER 60

Day Four: 8:45 a.m.

D re and his buddies left the warehouse in Gardena and spread out to search each of the six locations found in Clint's phone. After their skirmish at the club, Gus and D'wan drove straight to the Valley and waited for Dre's call. He directed them to check out the house on Wardlow Circle, while Dre and Mossy covered three addresses in L.A., and Terrell and Bobby split up to search the remaining two.

The first house Dre and Mossy checked appeared to be abandoned, the second looked lived in, but there was no one there. Dre's confidence was waning when he received a call from Gus.

"She ain't here," Gus said. "Whoever was here left in a hurry."

Seconds later, Dre got a similar call from Terrell and Bobby.

Dre and Mossy were only a few blocks away from the last location. "She ain't gonna be there," Dre said dejectedly. "I don't know why we're even lookin'. As soon as we grabbed Clint, The Shepherd probably moved all of the girls out."

All Dre wanted to do right now was go back to the warehouse and beat Clint to death.

"We're almost there," Mossy said. "So we might as well check." Dre could tell from his somber tone that Mossy didn't believe Brianna would be at the last house either.

As he drove through an intersection on Broadway, Dre's smartphone rang. The caller ID showed a blocked call. Dre answered it, but didn't say a word. It was several seconds before the caller spoke.

"You obviously don't understand who you're messing with?" The Shepherd said evenly.

"No," Dre replied with equal cool, "I think *you're* the one who doesn't understand."

He hit the speakerphone button so Mossy could hear the conversation.

"You're really disrespecting me." The Shepherd was clearly agitated. "I don't tolerate disrespect."

Although Dre hadn't been in the club when Clint was grabbed, he'd assumed that The Shepherd would have no trouble linking him to the abduction.

"I had to do what I had to do."

"I figure Clint's probably already told you where Brianna is," The Shepherd said. "He's weak. But don't waste your time going over there. She's been moved to a different location."

Of course, Dre knew that now.

"Clint gave us a lot of information about your business," Dre lied. "You run a very lucrative operation. The police will be quite interested in all the stuff your boy told us."

The Shepherd was silent for so long that Dre was certain his threat had registered with the force he'd intended.

"So you want your boy back?" Dre pushed.

The Shepherd laughed. "Naw. You can keep him. Do you want your niece back?"

Dre's fingers tightened around the steering wheel.

"I can't hear you," The Shepherd taunted.

"What kinda dude are you?"

"I'm a businessman, just like you. You didn't answer my question. Do you want your niece back?"

Mossy tapped him on the forearm and gave him a look that ordered him to play along.

"Yeah, I want her back."

"Well, because you disrespected me the way you did, I'll have to decide now whether I actually want to give her back. I've been shipping a lot of girls down South. The brothers in Birmingham or Atlanta would love a little tender like Brianna. Or I might just ship her across the border to Mexico and let my brown-skinned brothers have a go at her."

While the threat of Brianna being transported out of state terrified him, there was something about hearing The Shepherd speak her name that turned his feelings of fear into fury.

Mossy held up a hand, signaling Dre to stay calm. Loretha's advice came back to him and he knew that he needed to play to The Shepherd's ego. Dre tried, but he couldn't do it.

He spoke with total calm. "I'm going to kill you."

Mossy threw up his hands.

"Don't make threats you can't back up, Businessman," The Shepherd said with a chuckle.

"I have somebody headed over to your house in Newport Beach right now." The false threat eased his anxiety a bit.

"Don't play me," The Shepherd seethed.

Dre happily recited his Newport Beach address.

"Clint gave up your address quick too," he said. "You should be more careful selecting your underlings. That boy is weak. He'll probably tell the police everything he knows."

Once again, The Shepherd did not have a quick retort.

"So if I were you, *Rodney*," Dre continued, "I'd do the right thing and let Brianna go. You don't want me on your ass for the rest of your life."

The Shepherd finally found his voice. "Like I said, I'm not quite sure what I want to do with the little whore. I need to give this some additional thought. In the meantime, tell Clint he's fired."

The line went dead.

Dre jerked the steering wheel to the right and lateraled across two lanes, coming to a stop in front of a dry cleaners.

"Dude, you okay?" Mossy asked.

Dre was wound way too tight to speak right now, much less drive. He felt like ramming his car into something, anything. But for Brianna's sake, he knew he couldn't lose it.

"Look, man, you gotta get some sleep. Even if it's just for a couple of hours. That way you'll have a clear head and we can figure out our next step. And I'm driving from now on. Let's trade seats."

"I can't sleep. I have to—"

"Dude, you've been up for four straight days. You need to sleep and you also need to take a shower because you're funky as hell."

Mossy climbed out of the car and walked around to the driver's side.

"I'm not playin', man. Get out. I'm taking you home."

CHAPTER 61

Day Four: 9:00 a.m.

In nearly three decades of teaching, Bonnie Flanagan had never seen kids like this.

"Daunte, if I have to tell you to sit down one more time, I'm sending you to detention! I mean it!"

Bonnie had a splitting headache, and the day had just started. She had no idea how Ms. Williams handled these kids without losing her mind.

"Michael was standing up too," Daunte said with a pout. "Why you only pickin' on me?"

"Just finish your test!"

Although this was a seventh-grade class, these kids were reading at the third-grade level. Bonnie had been determined to show Manuel Ortiz that he hadn't beaten her. She'd planned to whip these kids into shape to further prove that she was an incredible teacher. If she could just get the troublemakers under control, she might actually be able to teach them something.

A hand shot up in the air near the back of the room.

"Ms. Flanagan, I'm finished," Chiquita Gomez announced happily. "Can I leave?"

"My goodness," Bonnie mumbled to herself. When did the Mexican parents start giving their babies crazy names? She had a hard enough time with all the Shaquishas and Tyeshas. Why would somebody want to name their child after a banana?

"No, you cannot leave. Class isn't over yet. Review your answers to make sure they're correct."

Chiquita had long Snooki-looking hair and a rose tattooed on her neck. She was barely thirteen and already a D-cup.

"She just wanna go see her boyfriend, Mr. Ortiz," Daunte said.

"Stop saying that!" Chiquita yelled.

"Ain't my fault you got an old, fat boyfriend with a big stomach."

"I ain't got no boyfriend. So stop saying that! He just let me work in his office."

Bonnie's radar shot straight up. *Since when were students allowed to work in the principal's office?*

"Daunte, please turn around and finish your test."

She walked over to Chiquita's desk. "I need you to come outside with me, young lady."

The whole class started to snicker.

"Chiquita in trouble now!" Daunte teased.

Bonnie pressed two fingers against her throbbing temple as she led Chiquita out of the classroom. They stepped into the empty hallway. Bonnie didn't close the door because she feared the students might ransack the room. She motioned Chiquita several feet away from the door.

"How long have you been working for the principal?"

"About a month," she said, clearly proud.

"And what do you do?"

"I put papers in alphabetical order and stuff like that."

Alphabetical order? He has two administrative assistants to do that.

"Does he pay you?"

"Yep. He give me forty dollars every time. But Mr. Ortiz told me not to tell nobody because the other students would be jealous." She stuck out her lower lip. "But I messed up and told Marquon. That big mouth had it all over the school by the next day."

This was highly inappropriate. *Was the man just plain stupid?*

"Who else is in the office when you're doing your work?"

Chiquita shrugged. "I don't know. I'm busy doing my work."

"When do you work for him?"

"After school on Mondays and Thursdays. I have to go to work today."

Bonnie wasn't sure whether to ask the next question. But she had to know.

She looked the girl dead in her eyes. "Has Mr. Ortiz ever done anything inappropriate when you're helping him out?"

Chiquita's face scrunched up. "Like what?" It took a few seconds more, then something registered.

"Ms. Flanagan! I can't believe you asked me that!" Chiquita exclaimed. "Mr. Ortiz is a very nice man! He wouldn't never do nothin' bad to nobody."

"I know," Bonnie said. "I just wanted to make sure. You can go back inside now. And don't tell anyone I talked to you about this."

That was a wasted directive. Chiquita would be spilling her guts as soon as the bell rang.

Bonnie remained in the hallway. She could hear the students inside cutting up as Chiquita walked back in.

Bonnie wasn't convinced that the girl was telling the truth. If something inappropriate was going on between Chiquita and Mr. Ortiz, the girl probably wouldn't admit it. Why in the hell would he have a student alone in his office after hours? Especially a student like Chiquita, who had a body more shapely than many grown women.

This time, Bonnie would not just push her suspicions aside. She would hang around after school ended today and pay Mr. Ortiz a visit. She would find out for herself just what kind of *work* Chiquita was really doing.

CHAPTER 62

Day Four: 9:25 a.m.

"It's okay, sweetie," Loretha said to Peaches outside the courtroom. "We know you tried. Don't worry about it. It's okay."

Loretha held Peaches close.

"I'm sorry. I'm so sorry," Peaches cried. "But I was too scared."

Angela rubbed her back. "We know, we know. It's okay. Let's get out of here."

Angela did not want Peaches to have to face Gerald when he walked out of the courtroom.

But it was too late. Gerald stepped into the hallway and marched right up to her.

"Hey, Peaches," he said. "Thanks for telling the truth in there."

Angela stepped between them. She could see the top of Gerald's head. "Get the hell away from us."

Gerald smirked. "I don't know who the hell you are, but you need to stay out of my business."

His red-faced attorney stood off to the side. "Uh...Mr. Walker...I uh...I think we should leave."

Gerald looked over his shoulder at his attorney. "You shut up too."

"You lookin' good girl," he said to Peaches. "I really like your hair. You look really pretty today."

Peaches pulled away from Loretha. She looked at Gerald, then touched her hair.

"If you wanna come home, I won't be mad at you. I know these nosey bitches tried to make you testify against me."

"She's got a home," Loretha hissed.

"I still love you, Peaches." Gerald winked, blew her a kiss and walked off down the hallway.

Loretha gritted her teeth. "That piece of low-life scum."

Peaches craned her neck and watched Gerald as he strolled down the corridor.

"At least he ain't mad." She reached up, patted her hair and smiled. "He said my hair was pretty."

Loretha closed her eyes and shook her head. "Lord, give me strength."

* * *

After leaving the courthouse, Loretha and Peaches returned to Harmony House. Angela went to her car to make some calls and arrived thirty minutes later. She found Loretha in her office, gazing out of the window.

"I don't think I've ever seen you look so sad," Angela said, stepping into the office and closing the door behind her.

It took a while before Loretha responded.

"This has been a pretty sucky day," she began, her voice low and raspy. "And not just because Peaches failed to testify against her pimp. I just got the news that one of my girls is HIV positive." She picked up a piece of paper from her desk and handed it to Angela. "And about ten minutes ago, Anamaria handed me this."

Ms. Loreeta—

i'm going back to my Daddy. he sorry for what he did. he not going to beet me no more. Thank U for helping me.

Lotta Luv, Peaches

Angela fell onto the couch across from Loretha's desk as if someone had knocked the wind out of her.

Loretha forced a smile. "My sentiments exactly."

"What happened?"

"What happened? It's pretty simple. You heard her pimp tell her she was pretty. That made her forget everything he'd done to her. I would suspect that since her parents died, he's the only person in her life to give her any kind of positive reinforcement. Doesn't matter that just a couple of days ago he practically beat her half to death. These pimps know how vulnerable these girls are and they use that to their advantage."

"We should call the police," Angela said.

"Even if they brought her back, it wouldn't do any good," Loretha said wearily. "This isn't my first girl to go back and it won't be my last. But I swear, every time it takes something out of me. I just pray the next time I hear about her—and there will be a next time—that scumbag hasn't killed her."

"We have to do something?" Angela said. "She's a minor. If we can't get him on assault or pimping, why can't they arrest him for statutory rape?"

Loretha laughed. "You're the lawyer, aren't you? We're not talking about some cute kid from the suburbs who's caught sleeping with her teacher. These girls are labeled prostitutes, so nobody cares that they're being bought and sold by adult men. Even though they're underage."

Tears slid down Loretha's cheeks.

"She has my number," Angela said. "Maybe she'll call me."

"She won't have your number for long unless she memorizes it. Gerald will make sure she doesn't have contact with anybody except him, his other girls and their clients. Unless she runs away again, she'll be totally isolated."

"I guess my taking her back to her aunt's house didn't help. After talking to warm, fuzzy Aunt Gina, I understand how she could gravitate toward Gerald. She doesn't have anybody else. At least he pretends to care about her."

"Don't beat yourself up about that."

Angela slumped further down on the couch. "I still don't understand how you can do this heartbreaking work day after day."

"Sometimes I wonder myself," Loretha said, smiling. She grew quiet again.

"Peaches is a bright girl," Loretha continued. "Over the years, I've developed a knack for being able to spot the ones who have the strength to change their lives. I saw it in Anamaria. The ability to wake up one day and realize their own self-worth. I have faith that Peaches will ultimately be another one of my success stories."

CHAPTER 63

Day Four: 9:45 a.m.

Apache was pissed off. They were treating him like a friggin' babysitter. He needed to be where the action was.

"You sick. You know that?" Apache leaned forward and spit in Clint's face. "Anybody who mess with little girls is a pervert. And I don't like perverts."

Clint was all cried out now. "If you let me go," he said in a whiny voice, "I swear, I'll pay you."

"I don't want no pervert's money. I wish I had my stun gun. I'd electrocute your sorry ass. I can't believe you wimped out in two zaps. You a little punk."

Apache punched him in the jaw and he tumbled to the ground again.

"Get your ass up," Apache said, kicking him.

Clint tried, but couldn't seem to balance himself with his arms tied behind his back. He managed to get to his knees, then fell back to the ground.

Apache grabbed him by the arm.

"Owwww! My arm!" Clint squealed. "It must be broken."

Apache threw him back into the chair. "How many girls you snatched?"

Clint hung his head.

"Did you hear what I said?"

"I…I don't know."

"You do know. Now tell me!" Apache slugged him again and this time, Clint hit the ground, headfirst.

Instead of crying out, this time he went quiet. Then all of a sudden, his body began to spasm like a fish flopping around on dry land.

Apache jumped back. "What's wrong with your dumb ass?"

Clint's body finally stopped moving and he was completely still.

"You ain't fooling nobody. Get your ass up!"

Apache was about to grab him by the arm again when Clint started writhing again. He was now turning grayish blue and foaming at the mouth.

"What the—!"

Apache pulled out his smartphone and called Dre.

"Hey, man, this dude is having a seizure or something."

"What did you do to him?" Dre yelled.

"All I did was hit him a couple times. He can't even take a punch."

"Man, you better pray that that dude don't die."

"He ain't gonna die. He's probably just fakin'?"

Dre released a string of curse words into the smartphone.

Apache grew even more nervous as he watched Clint continuing to shake and foam at the mouth. He'd shot a few dudes in his time, but he'd never hung around to watch 'em die.

"I'm outta here," Apache said. "This pervert deserves to die."

Dre didn't respond.

"Did you hear me?" Apache asked. "He's probably gonna die."

He heard Dre inhale through the phone. "You got your throwaway cell phone with you?" he finally said.

"Always," Apache said.

"I'm the one who got everybody mixed up in this," Dre said. "And if he dies, all of us'll go down. I can't let that happen. Call nine-one-one and tell 'em where he is. The warehouse is at the end of the cul de sac at Alondra and Maple. Leave the door open and bounce."

CHAPTER 64

Day Four: 10:05 a.m.

With so many girls to watch over, it had been easy for Peaches to slip out of the back door of Harmony House unnoticed. She speed walked past all the impressive Lafayette Square mansions. Peaches wished she'd had time to look around. The only black people she knew who lived in mansions like this were on *The Real Housewives of Atlanta.*

When Peaches reached St. Charles Place, she started running at top speed. She got to Crenshaw and looked right, then left. She spotted a Jack 'n the Box and a Mobile gas station a block away. She jogged to the corner and repeatedly pressed the button on the traffic pole. The light finally changed and she dashed across Washington Boulevard. Thank God there was a pay phone behind the gas station. She called Gerald collect.

In no time at all, Peaches spotted Gerald's shiny black Mercedes SUV with the twenty-three-inch rims.

"Hey, boo!" he said, hopping out. Gerald pulled Peaches into his arms and squeezed her tight.

He was out of his courthouse suit now and sporting jeans and a white T-shirt that came to his knees.

"I really missed you, girl. Don't you ever leave me again, you hear?" He kissed her deeply on the lips.

Peaches felt so good when Gerald hugged her. She wanted to tell him that, but the words got stuck in her throat.

"What's going on? The cat got your tongue. You need to tell Daddy you missed him too."

"I missed you," Peaches said, suddenly shy.

"You hungry? You want something to eat?"

"Yep."

"I'ma take you to a nice restaurant."

Peaches jumped in the car and they drove the short distance to Roscoe's Chicken and Waffles on Pico.

Gerald parked in back and took her by the hand as they walked inside the restaurant. They were seated in a back booth. He threw his arm around her shoulder and kissed her in the crook of her neck.

"I really do like that new hair of yours," Gerald said. "You look so pretty, boo. But I gotta get you back into some sexy clothes. I like my girls to show what they workin' with."

Peaches stared down at her sweatpants. She'd actually gotten used to having her body covered up.

They sat on the same side of the booth, with Gerald stopping every few seconds to give her a kiss and tell her how pretty she was. Peaches couldn't remember the last time she felt so special. This was like a real date. The other girls would be so jealous.

Peaches ordered waffles and chicken wings and Gerald had the same thing. They finished their food and walked hand-in-hand back to the parking lot. When they were seated in the SUV, Gerald reached into the backseat and pulled out a shiny gift box.

"I bought something for you, boo."

Peaches couldn't believe it. Gerald had never given her a present before. Not even on her birthday.

"Go ahead. Open it."

She tore through the wrapping paper, lifted the lid and pulled out a sheer, red dress.

"That's gonna look hot on you tonight, baby. And I don't want you wearing nothing but flesh underneath it."

Tonight!

Now she was really excited. Gerald was going to take her on a date too. Maybe they would go dancing. She was so lucky that he wasn't mad at her.

"I wanna see it on you now, baby. Climb in the backseat and put it on for me."

Peaches didn't move.

"Did you hear what I said?" The familiar sharpness in Gerald's voice frightened her.

Peaches climbed between the seats into the back of the SUV. She took off the sweatpants and T-shirt Loretha had given her and slipped on the sheer dress. It was low cut in the front and barely covered her rear end.

"Take them panties off," Gerald scolded her. "I told you I didn't want you wearing nothing underneath it."

Peaches obeyed and pulled off her panties.

"You lookin' good, boo," Gerald said with pride. "You gonna make Daddy a whole lot of money wearing that."

Peaches smiled and started to pull the dress back over her head.

"Hold up. What you doin'?"

"I'm putting my other clothes back on. I'm cold."

"You won't be cold after you walk around a little bit. I brought your red sandals. The ones that make your calves look big. Put them on."

Gerald started up the car and eased out of the parking lot and into traffic. He turned right then headed south on LaBrea.

"Where we going now?" Peaches asked.

"Where do you think? We gotta make up for lost time. You know how much money you cost me pulling this mess? I had to hire me a lawyer and everything. I'm makin' you pay me back every dime. Don't you ever pull no crap like this again. If you do, next time I won't beat your ass, I'll kill you."

Peaches was stunned into silence.

"I…I can't work tonight," Peaches whined.

Gerald took his eyes off the road and looked over his shoulder at her. "Why not?"

"Cuz...I'm...I'm tired."

"Tired? I'm tired too. But we gotta eat. So you gotta work."

He drove for close to thirty minutes, then pulled to a stop on Long Beach Boulevard. Peaches saw two other girls she knew prancing up the street in stilettos and shorts.

"Now get out there and make me some money."

"Gerald, please. I...I can't. It's cold out there!"

"If you wanna get out of the cold then pick up a trick."

Gerald climbed out, opened the back door and jerked her out of the car.

"Now get your ass out there and go get my money."

Peaches stumbled out of the SUV, twisting her ankle as she landed hard on the curb.

"I'll be parked across the street watching you," Gerald warned. "And you better not let no dude run off without paying you again."

Peaches was crying now. Crying over her sore ankle as well as how mean Gerald was treating her. She wished she was back in that courtroom. If she had another chance she would answer every one of that prosecutor's questions.

Yes, Gerald was my pimp.

Yes, Gerald busted my lip.

Yes, Gerald treated me worse than a dog.

Peaches wobbled down the street, her teeth chattering, brushing her hands up and down her forearms to warm herself up. The cold air breezed right through her dress. Her tears only made her colder.

I'm so stupid.

Halfway down the block, she eyed the bus bench where Loretha had left her business card.

That only made her cry harder.

CHAPTER 65

Day Four 10:30 a.m.

Dre lay prone on his living room couch, his eyes shut, massaging his forehead. Mossy was stretched out in an arm chair across from him, his thick arms locked across his chest.

"You don't have to say a word," Dre said finally. "I never should've let Apache guard Clint. I know that."

Truth be told, Dre wouldn't have a problem if Clint did end up dead. Maybe subconsciously he'd left Clint with his cousin because he knew there was a good chance that Apache *would* kill him.

Mossy's chest rose as he took in air. "You brought me into this to help you get your niece back. I ain't trying to catch no murder rap."

Dre finally met Mossy's glare. "Okay, fine. You can leave then. If it all blows up, you were never here."

Mossy sprang forward in his chair. "Man, it ain't like that. We go way back and you know I would never leave you hangin'. But you also know your cousin is a fool."

"It is what it is," Dre said, his voice hoarse. "Hopefully, an ambulance will get him to a hospital in time."

The silence returned, filling up the small apartment. Dre was glad that Mossy had convinced him to get some sleep. Just an hour of shut eye left him feeling re-energized.

He sat up and pulled a bottle of 5-Hour Energy from his pocket.

"Dude, you can't drink no more of that stuff. You already got the shakes."

"I'm fine."

"No, you're not. Look at your hands."

Dre stared down at his trembling fingers, unwilling to believe that they were his. He set the small bottle on the coffee table and rested his head on the back of the couch.

"I'ma run over to Popeye's to get us something to eat," Mossy said, standing up. "If The Shepherd calls back, please don't go off on him. Just say whatever you gotta say to get your girl back."

When the door closed, Dre eyed his smartphone. He wanted to check on his sister, but he couldn't face telling her he had not found Brianna yet. The smartphone suddenly began to ring as if he had somehow willed it to. He checked the display.

It was Donna.

Dre started rubbing his forehead again. It rang three more times before he finally answered the call.

"Hey, sis. How you doin'?"

"This ain't your sister. It's your mama."

"Hey, mama. How's Donna doin'?"

"Goin' stone crazy. She called all the TV stations and accused 'em of racism because they wouldn't run a story about Brianna. She calmed down a little bit after Reverend Robinson dropped by to pray with her."

Dre hung his head.

"But what I wanna know is how are *you* doin'?"

"I'm fine, Mama."

"No, you're not. I had a bad feelin' come over me late last night. I know you doin' everything you can to find Brianna. I just want you to be careful."

"I am being careful, Mama."

"I have faith that the Lord is gonna take care of Brianna and you gotta have faith too. I don't want you out there doing anything stupid."

Dre grumbled. "Mama, what did Anthony tell you?"

"Nothing. I asked your brother a dozen times to tell me what you were up to, but he wouldn't say a word. That's how I knew you were in trouble. Then this chill just came over me. So I got down on my knees and started praying."

When Dre was a kid, he used to think his mother was psychic. She seemed to know when something was wrong with him even before he did. He knew what was coming next. He could not handle one of his mother's sermons right now.

"Yeah, okay, Mama. I gotta go."

"Don't rush me off the phone. I'm ain't done yet."

Dre closed his eyes and rubbed the back of his neck.

"I've never said it before," his mother continued, "but I want you to know that I'm really proud of you. You stopped sellin' them drugs and turned your life around. I ain't seen too many young men do that. You turned out to be a fine young man. If your daddy was alive, he'd be proud too."

Dre felt a lump the size of an orange expand in his throat.

"But then again," his mother said with a chuckle, "you are *my* son."

Dre laughed. Though he couldn't bring himself to say it, he could really use a hug from his mama about now.

"I love you boy, and I've been praying to God that you don't do something stupid and end up back in jail."

"I won't, Mama," Dre said.

Not unless that's what it takes to bring Brianna back home.

CHAPTER 66

Day Four: 10:45 a.m.

Freda paced up and down the hospital corridor, her smartphone pressed to her ear.

She was trying to reach The Shepherd to give him an update on Clint's condition, but he was deliberately ignoring her calls. When Shep had called her earlier to report what had happened at the club, Freda couldn't believe it when he started ranting about Clint being an idiot. This wasn't Clint's fault.

A nurse walked past, looking her up and down. Freda was wearing a slinky, silver T-strap dress that looked more like a top than a dress. She wasn't wearing a bra and her nipples stuck out like headlights. Her bright-blue eye shadow matched the large flower she'd pinned in her hair.

"You got a problem?" she said to the nosy nurse.

"Ma'am, we don't permit cell phones in ICU." The woman pointed at a sign on the wall.

"I know that." Freda shoved her smartphone inside her purse. "I can read."

A young Asian man in green scrubs approached from the far end of the hallway and slowed near Clint's room. "Are you Clint's doctor?" Freda asked.

"Uh…yes, I am." The man was having trouble keeping his eyes on Freda's face.

"Can you tell me how he's doing?"

"Are you a family member?" the doctor asked.

"Yes. I'm his wife."

"Your husband suffered a very brutal beating. He uh…" The doctor seemed to lose his train of thought.

Freda put a hand on her hip. "Can you please take your eyes off my titties long enough to tell me whether Clint is going to live or die?"

The doctor's face turned crimson.

"Oh, uh…he's got several broken bones and he suffered severe damage to his internal organs. He's no longer critical, but still very serious. The police are going to want to talk to you."

Freda didn't want nothing to do with the police. If they started sniffing around, they might stumble upon something they didn't need to know. She had to leave before they got there.

"Is Clint able to talk to me?"

"I'm afraid not. He's conscious but his jaw was broken, so his mouth is wired shut. And he really does need to rest."

"Can I see him anyway? I won't stay long."

The doctor stole another quick look at her chest. "Uh, sure."

She entered the room and grew frightened by all the beeping lights. Clint's face was a big, swollen ball. His eyes were bloody slits.

"Oh my goodness!" Freda hadn't been all that close to Clint, but she didn't want to see him like this.

She walked closer. "Can you hear me, Clint? If you can, just lift a finger."

Clint raised the index finger of the hand closest to her.

"You're gonna be okay," she said stroking his head. "Shep's gonna get whoever did this."

Though Brianna's uncle hadn't been one of the men who entered the club and kidnapped Clint, they'd known immediately that he was responsible. This was Shep's fault as far as Freda was concerned. They should've given Brianna back the minute they learned about her uncle. Now they were in the middle of a street war. And for what? They had dozens of girls like Brianna.

A single tear rolled from the corner of Clint's eye back toward his hairline.

"That little heffa," Freda seethed through clenched teeth. "I hope Shep makes her ass pay."

CHAPTER 67

Day Four: 11:35 a.m.

Angela and Loretha sat in her office for over an hour, talking about Peaches and the other girls in the house, alternately laughing and crying.

For the third time, Angela checked her smartphone, hoping Dre had responded to one of her many calls and texts.

Loretha pursed her lips. "That's a tough situation you're in."

Angela nodded sadly. "I know."

"You'll get her back."

"I certainly hope so because I don't think Dre will be able to handle it if he doesn't. If something happens to Brianna, he'll kill Shep."

Loretha turned away and stared out of the window. "That might not be a bad thing."

They were both quiet for a long time.

"I want to thank you again for your willingness to take Peaches under your wing," Loretha said. "A lot of people tell me they want to mentor my girls, but few actually mean it."

Loretha stood up.

Angela stayed put. "You're putting me out? There has to be somebody else in this house I can mentor. Who else you got?"

"You serious?"

"As a heart attack. And I was serious about helping you start a mentoring program too."

Loretha seemed to be thinking for a minute. "I do have another girl who could use some mentoring. You briefly met her yesterday. She's all bravado, but she's nothing but a baby underneath. I see something in her that you may be able to bring out. She's Latina, only fourteen. You game?"

"Absolutely." Angela hopped up from the couch. "Let's go meet her."

They walked out of Loretha's office and up the stairs. Loretha knocked softly on Carmen's door, paused a second, then walked in without waiting for the girl's okay.

Carmen was sitting at a small desk, drawing on a scratch pad.

"Carmen's our resident artist," Loretha bragged.

The girl looked up at Angela, rolled her eyes, then went back to her work.

"What are you drawing?" Angela asked.

"My new house. The one I'm gonna have if I can ever break out of this prison."

Angela and Loretha smiled.

"Angela's your new mentor," Loretha said. "I'm going to leave you two alone so you can get to know each other."

Angela sat down on the bed behind the girl.

"So tell me something about yourself?" Angela began.

Carmen turned around. "Look, I don't even wanna be here and—"

The girl took a long look at Angela. "Uh, I don't mean to be rude or nothin', but you look whipped. Your mascara is a mess. You been cryin'?"

Angela stood and examined her face in the mirror on the back of the door.

She tried to wipe the black mascara from underneath her eyes with her fingers.

"Actually, I have," she replied.

Maybe if she showed her own vulnerability, the girl might open up to her.

"So why you cryin'?"

"One of the girls I was mentoring went back to her pimp. I was hoping I could help her see a different side of life."

The girl hunched her shoulders and turned back to her artwork. "Y'all need to understand that being in the life ain't that bad. She's probably like me. She'd rather be with her Daddy than be stuck up in here. It's boring."

Angela knew that now was not the time to try to reason with the girl.

"Also, my friend's thirteen-year-old daughter was kidnapped by a pimp three days ago. We've been trying to find her."

Carmen turned around and faced Angela again. This time, her face showed sympathy.

"See, that's crazy. My daddy don't do that. All his girls wanna be with him. He don't be kidnappin' nobody. Who's her pimp?"

"A guy they called The Shepherd."

Carmen's young eyes expanded. "O-M-G! That girl is in big trouble!"

Angela moved to the end of the bed, closer to Carmen. "You know him?"

"I heard of him. One of my wives-in-law, Shareese, used to be with him. She ran away to be with my daddy. The Shepherd makes his girls work like slaves. All he cares about is money. My daddy never makes us do more than five or six johns a day."

Angela wanted to explain to Carmen the many reasons her *daddy* didn't deserve her praise. But right now, it was more important to find out if she had any information that could help Dre find Brianna.

"Yeah, I heard The Shepherd was hard on his girls," Angela said.

"Hard don't describe it."

"Do you know where his girls live?"

Carmen shook her head.

"Do you think your—" she could barely bring herself to say the word, "wife-in-law Shareese could help us find out where The Shepherd's girls live?"

Carmen shook her head vigorously. "No way. We don't never tell on our daddies. And anyway, Shareese said The Shepherd makes them wear hoods every time they leave the house. They don't even know where they live. The Shepherd is rich. He has lots of houses and he moves his girls around so the po-po can't catch 'em. Y'all just better find her before he breaks her down."

"What do you mean?"

Carmen tapped her index finger against her temple several times. "Get in her head. Your daddy knows how to get into your head and make you loyal. Once they do that, you don't never want to leave the life."

Angela swallowed. This world seemed so unreal. She was sitting here talking to a fourteen-year-old about a pimp. Her eyes moistened at the thought of Brianna, a child she'd never met, being repeatedly raped by grown men.

Carmen noticed Angela's tears and seemed to soften a bit.

"I know one way you might be able to find her," Carmen said empathetically.

Angela wiped her face with a tissue from her purse. "How?"

"Just make a date."

"What do you mean?"

"Everybody know The Shepherd don't have his girls walking the track unless they mess up or mouth off. That's why they think they're better than everybody else. Shareese told me he own his own motels in the Valley. His girls just be in the rooms waiting for the johns to show up. He do everything on the Internet. My daddy don't know how to work a computer that good, but he said he might try to learn one day."

"So how would I go about making a date?"

Carmen huffed in exasperation. "Just go on MyBackPage.com."

"What's that?"

"You really are clueless. It's an Internet site where johns go to make a date. A dude can put in the city and get a list of girls to go on a date with."

Angela was stupefied.

"They pay the money on their credit card, then go to the motel and have their date."

Angela could feel her pulse start to race. "But how would I know I'm getting one of Shep's girls?"

"Cuz he got his brand tattooed on his girls."

"Do you know The Shepherd's brand?"

"It's the letters S and H with a dollar sign."

Angela snatched her purse and pulled her iPad Mini from her purse. Her hands shook as she typed in the letters of the website. It seemed to take forever for the page to load. Angela's shock intensified as she realized what she was looking at. The site did indeed advertise girls for *dates.*

Carmen had joined her on the bed and was looking at the screen too. "If you see a girl's body and her face blurred out like that, it means she's probably under eighteen."

Angela's mouth fell open as she scrolled through screens and screens of girls with blurred faces.

How could this be going on?

"You can't put in no age or nothin'. But say you want somebody with long hair or big tits, you can search for that."

Angela doubted that she would be lucky enough to find Brianna on this site, but if she could identify one of The Shepherd's girls and make a date, that might lead them to the location of one of his motels, and possibly, Brianna.

This seemed so incredibly simple. If this fourteen-year-old knew this, why didn't the police?

"Just put in L.A. and look for one of the young girls with The Shepherd's brand and make a date," Carmen directed her. "He might have her working at his motel tonight."

Carmen had no idea how valuable this information was.

"Y'all coulda found her a long time ago," Carmen said. "All you needed to do was make a date."

Still stunned, Angela stared at this womanly child and shook her head.

Out of the mouths of babes.

CHAPTER 68

Day Four: 12:10 p.m.

The Shepherd finally took Freda's call giving him an update on Clint's condition. He listened, expressing no sign of emotion or concern.

"I don't care whether Clint lives or dies," he said coldly, when Freda had finished. "He betrayed me with his stupidity. Just make sure that girl is on lockdown."

He hung up without saying good-bye.

The events of the last few hours were not reason for alarm or panic. They dictated calm deliberation. Fools and amateurs panicked. He could not run successful operations by freaking out at the first sign of a glitch.

The Shepherd could not deny, however, that Andre "Dre" Thomas was turning out to be a much bigger problem than he had anticipated. It wasn't often that The Shepherd underestimated his opponents. Few had ever challenged him over the years. It was his fault for becoming lax, for handing his operation over to men who did not have the appropriate mental acumen. He would fix that.

The Shepherd showered and dressed in black slacks and a white Polo shirt. Black men in the hood were always complaining about being hassled by the cops. If they didn't want to be harassed, then they shouldn't dress like hoodlums and speak as if they'd never gone to school.

Standing in the foyer of his great room, Shep surveyed his magnificent surroundings. His intellect and drive had earned him millions. He would not lose this. He would not lose his freedom. He would fix this problem.

He walked outside and spotted a large Italian who was pretending to paint his home. He was actually a bodyguard The Shepherd had hired just in case Andre Thomas was foolish enough to actually come to his neighborhood. He couldn't believe Clint had actually given up his address.

The Shepherd waved to his neighbor.

"Good afternoon, Bill," he said to the lawyer who was finishing his mid-day walk.

"Hey, Rodney," Bill called back. "Beautiful day in paradise, isn't it?"

The Shepherd laughed. "Yes, indeed."

Sliding behind the wheel of his Bentley, The Shepherd headed for City Stars. It was over an hour before he arrived at the club. The Shepherd reminded himself to keep his emotions in check once he got inside. A true leader never lost his composure.

It was well past the lunch hour, but the club was still packed with businessmen. At this time of the day, his clientele was mostly white and Asian. These men had jobs that did not require them to punch a time clock. By evening, the club would be all black.

The Shepherd stopped to admire the new girl on stage. He would definitely have to try her out.

He ascended the back staircase to his private office on the second level. He had not taken the time to greet any of the workers whose bills he paid, though they all smiled his way. They knew he was the owner, but little else about him. He preferred it that way.

Large followed him into the office and closed the door. He waited in silence as The Shepherd settled into a red leather chair behind a massive, black lacquer desk. Shep steepled his fingers, then looked up at his underling.

"How did this happen?"

"Uh...the dudes weren't even carrying. They grabbed Clint and dragged him out the back door before anybody even knew what happened."

"How many bouncers work here?"

"Four."

"And where were they?"

"Two dudes started fighting. Everybody went to deal with that."

"And who do you think set up that fight?"

"I...uh..." Large's vacant eyes indicated that he'd just put two and two together.

A warrior must take the blame for the mistakes of the weak.

"Never mind." The Shepherd inhaled. "You can leave."

He would deal with the inadequate security of his operation after he had discussed this problem with the one person who was ultimately responsible for this entire ordeal.

The Shepherd took out an untraceable cell phone and dialed.

"You've created a tremendous problem for me," were his first words to the man. There was no need for introductions or niceties.

"What are you talking about?"

"The last girl you gave us did not fit my criteria."

He could sense the man's nervousness through the phone line.

"Her uncle is causing problems for me. And if he's causing a problem for me, he's also causing a problem for you."

The Shepherd's operation had worked smoothly up until now because he targeted the right girls.

The man finally spoke. "She *did* fit the criteria. She didn't have a mother or father in the picture and lived with her grandmother. I didn't know about her uncle. It wasn't my job to check out the whole family tree."

The Shepherd's teeth clenched at the man's lack of respect.

"You must be more careful in the future."

"You're going to keep my name out of this, right?"

Shep chuckled. He was surrounded by weakness.

"Just send the girl back home," the man said. "Leave it at that. We have others in the pipeline."

"Maybe you should send back that thousand-dollar finder's fee I paid you."

That suggestion was met with silence.

"I just don't want any trouble. Everything has been running smoothly. Just give her back."

"You must be more careful in the future," The Shepherd admonished him. "For your safety as well as mine."

CHAPTER 69

Day Four: 3:30 p.m.

Bonnie remained in her classroom after the ending bell, hoping to get a few papers graded. She couldn't concentrate, however, because her mind kept wondering what she was going to stumble onto when she walked into the administration office.

She eyed the clock on the wall at the back of the classroom. Chiquita had been on the job for about thirty minutes. Now would be a good time to find out what kind of *work* Chiquita was really doing.

Bonnie stuck the papers she was grading into a folder and slid it into her oversized purse. She looked around the classroom to make sure everything was in place, then turned out the lights.

Bonnie wanted to talk to Wainright about her suspicions, but figured she should have some evidence before going to him. The hallway outside was deserted and the school was quiet. This was the time of day she liked most.

Her steps slowed the closer she got to the administration office. She knew the staff would be gone. They hightailed it out the minute their shifts ended. If anybody else was still around, she hoped it would be Wainright. She would need a credible witness.

When she entered the office, she did not see Chiquita behind the counter. No one was present.

My goodness! Please don't tell me that fool has the audacity to be alone with that girl in his office.

Bonnie reached down and unlocked the latch on the swinging gate that allowed her to enter the area behind the front counter. The door to Principal Ortiz's office was closed.

So where was Chiquita?

Bonnie peered down a hallway, but did not see or hear any signs of life.

Gathering up her courage, she knocked on the door of the principal's office.

"Who is it?" he yelled through the door.

Was that rustling inside the office?

"Ms. Flanagan," she yelled back.

A full minute passed before Ortiz's door opened. He stood in the way, blocking her view of the office's interior.

"Can I help you?" He was not happy to have been disturbed.

"I'm looking for Chiquita Gomez."

"And why would you be looking for her in my office?"

"She told me she was working in the administration office after school today."

"Yeah and?"

"So where is she?"

"She already left."

Bonnie turned to look at the clock on the wall behind her. "School's barely been out for forty-five minutes. How long did she work?"

"I didn't have much for her to do today, so she left early."

You liar. That girl is hiding in your office right now. That's why you won't open the door.

"Is that right?"

"Yeah, that's right."

"Are you sure she's not in your office?"

"Ms. Flanagan, you're way out of line. I've been tolerating your disrespect because you're a good teacher. But you're really pushing it. Exactly what are you implying?"

"I'm just wondering why you'd have a student working alone in your office when no one else is around. That seems highly inappropriate."

"Look, Chiquita has a rough family life. The free lunch she gets at school is the only meal she has on most days. I made up some work for her to do as an excuse to give her a few bucks. She's a good kid."

"I don't believe you."

"And just what do you believe?"

"I believe there's something inappropriate going on between you and that child."

Ortiz's eyes shot rays of fire into hers.

"Do you understand that I hold your career in my hands, Ms. Flanagan? I could have you out of here just like that." He snapped his fingers.

"You'd have to have a reason to get me out of here."

"I could make one up."

Bonnie wished she'd been smart enough to turn on the tape recorder on her smartphone.

"That would be retaliation."

"So? Happens all the time."

"If there's nothing inappropriate going on between you and that girl, open the door and let me check your office."

"What you're insinuating is both outrageous and defamatory. I'm not letting you in my office."

"You would if you didn't have anything to hide."

Ortiz angrily stared her down, then stepped back and flung open the door.

Bonnie stepped inside and to her shock, Chiquita was not in the office. She was about to turn and leave when she remembered the principal's private bathroom. Without asking, she charged into it. Empty.

"You satisfied now?"

No, I'm not satisfied.

"Okay, fine," she said. "I was mistaken. I apologize."

Ortiz's nostrils flared. "Just like you were mistaken about those missing girls. You can leave now." Ortiz slammed the door a second after she stepped across the threshold.

Bonnie still wasn't convinced that nothing was going on. Chiquita probably told Ortiz about their conversation. Maybe that was the reason he sent her home early.

Now Bonnie was even more worried. Ortiz was a fundamentally vindictive man. She wouldn't put it past him to make up something to get back at her. He practically said he would. To protect herself, she would report the incident to Wainright first thing in the morning.

In the meantime, Bonnie would just have to watch her back. The next time she confronted that pervert, she'd be sure to get his fat butt on tape.

CHAPTER 70

Day Four: 3:45 p.m.

Dre wolfed down the food Mossy had picked up and drank almost a liter of water. A few hours of sleep, plus the food was exactly what his body craved.

"I wanna go back to some of those houses," Dre insisted. "They're probably moving Brianna around. We can stake out a couple of 'em and maybe we'll get lucky."

"Man, luck ain't on our side," Mossy said. "I think we should stay put until The Shepherd calls back. The ball's in his court now. He ain't gonna hurt Brianna cuz he don't want you on his ass for the rest of his life."

What Mossy was saying made sense. He just wished he could make himself believe it.

"When The Shepherd calls back," Mossy advised for the ump-teenth time, "you can't piss him off. Just suck up to him. We'll get his ass later."

Dre flinched when he heard the ringing of his smartphone.

Mossy grabbed it from the coffee table before Dre could reach it. The caller ID showed that it was a blocked call.

"This is probably him again." Mossy turned it on and pressed the speakerphone button.

"Yeah?" Dre said.

"I've had some time to think," The Shepherd began.

"Just give me my niece back," Dre said, "and we can both go our separate ways. If you want a war, I can give you that. But from what I hear, you're not big on violence." *Unless you're beating up some innocent kid.*

"You hear right, my brother. There's no need to resort to violence. I use my head. That's what's made me a very wealthy man. But I'm a little leery since I thought we had a deal, then you and your boys came onto my property disrespecting me."

"I guess I didn't trust you to hold up your end of the bargain."

It was suddenly clear to Dre that Shep wanted an end to this battle as much as he did. That was the only reason he'd called back. Loretha had described him as a punk at heart. As hard as it was to do, Dre decided to follow Mossy's advice and appeal to the man's ego.

"I'm ready to call it quits," Dre said.

His voice broke in a manner that Mossy probably thought was feigned, but it wasn't an act. His emotions were slipping away from him.

"You know what? This is the first time I truly believe you, my brother. You finally sound like a man who realizes his limitations."

"I do," Dre said, deciding to pour it on even thicker. "I...I just want Brianna back. I'm beggin' you."

"Now that's what I'm talking about," Shep said. "Act like you understand the situation."

"I do. So let's do this."

"You got my money?"

"Yeah. Just tell me where I can meet you to pick up Brianna and that's where I'll be."

Shep was quiet. Mossy gave Dre an encouraging nod and a smile, then hit the mute button on the smartphone.

"It's working," he said. "This brother don't want no more trouble from us. Just continue to play it his way."

Mossy tapped the screen again, unmuting the smartphone.

"Tonight," Shep said. "We can do the exchange tonight."

"When and where?"

There was a long gap of silence.

"The Westfield Mall on Slauson."

Dre gave Mossy a puzzled look. Mossy opened his hands palms up and shrugged.

"Why there?"

"In a crowded place like that, neither of us has an advantage."

"Okay," Dre said tentatively. "What time?"

"Nine-thirty. The mall closes at ten. That should give us enough time. I'll have Brianna near the entrance of JC Penny's."

"So you'll be there?"

He chuckled. "Hell no. I'm sending one of my guys. You wait on the top level in the food court. You'll be able to look down and see her. One of my guys will meet you up there and take the money. Put it in a duffle bag. Once he checks it out, the guy on the first level will let Brianna go and walk away."

"You make it sound pretty simple."

"It will be. And if you're stupid enough to try any heroics, I'll have somebody slit her throat right then and there."

"You'd do that in the middle of a crowded mall?"

"I'm not doing a thing. You'd be amazed at what you can get people to do for you."

Dre prayed that this was simply a bluff. "Okay. I'll be there. You'll get your money and I'll get Brianna and we can both go our separate ways. Otherwise the violence could get rough."

"You threatening me?"

Mossy raised his hand in a slicing motion across his neck.

"Uh, no. That wasn't what I meant. We both need to abide by the code of the street. You give me your word, I'll give you mine."

"In light of your recent conduct, your word means nothing to me," The Shepherd said.

"We both understand business," Dre replied. "You don't want a war that will never end and I want Brianna back. So let's do this."

Shep took his time responding again. "Then I guess we got a deal, Businessman."

CHAPTER 71

Day Four: 4:30 p.m.

"Okay, who wants to start?"

Loretha surveyed the eight girls gathered in the living room at Harmony House. They were all suddenly mute. The group sessions were always slow to get started. But in another fifteen minutes, she wouldn't be able to shut them up.

"Carmen, why don't you begin," Loretha prodded. "Tell us three things you like about yourself."

She shrugged. "I don't know."

"I'll help you," Loretha said. "You have a beautiful smile."

"Yeah, I do, don't I?" Carmen flashed a wide grin.

The other girls laughed.

"Now tell me something else about yourself that you like."

Carmen stared at the ceiling as if she was trying to think up something. "Oh, I know. According to the johns, I have very nice chi chis."

The other girls laughed again. Loretha did not.

"No," she said gently, "I want to hear something *you* like about yourself."

Carmen cupped her forehead as if the assignment made her head hurt. "I can't think of nothing, Ms. Loretha."

"Okay, I'll help you out again. You're very smart."

Carmen responded with a look of disbelief.

"You are," Loretha insisted. "You helped Angela out on the computer. She told me she couldn't believe how smart you were."

"For real?" Carmen said with a stunned expression. "That lady lawyer said I was smart?"

"She sure did. I can't believe you're forgetting the one thing you're extremely good at."

Carmen was genuinely baffled. "What?"

"Who's the best artist in this house?"

"Oh, snap!" Carmen said. "I can't believe I forgot. I'm definitely good at that." Carmen stood up and took a bow.

This time, Loretha laughed along with the girls.

"Sometimes, when we've had a hard time in life, we tend to only think about the bad things that've happened to us, instead of remembering about all the good things too. I want you girls to focus more on the good than the bad."

Another girl's hand shot up.

"Okay, Melody. You want to go next?"

"My social worker told me I'm strong cuz of everything I been through."

"You got that right," Loretha said.

"And what else?"

"Uh, I think that's about it."

"No, it's not. I'd say you're very helpful."

Melody grinned. "I am?"

"You're always the one volunteering to help Anamaria clean the kitchen, even when it's not your day. And whenever a new girl arrives, you're always the first one to reach out to be her friend."

Melody pressed a finger to her chin. "You right, Ms. Loretha. I am helpful, huh?"

"I want everybody to grab a piece of paper and a pen and write down five things you like about yourself."

"Five?" The girls all moaned in unison. "That's too many."

"I'm going to the kitchen to get cupcakes. And you'll only get a cupcake if you have five things on your paper."

"That ain't fair," another girl protested. "You already gave Carmen and Melody some of theirs."

"You're right," Loretha replied. "Carmen you come up with five more since I came up with the first three and Melody, you come up with four more."

Carmen folded her arms. "Aw, that's cold, Ms. Loretha."

"Just do it."

Loretha went into the kitchen and pulled paper plates from the cabinet. She'd only been gone a couple of minutes when she heard a commotion coming from the living room. She hurried back to the girls.

When she entered the living room, she found them all gathered around the front door, trying to get a look through the peephole at the same time.

"What are you girls doing?"

"There's a homeless man on the porch," Carmen said. "He might be trying to break in."

Loretha leaned in and looked through the peephole herself. The man was standing so close to the door she could not get a good look at him.

He knocked hard and Loretha jumped back, bumping into one of the girls. Her first thought was that the man was some pimp trying to disguise himself as a homeless bum so he could break in and snatch one of her girls. She needed to get her gun. But not in front of the girls.

"Go to your rooms," she yelled at them, before turning back to the door. None of the girls moved.

"You might need us to help you beat him up," Carmen said.

"What do you want?" Loretha yelled through the door.

"It's me," the gruff voice answered.

"And who the hell is me?"

The voice was barely audible. "Rena."

Loretha stiffened and didn't say anything for several seconds. "Step back so I can see you better," she said.

Rena did and Loretha started bawling.

Melody patted her on the back. "You okay, Ms. Loretha? What's wrong? Who is it?"

Loretha opened the door and stared lovingly at Rena. Loretha leaned forward to give her a hug, but Rena backed away. Her hair was matted to her head and there were open sores on her cheek and forehead. Her clothes were smudged with dirt, and she smelled like a dead animal.

"Yuck!" one of the girls said. "I hope she ain't comin' in here cuz she stank."

"C'mon on in. I'm so glad to see you!" Loretha gushed through her tears.

Rena stepped across the threshold and Loretha was about to close the door when Rena pointed behind her.

"What?"

"My stuff," she mumbled, pointing to her grocery cart.

"It'll be safe there," Loretha said.

Rena's eyes flickered with alarm and she took a step back onto the porch.

"Okay, okay," Loretha said. "I'll help you bring it inside."

The girls just stared at the exchange, keeping their distance as if Rena's stink might rub off on them.

"This is Rena," Loretha said, introducing her to the group. "She's an old friend of mine. She went through some of the same things you all went through, but it went very, very badly for her."

Loretha was quietly weeping, and didn't try to hide her tears from the girls. "But she's here with us now and we're all going to rally around her and help her heal, okay?"

The girls kept their distance.

"Why you crying, Ms. Loretha?" Carmen asked. "You okay?"

"I'm fine," Loretha said. "I need someone to help me get Rena upstairs and washed up."

Melody's hand shot up in the air.

"I'll do it," she said, stepping forward. "Cuz I'm good at helping people."

CHAPTER 72

Day Four: 4:45 p.m.

Freda leaned against the kitchen counter, drinking straight from the Vodka bottle. Everything was such a mess. Clint was practically on his deathbed and Shep couldn't care less. She would never forgive him for his callousness. Not the way Clint slaved for him.

She checked her smartphone again, wondering if she had missed Shep's call.

In the two years since she'd become part of Shep's inner circle, no one had ever come looking for any of the girls they'd abducted. So the situation with Brianna made them all nervous. Freda had spent a few days in lockup when she was walking the track, but she had never done any real time. That possibility made her shudder.

Her smartphone rang and she jumped.

"How's the girl?" Shep asked when she answered the call.

"She's here with me. She's tied up *and* drugged. What are we going to do with her?"

"We're going to give her back."

This surprised Freda. Shep did not like being challenged. If he was folding, the situation was likely more serious than even she had imagined. She thought of Clint, broken and bruised.

"If we do, is this guy going to just go away?"

"I suspect he will. He's a former drug dealer. So neither the cops nor a prosecutor are likely to believe anything he says. And the fact that he nearly got Clint killed is another reason I think he'll walk away once he gets her back. Businessman could be charged with assault and attempted murder, which would mean an automatic suspension of his parole."

That made Freda feel much better. Shep always had a plan. The sooner Brianna was gone, the better for all of them.

"Okay," Freda said. "Where do you want me to take her? Should I just drop her off in a parking lot somewhere."

"Nope. She's going to the Wyndgate."

That surprised her. The Wyndgate was The Shepherd's busiest motel. They should drop her off someplace with no connection to them.

"The Wyndgate?" she asked.

"Yes."

"You're having her uncle pick her up there? That's nuts."

Shep did not speak, which was a sign that he was angry. She had not meant to disrespect him and she knew Shep had interpreted her comment that way. But what he was suggesting *was* nuts.

"Do you believe in me, Freda?"

"Yes, of course."

"How much money would you say I've made you?"

"Lots," she said. "I'd say at least eighty grand so far this year."

"Yes."

"You never made money like that before you met me."

"No," she said softly.

"So trust me to know what I'm doing."

There was another break in the conversation, this one, much longer. Freda knew better than to open her mouth.

"Have Brianna dressed for a date and ready at five."

Freda lifted the bottle to her lips and took a long gulp. "Okay."

Shep chuckled. "Brianna's going to have a little fun before heading back home."

Freda didn't understand why Shep didn't stop playing around and just give the girl back. But she wasn't about to say that.

"Large will pick her up," he said. "I've already spoken to him. After she's done with her date, he's taking her to meet her uncle."

"Are you setting her up with one of our regulars?"

"Yeah."

"Her face is all black and blue. I'll do my best to cover up her bruises."

"Don't waste your time," Shep said with a laugh. "This client'll like that."

"Who is it?" Freda asked.

"Little Ms. Brianna's going to get a real treat this evening. She's going on a date with Demonic."

CHAPTER 73

Day Four: 5:15 p.m.

Dre and Mossy had just pulled out of the parking lot of Dre's apartment complex and onto LaBrea Boulevard. Despite his agreement with The Shepherd to exchange Brianna for cash later tonight, Dre refused to sit still and wait. He insisted on checking The Shepherd's houses again to see if anybody was there. Mossy thought it was a bad idea, but relented after Dre agreed to let him drive.

Dre's smartphone rang. He picked it up from the center console of his Jetta and saw that the call was from Angela.

This was her third call in less than an hour. His energy and his focus had to be completely on the job ahead of him. He would call Angela back later. After he had safely rescued Brianna.

The second he set the smartphone back down, it buzzed, announcing an incoming text.

"That your girl again?" Mossy asked.

"Yeah."

"You need to call her. She's worried about you."

He reached for his smartphone and read the text.

Angela: I know how 2 find b!!! where r u

Dre read the screen twice. Both times, in disbelief. Maybe Angela was just trying to trick him into responding. A second later, another text came in.

Angela: where the hell r u???

He turned to Mossy. "Angela says she knows how to find Bree."
"What? How?"
"Hell if I know."
Dre fired off a return text.

Dre: just leaving house
Angela: meet me at Starbucks on Crenshaw
Dre: why
Angela: just call me now!

Dre didn't know what to make of Angela's message. He dialed her number, but as soon as she picked up, his smartphone went dead.
He was out of juice.

* * *

Dre and Mossy waited inside the Starbucks, eager for Angela to arrive. When Dre had called her back on Mossy's smartphone, Angela rushed him off the line, saying she would explain everything when she got there.

Dre was too nervous to sit or stand, so he paced in a tight circle. Mossy had just picked up their coffee orders when Angela sprinted in.

"I know how to find Brianna!" she said, her face flush. "You need to make a date online!"

Dre's face went blank. "What?"

Angela led them to a small table in a corner of the store. She pulled out her iPad and started tapping the screen as Dre and Mossy stared over her shoulder.

When MyBackPage.com popped up, Angela explained what she was doing.

"This is a site where guys go to buy sex. The Shepherd puts his girls on here."

She tapped the screen, scanning through girl after girl—all of them wearing next to nothing. "Every time you see the girl's face blurred out, it probably means she's under-aged."

"How could this be legal?" Mossy asked, taking a sip of his coffee.

"Technically, these sites aren't selling sex, they're selling *dates*. Despite the fact that the girls are posing with their legs spread open and their breast exposed, these ads say nothing about sex. So technically they're not breaking the law."

Dre grabbed a chair and sat down next to her.

"I'm narrowing our search to the L.A. area and we're going to look for a girl who meets Brianna's physical characteristics," Angela said. "And then you're going to make a date."

"How do we know Brianna is on there?" Dre asked.

"We don't. But even if she's not, we may find one of The Shepherd's other girls, which could then lead us to Brianna."

Dre's head swirled with excitement. "But wait a minute. How do you know which girls are Shep's?"

"He brands his girls. Most of them have tattoos of the letters *SH* followed by a dollar sign." Angela pointed at a scrawny white girl whose face was blurred. "Look right there, you can see it just below her neck."

The tattoo looked as if it hadn't even healed yet.

"How did you learn all this?" Mossy asked.

"I'll explain later. Give me your credit card," she said to Dre. "We're going to make a date with her. Since her face is blurred out, she's probably a minor."

Dre eased his wallet from his back pocket, slipped out his Visa and handed it to Angela. She punched in his email address, credit card number and the other requested information.

"Okay," she said, "somebody's going to call you on Mossy's cell and arrange a date."

"I don't understand why the cops don't shut this stuff down," Mossy said.

"There aren't enough vice cops in the world to monitor these sites," Angela said. "Oh, and if you just want a live strip show from the comfort of your home, you can have that too. Angela hit a few keys and a soft female voice purred at them.

Hey, you! Thanks for visiting my website, Any Way You Want It. Would you like to see what I have to offer? Well, how much time do you have and how much are you willing to spend? Just put in your credit card number and I promise to make it worth your while. It'll cost you five dollars a minute or two-fifty for a whole hour. Whether you want ten minutes of my time or ten hours, I promise to blow your mind!"

The woman took out one of her boobs and licked her nipple. Angela muted the sound.

"This is unbelievable," Mossy said.

"Just type in your credit card number and you can watch her masturbate, have sex with a man or another woman or you can make a special request and she'll do whatever you tell her to do. And it's all live."

"Is some pimp behind this too?" Dre asked.

"I doubt it. She's probably a soccer mom just trying to make some extra money on the side. You'll find a lot of married couples on here willing to have sex online to help pay the monthly bills."

Angela glanced at her watch. "We should get a call to set up a date any minute."

At that very second, Mossy's smartphone rang. Dre hit the speakerphone button, then lowered the volume so no one around them could overhear.

"Yeah?"

"Hi, sweetie, I understand you want a date tonight."

The woman on the phone sounded much too mature to be the girl shown in the picture.

"Yeah," Dre said.

"You're not a cop, are you?"

"Naw," Dre said.

Angela spun her finger in a circular motion, nudging him to embellish. "I saw your picture and I liked…I really liked your body." He could not stomach talking this way to a stranger.

The woman's voice changed. "It ain't my picture. I just schedule the dates. And just so you know, our girls don't have no sex," she said sharply. "It's just a date. If you want sex, you need to call somebody else cuz that's illegal."

The woman had obviously been properly coached.

"I know that," Dre said. "I just want to spend some time with you. Get to know you. When can we get together?"

The woman hesitated. "You sure you're not a cop."

Dre realized that he had to assure her that he was on the up-and-up. So he discarded his disdain and played the role that would get him the date he needed.

"I already told you. I ain't no cop. So when can I meet—" he glanced down at the screen, looking for the girl's name— "Ms. Prissy 8942? Can we do it today?"

Dre heard a muffled male voice in the background. The woman was obviously being told what to say. Dre just hoped they'd lucked up and this was indeed The Shepherd's operation.

"As long as you ain't playin' no games," the woman chided him.

"I'm ready right now. Where are you located?"

"In the Valley."

Dre shook his fist. This was a good sign. "I can be there in less than an hour. What's the address?"

Dre wrote it down and shot up from the chair.

"Let's roll."

CHAPTER 74

Day Four: 5:40 p.m.

Dre sat in the passenger seat, pressing his right fist into the palm of his left hand, cracking his knuckles.

"Man, you gotta stop fidgeting," Mossy said. "You're making me nervous. We're going to find her."

It had only taken them forty-five minutes to get to the address the girl had given him. They'd exited the 101 Freeway at Laurel Canyon and drove another four miles before locating the motel.

"Keep going," Dre said, quietly. "Park up the street." He needed to get himself mentally ready for this.

Mossy did as instructed. Unlike Apache, his buddy knew when to ask questions and when to keep quiet. Right now, Dre needed quiet.

They parked half a block away on the opposite side of the street. They still had a clear view of the Vegastown Motel. The two-story building appeared long neglected, with peeling paint, cloudy windows and railings in need of repair. There was a lot adjacent to the motel with parking for a dozen or so cars and a few more parking spaces directly outside the first-floor rooms.

Dre glanced at his watch. "It's time."

Just in case he was being watched, Dre decided to arrive alone. Mossy got out of the car and started casing the area on foot.

Dre eased his Jetta into a parking space near the room he'd been given. He told himself not to get his hopes up. It wasn't like he was going to walk into the room and have some girl tell him exactly where to find Brianna. But then again, maybe God would show him some mercy. He'd been praying so hard, maybe it would be just that easy. He climbed out of the car and walked slowly toward room 5.

He braced himself, then knocked on the door. He looked over his shoulder, but did not see anyone watching him. Within seconds, the door opened and he stepped inside.

The tiny white girl standing before him looked as if she belonged in elementary school.

"Hey, uh…hey, baby," the girl said. Dre could tell that she was just as nervous as he was. Her tiny hands were actually trembling. "You ready for your date?"

Dre wanted to pick her up and shake her until she started behaving like the child that she was. She should be home playing with a Barbie doll.

Dre swallowed. "What's your name?"

"Kaylee. So what kind of date do you want?"

Dre wasn't sure how to answer. "What kind of dates do you have?"

"Uh, blow jobs are fifty. Missionary position is one hundred and doggie style is two hundred. But you have to wear a condom."

The girl spoke as if she was reading from a script.

Dre felt sick to his stomach. After he got Brianna back, he was going to stay parked at this roach motel and beat down every pervert who showed up to have sex with one of these kids.

He glanced over his shoulder. Though he hadn't seen anybody, he assumed the girl's protection was just outside. He had to be careful about how he approached her. He didn't want her to scream for help.

"I just wanna talk for now." He sat down on the bed, facing her.

"Okay, that's good," the girl said nervously. "But if I don't get no money, they gonna beat me."

Dre pulled out his wallet and gave her three twenty-dollar bills.

The girl looked relieved. She turned around and protruded her rear end toward him. "Do you wanna touch me?"

Dre pounced from the bed. With one hand, he grabbed Kaylee from behind, locking her arms at her side, lifting her off the floor. With his other hand, he covered her mouth.

Kaylee twisted and struggled, trying to get away, but was easily restrained.

"Relax," Dre whispered. "I'm not going to hurt you. I just need you to answer a few questions for me," he said gently. "When I take my hand from your mouth, you better not scream. Okay?"

Dre felt her tears dampen his fingers. He slowly lifted his hand.

"Please don't hurt me," Kaylee cried. "I'll do whatever you want me to do. Just don't hurt me."

"I just want to talk to you, okay?"

She nodded.

Dre lowered her to the ground, then turned her around so she was facing him.

"I'm not going to hurt you," he said firmly. "All I want is information and then I'll leave. Okay?"

Kaylee stared into his eyes for several seconds, then took off for the door. Dre had his hand back over her mouth before she'd managed to cover two feet.

The girl was sobbing hysterically now.

"I'm trying to find my niece," Dre said, holding her from behind. He could see her face in the mirror across the room. "Are you one of The Shepherd's girls?"

He could feel her quaking in his arms.

"Are you?"

When she nodded, Dre removed his hand from her mouth. "Please don't scream," he said.

He returned to the bed and swung her around so she was facing him again. Though he was sitting and she was standing, they were practically eye level. It was only then that he spotted The Shepherd's brand near her collarbone.

"Do you know where I can find The Shepherd?"

Kaylee shook her head.

"Don't lie to me. I promise I won't hurt you."

"The Shepherd don't never come to the house," she cried. "I don't know where he live. I swear."

"Where does he keep his girls? Where do you stay?"

"I don't know. They always cover our heads when we leave the house. But it's not too far from here because it only took us a few minutes to get here. I swear I don't know where it is."

The girl's eyes wandered toward the door. "You takin' too long. You gonna get me beat. He's gonna check on me in a minute."

"Who?"

"Darnell. He drove me here."

Dre pulled up Brianna's picture on his smartphone. "Have you seen this girl before?"

"Oh my God!" Kaylee covered her own mouth this time. "That's Brianna. Are you her Uncle Dre?"

Dre's mouth fell open.

"How do you know my name?"

"Brianna kept tellin' everybody you was gonna come rescue her. She wouldn't do nothin' they told her to do."

That news made Dre feel good enough to float right out of the room. Brianna wasn't only alive, she was giving them hell.

"Do you know where she is?"

"They don't let us stay in the same room no more. But she was at the house when we left. But I swear I don't know where it is."

"Is Darnell taking you back to the house?"

"Yeah, but I have three more dates."

Three more dates?

He wanted to grab the girl and take her with him.

There was a pounding on the door. "Kaylee, you okay in there?"

Kaylee's eyes met Dre's.

"Yeah, I'm okay," she yelled toward the door. "We almost done."

She turned back to Dre. "You have to hurry up! He gonna expect me to make a lotta money after all this time."

Dre took another forty bucks from his wallet and gave it to her.

"Thanks for helping me," he said, starting for the door.

"So you don't want no date?" Kaylee asked in surprise. "You already paid me."

"How old are you?" Dre asked, walking back over to her.

"I'm eighteen," Kaylee said half-heartedly.

"How old are you for real?"

Kaylee's eyes fell to the ratty carpet. "Twelve."

"Why aren't you in school?"

"I didn't like school. Everybody made fun of me because I lived in a foster home. Jaden was gonna take me away. But he was just fake."

Based on all the things Loretha had told them, he knew this girl had a tragic story just like all the others. His eyes bounced around the room until he spotted what he was looking for. He picked up a discarded store receipt from the end table.

He scribbled down his cell number on the back and gave it to her. "You ever heard of Harmony House?"

Kaylee hitched her shoulders. "Nope."

"They help girls like you get away from their pimps. They'll give you a safe place to stay. When you're ready to leave, I want you to find a way to call me and I'm going to help you escape. I want you to memorize my number, then tear up that paper so nobody'll see it."

Kaylee stared down at the paper, then looked up, dumbfounded. "Why you wanna help me?"

"Because you don't deserve this," Dre said. "So when you're ready, I want you to call me."

CHAPTER 75

Day Four: 6:30 p.m.

Dre stepped out of the motel room and was almost nose-to-nose with Darnell. The dude looked like a Skid Row bum. His skin was a pimpled mess and his teeth were way past rotten.

"Hope you had a good time, my brother," Darnell said, grinning. "We got a large selection of youngsters, if that's your thing. And we give repeat clients ten percent off."

Dre did everything in his power to restrain himself from pushing the skinny man's head through the window. He walked past him without responding.

Just as he reached his car, Mossy appeared from nowhere and climbed into the passenger seat.

"You find out anything?" Mossy asked, once they were inside.

"The girl recognized Brianna. She's definitely at one of The Shepherd's houses. But she doesn't know the address. They cover the girls' heads every time they leave so they don't know where they're going."

Mossy smiled. "Well, don't sweat it, my brother. I—"

Dre cut him off. "We're going to stay here until she's done. When that dude up there takes her back home, we're following them back to the house."

Mossy smiled wider this time. "Great minds think alike. See that white 4Runner over there?" He pointed at an SUV parked right outside the room Dre had entered.

"That's the ride of the dude who knocked on the door when you were in the room with that girl. I'm assuming he's the one transporting her. We'll have no trouble following him because I stuck a GPS tracker underneath his truck. He's going to lead us straight to Brianna. All we have to do is wait."

Dre smiled and extended his fist to Mossy, who bumped it against his own.

"I just hope we can wrap this up before nine. Because if she's not there, we have to make it back over to the Westfield Mall."

"I told you, man, we're going to get her back," Mossy said.

For some reason, this time, Dre believed him.

* * *

It was another forty minutes before they saw Darnell and Kaylee leave the motel room. Darnell also hustled two other girls from upper rooms into his SUV. They could actually see Darnell give the girls hoods to put over their heads. He must have instructed them to lay down because they could not see them through the window.

Despite Mossy's objections, Dre had called Apache, who was now sitting in the backseat.

"Man, once we got little shorty back, The Shepherd gonna have to deal with me," Apache announced.

Mossy gave Dre a look. He knew the risks posed by having Apache join them. But neither Mossy nor Dre was strapped. If things got ugly they needed someone who had fire power and wasn't afraid to use it.

Thanks to the GPS device, they did not have to follow Darnell very closely. The 4Runner drove down Ventura Boulevard for several miles. The traffic most of the way was stop and go.

"Hey, man," Mossy said, "I forgot to tell you I took pictures of the dudes going into the other girls' rooms. I assumed they were johns, but you never know."

Mossy pulled out his smartphone and held it up so Dre could see it. "You recognize that guy?"

"No."

Mossy scrolled to the next picture. "What about this cat? He didn't go into any of the rooms, but I saw him talking to the guy transporting the girls."

The picture was taken from several yards away and showed a side view of the man.

Dre stared at the screen for way too long. "I think I do know him."

Mossy seemed surprised. "You do?"

"Yeah, but I can't place him."

Dre's eyes went to the road, then back to the picture.

"Wait a minute." Dre pounded the steering wheel with the heel of his fist.

He snatched the smartphone from Mossy and examined the photograph more closely.

"Who is he?" Apache asked. "We can get his ass too."

It had never made sense to Dre that The Shepherd had targeted Brianna. She didn't fit the profile of the girls he went after. She wasn't a runaway or a foster kid. She was a good student from a good home. But now Dre understood exactly how Brianna had gotten caught up in this nightmare.

"Somebody with access to children is steering girls to The Shepherd," he fumed. "And that's the pervert who's doing it. As soon as we get Brianna back, I'm goin' after his ass."

CHAPTER 76

Day Four: 7:30 p.m.

"Wake up," Freda grabbed Brianna's upper arm and pulled her to her feet. She managed to stand unsteadily, then slithered down the wall.

"I told you to wake up!" Freda screamed. "You're going on a date."

Brianna was sluggish from whatever drugs they had pumped into her system.

"I don't wanna go on a date. I wanna go home."

"You *are* going home," Freda said. "Right after your date. Your uncle's been causing us too many problems. We're sending you back."

Freda's words seemed to energize Brianna.

"I'm going home?"

"Yep, right after your date."

Brianna didn't trust Freda, but maybe she was telling the truth this time. She had been praying to God harder than she had ever prayed in her life.

"Here," Freda handed her a black leather skirt and a pink halter top. "Put this on."

When she didn't take the clothes, Freda backhanded her.

Brianna slumped back to the bed.

"I'm tired of messin' around with you. Just do what I told you to do."

Brianna took the clothes and wiggled into the skirt, which fit so tight it cut off the circulation in her legs. The top hung loosely from her body like extra skin on a piece of raw chicken.

Freda opened the door and yelled out into the hallway. "Tameka! Get in here."

Tameka appeared in the doorway. Brianna was glad to see her. She was the only girl in the house who was nice.

"Put some makeup on this girl," Freda ordered, as she headed out of the room. "She needs to be ready when Large gets here in ten minutes."

Tameka disappeared then returned carrying a small duffel bag. She set it on the floor and opened it up. It was filled with makeup, foundation, lipstick, eye shadow and blush in all colors. Brianna hadn't seen this much makeup in a department store.

"You doing okay, girl?" she gently asked.

"No! I wanna go home!"

"I know, I know. You gonna be okay. Just do what they tell you to do. You can't be biting clients," she said with a laugh. "I wish I coulda been there to see that john hopping around the room holding his dick. We was all crackin' up when we heard about that."

"Please help me escape," she begged.

"C'mon, girl. It ain't that bad. Stop actin' like a baby."

"Yes, it is," Brianna sobbed. "I can't do this."

"Please stop all that crying, girl." Tameka gave her a hug. "I can't make you pretty if you crying."

Tameka dug a compact out of the suitcase and began patting foundation on Brianna's face.

"Ow!" Brianna winced when Tameka pressed a sore spot on her cheek.

"It's a shame what Clint did to your face. But I heard that your uncle got him back good."

"What?"

"Your Uncle Dre got Clint beat up bad. He's in the hospital."

"Is my Uncle Dre comin' to get me?"

Tameka glanced toward the door.

"I think so. Freda told me to make you pretty cuz they gonna let you go. I guess they don't want your family to see you lookin' all beaten up."

Brianna wanted to smile, but it hurt too much. "I'm really going home?"

Tameka nodded, excited for the girl. "Yep, that's exactly what I hear."

CHAPTER 77

Day Four: 7:45 p.m.

Darnell's truck pulled into the driveway of a two-story house off Sherman Way. Electronic gates opened and closed behind him.

Mossy drove past the house and circled the block, then parked several houses away.

Apache whistled. "This dude must be making some big cash to be livin' large like this."

Dre looked at his watch. He was supposed to meet The Shepherd to exchange Brianna for the cash in less than two hours. If they busted into the house and Brianna wasn't there, Shep might follow through on his threat to ship her out of state. Dre was now questioning whether this was the right move.

Dre had been a risk taker for all of his life. Now was not the time to start playing it safe. The odds were good that Brianna was inside that house. Kaylee had seen her there that very morning. For all Dre knew, The Shepherd planned to stiff him when it came to the exchange. He had to act now.

He turned to Mossy. "I want you to stay in the car, engine running."

Mossy looked at Dre as if he had lost his mind. "You going in there with *him* rather than *me*?"

Apache glowed with pride. "My cuz know when he needs the real deal. This ain't no joke."

"It might get ugly in there," Dre said. "There's no reason for you to go down if it does. It's a different situation for us. Brianna is family."

"The only way something's gonna go wrong," Mossy said, "is if Rambo back there pulls out his gun and starts cappin' people."

"I'ma do whatever needs to be done," Apache declared.

"Let's stop talking negative," Dre said. "I'm planning on running out of that house with Brianna in my arms. I need you to be ready to roll when we come out."

All three men climbed out of the car. While Dre and Apache crept toward the house, Mossy walked around to the driver's side and slid behind the wheel. He watched as Dre and Apache jumped the fence.

They landed on the lawn and charged straight toward the front door, kicking it in.

Darnell shot into the entryway from an adjacent room. Before he could reach for his gun, Apache's Glock was aimed squarely at his forehead.

"Don't move punk ass!" Apache said.

Dre snatched Darnell's gun from his waistband and punched him in the Adam's apple. As he fell to his knees, grabbing his throat, Dre gripped him in a chokehold and pressed the gun to his temple.

"Where's Brianna?"

"What? I don't know no Brianna."

Apache stepped past him, holding his gun with two hands. "Hand over Brianna and we'll be out of here," Apache called out as he headed down the hallway.

Pushing Darnell ahead of him, Dre followed after Apache.

They entered a large den. A woman and five young girls were huddled in a corner of the room. Dre recognized Kaylee, whose eyes were so wide he thought they might pop out of her head.

Still holding the gun to Darnell's head, Dre stepped toward them. "Where's Brianna?"

"We don't know nobody named Brianna," the woman answered. There was anger, not fear, in her voice.

Apache aimed the gun to the right of where the girls were standing. He fired two shots into the wall, setting off a chorus of screams.

"She ain't here no more!" one of the girls cried out.

"Check the rest of the house," Dre said to Apache.

Apache stormed through the house, charging in and out of rooms. He hit the stairs and tore through the second level like a crazed commando. "She ain't here," he yelled down to Dre.

Apache reentered the den and raised his gun high in the air. "Somebody better tell me where my little cousin is cuz I really do feel like shootin' somebody right now."

"They took her to see Demonic," one of the girls blurted out.

Loretha's story about Demonic instantly came back to him. Dre tightened his grip around Darnell's neck.

"Where is she?" he yelled into Darnell's ear. "Tell me or I swear I'll choke you to death, then shoot you with your own gun."

"I don't wanna die," a chubby girl wailed. "They took her to the motel."

"Which motel," Dre said to Darnell.

"I ain't tellin' you nothin'!"

"Can I shoot him?" Apache pleaded, bouncing on his tiptoes. "Please let me shoot him."

Dre's eyes met Apache's. He released Darnell, then pushed him a few feet away. Dre nodded and Apache fired a single bullet into Darnell's right foot.

Darnell hollered and rolled to the floor.

"You shot me!" Darnell yelled, staring in disbelief at his bleeding foot. "I can't believe you shot me!"

All of the girls were wailing now. Even the hard-looking woman.

Dre looked around the room and spotted both rope and tape. It was probably what they used to restrain the girls they abducted. He started unraveling the rope.

Apache stepped toward the cringing girls, brandishing his gun.

"After he's done tying y'all up," Apache said, "I'm shooting you one by one until somebody talks."

The woman finally cracked. "Please don't shoot us! Brianna's at the Wyndgate on Ventura."

"You're comin' with us," Dre said, pulling the woman away from the group.

While Apache lorded over them with his Glock, Dre took each of the girls and linked them together with their hands tied behind their backs. He did the same to Darnell, who was sobbing and close to passing out.

"I want everybody's cell phone," Dre yelled, as he scanned the area for a house phone.

He wanted to prevent them from alerting someone at the Wyndgate before they could get there. This time, he was going to find Brianna.

Dre was sure of it.

CHAPTER 78

Day Four: 8:15 p.m.

B rianna crouched in the backseat of an SUV, her spirits lifted sky-high because she was on her way home.

What Tameka had said made sense. They wanted her to look presentable when they sent her back. That's why Tameka had put all that makeup on her face. Brianna wished she could wash it off, but she didn't want to scare anybody with all the bruises on her face. She couldn't wait to see her mother and grandmother. She knew her Uncle Dre was going to rescue her!

When the SUV finally stopped, Brianna lifted her hood and peered out of the window. Freda had given her a shot, which made her feel nice and relaxed. But it also made everything blurry. She was hoping to spot her Uncle Dre's car. But all she saw was the bright light from the motel sign. *The Wyndgate.*

Maybe Uncle Dre would be in the room waiting for her. She was so happy!

"C'mon, get out," a man said, opening the back door.

When she glared up at the big man, her happiness vanished. He looked like a giant monster. She remembered Freda dragging her out to the car, but she'd never seen this man before.

The man reached down to grab Brianna's arm, but she shrank away to the opposite side of the car.

"Where's my Uncle Dre?" she demanded.

He ignored her question and easily pulled her from the car with one hand. He practically dragged Brianna behind him. As they started up the stairs, one of her high-heeled shoes flipped off and landed on the ground below.

"Can't you even walk straight?"

The man headed back down the stairs to retrieve her shoe, gripping Brianna's arm even tighter.

She tried to pull away. "You're hurting me!"

"Little girl, you don't even know what hurting is. This ain't nothin' compared with what you gonna get tonight."

"My Uncle Dre's comin' to get me!"

"Yeah, okay."

They continued up the stairs, then down the walkway. The man stopped, pulled out a key and opened the door. He flicked on a light and shoved Brianna inside.

"You wait right here. Have a good time." He closed the door and locked it from the outside.

Brianna looked around the room. It reminded her of the same sad room where the man had tried to rape her. She sat down on the bed, overcome with emotion. She couldn't wait to see her Uncle Dre. She was so sleepy, but she had to stay awake.

A few minutes later, Brianna heard the rattle of the door being unlocked. She stood up and covered her mouth with both hands. She was ready to run straight into her uncle's arms.

When the door finally opened, the man standing in the doorway was not her Uncle Dre. She squinted at the hazy image. This man was fat and old. Older than her granddaddy who died before she was born. He was wearing a suit like a businessman and his short afro looked as if it had been freshly cut. He smiled at her in a way that made her feel dirty. A red duffle bag was tucked underneath his arm.

"Hi, Brianna." His voice was gruff.

"Where's my Uncle Dre?"

"I'm your uncle tonight," the man said with a creepy smile. "Come here and give me a hug."

He tossed the bag onto the bed and pulled out a short stick that looked as if it had been cut from a broom handle. Brianna backed away.

"Please," she began to cry. "Please leave me alone. I'm just a kid."

The man licked his lips. "I like kids."

He unbuckled his belt and stepped out of his pants. He was wearing red silk boxers.

Brianna continued to back away. "Please don't hurt me."

"We're gonna have some fun tonight," he said, waving the stick at her. "Take off that top so I can see what you got."

"Leave me alone!"

The man charged forward and snatched Brianna's halter top, ripping it from her body.

She folded her arms across her chest, shielding her breasts.

Still holding the stick, the man dug into the duffle bag again and removed a small boom box. He pressed a button and blues music blasted from the speakers. He turned it up as high as it would go.

"I don't want nobody to hear you screaming," the man said.

"Turn around," he ordered

Brianna didn't move. She couldn't move. All she could do was cry.

The man gripped the stick like a weapon, leaned forward and tried to ram it between her legs. Brianna darted away just in time, scampering across the bed to the other side of the room.

"Help me!" Brianna tried to yell over the music. "Somebody help me!"

CHAPTER 79

Day Four: 8:30 p.m.

Dre and Apache ran from the house, carrying Freda by her forearms.

Mossy started the engine the second he saw the huge gates surrounding the house swing open.

"Who the hell is that?" Mossy asked.

Dre didn't have time to provide an explanation. He shoved Freda into the backseat, while Apache entered from the opposite side. They tied Freda's arms with a rope, then shoved her down on the floor.

"This is kidnapping!" Freda yelled. "You're going to jail!"

"You ain't calling no police," Apache said. "Cuz if you do, you gotta explain what you been doin' to them girls."

"Maybe now you understand how it feels to be kidnapped," Dre yelled at her. "Now tell us how to get to the Wyndgate!"

* * *

They reached the motel in about ten minutes.

"Which room is she in?" Dre demanded.

"I don't know."

Apache pulled his gun from his waistband and pointed it at her foot. "You want me to shoot your foot off too?"

"I swear I don't know which room!"

"She better be here!" Dre said. "Or I'm coming back and cappin' you myself."

After making sure Freda was securely tied to the driver's seat, the three men jumped from the car.

Dre looked up at the building. The motel had three stories with at least a dozen rooms on each level.

"We gotta check every room. I'll take the first floor. Mossy you take the second. Apache you take the third."

Dre ran toward the first door, while Apache and Mossy took off up the stairs.

"Open up! Brianna, are you in there?" He banged on the door with both fists until he heard the doorknob turn.

A lanky man wearing nothing but a T-shirt eased the door open. "What the hell?"

Dre pushed his way inside. "Brianna! Are you in here?"

"Man, ain't no Brianna in here."

A woman sat in the middle of the bed, a sheet clutched to her chin covering herself. Dre checked the bathroom and the closet, then ran to the next room.

The realization that Brianna was with Demonic pumped extra adrenalin through his body. He kept imagining all the sick things Loretha had described. He had to find her.

Dre ran from room to room, pounding on the doors and windows. If the door didn't open fast enough, he kicked it in.

"Brianna! Brianna, where are you?"

"What's goin' on out here?" A barrel-chested man stepped out of room 5.

Dre recognized him as one of the bouncers from City Stars. He bum-rushed the man, grabbing his huge head and pounding it into the wall until he passed out.

CHAPTER 80

Day Four: 8:35 p.m.

Demonic was grinning now, his eyes glistening with lust as he stared at Brianna. This little girl was as slippery as an eel. Each time he thought he had her, she scurried to the other side of the room.

"I've been needing a good workout," he wheezed, dropping the broomstick to the floor.

"Let me go. Please let me go!" Brianna begged, her hands covering her bare breasts.

He shot across the bed again, his hand reaching out and grabbing the tail end of Brianna's skirt. He ripped it from her body, leaving her completely naked.

"Get away from me!"

Again, Brianna managed to dart away.

Demonic charged across the room, this time, catching her. He easily lifted her high above his head and threw her down on the bed. He was about to pounce on top of her when Brianna rolled away and sprinted toward the door.

She had the doorknob in hand just as Demonic grabbed her by the waist and pulled her to him, her back pressed against his hairy chest. He kept one hand locked around her waist, while his other hand roamed her breasts.

"You're a tough one, little girl."

Brianna turned sideways and bit him hard on the shoulder. When his free hand went to massage the bruise, Brianna swung her right foot backward, kicking him in the groin. He loosened his grip and she squirmed free. As he bent over in pain, she grabbed the broomstick and jabbed it in his eye.

Demonic screamed like a wounded hyena and weaved from side to side. But he didn't go down.

"They told me you had a lot of fight in you," he said, pressing his palm to his eye.

Brianna had hoped this would end like her first outing, with the john too wounded to continue. But Demonic kept coming at her.

"I like pain," he said, spitting over his shoulder. "I like taking it as much as I like giving it. Come here, little girl. I'm ready to get this show on the road."

Brianna scampered away from him again, hopping over the bed. She surveyed the room and tried to plot an escape. If she could make it to the bathroom, she could at least lock herself inside. But he would probably just kick the door in, then she would really be trapped. The only window faced the back side of the room. If she jumped, it would be two stories down to the alley below. She would certainly die.

She had to keep the man moving. Based on how hard he was breathing, he was not in good shape. If she kept him running after her, maybe she could make him have a heart attack. The man was big, but he was also as fast as a panther. If he caught her again, she probably wouldn't get away.

Brianna spied the boom box and realized why no one had responded to her screams. She grabbed the box and hurled it through the window. It easily broke through the glass, rendering the room silent except for Demonic's raspy wheezing.

"Now why'd you do that? Now we gotta be quiet. You're about to make me get mean."

Brianna eased toward the bathroom door. Maybe that would be her best bet. She'd almost made it inside when the man's hand reached out and picked her up by one shoulder and slammed her onto the bed.

She inched back toward the headboard. "Please don't hurt me!"

Demonic picked up the stick with one hand and grabbed Brianna's right foot with the other.

"Open your legs, you little slut," he said, dangling her in the air. "I got something for you."

"Help me!" Brianna pressed her lungs for everything they had. "Uncle Dre, please help me!"

CHAPTER 81

Day Four: 8:40 p.m.

Dre stepped over the unconscious bouncer and hurried into the room. Brianna wasn't there.

Just as Dre was about to break down the door of the neighboring room, he was certain he heard Brianna scream. He ran outside and looked up at the building. He couldn't be sure whether her voice had come from the second or third level.

"I'm here, Bree!" Dre yelled back. "Where are you, Bree? Where are you?"

There was no response.

"Up here," Mossy hollered from the second floor. He pointed to the far end of the building. "The scream came from down there!"

Mossy took off in that direction as Dre flew up the stairs three at a time. Apache ran down the staircase from the third level.

"Break down every damn door!" Dre yelled, as he reached the second level.

He slammed his shoulder into a door, which easily flew open. He ran inside and checked the room. Empty.

"Where are you, Bree!" Dre was crying now, fear and rage about to devour him.

He kicked in another door. It, too, was empty. Motel guests were now peeking out of doorways and peering over the railing. But Dre didn't care. If he spent the next ten years in jail, so be it. As long as he brought Brianna back home.

"This is it!" Mossy yelled from one of the rooms.

Dre was several yards away. He ran at top speed, barely able to stop when he got to the room.

From the doorway, he saw a fat black man sitting on the edge of the bed, a stick in his hand, gasping for air.

"Where is she?" Dre screamed. "Where is she?"

Dre pivoted, taking in the entire room. He rushed into the bathroom. Then he noticed Mossy. His friend had one palm pressed against the wall, his head lowered.

"Nooooo!" Dre yelled. "Where is she? What happened?"

Mossy still didn't speak. Dre saw tears in his eyes.

The man sitting on the bed dared to respond to Dre's question.

"That girl—" The man could barely speak. "That girl must'a lost her mind."

Dre spun around. That was when he noticed the broken window facing the back of the motel. He walked unsteadily toward it.

Two stories down, the spotlights along the back of the building provided a crystal clear view of something Dre did not want to see.

Brianna's frail, twisted body lay sprawled in the alleyway atop a heap of trash.

When Apache entered the room a second later, he ran over to the window where Dre was standing and peered down.

Apache pressed his fist to his lips. "Aw, hell naw!"

Dre bolted over to the bed and started pounding the man in the face with a flurry of two-handed punches. Apache picked up the stick and joined in, wielding it like a baseball bat.

"I didn't even touch her!" the man cried, holding up his hands in a fruitless effort to ward off the blows. "She jumped out that window on her own!"

CHAPTER 82

Day Four: 8:45 p.m.

A low, guttural roar gushed from Dre's lungs as he ran down the stairs, nearly tripping over his own feet.

When he reached Brianna, Dre dropped to his knees, cradling her in his arms. He sat there atop a smelly mattress stacked with trash, rocking and wailing.

Dre had no idea how much time had passed before he noticed Mossy staring down at him. He watched as his friend bent and pressed two thick fingers to Brianna's neck.

"I feel a pulse! She's alive!" Mossy yelled. He pulled out his smartphone and called 911.

Dre could not seem to comprehend or react or move. But when he saw Brianna's eyes blink open, he came out of his stupor.

"Bree! I love you, Bree!"

He pulled her close to him, sobbing into her wild mass of hair. But when he looked into her face, he saw terror in her eyes.

Brianna suddenly started yelling and kicking and flailing her arms, struggling to get away from him.

"Don't touch me!" she screamed. "Let me go! Get the hell away from me!"

Dre wrestled to hold on to her. "Bree, it's me. It's Uncle Dre. You're okay, baby. You're safe now."

His words did not calm her.

"Get away from me! I'll kill you!"

She scratched at him and bared her teeth, then started making sounds like a deaf-mute. With her wild, uncombed hair and her bloody, battered face, she looked like a rabid dog.

Dre refused to let her go. He tried to stand up, but she fought so fiercely, that he stumbled and they both fell deeper into the trash pile.

"Man, put her down!" Mossy yelled. "She's in shock. She doesn't know who you are. Put her down and just back away."

Dre finally released her and stood up. He took several steps away from her.

Brianna sat there for several seconds staring up at him with glazed eyes. She was panting and crying, then started crab walking away from him.

"It's okay, Bree," he said softly. "It's me. Uncle Dre. You're safe now. Everything's gonna be okay."

Brianna seemed to be calming down and Dre prayed that she would finally recognize him.

Apache ran up to them. "I gave that freak everything he deserved. He won't be messin' with nobody else's kid."

At the sight of Apache, Brianna's nostrils flared and she started wailing and swinging her arms again as if she was fighting off an invisible attacker.

Apache started toward her, but both Dre and Mossy grabbed opposite arms, pulling him back.

"She doesn't recognize us," Dre cried.

Dre stood there in the middle of the alley, feeling totally helpless.

Brianna's eyes darted all around the alley. Before they could react, she backed away and slid behind a large trash dumpster.

Dre dropped to his knees. "Where's the friggin' ambulance?" he wailed. "Somebody help us!"

DAY FIVE FOUND

"Victims of human trafficking have limited access to help and often do not self-identify, especially when they have been isolated from friends and family for long periods of time. Feelings of shame and fear of reporting to law enforcement may also add to a reluctance to seek help."

—*National Human Trafficking Resource Center*
Annual Report

CHAPTER 83

Day Five: 6:50 a.m.

It was more than two hours before the start of visiting hours at Northridge Hospital Medical Center. Yet the hospital's visiting area was already standing room only. Close to two dozen of Brianna's relatives and friends were anxiously awaiting an update on her condition.

At the far end of the room, Angela sat on a couch next to Dre, who kept rubbing his forehead and muttering to himself.

"If only I'd gotten to her just ten minutes earlier. I could've kept her from diving out of that window."

"You can't blame yourself," Angela said softly. "You got her back. That's all that counts."

"I just wish I'd gotten there before that freak messed her up. If only I had—"

A woman in a white coat stepped into the room. All conversation stopped as everyone's eyes focused her way.

"I'm looking for the family of Brianna Walker," she announced.

Donna stood up, her mother along with her. "We're her family."

Dre and Angela made their way over to her as well.

"Should we talk in private?" the young female doctor asked, taking in the intimidatingly large group.

"No need to do that," Donna said, gripping her mother's arm. "We're all her family. Just tell me how my baby is."

The doctor clasped her hands in front of her.

"Your daughter survived a two-story fall, but her most serious injury is a broken leg. She's got lots of cuts and bruises, but no internal injuries. Landing on that pile of trash saved her life. She's a very lucky little girl."

"Lucky my behind!" Brianna's grandmother exclaimed, raising both of her hands in praise. "That baby is blessed!"

The room exploded with clapping, followed by a chorus of praise from the group.

"Amen on that!" someone shouted.

"Thank you, Jesus!" a woman standing behind Angela called out.

"The Lord answers prayers!" said a man wearing a preacher's collar. "Yes, He does!"

The doctor looked nervously around the room, then cleared her throat. "While she's doing great physically, her emotional recovery is going to be long and slow. She's had a very traumatic experience."

"Can we see her?" Donna asked.

"She's been sedated, but you can see her." The doctor's wary eyes returned to the crowd. "But only two or three of you."

Dre began trailing after Donna and their mother, but the doctor gently stopped him.

"I'm sorry, sir. Brianna's not ready to have any male visitors just yet."

"I'm her uncle," Dre said, defensively. "She knows me."

"I'm afraid that she's been so traumatized by this ordeal that she gets hysterical whenever she sees any male. I was called in to replace Dr. Maravich, her initial treating physician. When she woke up and saw him, she started screaming and trying to climb out of bed. The same thing happened when a male nurse tried to approach her in the emergency room. She's suffering from an extremely severe case of post-traumatic stress disorder. We shouldn't do anything that could possibly traumatize her any further. Waking up and finding you there might. We're only assigning female staff to care for her."

Dre turned away, his face crushed.

"It's okay," Angela said, squeezing his forearm. "You'll see her soon. She'll be back to her old self before you know it."

"I gotta go."

Angela frowned. "Go? Go where?"

Dre looked away.

"Please don't do anything stupid. You need to let the police handle this."

"Police, my ass!"

The volume of Dre's voice drew stares from everyone in the waiting area, but Dre didn't bother to lower it.

"This Shepherd asshole has been pimpin' children for years. Years! The police obviously don't care or they'd be doing something about it."

Angela took a step closer to him. "And just what are you going to do?"

"Trust me," Dre said, moving toward the bank of elevators. "You don't wanna know."

CHAPTER 84

Day Five: 8:30 a.m.

It took Dre well over an hour in rush-hour traffic to make the drive from the hospital in Northridge to City Stars.

He wasn't sure exactly what he planned to do when he got there. But in his fantasy, his first move would be to torch the club. Then he'd find every sleazy motel The Shepherd owned and burn them to the ground too. What he wanted most was to find The Shepherd and pound him in the face until his last breath was gone.

It tore Dre up inside that Brianna was so traumatized that she couldn't even face him. That cut him deep. The doctor's words were like a sucker punch in the stomach.

"We shouldn't do anything that could possibly traumatize her any further. Waking up and finding you there might."

Dre couldn't bear to imagine what had happened to Brianna inside that room with Demonic that would force her to leap from a two-story window. As hard as he tried, he could not erase the horrible image of her battered body lying in that alley.

Five minutes after Dre exited the Harbor Freeway on El Segundo and spotted City Stars, he was surprised to see police cars parked up and down the street. The entire block had been cordoned off by a police barricade. Dre parked as close as he could get, then walked over to join the growing crowd of looky-loos. He had trouble seeing much since everybody else was rubbernecking to get a peek at what was happening.

"What's going on?" Dre asked a pudgy teenager who was holding his smartphone high in the air videotaping the scene.

"They raided the place about an hour ago," the boy said, excitedly. "The cops have been walking out with boxes and boxes of stuff. I heard they've been pimping little girls out of the place."

The news of the raid did nothing to ease Dre's anguish over what had happened to Brianna.

A buzz swirled through the crowd as two cops walked out tugging a man in handcuffs.

Dre craned his neck to get a better look. "Who's that?" Dre asked the teenager with the camera phone.

"That's The Shepherd," the boy said. "He owns the place."

Dre was stunned at the physical stature, or lack thereof, of this pip-squeak. He had not appeared to be such a small man on Skype. Rodney Merriweather couldn't be any taller than five-five, if that. His hair was closely cropped and he was dressed in khakis. The collar of his Polo shirt was flipped up. He could've easily passed for a USC student.

It was hard to believe that this little twerp was the man who had destroyed the lives of so many young girls. Dre pushed his way through the crowd.

Just before an officer forced The Shepherd into the backseat of a squad car, Dre cupped his hands around his mouth and called out to him. "Hey, Shep!"

Shep's head jerked sideways and their eyes met.

"I got some buddies waiting for you in lockup," Dre said with a taunting smile. "They got an extra-special welcome planned for you."

Dre turned around and trudged back toward his car. Jail wasn't good enough. He wanted The Shepherd to feel some pain. When he glanced down the street, he saw Angela leaning against the hood of his car, smiling. He picked up his step.

"How'd you know where to find me?" Dre asked, trying not to smile back at her.

"Wasn't very hard to imagine where you might go."

"Did you have anything to do with this?" he asked, angling his head toward the club.

"Yep," Angela said, not hiding her smugness. "I called my contact with the LAPD's Human Trafficking Task Force. I passed on everything you told me last night, including all those addresses. They're executing search warrants right now at every piece of property The Shepherd owns."

Dre appeared genuinely shocked. "So your call put all of this in motion?"

"Not exactly," Angela said. "As it turns out, Loretha's been working with the task force as a confidential informant for well over a year. They were close to busting him, but my call just expedited things a bit. Loretha's going to be the primary witness against The Shepherd. She's been granted full immunity from prosecution."

If he'd had it his way, Dre would've preferred to mete out a little street justice. And he wouldn't have needed Mossy or Apache or anybody else to help him with the job. The pleasure would've been all his.

Dre shrugged. "With all the money he's got, he'll hire some high-priced lawyer and buy his way out of any jail time. He'll probably be back on the street snatching girls before Brianna gets out of the hospital."

"Not this time. They're bringing in the feds. He's going to do some serious time. He apparently kept very good records of his Internet operation and he also did a lot of videotaping. Even if the girls are too afraid to testify against him—and I suspect they will be—all the records he kept are going to bury him."

"I wish I could be the one to bury him."

"Yeah, I know. That's why I'm here. To keep your hotheaded butt out of trouble."

Dre smiled. "Thanks. I always wanted another mama."

"You're welcome." Angela grabbed his forearm. "Let's go. I'm treating you to breakfast at the Serving Spoon. You're looking kind of skinny. I like my man to have meat on his bones."

Dre's chin jutted forward as a smile tickled his lips. *My man.* He liked the sound of that.

"How about lunch instead of breakfast?" He pulled his keys from his pocket. "I have something else I need to take care of."

"And what's that?"

He smiled. "You don't wanna know."

The playfulness disappeared from Angela's face and she took a step closer to him.

"Brianna isn't the only one who's been through a traumatic experience, Dre. You've been through a lot too. I bet you haven't had eight hours of sleep since she was taken. The best thing for you to do right now is to eat and get some rest."

"This won't take long," Dre said. "I'll meet you at the Serving Spoon at one."

"Okay," Angela said, walking around to the passenger side of his car. "Lunch it is. But wherever you're going, I'm going too."

Dre laughed. "Why are you so stubborn?"

Angela cocked her head. "Wow. I was just thinking the same thing about you."

"Fine," Dre said, hitting a button on his key ring to open the doors. "Get in. I might as well let you keep me from killing this scum too."

CHAPTER 85

Day Five: 9:50 a.m.

During their drive to Compton, Dre filled Angela in on the reason they were headed to Maverick Middle School.

"I can't believe it," Angela said. "I mean, it's unbelievable. I just hope you're right."

"I *am* right," Dre said.

They pulled to a stop in the school's parking lot. Before Dre could turn off the engine, Angela grabbed his arm.

"I know I sound like a broken record," she began, "but I'm going to try this just one more time. I really think we need to turn this information over to the police and let them handle it."

Dre's face grew stern. "We'll talk to the police *after* I do what I came here to do."

Angela huffed. "Promise me you'll go in there, say what you have to say, then leave."

"Okay."

"So you're not going to do anything crazy? You're going to be nice, right?"

"Yep." Dre smiled and opened the car door. "As nice as I can possibly be."

They found their way to the administration office.

"I'm here to see the principal," Dre said, after signing in.

"Do you have an appointment?" the receptionist asked.

"Nope."

"I'm sorry, but—"

"Tell Mr. Ortiz that Brianna Walker's uncle is here and that he definitely wants to see me."

"He's in a meeting."

Dre shrugged. "Does it look like I care? Pull him out of his meeting."

The receptionist backed away, her eyes flashing alarm.

Angela gave him a chiding look. "They're going to call security on your crazy butt," she whispered.

"That's fine. I could probably take three or four of those rent-a-cops all by myself."

They watched as the receptionist placed a call. She turned her back to them and lowered her voice. Five minutes later, two women walked out of the principal's office, followed by Ortiz.

"How can I help you?" Ortiz trudged up to the counter, his face strained with a tight smile.

The two women who'd been in the principal's office hovered nearby. There were five other people in the area, including a student.

"You remember me?" Dre said. "I was here with my sister a couple of days ago to talk about my niece, Brianna."

"Oh yes, yes," the principal said. "I understand she's been found. You must be so relieved."

"Yep, we are." Dre struggled to hold his anger in check. "We need to talk in the privacy of your office."

"About what?"

"About some criminal activity going on at your school related to Brianna's kidnapping."

Ortiz's indulgent demeanor disappeared. "Now isn't exactly a good time."

"It's the perfect time for me," Dre said. "So we can do it out here in front of all these people or we can go in your office and talk in private. Your choice."

Ortiz exhaled. "Fine." He turned to the receptionist. "Please ask Mr. Wainright to join us."

Dre raised his hand and pointed at one of the women who'd walked out of Ortiz's office. "Ms. Flanagan, why don't you join us too?"

Bonnie gave the principal an uncertain look, as if she wasn't sure she really wanted to be invited in.

Dre, Angela and Bonnie followed Ortiz into his office. Dre and Angela took seats in front of his desk. Bonnie sat at a circular table off to the side.

"And who are you, young lady?" Ortiz said to Angela.

"Angela Evans. "I'm—"

"She's my lawyer," Dre interrupted. "We're thinking about suing the school district."

Bonnie gasped. Ortiz shifted his roly-poly body in his leather chair.

"Exactly what is this about?" Ortiz asked.

"I've uncovered information that someone who works at this school has been feeding information about female students to traffickers who kidnap them and force them into prostitution."

Bonnie gasped. "Oh my God! I knew you were up to no good."

Ortiz sat up and started to sputter. "That's outrageous."

"No, it's not," Dre said. "Brianna was the fourth student to go missing from this school."

"That's also untrue," Ortiz replied. "Those other girls didn't disappear."

Dre cracked his knuckles. "Somebody lied. We were told that Leticia Gonzales' family believed that she'd been taken back to Mexico by her mother. Imani Jackson had supposedly been sent to Birmingham to live with her grandmother. The story we got about Jasmine Smith was that she'd been found living with an older boyfriend and was placed in foster care. None of those stories are true."

"But that's what Mr. Wainright told me," Bonnie said, confused.

"My sister got in contact with the families of each of those girls," Dre said. "They didn't back up any of those stories. All three of those families are still grieving over the unexplained disappearances of their daughters."

"Let's just get to the bottom of this," Ortiz said. "Exactly who do you claim is feeding information about our students to traffickers?"

Bonnie pointed a finger across the desk. "Don't sit there and act like you don't know."

There was a quiet tap on the door and Assistant Principal Wainright stepped into the room.

"You wanted me to join you?" he said to Ortiz.

"Get in here," Bonnie said excitedly. "This is Brianna Walker's uncle and his attorney. Just wait until you hear what they have to say."

Wainright remained standing, casually leaning his shoulder against the wall.

"As I was just saying, somebody at this school's been giving the names of troubled female students to human traffickers," Dre repeated. "The traffickers then connect with the girls on Facebook, abduct them and force them to work as prostitutes."

Wainright looked incredulous. "I can assure you, no one connected with this school is doing anything like that."

Bonnie puckered her lips. "It's no surprise to me. I've been telling you all along something wasn't right."

"Let's stop all this innuendo," Ortiz said. "Exactly who are you talking about and what evidence do you have to support these claims?"

Dre let the room settle into an uneasy silence.

"Why don't you tell them about your little side business?" Dre said.

He locked eyes with Ortiz, then slowly turned to Wainright.

"Me?" he blubbered. "How dare you?!"

Ortiz laughed, then rocked back in his chair. "You think *he's* doing this. You're nuts. That man's a saint."

Bonnie was bouncing in her chair, barely able to contain herself. "You've got it wrong." She pointed at Ortiz. "That's the sexual predator over there."

"Both of you are crazy," Ortiz said, standing up. "Everybody out of my office. Now!"

Dre slowly rose to his feet and so did Angela.

"No problem." A mock smile rested on Dre's lips. "We're running late for our appointment with the LAPD's Human Trafficking Task

Force." He kept his eyes on Wainright. "Human trafficking is a federal crime. You're looking at the possibility of life in prison."

Wainright was now blood red with anger.

"How dare you malign me like this? You have no evidence of these insane allegations. I'm suing you for defamation."

Bonnie started to speak, but Dre held up a hand, quieting her.

"Hold on a minute." He pulled his smartphone from the pocket of his jeans and began tapping the screen.

"When you do sue me for defamation, I'll be using this little piece of evidence in my defense."

Dre held up the smartphone, showing it first to Bonnie, then to Ortiz. When he turned to Wainright, he shoved it in his face.

"This is a picture of you at the Wyndgate motel on Ventura in the San Fernando Valley. The Wyndgate is one of the motels operated by the traffickers." Dre turned back to Ortiz. "This picture was taken yesterday around six-thirty."

Ortiz was speechless.

Dre pointed at the screen. "I have a nice shot of you talking to one of The Shepherd's henchmen. You *do* know who The Shepherd is, right?" he asked Wainright. "Since you're his real estate agent, you probably know him by his real name, Rodney Merriweather."

Wainright's left hand started to shake like he had Parkinson's disease.

Ortiz was so flabbergasted, he had to sit back down. "Rich, is this true? If you've damaged this school's reputation, ruining my chance to become Superintendent, I'll—"

Bonnie threw up her hands. "You arrogant pig!" Bonnie shouted, throwing up her hands. "Did you hear what this man just said? Our girls are being trafficked and you have the nerve to be worried about a darn job?"

Ortiz swept a strand of his thinning hair off his forehead. "Oh, well, I uh...I...of course I'm concerned about the girls."

Dre could only shake his head. He turned back to Wainright.

"It won't be hard for the cops to gather more evidence against you. I suspect all they have to do is check your phone records and computer. It took me a little while to figure out how you did it. But when I checked Brianna's Facebook account, I saw that you were one of her Facebook friends. That's how The Shepherd got the Facebook names of Brianna, Leticia Gonzales, Imani Jackson, Jasmine Smith and no telling how many others. You friended them and helped The Shepherd target them for his Jaden scam."

Wainright started to hyperventilate. "You've absolutely lost your mind!"

"And in case you hadn't heard, The Shepherd was arrested this morning. Cowards like him tend to fold fast. He's probably in an interrogation room right now, crying like a baby and pointing the finger at you."

"This is ludicrous!" Wainright tugged at his tie. His armpits were soaked with perspiration and beads of sweat dotted his forehead.

"Wait a minute," Ortiz said, pointing up at Wainright. "You told me you spoke to the families of each of those girls and found out that they weren't victims of foul play."

"That's also what he told me," Bonnie said.

"He lied to my sister and to both of you," Dre said. "He did that because he wanted Bonnie to stop making a stink about those missing girls. He couldn't risk anyone drawing a link between them. But the truth is, they're all still missing. No telling where The Shepherd has shipped them off to."

Wainright was gasping like somebody had stuffed a vacuum cleaner hose down his throat.

"So how'd you take your cut?" Dre asked. "Did The Shepherd give you a finder's fee for every girl you referred? Or are you partners with him in his operation?"

Bonnie nearly fell out of her chair.

"You're a disgrace," Bonnie screamed. "I wish they could bring back the electric chair just for you."

Wainright tried to collect himself. "This…this…is insane."

"Yes, it is," Dre continued. "See, you messed up when you targeted Brianna. She didn't have a father, but she had me. The other girls' families didn't know what to do when they disappeared. I'm a reformed criminal. It takes a criminal to know a criminal."

Dre moved toward the door, his eyes still on Wainright.

"I had actually planned to come in here and beat you down, but my lawyer here made me promise to be nice. And luckily for you, I'm going to follow her instructions."

Angela responded with a relieved smile.

Dre reached for the doorknob, pivoted, then coldcocked Wainright so hard, his head went flying into the nearby file cabinet. The force of the collision sent teeth and blood exploding from his mouth.

"Oooooowww," Wainright wailed. "You broke my jaw!" He shrank to the floor, cupping his jaw with one hand.

Bonnie and Ortiz gasped in unison.

Angela grabbed Dre's arm and tugged him out of the office.

"I know I said I'd behave," Dre said, smiling like a remorseful child. "But I couldn't help it. So you mad?"

"Yep." Angela smiled right back at him. "I'm mad because you didn't take an extra swing for me."

EPILOGUE

Three Weeks Later

As Angela climbed out of her car a few yards away from Harmony House, she could hear a chorus of young voices singing at the top of their lungs. She hurried up the front walk, the smile on her face widening with each step.

She instantly recognized the melody of the Destiny's Child song, *Survivor*. Except that the girls had apparently come up with different lyrics. The significance of the song for the Harmony House girls sent goose bumps of delight up and down her arms.

> *Now that we're away from you*
> *We're so much better*
> *Learnin' to love ourselves*
> *Is how we did it*
> *Thought that we would fail without you*
> *But we're hangin'*
> *Thought that we'd be nothing without you*
> *But we're something*

When Angela eased the front door open and stepped inside, she found the living room packed with women—young, old and in-between. Carmen was holding center stage, standing on a folding chair, waving a chopstick through the air. Although she played the role of choir director, she was singing the loudest.

We are survivors
We're gonna make it
Gonna survive
And keep on survivin'

Angela spotted a proud Loretha at the back of the room and snaked her way through the crowd, extending greetings along the way.

"Now this is what I call a party!" Angela said, giving her a hug.

"Thanks so much for organizing it," Loretha beamed. "It's so important for the girls to be exposed to women who can show them options that are different from the dysfunction they grew up around."

Angela had kept her word about forming a mentoring program for the Harmony House residents and this was their very first gathering. The room was crammed with members from Black Women Lawyers of Los Angeles and California Women Lawyers, as well as current and former residents of Harmony House.

After the group responded to the girls' performance with rousing applause, Angela spent the next few minutes thanking her friends and colleagues for their support.

Angela felt a tap on her shoulder and turned around.

"I have a surprise for you in the kitchen," Loretha said, looping her arm through Angela's. "Close your eyes."

"A surprise? What is it?"

Loretha grinned. "Just close your nosy eyes."

Angela did as instructed and allowed Loretha to steer her out of the living room and into the kitchen.

"Okay, you can open your eyes now."

When she did, Angela found every inch of counter space crowded with food. She saw fried chicken, barbecue, potato salad, mac 'n cheese, cakes, pies and more.

"Wow. Who donated all the food?"

"Girl, that's not the darn surprise."

At that instant, someone shot up from behind the island, causing Angela to jump an inch or two off the ground.

"Oh my God!" Angela ran over and pulled Peaches into her arms, squeezing her hard. "I'm so glad to see you! How are you doing?"

"I'm good," Peaches said, smiling shyly.

Angela grabbed her by the shoulders, leaned back and just looked at her. "You look so good. I love that hair."

Peaches patted her kinky coils and laughed. "Me too."

"What did I tell you about this girl?" Loretha grinned. "She's back in school and doing quite well."

Angela gave Peaches another hug, then the three of them walked arm-in-arm back into the living room. A few of the girls were now involved in a little one-upmanship.

"Oh, no, no, no, no, no," Carmen said, hands on hips, "*my* mentor ain't just a lawyer, she's a partner with a big-shot law firm. Let me introduce y'all to Ms. Anna Segobia Masters of Winston and—" Carmen paused. "Hell, I can't remember the name of her law firm, but take my word for it. It's off the chain."

Carmen extended her arm like a game show model toward an attractive Latina in a red and gold St. John suit.

"Excuse me," said one of the youngest girls in the room, "but I got me *two* mentors, one on both sides of the law. Let me introduce y'all to Ms. Public Defender Tami L. Warren and Ms. Prosecutor Linda Rosborough. Holla!"

The girl raised both hands, simultaneously high-fiving Tami and Linda.

Another girl threw an arm around her mentor. "This right here is Ms. Janet Swerdlow. She owns her *own* law firm. Thank you very much. Swerdlow—" The girl paused. "Give me a second cuz this is a mouthful, but I've been practicing. Swerdlow Florence Sanchez Swerdlow and Wimmer. How you like me now?"

As Janet clapped her approval, the girl did a short celebratory dance, swinging her hips from side to side.

"All y'all hood rats need to step aside," Melody said, "*my* mentor is a judge. This is the Honorable Marguerite Downing. And if any of y'all get out of line, I'ma have her put you under the jail and give *me* the key."

The room vibrated with laughter as Melody and the judge embraced.

Loretha tapped Angela on the shoulder. "I have someone else I want you to meet."

Angela followed Loretha into a room off the hallway where a woman sat alone watching TV at a barely audible level. Her head was covered with a scarf and it was hard to see her face. Angela wondered why she hadn't joined the party.

"Angela, I want you to meet Rena."

Angela extended her hand, then froze and turned back to Loretha. "Is this—"

"Yes," Loretha glowed. "Yes, it is."

"Nice to meet you, Rena," Angela said.

Rena didn't shake her hand, but smiled bashfully.

"Wow!" Angela said, as they headed back to the living room. "I can't believe she's here."

"Me either. And guess who else is here." Loretha pointed across the room. "See the girl in the blue T-shirt. That's Kaylee, the girl Dre met at the motel."

"Oh my God! Dre told me you arranged a rescue after she called him. I'm so glad you had space for her."

Kaylee was laughing and joking with the other girls. Angela took a moment to examine all of the young faces in the room. Every single girl looked like any average, well-adjusted teenager. But they were not. They were survivors.

"I'm working with social services in the Oakland area," Loretha said. "Kaylee's mother told the social worker she didn't want a prostitute in her house." Loretha shook her head. "But it looks like they've found a distant cousin who's going to take her in."

A wave of sadness for Kaylee fell over Angela.

"I just pray the cousin's home is a healthy place for her to be," Loretha said.

After another hour of partying and catching up with old friends, Angela cornered Loretha in the kitchen. "I'm so sorry that I have to cut out early."

"I completely understand," Loretha said, giving her another hug. "You've been such a blessing to us. Thanks for everything."

Angela said good-bye to Peaches and promised to drop by to check on her later in the week. Thirty minutes later she had arrived at her second celebration of the day.

Angela entered the living room of Brianna's home and found it as crowded as Loretha's had been. She searched through the faces for Dre, finally spotting him in the kitchen. When their eyes met, he headed her way.

"Hey, gorgeous lady," he said, bending to kiss her. "How was the party?"

"Fabulous. I met Kaylee. She told me to tell you thanks and asked how Brianna was doing. In the midst of what you were going through, it was incredible that you took the time to try to save her."

"All I did was give the girl my number." Dre's expression turned solemn. "What happened to all the other girls they took from The Shepherd's houses?"

"Most of them were sent to county facilities. A few were reunited with their families." She craned her neck. "Where's Brianna?"

Dre pointed over Angela's shoulder. Brianna was standing in the den, both arms wrapped tightly around her mother's waist. She had a thigh-high cast on her left leg. Bruises were still visible on her face and neck.

"How's she doing?"

Dre shrugged. "Better, but nothing like she was. She's still jumpy and she can't sleep through the night. She's basically scared to leave my sister's side. My mother's going to home school her for now. She's also still afraid to be alone around men." He paused. "Even me."

Angela gave him a hug. "It's going to take some time for her to heal. You'll get her back."

"I hope so. We used to be tight. Now I can barely get her to talk to me. Every time I think about what they did to her, I want to find Wainright, The Shepherd, and everybody else in his operation and take 'em out to a field and shoot 'em."

"You have to let that go. The system will deal with them. I'm sure they'll get everything they deserve. I'm thrilled with all the media attention the case is getting."

The arrest of Rodney "The Shepherd" Merriweather made national news, including a special report by CNN's Anderson Cooper. The feds stepped in and indicted him on fifteen different charges under the federal Human Trafficking Act. He was actually facing the very real possibility of life in prison. The rest of his cronies, including Wainright, Clint, Freda, Large and Darnell, would also be facing some serious time. Unfortunately for them, The Shepherd kept such good records, a conviction for every one of them was a certainty. Demonic, who was also behind bars, was placed in protective custody after two inmates nearly beat him to death.

Dre took Angela's hand and led her into the backyard. They sat on a long bench and quietly enjoyed the summer breeze along with the Motown sounds wafting from the house.

"Uncle Dre?"

Brianna's voice was so soft, they barely heard her.

Dre glanced over his shoulder, his expression suddenly hopeful. "Hey, Bree."

Brianna limped around the bench until she was facing him.

"I just wanted to say thank you again for comin' to get me. I knew you were gonna come." A single tear rolled down her cheek.

Dre's eyes began to water too.

"You don't have to thank me, girl. Of course I was comin' to get you."

Brianna leaned forward, then awkwardly threw her arms around Dre's neck, giving him a stiff hug. He held onto her for a long, long time.

"I love you, Bree," Dre said. "Don't you ever forget that."

When Brianna hobbled away, Dre sniffed and wiped his right eye with the heel of his hand. "I think you've seen me cry more this week than I probably have my whole life. I don't want you to think I'm weak."

Angela laughed. "It's okay. I love sensitive men."

Dre smiled and arched a brow. "I'm not sure I would've found her without your help."

"Glad to do it."

He threw his arm around Angela's shoulder and she snuggled close to him.

"You know, we never got a chance to finish our dinner date," Angela said. "You owe me."

Dre leaned down and kissed her deeply. "How about tomorrow night?"

Angela smiled. "Sounds like a plan."

AUTHOR'S NOTE

"I freed a thousand slaves. I could have freed a thousand more if only they knew they were slaves."

—Harriet Tubman, Abolitionist, Humanitarian

Without question, of all my books, *Anybody's Daughter* was the most difficult for me to write. Not from a technical standpoint. The story came to me fast and furious, the characters materialized easily. The hard part was dealing with the emotion of knowing that the atrocities I was writing about are real and happening every day. Visiting the track in Compton as well as the STAR court in Watts was both eye-opening and gut-wrenching.

So unlike all of my prior novels, I couldn't just type *the end* and move on to the next project. I plan to lend my voice to the fight to end all forms of human trafficking, be it sex trafficking, labor tracking or domestic servitude. But I must admit, that saving the youngest victims is where I plan to devote most of my energy.

It is my hope that my fictional account of what is going on in real life in cities across the U.S. and around the world will also move you to join the fight. Albert Einstein said it best:

"The world is a dangerous place, not because of those who do evil, but because of those who look on and do nothing."

—Albert Einstein, Renown Scientist

Unless we all become enraged enough to do something about this tragedy, anybody's daughter could end up being a victim—even yours.

How can you help? One of the biggest needs is adequate housing for girls who are rescued from this horrific life. I have listed below some of the organizations I came across during my research for this book. These groups, via their website resources as well as personal contact, provided information that helped me understand this tragedy from the victims' perspective—which is crucial. There are many, many more organizations out there fighting for our daughters and sons. And yes, we must not forget that our sons are being victimized too. Forgive me for not being able to list each and every worthy organization.

Please visit these websites and consider donating both your time and financial support.

Motivating, Inspiring, Supporting and Serving Sexually Exploited Youth (MISSSEY)
www.misssey.org

Girls Educational & Mentoring Services (GEMS)
www.gems-girls.org

Courtney's House
www.courtneyshouse.org

More Too Life
www.moretoolife.org

Saving Innocence
www.savinginnocence.org

Global Center for Women and Justice, Vanguard University
www.gcwj.vanguard.edu

The Polaris Project
www.polarisproject.org

The Coalition to Abolish Slavery & Trafficking (CAST)
www.castla.org

To report suspicions of human trafficking, connect with anti-trafficking resources in your area, request training or obtain general information, call the National Human Trafficking Resource Center's toll free hotline at 888-3737-888 or text HELP or INFO to BeFree (233733).

DISCUSSION QUESTIONS FOR
ANYBODY'S DAUGHTER

1. Did you approve of the tactics Dre used to find Brianna? What would you have done?
2. Despite Dre's criminal past, do you think he's a good match for Angela?
3. Do you think enough is being done to stop all forms of human trafficking? If not, what more should be done?
4. Why do you think greater focus isn't placed on the clients who drive the demand for sex trafficking?
5. Do you believe under-aged girls should be arrested for soliciting prostitution?
6. What can be done to help young girls develop the level of self-esteem that might keep them from being such easy prey for sex traffickers?
7. What steps can parents take to protect their children from predators on the Internet?
8. What do you think the penalties should be for individuals involved in sex trafficking?
9. Why do you think sex trafficking, particularly minor sex trafficking, has reached such epidemic levels?
10. What were some of the things you liked/disliked about *Anybody's Daughter*?

We hope you enjoyed *Anybody's Daughter*. Pamela's novels are available in print, e-book and audio book formats everywhere books are sold.

To read an excerpt of all of Pamela's thrillers visit www.pamelasamuelsyoung.com.

Vernetta Henderson Mysteries

Every Reasonable Doubt (1st in series)

In Firm Pursuit (2nd in series)

Murder on the Down Low (3rd in series)

Attorney-Client Privilege (4th in series)

Angela Evans Mysteries

Buying Time (1st in series)

Anybody's Daughter (2nd in series)

Short Stories

The Setup

Easy Money

Non-Fiction

Kinky Coily: A Natural Hair Resource Guide

ACKNOWLEDGEMENTS

As always, I'd like to start by thanking the smart, supportive, and insightful group of friends and family members who critiqued the early drafts of this book: Joy Lottie, James White, Diane Mackin, Randy Bauer, Debbie Diffendal, Ellen Farrell, Paul Ullom, Shelby Ullom, Olivia Smith, Cynthia Hebron, Pamela Goree Dancy, Jocelyn Tubbs-Turner, Valerie Lamar, Donny Wilson and Jerome Norris. I couldn't do it without your support and encouragement (and frankly, I never plan to).

To the two Los Angeles area book clubs who read an early draft of *Anybody's Daughter* and provided me with an invaluable critique: Bookalicious Book Club members: Arlene L. Walker, Judi Johnson, Saba McKinley, Kamillah Clayton, Helen Jingles, Raunda Frank, Claudette Knight, and Lesleigh Kelly; and Sisters with Books Book Club members: Cheryl Finley, Bunny Withers, Gloria Falls, Helen Merrick, Freida Smith, Janice Criddle, Debra Hardy and Beverly Newton. Can't wait to visit your book clubs again. And to an extra special book club member, Sharon Lucas of the Reading Divas in Bowie, Maryland, you have been an incredible friend and fan. I truly appreciate all your enthusiastic support.

To my do-it-all assistant, copy editor, handler, publicist, personal shopper, and friend Lynel Washington, thanks for all you do. You help keep me sane! To Ella Curry of EDC Creations Media Group, LLC, the best publicist I know. Thanks for helping get my books to the world.

And as always, to my parents, Pearl and John, thanks for being so proud of me. To my husband, Rick, thanks for your support and especially for helping make sure the characterizations of "the bruthas" in my novels are always on point.

To my fans, thanks for reading my novels. I love hearing what you think, so email me!

ABOUT THE AUTHOR

Pamela Samuels Young is a practicing attorney and bestselling author of the legal thrillers, *Every Reasonable Doubt, In Firm Pursuit, Murder on the Down Low, Buying Time, Attorney-Client Privilege,* and *Anybody's Daughter.* She is also a natural hair enthusiast and the author of *Kinky Coily: A Natural Hair Resource Guide.*

In addition to writing legal thrillers and working as an in-house employment attorney for a major corporation in Southern California, Pamela formerly served on the board of directors of the Los Angeles Chapter of Mystery Writers of America and is a diehard member of Sisters in Crime-L.A., an organization dedicated to the advancement of women mystery writers. The former journalist and Compton native is a graduate of USC, Northwestern University and UC Berkeley's School of Law. She is married and lives in the Los Angeles area.

Pamela loves to hear from readers! There are a multitude of ways to connect with her.

Facebook:	www.facebook.com/pamelasamuelsyoung and www.facebook.com/kinkycoilypamela
Twitter:	www.twitter.com/pamsamuelsyoung
LinkedIn:	www.linkedin.com/pamelasamuelsyoung
Pinterest:	www.pinterest.com/kinkycoily
YouTube:	www.youtube.com/kinkycoilypamela
MeetUp:	www.meetup.com/natural-born-beauties.

To schedule Pamela for a speaking engagement or book club meeting via speakerphone, Skype, FaceTime or in person, visit her website at www.pamelasamuelsyoung.com.

54343592R00230

Made in the USA
San Bernardino, CA
14 October 2017